Praise for
The Outside Boy

"In Hibernian society, there's hardly a creature lower than the Irish tinker, a nomadic group 'tis said was driven into the barren country by the fundamentalist Cromwell to starve. Regardless, the modern diminutive hero Christy, in Jeanine Cummins's gloriously poetic novel, will burrow his way into your heart. It's not often I hug a book, but with moist eyes and beginnings of a song in my heart, I followed Christy's journey from a death to hopeful life. Read this lovely book and you will hug yourself."

—Malachy McCourt, bestselling author of
Malachy McCourt's History of Ireland

"*The Outside Boy* is a poignant and magical tale about the travelling people in Ireland, a way of life all but vanished. Cummins captures that world in pitch-perfect prose, charming and beguiling till the story nearly breaks your heart."

—Keith Donohue, author of *The Stolen Child*

"*The Outside Boy* is such a powerful read. I identified so strongly with this story of a strange and gorgeous and vanishing way of life. It's an adventure and, yes, a eulogy, but it's also a full-throated song of praise. I loved it."

—Sherman Alexie, National Book Award–winning author of
The Absolutely True Diary of a Part-Time Indian

"Truly charming at times, heartbreaking at others, but *always* captivating. An atmospheric coming-of-age story set in the world of the Irish travellers, it will stay with you long after you've finished the last page." —Lesley Kagen, author of *Land of a Hundred Wonders*

continued...

"A lyrical journey along the twisting path of Gypsy life, *The Outside Boy* is part coming-of-age novel, part mystery, and all heart. It's easily one of the most beautiful and satisfying books I've read this year."
—Jennie Shortridge, author of *When She Flew*

"*The Outside Boy* will charm you, fascinate you, delight you, snake into your heart, and bust it wide-open. I'm hard-pressed to think of a narrator more lovable than Christy Hurley, who describes his lost, beautiful world—that of the Irish travellers in the late 1950s—in prose that's as profound as it is funny. What a graceful, perfect book."
—Carolyn Turgeon, author of *Godmother: The Secret Cinderella Story*

"Jeanine Cummins's debut novel is a multilayered, meticulously researched journey into the elusive lives of the Irish travellers. Lucky for those of us along for the ride, her dynamic tale unfurls through the singular lens of the clever and charming Christopher Hurley, a wise-beyond-his-years boy coming of age in a tiny corner of history, but trying to answer the most universal of questions: Who am I and where did I come from?"
—T Cooper, author of *Lipshitz Six or Two Angry Blondes*

"You do not need to love Ireland to love *The Outside Boy*. You only need to love life and to have once been as young and fresh of heart as the book's marvelous narrator. You will enter the rare realm of the travellers, yet feel completely at home, living Christy's youth as if it were your own, laughing with him and feeling his heart race and suffering his hurts and rejoicing at his ultimate triumph. You will reach the last page smiling through tears and give thanks for a writer of uncommon talent. And it will stay with you, making you Irish in the very best way, even if you are not."
—Michael Daly, author of *The Book of Mychal*

"*The Outside Boy* has found a permanent home in my head and heart and on the shelf with authors like J. M. Barrie, Roddy Doyle, and Sue Monk Kidd. A flawless coming-of-*rage* story overflowing with talent, heartbreak, and joy."
—Jennifer Belle, bestselling author of *Going Down* and *High Maintenance*

THE **OUTSIDE** BOY

JEANINE CUMMINS

NEW AMERICAN LIBRARY

New American Library
Published by New American Library, a division of Penguin Group (USA) Inc.,
375 Hudson Street, New York, New York 10014, USA
Penguin Group (Canada), 90 Eglinton Avenue East, Suite 700, Toronto, Ontario M4P 2Y3,
Canada (a division of Pearson Penguin Canada Inc.)
Penguin Books Ltd., 80 Strand, London WC2R 0RL, England Penguin Ireland,
25 St. Stephen's Green, Dublin 2, Ireland (a division of Penguin Books Ltd.)
Penguin Group (Australia), 250 Camberwell Road, Camberwell, Victoria 3124, Australia
(a division of Pearson Australia Group Pty. Ltd.)
Penguin Books India Pvt. Ltd., 11 Community Centre, Panchsheel Park, New Delhi - 110 017,
India
Penguin Group (NZ), 67 Apollo Drive, Rosedale, North Shore 0632, New Zealand
(a division of Pearson New Zealand Ltd.)
Penguin Books (South Africa) (Pty.) Ltd., 24 Sturdee Avenue, Rosebank, Johannesburg 2196,
South Africa

Penguin Books Ltd., Registered Offices:
80 Strand, London WC2R 0RL, England

First published by New American Library,
a division of Penguin Group (USA) Inc.

First Printing, June 2010
10 9 8 7 6 5 4 3 2 1

 REGISTERED TRADEMARK—MARCA REGISTRADA

LIBRARY OF CONGRESS CATALOGING-IN-PUBLICATION DATA

Cummins, Jeanine.
The outside boy/Jeanine Cummins.
p.   cm.
ISBN 978-0-451-22948-9
1. Family secrets—Fiction.   2. Ireland—History—20th century—Fiction.   I. Title.
PS3603.U663O88   2010
813'.6—dc22   2010003853

Set in Palatino
Designed by Ginger Legato

Printed in the United States of America

PUBLISHER'S NOTE
This is a work of fiction. Names, characters, places, and incidents either are the product of the
author's imagination or are used fictitiously, and any resemblance to actual persons, living or
dead, business establishments, events, or locales is entirely coincidental.
    The publisher does not have any control over and does not assume any responsibility for
author or third-party Web sites or their content.

For Grandma Polly and Grandpa Art,
who came from different worlds.

life on the road. Thank you all for your sincerity, warmth, and inspiration.

And most especially, I want to thank Winnie Kerrigan, who taught me more about the hearts of travellers than I could have learned in a thousand books. Thank you for welcoming me into your home in Dunsink, and for sharing your wonderful family, your stories of hardship and happiness both, and yourself with me. You are a rare and honest soul, and I hope you will recognize pieces of yourself in these pages.

And to my friends and family, who stuck with me (no easy feat) throughout the writing of this book:

All of my Matthews family, you know who you are, and you are indeed funny-handsome. All my extended Cummins family, for persevering past the difficulties so that we might remain a *family*. And my newer family, the Kennedys, who all become dearer to me with each passing day: Joe, Margaret, Loretta, Ru, Aine, Aisling, Jimmy, Caoimhe, Saoirse, Brianna, Shane, Joan, and Darragh.

My immediate family: my awesome parents, Gene and Kay Cummins; my brother, Tom Cummins, and his beautiful family, Whitney, Riley, and Declan; my sister, Kathy Lopez, and her gorgeous boys, Tom, Eamonn, and Oisin. You guys are the best, proudest, most ungrudgingly supportive family *ever*.

The best friends a girl could ever hope for: Evelyne Faye, Nikki Stapleton, and Charlotte Jack.

And the loves of my life, Aoife and Joe. You two are Every Happy Thing in the world to me.

AUTHOR'S NOTE

I have endeavored to remain true to the culture, the humor, and the way of life of the people portrayed in this work of fiction: the Irish Travellers or *Pavees*. I must ask my readers to do me the kindness of suspending their disbelief in the moments where absolute authenticity was not prudent. For example, my narrator's voice is not strictly a traveller's vernacular, as that treatment would have rendered the book almost impenetrable to the American reader. I also opted for Americanized spellings throughout, with the exception of the word *traveller*, with its double-L, because that word has an entirely different meaning than its touristic American cousin, the simple traveler.

I hope that my efforts herein will pay homage to a mostly vanished way of life, and to the fortitude and grace of many of the travellers themselves. It was my goal in writing this book that I might depict the traveller character beyond the usual stereotypes, by illustrating some of their hardships without turning them into victims, and some of their flaws without turning them into caricatures of violence and immorality. Theirs is a culture like any other, with both goodness and badness dwelling therein.

Some academic research enhanced my understanding of the travellers' values, moral code, economy, customs, and daily life on the road. Thank you to the authors of these works, for their diligent insight:

1. *Puck of the Droms* by Artelia Court,
2. *The Road to God Knows Where* by Sean Maher,
3. *Nan: The Life of an Irish Travelling Woman* by Sharon Gmelch,
4. *Irish Travellers: Representations and Realities* by Michael Hayes,
5. *Irish Travellers: Racism and the Politics of Culture* by Jane Helleiner,
6. *The Irish Tinkers: The Urbanization of an Itinerant People* by George Gmelch,
7. *People of the Road: The Irish Travellers* by Mathias Oppersdorff,
8. *Irish Travellers: Tinkers No More* by Alen MacWeeney,
9. *Traveller Ways, and Traveller Words* from Pavee Point Publications.
10. *All Things Wise and Wonderful* by James Herriot was my veterinary bible.

ACKNOWLEDGMENTS

I need to thank the following people, who made this book possible.

My early readers: Dinah Prince Daly, Mary McMyne, Anton Strout, Eric Schnall, Joi Brozek, John Lawton, Brenna Tinkel, Sherman Alexie, Jeremy Tescher, Don Rieck, Eileen Stapleton, David Medina, Jane Park, and Layne Maheu. Jennifer Belle, who provided me with an invaluable workshop experience, and whose tremendously keen insight is matched only by her wit. And most especially the glamorous and glittery Ms. Carolyn Turgeon, who is always there when I need her, and who never complains about being asked to read *yet another* draft. Thank you all, for your unfailing encouragement and invaluable feedback.

My patient and loyal agent, Doug Stewart, and his ever-positive accomplice, Seth Fishman. Thank you for not giving up on me.

Wizards of publishing Claire Zion, Kara Welsh, and Leslie Gelbman. Thank you for second and third chances. Claire, I am especially grateful to you, for making this book even more beautiful than I hoped it would be.

My family at Penguin: Norman Lidofsky, Trish Weyenberg,

Patrick Nolan, Lisa Pannek, and the whole paperback sales department for everything. And I mean *everything*. Megan Lynch, for awesomeness. Craig Burke and your crack team of super-publicists. Rick Pascocello and your squad of unparalleled marketing geniuses. Thank you all for your friendship, support, and enthusiasm. And for being so good at what you do.

The Penguin sales force, which remains the greatest in the industry—my gratitude is boundless and bottomless. I miss working in your midst every day, but I am delighted that my career is safe in your hands.

Ann Marie Markey, for allowing me the physical and emotional freedom to write, knowing that my baby girl was safe in your care. And Zully Arias, who swooped in, late in the game, and won my daughter over.

Millord Levine and Robert J. Reed for heroically saving my deadline.

I thank the following people for sharing their critical expertise on various subjects:

Matt Trivett, Sean Bryan, Doug Hanson, Buz Brand, and all the guys at Station 6, who taught me about the properties and poetry of fire.

Lisa Thess, who has an astute tenderness for, and profound knowledge of, horses.

Artelia Court, who lent me her considerable wisdom about life among the travellers.

And hugely: Brendan ó Caoláin and everyone at Pavee Point in Dublin, who were open-minded and kind enough to overcome their likely suspicions of me, in order that I might learn from them. In particular, I am grateful to Martin Collins and John Paul Collins, and to the women of Pavee Point, including Kathleen, Sheila, Lisa, Nanny, Sheila, Caroline, Mag, and Sheila. Yes, that's three Sheilas. And to James Collins and his adorable grandson, who welcomed me into their home in Finglas, and spoke to me about tinsmithing, and

THE **OUTSIDE** BOY

PROLOGUE

IRELAND, 1959

I was dreaming of purple horses. Myself on one and Martin on the other, and we was bareback, and we was racing. These wasn't no strong, slow, piebald gypsy ponies like most of us travellers had in them days in Ireland, for pulling our wagon-homes behind us wherever we went. No, in this dream, me and Martin raced thundering thoroughbreds at a proper race meeting, like at Punchestown in Dublin. And the crowd waved their colors and they roared for us, never mind that we was travellers. They loved us anyway. Our purple stallions was sixteen hands high at least, and we was so swift on them we nearly took flight. I had the coarse thickness of my horse's mane wrapped full around my fist, and I squeezed his big, strong neck with my knees and kept my head down close beside his twitching ear. I whispered to him, "Go on, bucko," and he went and went, and we was leaving Martin and his horse in our dust. And then there was an almighty screeching howl that went up, and my purple horse vanished, and I was sitting up straight as a fencepost in the dark, my blanket wrapped 'round my fist and my heart hammering.

Dad was sitting up beside me, too, and we blinked confusion at each other in the dark. We wasn't sure what'd wakened us until we heard it again: a keen, raw and sharp. Dad's hands was like ghosts between us, and he gripping his own blanket close to his chest.

"What . . ." he started, but before he could finish the question, the wail rose up again and engulfed the camp. I could feel every hair on my body, and the wraithlike cry seemed liquid, seeping up through the planks of the wagon and into our clammy nighttime skins. There was a terror in that sound that was all new to me.

"Is it a *bansídhe?*" I asked Dad.

He looked at me like I was gone soft in the head. "Come outta that nonsense, Christopher," he said to me. "You know there's no such thing as a bloody *bansídhe.*"

He shook his head at me crossly, and I felt stupid, and was glad for the feeling stupid. Of course there was no such thing as *bansídhes.* I was nearly twelve years of age—old enough to know better. But then there was a sudden BANG BANG on the door of the wagon, and I could feel my heartbeat clamber into my throat. My heels stuck into the floorboards, and I did a backwards crab-gallop until I smacked into the wall. My chest was heaving as I stared past my dad at the wagon door. He was staring at it, too, with eyes as wide open as mine.

"Dad?" I said.

I wanted him to reassure me—just a word, a squeeze—that it would be okay.

"Wait there, Christopher," he said, and he started to move toward the door.

And now the clatter at the door grew louder, and there was nowhere for us to go, only to cower inside and await the doom of the shrieking specter who was rattling at our wagon door. I stopped breathing altogether, and the door creaked and swung on its hinge, gaping open into the frigid night. The cold air flew in at once and reached my bare ankles. I trembled over them, folded my arms around my scrawny knees, and shook like a wet hound.

"Christopher!" the specter shrieked, and it was my granny.

She was calling my dad, who I was named after. Granny, heaped in blankets outside in the not-yet pinkening light, her hair and eyes wild. Her mouth stood open and revealed all the gummy graves where her teeth used to be. She looked so unnatural that my terror was hardly relieved at all.

Dad was only in his bare feet, and he made a frantic silhouette, leaping out of the wagon after his mother. I crawled to the door behind him and watched Granny deliver her unholy cries into the dark camp. I pulled my blue ankles up and tucked my blanket 'round them while I watched the horrible scene unfold: Granny, down on her knees beside the deadened fire, rocking back and over so hard I feared she would topple into the ashes. The keen she let up was so thick and tender I could nearly see it coming out of her, her breath spiraling out violently in torrid colors, defeating the darkness and drenching the camp with grief.

"Mam," my dad said quietly.

He was in front of his mother now, and he'd his hands on her shoulders. He shook her a small bit, but she took no notice of him. She tore at her white hair until she looked like a proper *bansídhe* herself. I started shaking again, and I wanted to believe it was from the cold, but my stomach was turning too.

"Mam!" Dad said again, louder this time, and shook her more roughly.

For a moment, I thought he would raise a hand to her, to snap her out of the state she was in. I swallowed all the billowing colors and held them fast inside me, but my knuckles stayed white, gripping the doorframe of the wagon while I watched. Uncle Finty was there now, too, and they both looked small and helpless, standing beside the ruined fire watching their mother weep.

My cousin Martin's head popped up in front of me then, and without a sound or a word, he swung the full weight of his body up on one arm and into the wagon beside me. He pulled open my blanket and I was blasted with the cold again, until he burrowed and folded us in tight. In the closeness, he smelled like tree bark and moss. We watched our fathers; we tried not to watch Granny.

"Go and check the wagon, Christopher," Finty said to Dad.

My dad hesitated, put his hand on his brother's shoulder for a long moment, like he was gathering strength for what he knew he'd find. Then he nodded and turned toward Granny's wagon door. It was hanging open, too, and she howled again as he went. I shivered under our blanket, to hear the sound of that wordless pain, unleashed and raw, galloping around the camp. Granny was like a toothless wolf. We watched without blinking while my dad disappeared into the wagon. Martin squirmed in even closer beside me, and I could feel his elbow stuck between two of my shivering ribs, like we was twins for a minute, instead of cousins. We was joined at the eyes and ears, joined at the dread. Everything was silent and stretched—only the tidal rhythm of our shared breath pushed the seconds forward. I wished for my mother.

Dad came out again, shaking his head.

"He's gone," he said.

His face was pale in the moonlight. Gone. I knew what he meant. He meant my grandda.

My stomach clutched, but my mind resisted. I wasn't ready. My fingernails dug into the flesh of Martin's arm, but he didn't wince. He didn't even move—only a shiver in his neck. A gulp.

"Grandda," I whispered, and I could feel a flood in my head, a distant, unleashed roar inside me. I dammed it up quick.

"Will we waken him, do you think?" Granny said.

Martin and I looked at each other in horror.

"Is she gone as well?" he asked me. "Gone in the head, like?"

Martin was always asking me things, even though he was a couple months older than me. He was twelve already. I shook my head and tried to answer him. But just like Grandda, my voice was away.

We stayed there while the sky lightened lilac at the edges. Me and Martin, joined at the hair, joined at the knuckles. We didn't move, didn't speak. I think he felt it too—some unspoken sense that if we stayed very still, if we blurred into each other, it mightn't be real. We tried that elusive magic of stillness, hoping like we always did that we might capture it, and it might be the answer to everything. But in truth, we was children of motion, and we didn't know how to stand still then. We didn't even know that we could.

ONE

After a good bout of crying in the morning, Granny cleaned up Grandda. She shaved him and dressed him, and we got on the road late. All day long she drove their pony and wagon herself, and Grandda still inside, where she would usually be riding.

"Where will Granny stay?" I asked, as we prepared to make camp that night, in a thick darkness.

I hadn't ever known nobody who'd died before, only my own mam, and it didn't really count as knowing her, since we'd only shared seven minutes of breath in this world. The rain was close.

"How do you mean?" Dad asked.

"Where's she going to be sleeping?" I said.

"I imagine she'll sleep in her bed," Dad answered.

I knew I shouldn't ask no more. I really knew, but it was confounding.

"Can we go in and see him?" I asked.

Cleaned and shaved and dressed. But still quite dead.

"We'll go in when your granny invites us and not before," Dad answered.

It was two days' journey to where we would rest Grandda, to where we'd have to bury him, inside in the town where his own parents and grandparents was buried. I never fancied towns, the buttoned-up, closed-in feeling of them, the way the houses crowded theirselves onto the narrow streets, pressed their shadows forcefully on the passersby. I preferred the open *tober*, the road, out the country, where all the rain-fed colors would be washed fresh and green. But sometimes it couldn't be helped. You had to go where you had to go.

It was magnetic, that burial journey, the way we was marching the horses and ourselves there without thinking or talking or even eating. We filled our bellies with Granny's endless wash of tears, but I couldn't seem to find my grief as easily as the rest of them, even though I was Grandda's favorite. Or maybe because of that.

I thought maybe grief was like an egg that had to be cracked open, and I just hadn't smashed mine yet—I was still holding it, cradling it. Careful.

ONE RARE, DRY, IRISH SUMMER's night, when I was seven years of age, the buffers came for Grandda. We was all sleeping when them headlamps slid acrosst my face in the blackness and then hung their bright, round moons on the skin of the tent above me. My eyes was as wide as them luminous circles, but I didn't even twitch. Dad was still snoring beside me when I heard the car door open, and then two feet plant theirselves into the gravel of the road. The driver left the motor running.

"Dad," I whispered, elbowing him awake. "Somebody's here."

He sat up quick and silent, pulling his legs out from under the blanket to crouch beside me. He put a finger to his lips and motioned for me to scramble to the back corner of the tent, where I mightn't catch a rock in the head, if there was a shower of rocks coming.

Them headlamps never brought good news. If it was the gardaí, they'd only tell us to shift. They'd *encourage* us. They might even kick dirt acrosst the fire and raise their night-voices, their country accents.

But if it was some rowdy buffers instead, stumbling homeward after a night on the drink, there might be thicker words, slurred and vicious. There might be a pelting of rocks, to remind us not to stay too long in their town. There might be . . .

"Hurleys?" The voice was close outside the tent flap.

No slurring. No whiff of hostility. The voice was crouching like Dad, quiet. Dad lifted the flap of the tent, like the lids off the eyes of them headlamps, and now they shone into the tent directly, and there was no hiding, in them beams. We was lit like daytime. Dad shielded his eyes with one arm, and I could see the buffer, bent at the waist. He was lean, young.

"Are ye Hurleys, camping here?" the buffer asked. "I need Stephen Hurley."

There was something frantic in the voice, a tremble.

"Who's asking?" Dad said.

"I'm Joe Burke, my dad is Eamonn Burke from up the glen, and we've an awful sick mare, foaling."

He was just a kid, maybe sixteen, and his words came out in a cracked tumble. Dad stood out through the tent flap and Joe Burke moved back to give him space. Dad was a head taller than him at least, and twice the breadth.

"Please, we need help," the kid said. "Are you Stephen Hurley?"

But Dad was already moving past him, to stoop at Grandda's tent. Three minutes later, I was sat in the back of Joe Burke's sedan, clutching Grandda's magic black bag acrosst my knees. We bounced over ruts and flew over dips, and I was glad my stomach was empty, because it was my first time in a car, and it wasn't nothing like the easy pace of a horse and wagon.

"How long has the mare been laboring?" Grandda asked Joe Burke.

"It's hard to know," he said. "She's been agitated since last night, so it might have started as early as that."

"Last night, as in, before bed this evening?" Grandda interrupted him. "Or before bed yesterday?"

Joe Burke glanced in the rearview mirror, almost afraid to answer. "Yesterday," he said.

"Is she off her feed?"

"Yessir," Joe Burke answered. "But only from this afternoon."

It was the first time I ever heard a buffer call my grandda "sir." I watched moths dart and swoop through the ropy beams of light in front of us, like tracks we was hurtling down. We nearly squashed a fox on a bend in the road, but he dashed into the hedges just in time.

"How's my assistant?" Grandda turned to look at me over his shoulder, and I nodded.

And then we was pulling into the lane of a farm, and the tires went spitting out gravel, behind, and Joe Burke had to slow that car down. Grandda was out the door before the car even stopped.

"C'mon, Christy," he said to me, and I galloped out after him, lugging the black bag behind.

There was always something about walking into a glowy barn at night, like a church. There was the strong, sleepy smell of the gathered animals, of their skin and breath. The spiky odor of the kerosene in the barn lantern, hanging from a rafter above, with its wick trimmed tidy and low. The feed sacks, the neat's-foot oil, the saddle soap, the clean straw underfoot, all blending their scents together. Like summer and heat and sunshine and sweat on your neck, and a full belly.

The lantern cast a blush around the soft, splintery wood of the stalls. Oiled saddles gleamed from their racks on the walls, and I gleamed from the inside out, like I always did walking into a barn. Because the barn was that matchless balance of all things, where the outdoors came inside—comfortably, without getting stifled or restrained. Or maybe it was the other way 'round, maybe it was really the indoors coming outside, leaving plenty of space in the planks of the wood, the packed earth underfoot, so's you nearly couldn't tell was you inside or out. It was a harmony I never seen nowhere else on earth, like walking into a place that God carved into the world, just to accommodate the shape of me in it. A comfort and exhilaration, both. But the swoon was brief; there was work to do.

In a darkened corner of shadow, the mare stood quietly, her hot breath coming in gathered shifts while she worked. The farmer stood behind her, shirtless and sweating. He looked more troubled than the horse. He heard us and turned to glance over his shoulder. A flicker of relief passed over his face and then fled.

"Breech," he said through gritted teeth.

He was working inside the mare, his arm invisible to the shoulder, nearly. He grunted and heaved so's you'd have thought he was the one giving birth to the foal.

"I can't turn him for the life of me," he said, and then the mare contracted, and I seen how his arm got squeezed inside.

He slapped the horse's rump with his free hand, and made another groan. The sweat was tripping him, but the mare stood placid, waiting. I could see all of Eamonn Burke's squat, yellowed teeth, right back to his jaw, because he bared them at us while he waited for the mare to free him again. When she did, he allowed his arm to slip out of the horse and drop to his side. He grabbed a rag to wipe hisself down.

"I can't get him turned," he said to Grandda, who was stripping down now, too. "It's a bad one."

"Have ye any bailing twine?" Grandda said.

"We have, of course," Eamonn Burke said, looking a little puzzled. "Joe, get the bailing twine."

My grin leaked out; I couldn't help it. I'd seen Grandda do this a hundred times before. He was dunking his hands in the bucket of antiseptic when Joe Burke returned with the twine. Grandda dunked the twine in as well and, pulling it out, fashioned it into a knotted loop. He was talking quietly to the mare.

"You're doing everything right," he said. "You just need a bit of a push and pull, is all. I'll see if I can't help."

His voice was almost a hum, a melody. The horse made a hum of her own, in answer, a soft note in the back of her throat. Grandda patted her rump.

"Christy," he said to me, without changing his voice from the humming. "Come 'round over here and see if you can hold her tail for me. Just hold it up out of the way so's I can see."

I placed his black bag carefully on the floor and went to help him. I grabbed a nearby bucket and put it upside down, so's I could stand on top and be taller. I gathered up the mare's roughened tail and held it aside. Grandda handed me the loose end of the twine to hold, too, and then worked the looped end up inside the mare. She shuffled a back foot, but only lightly. She flicked her tail, but I managed to hold it, and all the while Grandda was working inside her and humming to her, talking her through it.

"That's a girl," he told her. "I'm just going to loop this 'round your little fella's feet . . . there. Now. We'll give him a tow out, from this end, if we can. Now. Just hang on a second there, I'll give him a shove from the other side. Just an encouragement. That's all he needs. A bit of persuasion. Now. Christy, come down here and pull on the twine."

I jumped down from the bucket and came beneath, beside Grandda. I held on to the twine where he showed me.

"Don't tug!" he said. "Just firm now, and steady as she goes. Wait for her. Wait. Wait. Now. Pull. Harder. A bit harder."

He never raised his voice from the hum. I could see his muscles working, all in Grandda's back and neck. His hand and arm was disappeared, but I could see him working anyway, and I pulled on the twine as solid as I could, and then was the miracle moment, two tiny little hooves appeared, ensnared by Grandda's twine loop. Eamonn Burke was astonished.

"How in the name of the Blessed Mother did you manage that, now?" he said, smiling. "I've been working that poor mare for the better part of three hours. I thought she was a goner. Feck."

He was shaking his head, flabbergasted. Grandda relieved his arm from the mare and cleaned it off, but his face hadn't broke into a smile, and I knew something was wrong. I could sense it, even before I seen Grandda's face. And then the mare was circling, and we all backed up to give her room. I moved the bucket aside so's it wouldn't trip her. She went down on her side, and her four legs poked out in rhythmic spasms: two heaves, and the foal slipped out, tiny and black in the straw beside its mother. He was a colt, slick and still except for the slightest rise of his little rib cage. The umbilical cord pulsed from the new mammy, who was glassy-eyed, now, and shattered.

"Didn't I tell ya she'd be grand?" young Joe Burke was saying to his father.

Eamonn twisted his head on his neck.

"Ah now," the farmer said. "It was a close one, all the same."

And you could nearly hear the two of them grinning at each other, in that glowy, lamplit barn. Not a speck of reverence between them. I never could understand how sometimes a farmer could be around animals for his whole life, grooming and feeding and doctoring and milking them, and yet still be so god-awful oblivious to their nature. The mare was closing her eyes.

"Grandda?" I whispered.

But he raised his fingers, and I knew to be quiet, to give him a minute to think. Instead, I looked at the tiny colt, easily the smallest, sickliest-looking newborn horse I'd ever seen. I could've lifted him with my two arms—seven years of age, I was. That foal wasn't no heavier than Grandda's black bag. And worse, he made no effort to lift his head. He still had the thick membrane of the veil wrapped 'round his neck and shoulders. He didn't try to wriggle free of it. He didn't try to do nothing. He only stayed laying there, hardly moving at all. Eamonn Burke was slapping his son's shoulder behind us, in a manly, congratulatory sorta way.

"It's a twin," Grandda said quietly.

Joe and Eamonn Burke went stock-still and silent behind us. Even in the lamplight, I seen their faces drain of color. They knew that twins was rare with horses, and that *surviving* twins was unheard of.

"Impossible," Eamonn Burke said. "She was bred before; we never . . ."

His voice trailed off, swallowed by the muffling straw. A mare rarely survived foaling twins, and on a small farm, where they depended on the sale of the weanling, and the annual breeding of the mare, that kinda loss could mean real hardship for a family. A season of hunger, at least. In the silence then, there was some communion between the dam and her foal. They breathed together. Outside, we could hear crickets.

In a moment, the mare dipped her neck and tried to stand, but it was too soon. Her tiny colt needed more blood from the cord, if he'd any hope at all of surviving.

"Hold her," Grandda said to Eamonn Burke, and he laid his large hands firmly acrosst her broad, flat cheek and her chin. "You're all right, girleen. Steady now and wait."

I unzipped Grandda's black bag, slid it into the light so's I could see inside.

"Christy, get the iodine ready," he said to me over his shoulder, but I already had the bottle in my hand, and was working the hard stopper out with my small fingers.

The tiny colt shuddered in the straw. We all knew what would happen if the mare stood now. That cord would snap, and the foal would bleed out, and the dam might, too. They both needed more time. But her distended belly was rolling like a tide, and she was trying to stand, to position the next baby inside, so's he could follow his tiny brother out into the world.

"Easy, girl," Grandda was whispering into the mare's twitching ear.

Her feet shuffled and scraped the ground, but she was weak after all the laboring, and the two men was able to hold her, between them. Eamonn Burke held on to her neck.

"Did you ever foal twins before?" he asked Grandda.

"Only once, years ago."

"And?"

Grandda shook his head.

"They both died?" he asked.

"All three of them," Grandda answered.

The mare was contracting. Her belly rolled. She had to stand.

"Just another minute, now; give your little fella a fighting chance," Grandda was humming to her.

And I watched as she flared her nostrils and blinked her eyes, and I thought I could sense a light going out in her, like she was about to give up the ghost altogether. And I guess Grandda sensed it too, because he leaned up, and signaled for Eamonn Burke to do the same.

"Go on, then," he said to the mare, nudging her rump. *"Hup!"*

The horse rocked onto her feet, jerking her colt and snapping the cord between them. There was a gush of dark blood, but it didn't spurt out, it only oozed. And then she was standing, awful close to the tiny colt, but she was careful of him—she knew where he was. She leaned her head down to nuzzle him, but then she was racked again, with the next baby coming, and she stood in a circle til she was ready to go again. Eamonn Burke tried to lead her, but Grandda shooed him away.

"Let her go where she will," he said.

And the mare backed into the darkest corner of the barn, leaving her first colt to fend for hisself. The tiny baby shivered, and I moved a bit closer with my iodine at the ready.

"Grandda?" I said.

I had the bottle and the dip cup in my hands. The colt needed it, to stop the blood and prevent infection. But usually Grandda always did this part. He was the expert, all the farmers said it. He'd birthed so many foals that they knew him now, to call for him if they was ever in a spot of bother, like tonight. He had some kind of a magic with animals—that's what they all said—that he was better than a vet by half, that he'd an instinct for it. But it all seemed obvious to me. Anybody could see what to do, if they would just open their eyes and look.

"You'll have to do it, Christy," Grandda said. "The iodine is already thinned, just dump it in the cup. You know how."

I knelt over the ailing foal, all on his own now, but I hesitated. He was so little. He moved his chin and looked up at me, but he still didn't lift his head. I'd never seen a foal who wouldn't lift his head. He was still on his side, where he'd landed when he'd fell out of his mam. His eyes was wet.

"Quickly, Christy," Grandda said to me over his shoulder.

Grandda was at the back end of the mare now, and there was a lot more blood than was normal. I dumped the iodine into the cup and lifted the colt's cord stump. It was sticky and warm, and the colt made a breathy mewl sound when I lifted the cord, but I couldn't tell if it was a pain or a comfort sound. I winced when I dipped the stump into the iodine, but the colt roused hisself and finally lifted his head, like a crow fluffing his feathers. He rolled onto his chest, and stuck his scrawny legs out at awkward angles beneath him.

"Hiya," I sang.

Grandda glanced over.

"Well done, Christy."

The colt blinked his eyes at me. His head looked too heavy for his neck, and it dipped and bobbed like a balloon on a string. He rested his chin in the straw. Joe Burke moved in for a look. He leaned close, reached out.

"Don't touch him," I said.

I don't know what made me say it. And more, I don't know what made Joe Burke listen to me, a seven-year-old boy. But he drew his hand back.

"Give him a minute," I said. "I need an empty feed sack."

Joe Burke left, banging the door of a nearby stall. I heard him upending a sack into a bucket, the scuffle of his boots as he returned with the empty sack. He held it out to me.

"Thanks," I said.

I peeled the veil back off the colt's shoulders to free him, and then I crumpled the empty feed sack into my fist. I started rubbing him with the coarse burlap, but I made my voice hummy, like Grandda's.

"Come on now, little fella," I said. "We've to get your breath going. Come on, let's hear it. Good and strong, boy-oh. Get the blood bumping."

I rubbed all up and down the colt's back, then flipped him over and did his tummy and his chest. He didn't resist at all. He was like a feed sack hisself, and so was Joe Burke, who stood watching. I rubbed harder, clapped my hands along the tiny rib cage. I was nearly afraid I'd break him, but I knew what he needed. A good, rough welcome, a jump start.

"Come on, let's get some fight into ya," I said.

Maybe I knew the mare was going to die. Maybe that's why I felt so connected to the little colt, because my mammy died, too, when I accidentally killed her as I was being born. I couldn't help wondering if it was a similar night to this, if everyone waited, wretched and breathless, for the horrible news that was my birth. Such a common truth: a travelling woman heaving her own soul heavenward while her baby boy slips, squawking and bloody, into the rough and dirty world to take her place. There's nothing worse than an ordinary grief.

Across the reach of the lamp, on the other edge of that rosy cone of light, in just a few minutes more, the second colt was born. Bigger and stronger than his brother. Except now there wasn't no time for dam and colt to haul their breath together in the hot night. The ending was gentle. The mare stopped kicking, stopped blinking. She stopped breathing. Her last movement was a soft flutter of her thick tail, peaceful enough.

Her new colt snuffled, charged his head about him. I got the baby bottle out of Grandda's black bag, and he collected the colostrum from the mam's still-warm udders. It had a heady scent, like butter and cut grass, filled all up with goodness. I wanted to feed the tiny black colt first.

"Don't bother with that one," Eamonn Burke said, when he seen where I was headed with the bottle.

I didn't even know what he meant.

"Don't go wasting the milk on him," he said. "He's not going to make it."

My mouth fell open and I looked at Grandda, who was busy tending to the new colt's stump. He was nut-brown, and nearly twice the size of his brother.

"How d'you mean?" I said.

I knelt down and touched the black colt's nose. He was still resting in the straw, but now he lifted his head again. He could smell the sweetness of his dam's milk, and he went seeking with his lips. He nosed the bottle in my hand.

"He's hungry," I said.

"He won't last an hour." Eamonn Burke took the bottle off me and went to feed the stronger brother.

"So you're just going to let him starve?" I said.

The farmer ignored me. Grandda came and stood beside me, put a hand on my shoulder. I shook my head. I jerked Grandda's arm, squeezed his hand. I was desperate. Grandda knelt down beside me for a look. The whites of the foal's eyes wasn't even white—they was yellow. But I could see him in there. I could *see* him. And I could count his fragile ribs beneath his skin, like glass. Them ribs lifted again, with his faltering breath. His head bobbled and swerved, and then collapsed into the straw again. But I knew, somehow, that he could survive. He had to.

"We'll take him, Eamonn," Grandda said quietly.

The farmer looked over at my grandda and shrugged.

"Suit yourself," he said. "Less work for me, getting rid of it."

"He needs a feed," Grandda said.

"It's wasteful," Eamonn Burke argued.

"It's only fair," Grandda said. "One feed, and then he's our responsibility."

The farmer shook his head and sighed, because he knew he owed Grandda a favor, because it was four o'clock in the morning and we was stood in his barn, covered in blood and muck. If either colt survived, it was only because of Grandda.

"I want to call him Jack," I whispered as I knelt to give the inky colt his first feed.

Grandda touched my arm."Don't go naming him just yet," he said.

But it was too late for them kinda warnings.

TWO

I never heard how it turned out with the other twin, but Jack thrived just like I knew he would. Grandda said it was touch-and-go there for a while, but I never had no doubts. He stayed that inky black color, but he grew to the size of a small rhinoceros, strapping and strong. He always seemed to know what we'd done for him that first night, how we'd saved him from doom. He was grateful.

Jack was a great comfort to me, them days after Grandda died. He seemed to soak up my grief like a sponge, and carry it with him so's I didn't have to.

On that journey to Grandda's burial place, it was two nights of stopping, of crowding into the wagon, gathering around his body inside, for to wake him. It was me and Dad, and then Martin and his parents—Uncle Finty and Auntie Brigid—and their two younger childer, Martin's four-year-old brother, John Paul, and his baby sister, Maureen. And we all crammed together inside Granny's wagon, where she was keeping watch over Grandda. There was drink and song both nights, and memories told in poetry, and Lord, the lament—that unshakable, feral keen. Grandda slept in the middle of it all, where he'd usually be playing the fiddle, telling jokes and stories, winking at us, and goosing Granny.

I'd never seen him so still before, not even when he was sleeping. And that stillness was a small gift. It allowed me to press Grandda into my memory like clay into a mold. I studied all of him in the lamplight: his strong, broad fingers with their knobby knuckles, like the roots of a tree, hard with calluses. His thick, hanging earlobes. His full head of white hair, raked back acrosst his head in deep, bright waves. And where the hair folded back from his forehead, his old-man spots—the mysterious marks that freckled his skin like a map of all the places he'd been. I was sat so close to him that I could see the tiny holes in his skin where the hair had growed out of his cheeks and chin, before Granny'd shaved him. I could see the wrinkles shooting out from the corners of his eyes, like rays coming out of the sun.

By the second night looking at him, I felt like a skinned apple, turning brown and starting to rot. I couldn't reconcile it—that the pure, barren stillness of that body was supposed to be Grandda. Martin and me went out into the pitch-black for a smoke, just to get away from it, but them relentless keens clawed their way after us in the dark.

Martin's face was lit orange from the fag we shared. His eyes gaped, and I wondered if I looked as scraped out as he did. His cheekbones was starting to stand up in his face because that was the age we was—losing our baby fat. He had a constellation of freckles acrosst the bright skin of his nose, and his green eyes turned down at the corners, just like his mammy's. His hair was like mine, soft and curly brown. Honey in the summertime. It was good to see the shapes of him moving, breathing, the way they was supposed to. Everything else was in blackness.

"It's enough to do your head in," he said, blowing the silver smoke through his teeth.

We was sat up on a farmer's gate, our ankles locked 'round the

lower bar, and we could hear Martin's mammy—Auntie Brigid—
and Granny, wailing in the distance. I shivered, my arms folded
acrosst the front of me. Martin started to hum to hisself, to block out
the sound of our nomad grief.

"I can't believe they's going to bury him," I said, pinching the fag
off Martin. I took a deep drag.

Martin jumped down off the gate, grabbed up a fistful of gravel,
and then climbed back up beside me. "What else would they do with
him?" he said.

I shook my head and sucked the smoke as deep into me as it
would go. "I donno," I said. "Anything would be better than that.
Than being stuck into a box and left in the one place forever."

Martin stared at me. "What's wrong with you, thinking about
things like that?"

"What's wrong with you," I said, "never thinking about them?
You never worry about nothing."

"Maybe I do, Christy." He started throwing the gravel bits into
the darkness one at a time, listening.

"Do you ever not be able to sleep at night?" I said.

"Sometimes," he said, which surprised me. But then he said,
"When I do be hungry, like."

"But them is the only times?" I said. "Even since Grandda died?"

Martin shrugged. I handed him back the fag.

"Like sometimes I can't sleep," I said. "And then the loneliest
things do come into my head. Like if Dad might've left a tarp behind, I might worry over it, being all alone in the dark and the damp
and the cold. And, like, I might worry that a car will run over it and
rip it up or something."

Martin was quiet beside me.

"I do always think about the scrap heaps, too," I said. "After we
leave a place. There's some kind of a deep sadness in that, in things
being always left behind on their own."

He didn't laugh at me or nothing. He took another pull off the fag and then handed it back to me. "Christy, scrap heaps don't feel things."

"But it's still all alone out there," I argued. "Even if it doesn't feel it."

"It's all in your head," Martin said. "You're too soft, Christy."

There had to be a way to make him understand.

"Do you remember the time we stopped on Lough Ree?" I asked. "And we halted right there on the shore? It was summer."

"Yeah," he said. "That was one of the best camps ever. Remember we made them driftwood rifles with Grandda?"

"Yeah." I grinned. "And then the whole time we was there, we was fighting the black-n-tans."

"That was class," Martin said. "And we'd go marching out, patrolling the camp."

"Do you remember what happened them rifles?" I asked. "When we left?"

Martin rubbed his hand over his eyes. His face was changing. "I guess I don't," he said. "I haven't thought about them rifles in ages, Christy. I wonder whatever did happen them."

I had to bite my lip to startle a tear away. "Dad and Finty made us leave 'em behind," I said. "They said we'd enough truck to haul around with us, our whole lives packed up in the wagons, without collecting junk into the bargain." I handed the fag back to Martin.

"So?" he said, taking it.

"So I didn't sleep for three days, wondering about them rifles," I said. "If some other *Pavee* childer found 'em in the dirt after we was away, or if they got washed back into the lough and drowned, or if they was pitched onto somebody's fire the next night for tea."

I could hear a catch in Martin's breath.

"Feck, I wouldn't like to think of them bobbing around lost in the water," he said.

"Or worse." I shook my head. "Sunk down to the bottom of Lough Ree where nobody'd ever see 'em again."

Martin chewed on the inside of his cheek.

"It's the same with Grandda," I said. "Only worse because he'll be trapped inside a little box, like, and buried in under the dirt and grass."

Martin started shaking his head. "But it has to be okay," he said. "It has to, Christy, because that's what they've been doing with dead people forever. Why would they do it if it was so horrible?"

"Who's going to complain about it?" I said. "Grandda? I guess dead people don't whinge much. And you know, he had that wicked fear of small spaces."

"Did he?" Martin said.

"Do you not remember that time at the Balinasloe horse fair, and he was all in the middle of that crush of people when a fight broke out, and he lost the plot completely?"

"Yeah, he did," Martin said.

"Lost the nut altogether," I said. "Sure Granny threatened they'd throw him in the lunatic asylum if he didn't take it handy."

Martin sucked his breath through his teeth. "That was an awful press of people, that time," he said. "All in the lashing rain and the muck. You'd get trampled, so you would."

We was small then, I remembered. Belt-buckle height. We was able to get out, dodging between legs and pulling each other through.

"He told me afterwards why it petrified him," I said. "Why he panicked. He said one time when he was young, he got hired to muck out a silage pit for a farmer. But he got trapped inside, and he was in there for ages before they found him. He nearly died from the fumes."

Martin made some kind of a breathy "oh" sound.

"Yeah," I said. "It was horrible. That's why he never wanted to sleep inside, in the wagon, even after the doctor said he should, for his lungs."

"Feck," Martin said. "He really wouldn't like to be buried."

"No." I shook my head.

"It *is* awful cramped feeling, when you do be inside," Martin said. "I donno how them buffers do it all the time."

I flexed, instinctively. That was always my response to thinking about doorways and walls and ceilings. To stretch out the muscles of my body, to let them unfold. To feel the openness of the free air all around me, unbound. That was the purest form of reassurance—it was elemental.

We was quiet for a few minutes then, and we couldn't help but listen to Granny's cry, carried to us, as it was, on the high, dark wind.

"I just can't imagine it," I said. "When you see him laying there, I can't imagine him buried."

"He still looks alive," Martin whispered.

"I hate to think of him cooped up and folded into a box," I said. "A lid nailed down over his face." I winced, imagining.

"He can't breathe," Martin gasped. "Can't move at all. Can't sit, can't stand, can't even scratch."

"There's no music," I said. "No starlight, no firelight, no sun. No wind, no air. Just six feet of darkness. Silence. Dirt."

Martin dropped the fag. "Feck," he said quietly. He threw the rest of the gravel down on top of the dying fag, and brushed off his hands.

Then it was quiet again, and I sorta wished Martin would start up his humming, because the wind had shifted, and the keening was even louder than before. I curled over my knees.

"What would you do, then?" His whisper hung close beside me.

"How d'ya mean?"

"Instead of burying him," he said. "What do you think he'd want?"

"I donno," I said. "I mean, I guess the best thing would be for him to be still alive."

"But barring that."

"Barring that then, I'd say the best thing would be if we could just leave him. Like if we could leave him up on that bank above Lough Ree where we made the rifles. Out under the stars, like."

"But the animals would get him," Martin said. "Or he'd wash into the lough like the rifles."

"We could leave him inside the wagon, then. I mean, he'd still be inside, which isn't perfect, but it's bigger than a coffin, and he'd have all his things around him. He'd have his fiddle."

"That does seem better," Martin agreed. "But Granny would never go for it."

"No chance." I shook my head.

"But maybe," Martin said, and I could hear him thinking.

"Maybe what?" I said. "There's fuck all we can do about it, Martin."

"We could burn the wagon," he whispered.

I drew my breath into me like a sword. "Fuck," I said.

But he was right. Fire. The warm embrace of flame and light—that was better than a cold box. They was going to burn the wagon anyway, after Grandda was buried. That was our *Pavee* way: to burn up the wagon and all the belongings of the person who'd died. It was meant to free the living from the memories, to purify everything and wash away the death for whoever was left behind—the way a wildfire in a forest cleanses the ground for new growth. And for the dead, the remnant spirit, that fire was meant to free whatever stubborn soul might be left trapped inside them objects most beloved—to urge them on toward purgatory instead.

"You'd be free then," Martin said. "If you was burnt up with your wagon."

"You would," I breathed.

"Let's do it," he said. "What'd you do with the matches?"

"What?"

"The matches."

"You can't," I said. "You can't have them."

Martin looked at me, but all I could see of his face now was two points of light where his eyes would be. He twisted his head at me. A quick motion, a dismissal.

"Fine, then," he said. "We'll head back?"

He hopped down from the fence and his feet made a crunch in the gravel.

I climbed down after him, cautious. "Hang on, Martin," I said.

I reached for his arm, to stop him. I had been the one to make him see, and now I had to make him un-see. But my fingertips only brushed against the blackness between us. He was striding ahead, and I could make out the shape of him against our faraway campfire.

"Martin, you won't do nothing foolish," I said.

His grunt might've meant anything.

"Martin."

"'Course not," he said, but his voice was like a closed book, and I couldn't pry it open again.

THAT NIGHT, I SLEPT FITFUL in the shelter tent beside my silent dad, listening the whole time to the camp-noises. Listening for Martin's footsteps in the dirt, listening for the scratch and bite of a match flaring up to breath. But the mind can only hold the body captive for so long, and when sleep took me, I dreamed that we was moving, that the camp was mobile. Sliding, seeping, crawling, rolling, bringing Grandda home. In the night, I imagined a whole troop of them purple horses, hitching us up from our weariness, and ferrying us along, secretly and kindly, so that we might waken, well rested, and find all wicked journeys behind us.

From every corner of Ireland, I could feel the motion of horses and humans: all Wards and Cassidys and McDonaghs and Hurleys. All the fierce, intrepid clans was gathering. The word had gone out;

Granny sang it in her keen like a smoke signal, and in every county, the *Pavees* heard it and smelt it and read it in the raindrops, and they turned their horses 'round in the roads, and they came to us.

"SURE THERE'S BAD LUCK IN that wagon now, Christy," Dad said in the morning.

I didn't tell Dad that there was obviously quite good luck in the wagon, to've survived the night against me and my big, fat mouth.

"You wouldn't want your Granny yoked to a ghost now, sure you wouldn't?"

I shook my head, though in truth, I couldn't see what would be so bad about being yoked to a ghost, if that ghost was Grandda. His body was getting buried into the clay in just a few short hours now. And then every other trace of him would get burnt to smoke.

Granny and Grandda's wagon looked the loneliest I'd ever seen it, even with the two of them still inside. Outside, the ground was littered with the remains of last night's salute; there was always extra drink that came with death, because whiskey and grief begot each other. Even Granny'd had a few swallows last night, and the broken glass of the now-emptied bottle glinted in the bright morning sun, making blue-green sparkles all around the camp. I stood among them sparkles at the back door of the wagon and rested my elbows on the doorjamb.

"Come in, Christy," Granny said from inside.

She had a small wooden crate clutched in her arms, and she was moving slowly around the wagon, carefully weighing and selecting the items that would make it into the crate. I stepped back and clambered up the three steps into the wagon.

"He looks well, doesn't he?" Granny said, stopping in her work to gaze at Grandda.

I nodded, but I couldn't answer. He looked even more alive now, in the light of the burial day, and I wondered how that happened.

How he got livelier-looking the longer he was dead. It was unthink-
able that a few hours from now, we was going to 'prison him in the
ground and then walk away from him forever. I wanted to reach out
and squeeze his knotted fingers, and say, "Grandda?" But I was too
afraid. I could barely even breathe. I went and kneeled down by
him, and folded my hands in front of me.

"Arragh, there's a good boy," Granny said, because she thought I
was paying my respects.

And I was, in my way. Grandda was there, just inches from me
now, and I wanted to memorize him one last time in the daylight,
every dip and crease, every color. I traced the lines on his skin with
my eyes. *Open your eyes*, I thought. *Open them, Grandda.* But he didn't.
I blessed myself then, and sat down on the floor beside him. Granny
started talking to me midsentence.

"Nothing's fair," she said, as if it was a thing that needed saying.
"There's nothing fair in this life. Sure haven't I lost four children and
now their father."

That was a thing, for travellers, that we'd lived with for so long
that sometimes we couldn't really see it no longer—that things
wasn't fair on us. Like: I have ten fingers. I have ten toes. Nothing's
fair on us. But now it was like a revelation to her, and it made her
stop moving. There's nothing fair in this life. It was the same for all
travelling women—a handful of dead children, and then eventually,
their father. Granny rested her crate on top of the bread box; she
leaned on it. Then she blinked, swept the hair from her forehead,
and went back to her packing.

"You're really gonna do it, Granny?" I asked.

"Do what?" She looked at me sideways.

It was the same look Dad gave me when I asked him about the
bansídhes—like I was crazy.

"I mean, do we have to burn everything?" I said.

It suddenly seemed so drastic, such a complete disappearance of
his life, like bad magic. I looked at the fiddle standing mute in its

corner, its bow leaned up beside it in a lifeless embrace. Grandda always kept that fiddle so shined up you could see yourself in it. He restrung it whenever he could. Granny used to say that if he'd took half as gooda care of her as he did of the fiddle, she'd be fit for a museum.

She came and sat down beside Grandda on the tick. She didn't look at me; she looked at him instead. She touched his hand, and that made me wish I had the courage to touch him too. Her voice was steady and soft.

"It's the right thing to do," she said, so matter-of-factly that I nearly believed it.

She stroked his forehead, but her calm couldn't quench my rising panic. Nothing seemed like the right thing to do now—not the burying, not the burning. Not the dying. The whole world had gone arseways.

Granny blinked and looked around her, at the floor first, where I was sitting. Then at the blankets, at Grandda's clothes and his tin-smithing tools. She took inventory with her eyes: his wellies, the pot and kettle, the bread box and press. Their few bits and pieces of porcelain, so carefully saved and transported over the years. The Bible they couldn't read. Four different Jesuses and two Marys, all watching us from the walls. And one of my favorite memories of him, an embroidered handkerchief, tucked beneath the corner of the tick.

Granny had bought them hankies as a Christmas gift one year, and embroidered them herself in navy threads with Grandda's initials, S.H., which Dad drew onto the cotton for her with a stubby pencil. I used to tell Grandda that his initials made the sound "shhh," so he thought it was great *craic* to flip a hankie out and show it to us whenever one of us was getting a going-over. He'd stand behind Auntie Brigid or Granny or whoever was doing the giving out, and he'd dangle the initials over his forearm at us and put his finger to his lips, hushing us—delighted with his own joke. We would titter, of course, and then Grandda would get caught, and he'd fold the hankie back into his pocket quite soberly. "I don't know what these boys do be on about," he'd say.

I fingered the hankie, pulled it loose from its hiding spot beneath Grandda. Granny took it from me and used it to sop up the corner of my eye. Then she folded it neatly and tucked it back beneath the tick.

"We have to let him go now," she said then. "So he can be free of this world."

Her voice was thin, watery. She opened and closed her toothless mouth. Her eyes was shining in the faint light. Granny could do that, she could change, like. Granny of the Transformations. Right now in the grief-stricken wagon she was a mournful fish. Mouth opened and closed, opened and closed, in silence. I imagined that one more gape of the mouth and she would sprout fins and gills, and she would rend off her black funeral dress and reveal a breastplate of hard, beautiful scales beneath, like the blue and green glass scattered on the ground outside. And then she would swim away in a river of her own tears.

"It has to be done, so," she said with finality, breaking the spell. "But first things first. We've the funeral in just a couple of hours. We need to feed the childer, so."

And she stretched out her hand to me. She was ready, so I had to be ready too. How could she be ready?

I stood myself up and gave her my hand. Granny put her Bible into the crate, and left the whole thing down on the floor. I peeked at its meager contents as I passed: two teacups with their saucers and two spoons, half a dozen small glass vials and bottles with cork stoppers, a toothbrush, a comb, a pair of scissors, a deck of cards, a blue stone rosary, her pipe but not Grandda's pipe, and then the Bible. Apart from her clothes, which would be moved into Brigid's press for safekeeping, this was really it. This crate held all the seeds she'd have to grow forward from. The buttons on her beady pocket clattered against each other as she climbed down the steps in fronta me, and I was soothed by the sound.

For a traveller, the beady pocket was like a map of her memory. Every *Pavee* woman had one: a long, black pocket that tied 'round her waist and hung to the side of her apron, where she kept her personal artifacts. But really it was the outside of the pocket where the memories was stored, because them pockets was decorated all with bright-colored stitching, and then, pinned and sewed in among the stitching, there'd be all the collections of holy relics and medals, all the beads and buttons and brooches the women swapped along the *tober*.

Granny'd had her pocket since forever, and every button on it had a story attached. All you'd to do was put your finger on one, and off she'd go, telling tales. It was like a scrapbook of her life, that pocket, and it was a comfort to me, hearing it clack to the side of her hip while she walked. Like she couldn't never forget a minute of her life with Grandda so long as she had that memory-map to guide her.

GRANNY WENT OFF SOMEWHERE PRIVATELY then, for to get herself washed and dressed for the church. Dad and Finty was away into the town for to collect the coffin, and Auntie Brigid was sat at the fire, washing her baby Maureen in the warmed tub, where me and Martin and John Paul had all had our go's ahead of her. I was stuck close to the fire, too, just trying hard not to think. I blinked and I breathed, and in the next moment, there was an unnatural heat on my neck. I looked up from the campfire and turned. Behind us, all the daytime sky was alight with the colors of a hungrier flame. The heat roared up.

"*Holy God and Mary!*" Brigid screamed, and she dropped Maureen into the tub with a splash. "The wagon's on fire!"

The baby flailed and went under, but Brigid scooped her out

quick—naked and slippy—and then plonked her, crying, into the dirt.

"Help me, Christy!" Brigid shouted.

I was standing with my mouth open, and Brigid was on her feet then, too, struggling with the sloshy weight of the washtub as she dragged it toward Grandda's burning wagon. I hopped, and between us, we managed to lift it, just. We doused a single flame, but new ones filled in behind it at once, and we only left a feeble puddle of muck on the ground beneath the wagon, like drool off a corpse. The flames licked and raced up the sides of the tarpaulin. The speed of the destruction was shocking, and Brigid and me was driven back in blasts.

"That's some glimmer."

A voice. I turned, and there was Martin beside me, watching the gobble of flames with wide, hard eyes. My mouth fell open to meet him, and then the light grew hotter on our faces, and there was a whoosh of a sound as something lit inside—the tick, maybe, where Grandda lay. And I knew now that he was burning there, too, in that black belly of fire, and it wasn't nothing like I'd imagined it. There wasn't nothing peaceful or free in it—not at all. It was horrible: the wagon was like a wounded monster, its tarpaulin skin twisting into charred rags, hanging limp and clinging to the frame.

It was impossible not to see inside now, to the quilts as they lit in puffy blooms of color. I didn't want to see Grandda burning, but there he was, his form. Just the shape of him there on the tick, growing lighter and darker at once. Lit by flames and blackening to cinder. Grandda was fuel now, his soul whittled down to chemistry. We watched the colors of the flames as they popped and soared and gnawed the willing wood. And then the smoke became a blindfold, and I was grateful for that small kindness.

Maureen was crying hysterical, after getting plopped cold and wet from her bath into the dirt. John Paul hoisted her up onto a lawn chair and was trying to quiet her, but she was naked and trembling. Brigid was near running in circles now, clapping her hands together, wringing them—she didn't know what to do. She pulled at the kerchief on her hair.

And then, there was Granny. Just back from bathing, and clean, stepping down the road toward us. She paused for a moment before she broke into that clumsy, loping sprint. Fear has a terrible speed to it. There she was: Granny, holding up her skirts and flying—and the shrieks coming out of her, the wails that dwarfed any keen that ever came before. Her grief was so thick then that it smothered us. I breathed it; I gulped it.

"What did you do?"

Nobody heard my whisper in the chaos, but I could see the tricks on Martin's face, how he'd talk hisself into resolve. How he knew it would hurt them, but still, he'd reckon, it was the right thing for Grandda. Because that's what I'd made him believe. And now Granny was crumpling, and Brigid was over, trying to hold her, trying to lift her up and keep her, and I knew that, really, it was me who'd made her crumple like that. It was my fault, all of it. Her crate was still inside, packed with her scant comforts. The vision of it felt vital to me, like the bare minimum she would need in order to carry on. Something in me sprung.

I leapt forward until I was in among them flames, clambering up the steps and into the wagon, the dragon breath of smoke all around me. Everything was in mottled, char-choke gray, but I was down low and reaching. Feeling. The floorboards, the cooker, the belch of Grandda's ruined violin. The splintering cracks of wood popping all around me, the loud speech of flame in my ears—like the snapping of a cotton sheet on a clothesline in the wind. My family's shouts, distant now, behind all that. Wispy curtains of smeared gray. The bite of a flame by my ear—another at my shoulder. I couldn't breathe. The air was atremble with them hot and quivery vapors. Any second them vapors would light, and my trousers, my shirt, me. I had to get out. Now. I was out of seconds. And then, there: Granny's crate. Smoldering and threatening, but still intact. A hot miracle. I snatched it, started to shimmy back the way I'd came.

Then—bump. A wall where the door should be. I had to take a breath. I sucked air, felt the hairs in my nose singe. Then crack—clatter—wood and ash and dust rained down. Nothing fell on me. And then the clear sky of day was overhead. Smoke and boiled vapors rushed out in columns, and I could find myself, gulp a breath. I could find the door. I threw the smoking crate out in front of me and then I followed it out with a tumble, my skin feeling all full of cracks and splits and bubbles, coiling and pulling like the burnt canvas of the tarpaulin.

I could hear Granny loud again, shrieking and howling. And my name, too, falling from her lips in a keening wail: *Christopher*. That was me. And I was on my back on the ground, coughing up flame like a dragon. And everything was in blinding brightness and I had to wait, wait. Dizzy. But when I opened my eyes, there was Granny, quiet, her face blank and sunlit, painted soot-black by the smoke and the Irish wind, wet even this far inland, wet even on a clear, blue, sunny day. How could a wagon burn like that, in the dampness of this wind?

"Holy Mother of God, Christy," Granny said.

I blinked my eyes. I thought I might be dead, like Grandda. I had went toward the light.

"Christy." Granny was tracing a cross along my forehead.

"I'm all right." I coughed. "I'm grand."

My face was wet, but it was only snot. Granny helped me sit up, and I seen all her carefully packed life-seeds from the crate strewed acrosst the dirt and the muck. She had ash in her hair. Grandda-ash. My skin was hot and flushed, but not burnt at all, not the way it felt. There was a terrible dry heat in my mouth and my throat, like sand. But I was okay, really.

Then Brigid's hands was under my armpits, and I was standing.

The wagon groaned and cracked, dismantling itself in turns, until only half its skeleton was left, the wooden bones of the rib cage brutally exposed and reaching into the scrubbed blue sky amid the flames.

We all stood and watched and waited. How many wagons had we seen burn like this before, down to shadow and shape? All that would be left at the end was a shifting pile of blackened wood and a wending trace of smoke, almost a figment.

But this was different. Grandda was real inside that blaze. He was in there, his old-man spots, his eyebrows. The pores of his skin, turning to nothing. Like marks on paper, he was getting erased.

We stood in a circle around the wagon: Granny, Brigid, Martin, and me, helpless and grief-struck, thunderstruck. That terrible festive odor of woodsmoke crept and wound around us, invading our clothes, our skins, our hair. John Paul tried his best to hush Maureen, and she wailed and cried while we watched them flames climb only higher and hungrier into the bright, funeral sky.

THREE

In the middle of all that heat and flame and fear, there was a cool whisper. Grandda's voice, like he'd been swallowing snow and now he was leaning into my ear and he was whispering secrets to me, things nobody else could hear. And I was straining, straining for him, but I couldn't make him out, only the suggestion of him, that somehow I knew he was there. Maybe he'd say it was okay, that it didn't hurt. That he felt free—thanks to me and thanks to Martin—and this was his soul, escaping here on the shoulders of smoke and flame.

"Grandda?"

I held my breath. And then I seen it, cartwheeling and tumbling through that sun-riot of fire-color. Whipping along the gray smoke-tops of the flames, a small, unburnt miracle: a square of dancing paper. And I knew straightaway it was Grandda: his soul, flattened and lightened, but not yet quite free. Ghost-flotsam. He was trapped here, in this singed and ragged leaf.

I held my breath as I watched it dip and circle. Sparks swarmed the air like scorched bees. I didn't mean to, but I stretched my fingertips out into the hot sky like twigs off the bough of a tree. And just like that, with one fresh puff of Grandda's spirit-breath, the square of paper leapt and flew, and tangled itself through my branches. Stinging sparks. Blackened fingers. I grasped it to me, and nobody seen, only me. A newsprint photograph.

All grays and whites and blacks, all flat faces and fettered eyes. They was riddles, the three of them: a woman, with the hair standing out sideways from her head like a flag in the whipping wind. Her smile precarious, like it might slip into grimace with a clean, daytime shift of the light, a cloud skittering in front of the sun. And then a fella beside her with empty eyes, his hand clinging on to her elbow as if he was steering her, like a ship on the ocean. The angles of the bones in his face made sharp shadows that carved him up into pieces. And between them, the big, round bauble of a baby, with cheeks like two fairy cakes, baked plump and iced with pink sugar.

All three of them was strangers to me—nobodies. But I was holding them tight in my hand and they was staring off the page like a mystery waiting to be solved, like I could save them. And then I spotted it—dangling from a silver cord 'round the woman's neck—it was unmistakable, unique: a Saint Christopher medal.

Mine.

I gasped out loud when I seen it, and my mouth hung open. I could taste the acrid smoke off the fire, turning pungent and bitter. The stink of burning flesh strangled out the woodsier scent. Nobody was looking at me; they all stared into the fire. Brigid bent down to throw up, her gray braids tied together at the back of her head. And somehow at that moment, I felt like I had the answer, that the newsprint photo was like a magic wand in my hand. I didn't know how to use it yet, but somehow, I sensed it could fix everything; that it was the key to making things right for Grandda. Maybe I could still give him the ending he wanted.

I closed my eyes and felt the hot leftover breath of them flames against my eyelashes and cheeks. That trace coolness from a mo-

ment ago had vanished; all the air was ablaze, and I knew that
Grandda was gone from everywhere else on earth. I was his only
keeper.

I stashed the photograph right into my pocket. Beside me, Martin
started to cough, and when I opened my eyes again, they was stung
by ropes of woody smoke. All the colors was trembling and giving
way. Grandda and his wagon was leaving a thick, inky smudge
acrosst the sky.

I DIDN'T MEAN TO FIND the tin. I was walking out into the field for
a slash, because you still have to piss, even when the rest of the
world stops working. And I just kicked it. My toe landed against it
with a sickening, hollow clunk, and I bent down to pick it up before
I even knew what I was at. My hands reached before my brain could
tell them no. The tin was the same color as the grass and the weeds,
a bright green with the yellow ESSO logo stamped into its side. I
could feel Martin's fingerprints on it in a glowy red-warmth, as real
to me as Jesus, and I wanted to rub them off with my shirttail. As if
that could undo what I'd done. That's how it was that Granny seen
me when she glanced up, across the smoking pile of rubble that was
her life, and I was stood holding that empty tin of petrol in my
guilty, guilty hands.

She rushed me. I never knew Granny could move so fast until
that day. It was like she'd lost twenty years off her, like grief can
shave you down to something more essential than your body and
make you quick again. I tried to hide the tin behind my back, not
because I thought it would work, but because my body was more in
charge than my brain.

"Give us it," Granny said, reaching. "What've you found?"

She yanked my arm out from behind me, and we both stared at
the empty petrol tin. It didn't look criminal, not on its own. In fact,
it was past its prime, with rust along its back seam and no lid.

Granny tipped it by its handle, and it was still wet inside, still sharp with the tang of its petrol. It leaked a telltale dribble of recent fuel instead of the rainwater or emptiness I'd been hoping for.

"Where did you get this?" Granny said.

I stared at her, openmouthed. "I . . ."

"Where?" she demanded.

"J-just there," I stammered. "It was just there in the field, Granny."

"Did you see anyone?"

I shook my head, but I donno—either she seen my guilt or she smelled it off me or something, because the next thing I knew, she was shaking me. She twisted my arm.

"What did you see?"

"Nothing, Granny!"

She stared into my face. Searching. Rummaging. I tried to hide everything there, but I was no good at it. She clattered me on the ear.

"Out with it!"

"It was me," Martin said, his voice nearby. "It was me, Granny."

Granny let go my arm, her anger suspended by confusion. The empty petrol tin was still dangling between us. Martin was just a few feet away, staring into the ruined shapes of the wagon. It had collapsed in on itself, closed and locked Grandda inside. It might've looked like the cheerful leavings of a bonfire, smoldering like that, in the sunshine. A young fire, less than an hour old and already dying. Dad and Finty would be back now, any minute, with the coffin. What would we put in it?

"No, Martin," I said, but nobody was listening to me.

Granny was taking steps toward him, toward his back. "How do you mean, it was you?" she said, stupefied.

Martin shrugged.

"*What* was you?" Granny said. Her fingers had fallen open, empty. She was clutching the air.

"Grandda wouldn't've liked to've got buried," Martin said.

Granny was shaking her head. What was left of the wagon shifted again, breathing new life to the lingering flames. I could've fetched more water then. We could've doused it, with a few good buckets.

"You know the way he was always afraid of being closed in," Martin whispered.

I moved toward them. I'll never forget the way his face looked. I couldn't read what was there, but it wasn't regret.

"And?" Granny said.

"And I thought to set him free," Martin said plainly, as if there wasn't nothing poetic or insane about it in the slightest. "From the coffin."

"You?" Granny's hands opened and closed. She was making fists of air. "You did this?"

She had little trickles of water running down her face. Tears, maybe, but I didn't know if they was put there by the smoke or by Martin. My eyes was running, too, scraped by the dirty air.

"You did this?" she said again, her voice rising a pitch.

I feared for what would come next. I could hear hoofsteps down the road, the rattle of a wheel and cart. Grandda's coffin coming. I took more steps toward Granny. I seen the storm that was building in her.

"You!" And now Granny lunged for Martin, and she grabbed him by a fistful of his hair.

I made to stop her, to calm her, but she only slapped at me, smacked me away. She grabbed the petrol tin from my loosened grip.

"This?" she screamed at Martin. "This is how you set him free? With this?"

She swung the empty tin up acrosst Martin's face. He ducked too late, and his nose spouted a scarlet ribbon, a tiny geyser. She hit him again, acrosst the shoulder, the ear. His hands was up, but she was raining down on him, all her grief and her fury and her terror. And then Martin was down on one knee, and Granny should've stopped because she might really hurt him, she might kill him. But she couldn't see nothing, only the ruined and blackened shapes of Grandda and fire.

"How could you!" she was screaming. "You divil!"

And every time she hit him, she screamed it again. "You divil, you divil, you divil!"

And then Dad and Finty was there, and they was peeling her off him, but they didn't know nothing yet, and I knew the hiding he'd got from Granny was nothing, once Finty found out. I feared they might need that coffin for Martin before they was done with him. Martin's one eye was swelling, closing, but he looked at me from out the other one, the open one. And I thought he winked. But I couldn't be sure.

AFTERWARDS, GRANNY WAS LIKE AN inverted lamp—she sucked light outta the day instead of lending it. She was dressed all in her funeral blacks, with a thick rug draped acrosst her shoulders. Her skin was gray as smoke, and a light had gone out in her face. The sunshine parted around her.

Finty didn't beat Martin at all. Instead, when Brigid told him what happened, he only clapped his hand over his mouth and turned away before we could see his tears. Then he sunk into a fierce, white quiet that I'd never seen off him before. His jaw moved in new angles, like he was a different man than the one who'd wakened up that morning.

"Dad," Martin wanted to explain to him, to make him see, the same way I'd made him see, just last night. "Do you not remember how afraid Grandda was, of tight spaces? I did it for him, Dad. To free him. I didn't mean no harm by it."

But Finty was gone deaf to his son. He moved through him like as if he wasn't there.

We had to put the funeral off by a day, so we could sort Grandda out. Dad was sending me in with Granny and Brigid, to go and

talk to the priest, but they was making Martin stay behind to help
get Grandda's body out of the fire. Finty was leant on a shovel, and
Dad was beside him, his hands in his back pockets. You would've
known they was brothers then, even if you'd only been driving by
and seen them. The way they looked, standing there with their rugged brown faces, sharp jaws, and broad bodies. Finty's hair was gray
beneath his cap, but Dad's was still brown. They was waiting to start
their digging til we'd leave.

"I want to stay, too, Dad," I lied. "I should help." I didn't want to
see a single finger of burned-Grandda. I didn't want to know what
was left. Or what wasn't.

"Go in with your granny, son," Dad said. "She needs you."

In the church, Brigid told the priest there was a terrible accident
and a fire, and the wagon had burnt. "We need an extra day, so," she
said. "To get ourselves prepared for the burial."

Beside me, Granny leaked her gray and stony silence, and on the
way out of the church, Brigid stopped at the door to fill up a small
vessel with holy water. She went down on one knee after, and she
whispered, but I heard her.

"Mary, wash the demon wickedness out of him and make him
clean again."

I dunked my own hand deep and blessed myself five times for
good measure. "Mary, make me clean again, too," I said.

I avoided Martin all evening. He was the new ghost in our camp,
instead of Grandda. Nobody talked to him or even looked at him,
and when Granny doled out the spuds for tea, there wasn't none on
a plate for Martin. Instead of asking for one, he just stood up quietly
from the campfire and made his way alone into the shelter tent.

He found me before bed, though. I was pissing into the field, and
he unzipped beside me.

"Hungry?" I said.

"Nah."

"I could get you some bread or something."

"I'm all right," he said.

"Did Granny hurt you much?" I said.

"Not much."

But his hand went to his damaged nose, his swollen eye. Then it was quiet except for the sounds of us watering the grass.

"Did it work?" I whispered.

"Did what work?"

"You know," I said. "The fire. Grandda."

Martin took a deep breath. "It worked some," he said. "I mean, I think it did."

I blinked, and my face welled up. "Was there much left of him?"

"Yeah." Martin nodded. "But not like before. I think it freed him."

I zipped up, took a step back.

"You know." Martin's voice was deadly quiet and even, like a sacred stone. "It was only pieces of him left. A lot of pieces."

I zipped up my breath in my lungs. "And that's what's in the coffin now? Pieces?"

Martin nodded again.

"They made me fill the rest up with rocks."

IN THE CHAPEL THE NEXT day, Father Dougherty raised his hands above the crowd with his palms facing us, and his long robes spreading out behind him like linen wings.

"A bit of *ciúnas*, please, folks, please!" he said, louder than necessary.

I was in the third pew with Martin, and I still couldn't look at him properly, but from the corner of my eye, he seemed to've growed two inches overnight. Or maybe I'd shrunk. His shoulders was pushed back, and he'd a gash across the bridge of his nose, where Granny had hit him with the petrol tin. The eye on the far side was a puffy, purple slit.

The two of us was minding Martin's little brother, John Paul, and the baby Maureen, who was slobbering on the Mass card because Martin was letting her. He'd propped the baby up in the pew behind him and gave her the Mass card to play with, to keep her quiet. I'd to pry it loose from her sloppy little fingers, and the corner was soggy, twisted. It felt like a sacrilege to let her eat Grandda's Mass card. I tried to smooth it out on the rail in front of me.

It musta been Dad who'd arranged for them lovely cards, because nobody else could read. The left-hand side was a picture of Jesus, standing on a very pointy mountain with a lot of yellow smokes or gasses around him, and then some clouds under his feet. He was holding His robe open so's we could see His sacred heart, but He looked sad, even with the fluffy clouds and the gasses. Then on the right-hand side was a cross, with no Jesus on it, just a little one with stripes coming out from its middle like it was meant to be glowing. And then below that was all the words.

> *May Jesus have mercy on the soul*
> *of Stephen Hurley.*
> *Born: 1891—*
> *Died: 11 February 1959.*

Then, a long prayer about the gentlest heart of Jesus, and purgatory and judgment and redemption and flames.

In the front pew, two rows ahead of us, Granny stood taller than I ever remembered her looking before. The color was sinking back into her face again, and a black lace veil was squashing her wild white hair into shape. She stood square and straight, and all the buttons of her borrowed dress lined up perfectly along her spine. The black wool flattened itself neatly over her hips and her shoulders until the only crooked line left on her was her mouth, but that battle was well lost.

All of Granny's childer was there. Not just Dad and Finty, but all fourteen of them—all the ones we only ever seen when we'd meet up with them at Puck Fair and that, and then all the ones who was living up in Dublin now for to collect the dole. Uncle Michael came alone from Liverpool on the ferry, and he had a new set of teeth which was too big and too cheerful. He was trying not to show them, but his lips had to stretch for the job, and still a bit of white shone out from in between, like they was a torch, or a lighthouse. There was even a few people there I'd never met before, even though they was Dad's brothers and sisters, because they'd went off travelling on their own ages ago. That was the way, with *Pavees*—to split off into tidier groups for travelling. Because, like Dad said, if you couldn't count out your camp on your two hands, there was too many of you in it. There was only so much work, so much food to go around, and the bigger camps was hungrier camps.

Most of Martin's older brothers and sisters came, too, from their own far-off corners of country. There was five of them who was all married now and gone, and then a seven-year-gap where Brigid'd had a crowd of lost babies and two stillbirths, before Martin came along and broke the bad streak. "We're here to mark a very sad occasion indeed," Father Dougherty was saying, in front of all of us. "And I want to ask all of you gathered here today, out of respect for the townspeople, and out of respect for this man we're here to honor, please, I want to ask you to keep the peace this day."

Outside, our wagons lined the whole street of the town. They was beautiful, the line of them, like a parade of rioting color—the finer ones among them embellished in golds and greens and brilliant reds, with curlicues and loop-di-loos all rolling down their sides, giving them wagons perpetual motion. Even when the wheels was still, a well-painted wagon had the constant encouragement of the wind under its eaves.

At the front of the queue was me and Dad's wagon, where Grandda's should be. The horses whinnied softly and stamped their feet at each other. The rain was dropping down slowly, and the crowds of travellers who couldn't fit inside the church began turning up their collars on the steps outside. I could feel the walls of the chapel swell. I clamped my teeth together and watched Father Dougherty's limp robes sway beneath his outstretched arms.

"We want no fighting, no drunkenness, and no bad behavior," the priest said.

I glanced at Martin now, and his face was sober, resigned. He had took an almighty leap of faith, and accepted everything that came with it. He had done that terrible fire for Grandda, martyred hisself to Granny's grief. He was so brave and so stupid, and I felt like a coward beside him. That was the moment that swallowed me up then, like somebody had kicked the balls right up inside me, into my stomach, and folded me in half with pain. A sucker punch. Grandda was gone.

"The publicans of this town have a right to serve who they will and to refuse who they will, and you must respect that," Father Dougherty was saying, while the shadow from his outstretched arms rose and fell acrosst Grandda's box.

I hated the priest for talking like that, for droning his shite-talk over my suddenly dropped grief-egg. And I hated Grandda for leaving, for making me listen to this. And I hated Martin for being so different from me, when we was supposed to be exactly the same.

"You would all do well to remember that you are visitors to this place, and it won't do any good to have chaos in the streets."

Grandda was dead, and all this priest cared about was some imaginary, future rampage of travellers. Anger is easier than sadness, so my cheeks went hot. Even the horses was growing agitated outside, jingling their bells in the rising wind, until the sound grew into a travelling murmur that slipped inside and made its way around the church. All them *Pavees* stifled their rage, like we'd been learning to do since forever.

Father Dougherty only looked startled, only slightly. He snapped his two hands shut, let his arms drop down to his sides. Uncle Michael turned 'round to add his own voice to the din.

"Are we at a funeral or a school lecture?" he seethed. He worked his lips around his too-white teeth, and the effort was something of a contortion.

"We're not running riot," Martin called, shocking me, his voice ringing clear around the church. "For Jesus' sake, we're here to bury our Grandda." His words stood up, taller than everybody.

Father Dougherty glared down at him, waited for quiet. "Now, then." The priest went on when the moment had passed. "In the name of the Father, and of the Son, and of the Holy Spirit."

"Amen," we said.

It was an old Jesuit who came to give the eulogy, and Finty said he was sorta famous, for a priest. His name was Father Toohey, and Finty told us that *Pavees* was his pet project, and he was always going 'round the country, trying to get rights and publicity for travellers, and that he fancied hisself a real hero, but that he wouldn't never have spent a night on the *tober*, not if his life depended on it. He'd known Stephen Hurley well, he said from the lectern, even though I'd never seen him before. He talked about what a good, long life Grandda'd lived, and that part was true, anyway. Grandda was near seventy when he died, which was old enough to make him famous, too, for a traveller.

"Stephen Hurley saw and survived unimaginable changes in his lifetime," the Jesuit said. "There were changes common to all of his generation—the advent of the automobile, the telephone, air travel. These decades have seen wondrous advances in technology, and everyone loves these modern conveniences. But for travellers, there is only a sense of doomsday coming, the decline of an ancient way of life."

There was a reporter in the back pew, listening to the famous priest and taking notes. The next day, the headline in the local paper would crown Grandda, "the last great king of the gypsies," and we'd laugh at how gullible they was, how little they knew about us.

"After hundreds, perhaps thousands, of years," Father Toohey went on, "this travelling community, which has been so vital, so integral, to the economy of our rural nation, is on the brink of collapse. In a single generation, we've witnessed a shift in the attitudes of our people. Where once you were welcomed, now you're only tolerated. Where once you were tolerated, now reviled."

I tried to look around and read faces, but apart from Maureen, they was all stone-set. There wasn't no nodding heads or murmurs of assent. That churchful of travellers sat poker-faced.

"Many among you are finding," he said, "that your traditional customs are not sustainable in the New Ireland. Your position in society is disappearing, and modern travellers are choosing to settle and grow roots, to put their travelling days behind them. Indeed, there is little choice now."

The priest shook his head at the lectern. He pounded his fist, but even that seemed a hollow gesture, just part of the act. He had a point to make, and it wasn't about Grandda.

"But Stephen Hurley survived all of that," Father Toohey continued. "And it didn't defeat him. He was determined to fight for his way of life. To be a proud provider for his thriving family, a stalwart and independent man of faith. He was a witty and resilient mind, capable of adapting to whatever adventures Our Blessed Savior threw into his path."

The priest bowed his head. That couldn't be it, surely. He wouldn't leave it at that—a sketch, a dull speech, a flat account that could've been any traveller's story.

"And now," he said, "the Lord has taken him on the most wonderful journey of all, the long mile road. One last adventure for Stephen Hurley. Our Father has taken him home."

But what about Grandda? Never mind all that high-minded

Jesuit shite-talk. What about the real man? Grandda's fiddle, and his special hankies? What about how he'd got nicknamed Saint Francis, because of his way with animals, and how we all ripped the back out of him, that he'd start a zoo if he was allowed? And what about how, sometimes, he'd get laughing so hard that he'd cry real tears that would flood down the lines of his face and turn his nose red, and then we'd all catch it, and we'd near piss ourselves laughing, and it would go on for ages? What about his fears and songs and temper? What about everything we'd inherited from him, how we'd loved him so much that Martin had been willing to risk everything? We had *burned* him, for God's sake. What about that?

AFTER WE BURIED GRANDDA—OR what was left of Grandda—in that coffin weighted down with rocks, I rode up in the front of the wagon with my father. I gaped at the people who peeped out the windows of their houses at us. I stared at the scrawny, freckle-faced boy who gave us the finger from behind the safe barrier of his mother's kitchen window. She'd roady-dendrums planted in the window box outside, but her freckle-faced son didn't have no front teeth, and no amount of flowers would fix that. Still, they'd probably grow back. More's the pity. I pelted a pebble that cracked his reflection smack in the tooth-gap, and he hopped away from the window. Dad gave my arm a yank to warn me, so I let the rest of my pebbles fall into the *tober*. We passed the shuttered-down doors of the midday pubs, and I wondered how long they would wait—after we was gone—before they opened their doors again. They knew we'd no homes to go to, nor no place for us to gather. They saw that our grief was on display in that line of wagons, and yet there was no welcome nowhere for us.

I tried to tell myself that I didn't care, that apart from Grandda, I had everything I needed, and my life wouldn't be no better if we lived in a house with plumbing and wall-to-wall carpet. It wouldn't be no better for me if them buffers was kind to us—it didn't matter. But in truth, I didn't understand the why of it, why that unwelcomeness grew up between us, stronger than their walls and fences. Faster and easier, even, than the wheels beneath our wagons.

We camped in a large field down the bottom of the town, but there wasn't room enough, and there ended up being wagons lining both sides of the Tullamore road, so that anybody passing by would've had to run through a column of travellers. Before it was dark, we built the biggest bonfire ever, and all the childer shoved and fought to get nearest the front, where they could hear the men telling stories about Grandda. The real eulogy was only beginning, and there wasn't no Jesuit could take it from us. The mammies all hung back 'round their own, smaller fires so's they could boil the dinners and mind the bare-arsed babies.

We never seen the sun go down—the day was that gray you couldn't much tell the difference when evening came anyway. But the men brought out their long-saved bottles to help slack the angry thirst in the murky twilight. It wasn't enough, and the whole of the camp was dry before night truly fell. So all of them empty bottles was smashed, and all them still-thirsty tongues was loosened, and all them grief-stricken travelling men set off on foot into town, to try again for an open door, for a bar upon which to rest their elbows and drop their tears.

I COULD HEAR THE SHIFTING whispers of all the mammies in the other wagons and tents, settling their childer down to sleep. I wondered where Martin was, but I didn't go looking for him. Instead, I went for a walk with Jack on his own—no wagon or cart—just the two of us. And when I was sure we was out of earshot of the camp and there wasn't nobody around to see, I buried my face in his neck and I wept. I didn't need to tell him nothing. He understood; he rested his chin on my shoulder. We came back sleepy, but I couldn't get comfortable.

I wasn't used to such a gathered village, it being usually only the three wagons in our own camp: Grandda's, Finty's and our one.

There was a song, a hymn under everything, that'd keep you awake, even if you wasn't all hopped up on grief. A night breeze murmured through that parish of wagons carrying drifting snatches of conversation, and the lowing of unfamiliar animals, with their damp and heavy breath and blinking eyes. It reminded me how absent Grandda was from all that life, how absent he'd always be from now on. And that made me angry at them gathered mourners, that makeshift city of grief-thieves. Nobody would miss Grandda like I would. I still had the memory-scent of his burning skin sunk into me like breath.

Dad came back late and I was sleeping, but not properly. I'd no blanket on me, and I was asleep sitting up, waiting for him because I wanted him to see me when he came in, and I wanted him to feel guilty. I'd the lantern low when he finally opened the wagon door and fumbled in. He looked toward me but didn't see me.

"Dad," I said.

He was taking his shoes off.

"Dad," I said again.

He didn't hear me. He was scooting hisself toward the tick and blankets.

"Dad!"

"Hah? Oh, Christy—you're awake."

"I was waiting you," I said.

"Ah now. And here I am," he said, laying down, closing his blue-and-red eyes.

I took my shoe off and threw it. It made a bang and a ricochet and then plopped right down on top of Dad's recently discarded pair. He didn't even twitch. I took off the second shoe and stood over him. I lifted it over my head as high as I could. I stood on my tiptoes and raised it toward the ceiling.

Dad was already breathing deep and steady. His eyes was closed like Grandda's, but his face was swirling with ruddy life. I swung the shoe down as hard as I could, brought it down with a swoosh beside my own ear, and smacked it into the floorboard an inch from my father's head.

His eyes burst open and he grabbed at his chest. His breath was jagged as he tried to recover hisself, sitting bolt upright. He looked at my shoe on the floor beside him and he made for me with a lurch. I didn't try to move away.

"What the fuck is the matter with you!"

His fingers was pressed into the flesh of my arm. I looked at him but I couldn't speak. I could feel my mouth quivering, shaking, full. I let the tears go. Dad pulled me onto his knee—I was nearly too big, but he did it anyway—and I collapsed into him.

"Jesus, what is the matter with you, child?" he said again.

But now he was stroking my head, and I had my arms around his neck, and I could taste a little whiskey in his sweat until I cried so hard I couldn't taste nothing, for the snot that clogged my nose. Dad pulled the quilt acrosst us, making mountain ranges out of the lumps of our two figures, one big, one small. And he stayed with me like that, awake.

FOUR

We ran from that town. Ran, scuttled, scurried, hurried. That's what it felt like to me, anyway, though in truth, Jack's hooves was marking their usual pace in the dusty roadway. Nobody wanted to stay too long in the graveyard of Grandda's burnt-out shadow, so we got gone, and now we was one less, travelling. I counted out my family on my fingers: Dad, me, Granny, Finty, Brigid, Martin, and then little John Paul and Maureen. Eight. There was eight of us left after Grandda was gone. I drew myself within, into the dark belly of our barrel-topped wagon, where the light tilted and changed through the hanging gap of the window curtain. The wheels jerked and rattled beneath us, and Jack clopped his hooves ahead, measured our distance in the glistening memory of his strong, working legs, his lean haunches. Our treasured books, the half dozen of them, was tucked carefully into their crate for safekeeping. I listened to them shift and slide, seasick inside, whenever we turned a sudden corner or climbed a hill. Dad's favorite, *The Odyssey*, my favorite, *The Hobbit*, and their handful of friends all jostled for position inside.

In the middle of all that motion, I held myself as still as stone, a silent mutiny of calm. And I wondered, if I stayed like that, could I go invisible altogether? My hands like rocks, hardening to stone on my two knees. My eyes becoming two black pebbles in the riverbed of my face. I was so still that my heart was like mahogany inside me, beatless and silent. Dad sat up in front with Granny, singing a low song to Jack.

And then through a gap in the curtain, I seen, as we was rolling by, some town-childer gathered at the gate of their schoolyard. And it seemed to me that we was like seafarers, and the *tober* was the ocean. We was passing the landlubbers by. We gawped at each other, us from our ships, and them from their shores, but the gap between us was so big we couldn't cross it. It was high tide or low tide, or whatever tide would prevent us from dropping anchor and rowing out to them, to exchange gifts and brides, gods and diseases.

And then them town-childer stuck out their tongues like knives and sang out after us, "Tinnnnnnker, tinker!" But Dad only lowered his head and drove Jack on.

"We have to get the Communions now, for the boys," Granny said.

She'd sold her pony to the Wards that morning, and she was gonna start fresh with everything, she said. But she couldn't start fresh with nothing til we got to a town where she could spend that pony-windfall on a new life. A breathing, touchable life, with wheels and wood, a coarse mane and flaring nostrils, a wagon and horse of her own. Until then, she was riding with us.

"It's not as if we haven't tried, Mam," Dad answered her.

She was sitting beside him, up the front, and they thought I was reading Bilbo, but really I was being still, and eavesdropping.

"Well, it's different now, isn't it? Martin . . ." Granny clicked her tongue. "He has the divil in him."

I could hear the clay pipe clacking against the rings of her hand. There was a shadow-scent of sweet tobacco off it, and Dad was quiet now, so the only answer Granny got was the echo of Jack's hooves through the dirt of the road. Granny took a healthy suck off the pipe to loosen the tension out of her words.

"Whatever possessed him." She breathed them words out. "He needs them sacraments. He could be in awful trouble, that one."

"How d'ya mean, Mam?" Dad said.

"I don't know. I don't know," Granny said. "Is he in mortal sin, Christopher? Is he, d'you think? Oh. We've to get him fixed. They're so awful late for them Communions. How many years late, now? Maybe it's our fault, if he's possessed, if he's demons in him."

"Mam, go on," Dad said, lowering his voice so it wouldn't carry to Finty's wagon behind. "Don't talk like that. He's not possessed; you know he isn't. He's only mixed up. He thought he was doing the right thing."

Granny made sort of a strangled grief-noise in her throat, and Dad went quiet. I wondered what hell would be like for travellers, if me and Martin was going there. I wondered if we'd be together. Was it even damper in the wintertimes, maybe? Or did every second baby die instead of every third? Was there no fire? That would be it—no fire. A hell without fire would be way worse than a hell with loads of fire. At least we'd be warm and dry.

I could feel a heat in my pocket then, where Grandda's ghost-photo was. It hadn't cooled since I'd put it in there; it stayed with a glowy warmth. Not a flame-heat like the fire that borne it to me, but something more like you get off the fuzzy belly of a spring lamb.

I tugged my chain out from under my shirt, and pulled the photo from my pocket. I rolled over and propped myself on my elbows, smoothed the newspaper out on the quilt. Even in the soft light of the moving wagon, my medal shone like a moon, made its oval of light on the woman's face in the photograph. I unlooped the silver cord from over my head and let the medal fall onto the paper. The one the lady wore in the photograph was tinier. I leaned my eyeballs in and looked for any difference between the two medals, any detail that might distinguish them.

My medal was nearly large enough to cover the palm of my hand, with a golden disc at its center, which was mounted on a central post, like an axle. Two bands, one silver and one gold, was also mounted on the post so's they twisted in orbit around Saint Christopher. Just like the rings around Saturn, Dad said, only turned up sideways. The words "Saint Christopher, Protect Us" was etched into the orbiting silver band, and then the outer gold one was covered with stars. On the golden disc in the very middle stood Saint Christopher hisself, in the midst of a raging sea. He had a staff in one hand, and on his shoulder he carried the child Jesus.

It was unusual, unique in all the world, in fact. Dad said that there was never another one like it, and that it was made especially for me. But the woman in the photograph appeared to be wearing one exactly the same. True, the photo was in grainy black and white on softening newsprint. But the light caught the oversized medal clear and bright, and I couldn't see a single distinction between them.

I felt the wagon slowing, heard Jack's hoofsteps drawing down in the road. I sighed and tucked the photo back into the safety of my pocket. I'd felt so sure, during the fire, that this photo was meant for me, that it was a message from Grandda—the way it landed on me, flew to my hand like a carrier pigeon coming home. And the way, even now, it stayed ghost-warm in my pocket. But if it really was a message, I couldn't work out what Grandda was trying to tell me. Maybe I was just going mental.

"Who are they?" I said.

No answer. I slipped the chain back over my head, plucked at the collar of my shirt, and dropped the medal back inside. I liked the cold, familiar weight of it against my skin where it lived, in the hollow between my tummy and my chest. Saint Christopher, protect us.

———

GRANNY SAID IT WAS SERENDIPITY that brought us to this town after Grandda died, like as if serendipity was a carousel, or a train you could buy tickets for, and then decide for yourself where it was you wanted to get off. Granny was sure that this was the town that'd welcome us, where we could stay long enough for me and Martin to get our long-overdue Communions. Where we could hunker down and start the work of repairing ourselves.

I knew she was right, never mind how many failed attempts we'd already made. Nobody ever wanted us in their parish. Of course they wouldn't say that, exactly. Instead there was always an excuse, and usually, that excuse was me. Because Dad wouldn't never tell nobody how I'd killed my mam when I was born. And without that knowledge, them priests was free to imagine other things about where she might be. They demanded answers, and Dad's response was the same every time: we left. We was so late for the Communions now that the last priest had said we should just wait til we was old enough, and we could get our confirmations at the same time. Months and months had passed since that.

We made camp about a half mile outside the town on the Long Mile Road, where there was a broad gap in the hedgerow. Once we'd maneuvered the horses and wagons over the ditch, the ground cleared away, and then it was just a wide rise of packed earth that opened right up into the green working fields on the far side. There was a water pump right inside the camp, beside the road near the hedge gap. Some wild grass grew around the edges of the clearing, but mostly it was barren and rutted with the wheels of wagons gone before us. It would've been a popular spot for travellers, but it smelled whipped clean anyway, like wind. At this time of year, we could see three farmhouses acrosst the quilted fields, but I'd say there'd be times of year when them fields was tall with crop, and we wouldn't've seen nothing then, only the birds in the slate sky overhead.

We was only two wagons now, until Granny could get herself a new one sorted out, so we parked them end to end, well into the clearing, nearest the edge of the field where the crops would grow. Between us and the road then, was the thick line of hedges and trees, so's the camp was nice and hidden, except at the crossing-gap.

There was a climbing tree stood apart from the rest a bit, not in the middle of the clearing, but off to one side, like the yolk of an egg. Between that tree and the wagons, we pitched the shelter tents, all facing the fire. Me and Martin dug a bit of a pit and then lined it with large rocks. We covered that over with good dry wood to burn, and lit the glimmer for our tea straightaway. Granny and Brigid pulled out their assortment of bedraggled lawn chairs, and John Paul helped set them all up facing the fire. Baby Maureen poked around after a beetle while Dad and Finty went into town for to get provisions.

With luck, we'd be here for a while, so we made our camp homey and quick. It felt real cozy to be tucked inside them trees and in outta the road. It was a great, comfortable camp compared to a lotta times when we halted nearly in the road itself, just pulled up into the hedges as snug as we could get.

Everybody was treating Martin more or less normal again, except Granny. It would take her a while to get 'round what he'd done, or maybe she wouldn't never get 'round it, until he was made new by the sacraments. She seen him walking around like a gargoyle, and she couldn't even manage a smile or a fondness for him no more. He didn't seem too bothered by it.

"Maybe she'd take it easier on you if she knew it was my idea," I said to him while we was gathering firewood.

"How do you mean it was your idea?" he said.

"To burn the wagon."

"It was never your idea," he said.

"But—" My mouth hung open. Hadn't I talked him into it, with my speech about tight spaces and driftwood rifles? Why could I never be just a bit sure of things?

"And anyway," Martin said, "there's no point in her hating the two of us."

SAINT MALACHY'S NATIONAL SCHOOL WAS on the nearer edge of the town, less than half a mile from where we was halting, so that afternoon, as soon as we'd the camp organized, and after we was sure classes was finished for the day and the school would be quiet, we went in to see the headmaster. Me and Martin was sat in the front office, squirming in our seats, waiting for Father Francis to inspect us. It never got easier, these inspections, no matter how many times we went through them. We always failed.

I liked to blame Martin whenever I could, which was often, because he was easy to blame for most things. But if he'd really stopped to think about it, he woulda known it was my fault we was always getting tossed out on our ears. It was true he'd a gift for making a priest or a nun squirm with discomfort. He always said the wrong thing, picked his nose at the wrong moment, wiped that booger under the wrong chair. He was the one who made them feel prickly and disapproving. But I was the one with the tricky, hazy past, the dodgy origins, the stammering, answer-less dad. I was the one who gave them the reason they was looking for, to throw us out. I was the one with the missing mother.

Being tinkers was bad enough, but being a motherless tinker seemed to cross some invisible line of tolerance people had for us. Dad always explained that to me, and I'd growed accustomed to it. He'd told me not to mind it, that it was better to try not to think about her. He never, ever talked about her—not even when the priests asked. He refused to tell them she was dead, that she'd slipped out of life just as I was slipping in. Even when they raised their eyebrows and made their terrible guesses, he wouldn't tell them what I'd done, how I'd killed her. There was lots of ways that

Dad wasn't brave, that he wouldn't stand up to the buffers, but when it came to my mam, he always protected me like that.

I knew what them priests thought instead, since they didn't know the truth. There was a lot of fighting on the *tober*, and it happened often enough: a woman would leave her family and run away, back to her mother, after a bad fight or a beating at the hands of a drunken husband. It was on their faces, in priestly judgment: that we was a failing family. Maybe they even thought she'd ran off with another man, or that she was a drunk, or in jail. And then they rejected us. Dad refused to set them straight, even when they urged him to reunite with her, to save the marriage, to set a better example for his son. Even when they shook their heads and told us that a child without a properly wedded Catholic mother wasn't a good candidate for the sacraments. Even when time and time again, they turned us away.

Now we was waiting again, and Martin was annoying me that bad I prayed for Jesus to make a separate waiting room for him. Or a shed or a closet or any old spot where we could stick him to shut him up for a minute. This was a day I had waited lifetimes for. Lifetimes. Well. Since the last time. We had to get it right this time. I wanted a moment to myself, just to take some deep breaths and prepare myself for meeting the headmaster, so's this time, it could be different. I wanted this priest to be more impressed by me than he'd ever been by any student before in all his years, so's he couldn't resist letting me in to his school, never mind about my mother. Making that sort of impression on a person requires concentration.

"You help me with the answers," Martin was saying.

For all his confidence, school terrified Martin in a way nothing else could. He was trying to keep his voice down because he didn't want his mam to hear. I looked back at him and shrugged. Sometimes I didn't want to help him.

"You *have* to," he said again.

"Or what?"

Martin made a fist and punched it into the waiting palm of his other hand.

"You're a right Al Capone," I said, rolling my eyes. "Terrifying."

"All right," he answered. "So I'll tell the whole class you still suck your thumb because you've no mother and you was never properly weaned."

More empty threats. I hadn't sucked my thumb since last November. Not in front of nobody.

"I'm not getting caught cheating," I said, unmoved. "And anyway, you're getting ahead of yourself. What makes you think we'll even get into this school?"

Brigid eyed us suspiciously, but she was too nervous to intervene. Our voices wasn't accustomed to being trapped inside, and they bounced off the walls and carried back to us. We was louder than we meant to be. Dad was standing, shifting his weight around and clasping his hands first in front, then in back, then in front again.

"Come on, Christy," Martin kept on. "You can give them to me in *cant*, and they'll think you're only coughing or whatever."

Brilliant. I would translate whole sentences of the *Pavee* language into a series of chesty hacks. Before I had the chance to tell him what a stupid plan it was, we was interrupted by the school secretary, who was the tiniest grown-up I'd ever seen, even including nuns. Her habit must've been hemmed in half, to fit her, and still she was in danger of tripping, her sensible shoes invisible beneath the long robes. She walked with both hands slightly outstretched in front of her, making the distinct impression of a hedgehog as she came into the room—all beady eyes, stretched neck, and animal mistrust. We sat up straighter in our chairs.

"I don't suppose you could fill out some paperwork with the boys' names and ages and that," she said to Dad, lifting a clipboard from the room's lone desk, and forking it over.

Her nose even twitched when she talked in her squeaky, hedge-hoggy voice. I wondered did she have whiskers she had to trim before greeting guests.

"Or would you be needing a hand with the forms?" she suggested.

The clipboard hovered in the air for a moment, the tiny nun drawing it back from Dad's grasp just a fraction.

"Oh no, not at all, Sister—thank you," Dad said, smiling, proud. "We'll manage it."

I watched her face for the inevitable signs of surprise, but she was a great actress for a hedgehog. She granted Dad the clipboard and a warm pat on the forearm. Maybe she wasn't acting at all.

"Let me know if you've any questions," she said. "And I'll be back to collect you when Father Francis is ready."

I was glad Dad had the clipboard now, to keep him busy.

"Christy, please," Martin said, more urgently, when the nun was gone. "I won't manage it on my own."

He'd said *please*. Unheard of. I watched his nostrils getting bigger and smaller, and I thought about ramming something up one of them.

"We'll sort something out," I said. "Just whisht, will ya?"

Sister Hedgehog returned much faster than we expected, and Dad wasn't finished with the forms. *Don't rush them, Dad*, I willed, but I saw the pen speeding up.

"Father Francis is ready for yous now," the nun chirped, her tiny, outstretched hands making urgent gestures to get us moving.

Dad made some kind of a flourish and a full stop with the pen, and then handed the clipboard back to Sister Hedgehog, who ushered us into the headmaster's office. Beyond the door the carpet was thicker, so's I could feel my wellies sinking into it queerly as we walked. It was like entering a tomb, or a holy place, full of terror and possibility.

Inside there was four chairs arranged in a perfect half circle around the priest's desk. Instead of the books I'd been hoping for, the walls of the office was lined with maps, done all in ancient-looking browns and yellows. Even the seas was brownish, with fancy writing acrosst them. No fish in them oceans. And then beside the desk, there was a big, round map on a stand—three times the size of a football. In all the school offices we'd got kicked out of before, I'd never seen nothing like it.

Father Francis was wearing a long black dress, even though Dad always told us not to call them dresses, if it was a priest who was wearing it. But that's what it was anyway, like a manly looking dress, with the white square of cloth at his throat. He smelled like the Holy Ghost. His skin was darkish, like maybe he'd been a traveller once, and he'd spent loads of time outside getting colored. His head was a shiny, naked dome that hadn't got as colored as the rest of him, and what hair was left 'round the back of his head was trimmed real tidy so's you could barely see it. A shadowy, knocked-back, silver halo. He was standing, spinning the ball-map 'round on its stand, and he halted it midrotation as we approached, pointing a finger at a yellow blob with the words "The Free Republic of Ireland" handwritten acrosst it in thick ink.

"There you are, boys!" he said, so loud that Martin jumped.

Father Francis cruised toward Dad and Auntie Brigid then, leading with the bald dome of his head.

"Hallo and you're very welcome to Saint Malachy's," he said, looking up, shaking Dad's and then Brigid's hands in turn. "Very welcome indeed."

Brigid looked like she might be sick.

"I'm the headmaster here, Father Francis. Welcome, welcome, and please, have a seat."

He was awfully welcoming. Four welcomes already. Brigid nodded and sat down, making a clacking sound acrosst her knees while her beady pocket shifted and settled. She still hadn't said a word. Father Francis retraced his steps to the far side of the desk and plonked hisself down in his red leather chair. Sister Hedgehog deposited the clipboard into his hands and then tottered from the room. Beside me, Martin put his finger in his ear. Brigid reached acrosst me and smacked the stray hand back down to his side.

"A welcome to the *Hurley* family," Father Francis mused, reading from the paper in front of him.

He tipped his head down so's he could see over the tops of his glasses at us, and I tried to smile at him, in case that would help.

"Martin?" he asked, examining the two of us.

Martin raised a solitary finger and answered, "That's me, Father, and I'm very happy to be here at Saint Malachy's today, and we thank you for the fine welcome."

Brigid's mouth hung open as she looked at her son beside me—his nerves had done the trick of making him articulate and polite, the bastard.

"Very good," he said. "That's what I like to see—a boy who's not afraid to speak up for himself."

Martin beamed, and Father Francis turned his attention to me. I sat on my hands.

"And, Christopher," he said. "Named after the good Lord Himself, I see."

He looked to me for confirmation, and I said, "Yes, Father," but it came out more of a squick-squawk.

"Very good, very good," the priest went on, oblivious. "And how good of your parents both to come! It's so rare that we get the father and the mother both. Aren't you a lucky pair of boy-ohs to have such an attentive mam and dad?"

"Yes, Father," Martin said.

"No, Father," I said.

The priest looked at me with a frown, and I frowned back.

"No?" he said.

I shook my head, amazed at my own stupidity. This was usually Martin's part of the bargain; it was like we'd swapped brains.

"No, Father," I said again. "It's just, the thing is, Father, they isn't our parents."

My voice was like a caged ferret in my throat. Father Francis wrinkled his tan forehead in confusion while Dad started into a coughing fit and Brigid's knuckles went white against her knees. I stared into the priest's confused face and felt the weight of my escaped words fill the room. Feck. What had I said? It couldn't be going wrong like this already, not again.

"I mean, they *is*," I said.

Either they was or they wasn't. I couldn't stop the stupid spilling outta me. Maybe Granny was wrong about this town, maybe it wasn't meant to happen here. It was all going wrong again.

"I mean, *he* is." I pointed at my dad.

I was like a tornado of stupid. I took a deep breath and blinked my eyes in the slowest, most deliberate way. When I opened them again, I would start over, and everything would be okay. This *was* the place for us. It *had* to be.

I couldn't go backwards and do what I should've done, which was to keep my big gob shut and let the priest think my parents was whoever he wanted them to be. But I *could* now, if I was very careful, find a delicate way to explain myself, couldn't I? Did it need to matter so much, about me not having a mam? Did it *always* need to matter? I opened my eyes.

"That's my dad," I said, still pointing. "And that's my auntie Brigid. She's Martin's mam, and his dad is Uncle Finty, who's at home in the camp."

I tried to conjure my ghost-mother: some fragile, indefinite cross between Brigid and Granny, dressed in long black skirts and a beady pocket. I thought if I wished for her hard enough, she might appear in the room beside us and the priest might shout "There you are!" at her, too, and then everything would be fine.

Brigid was examining the legs of Father Francis's desk, and I looked hard at her, blamed her for not loving me more, so's we could all pretend quite easily that she was my lumpy, two-chinned mother. Why couldn't she do that? Dad's coughing petered out and then, with the absence of my stupid, cramped voice in the room, there was a horrible quiet, and I thought I would throw up for sure.

We'd lived and failed this moment eleven times already, in eleven different parishes. We never even got up the steps at Our Lady of Perpetual Hope in Cullohill. Never had a prayer at Saint Mary of the Visitation in Athlone, where the nuns overheard Martin swearing and spitting before we even unhitched the wagons. A few times, we'd managed to get so far as this. The office. The headmaster. The interview. The dismissal. Saint Malachy's was parish number twelve. I knew the others had stopped counting, but I hadn't. No matter how many times it went wrong, I never stopped hoping that the priest wouldn't ask where my mother was. Or hoping that Dad would say more than just "He doesn't have a mam." Or hoping I'd be so impressive with my reading that it wouldn't matter, and the priest would insist that I stay on as a boarder because I was so gifted, especially for a traveller.

"And where is this fine young fella's mother?" Father Francis asked, addressing Dad this time.

"He doesn't have a mother," I heard Dad saying—the usual account. "But he's very bright, Father. He can read and everything. He doesn't usually carry on like this, do ya, Christy?"

Father Francis smiled at me. "You're all right there, young Mr. Hurley," he said kindly. "A bit nervous, are you?"

I nodded.

"You're all right," he said again, and then he addressed Dad. "Well, we needn't talk about it *in front* of the boys, Mr. Hurley, if it's an upsetting subject, but we *must* ensure they are both properly prepared for their sacraments. Obviously, we need to be reassured that your son is the offspring of a union sanctified by the church. Surely his mother knows how important this is?"

Father Francis cleared his throat, but if he was waiting for Dad to reassure him, he'd have a long wait. The priest passed a sympathetic glance in my direction, then fixed hisself on Dad again.

"Mr. Hurley," Father Francis pressed, "I would like to help you, but I'm sure you understand that my hands are quite tied on this particular matter."

Dad nodded, and I felt panic wash over me. We was so close this time—I couldn't keep counting rejections. Thirteen was an unlucky number, and it was my fault, all of it, for killing my mam and letting Dad take the blame for her absence. I thought about Dad lowering his head when them kids called us "tinkers" on the *tober*. I'd thought he was a coward, but maybe I was the spineless one.

"I understand, Father," Dad was saying.

Through the window behind Father Francis, and acrosst the courtyard, I could see an empty, darkened classroom, its desks lined up and waiting. I couldn't watch it slip away again because of me. We'd be so good here, so perfect. It was what Grandda wanted, what Martin needed. What *I* needed. I jammed my hands into my pockets and, in Grandda's warming, newsprint photograph, found strength.

"I killed her!" I erupted.

Beside me, Auntie Brigid crossed herself. Father Francis stared at me aghast, but it was too late now. The truth would either save us or slaughter us.

"Being born," I explained, my voice like a brand-new Bible. "She died when I was born."

The words came out of me like as if God hisself had put them there, with that much certainty. It wasn't even hard or scary. A shout: there you are! Straightaway, my breathing calmed, my cheeks cooled.

Dad's face fell open, but he didn't say a word.

Father Francis looked stricken; he tutted and shook his head slowly. "Oh, young Christopher!" he said to me.

I studied my murderous toes.

"Mr. Hurley, why didn't you say so?" Father Francis continued. "I am sorry. And may God bless her and keep her, my child. What an awful burden for the two of ye to bear. I thought . . . Well, it doesn't matter what I thought. I'm so sorry for your loss."

He smiled at me then, and I had the flooding certainty that everything was going to be okay. Dad closed his mouth, his teeth clenched. I couldn't tell what he was thinking. I didn't care.

"Thank you, Father," I said quietly. "My mam would be very happy to know that I would take my First Holy Communion here at Saint Malachy's, and we won't be no trouble at all, Father. And we'll do all the work assigned, and all the readings and the maths and everything."

"That's very ambitious of you," Father Francis said approvingly.

"Yes, Father," I said. "If you'll just give us a chance."

I could hear everyone breathing in the room. "Of course," he said, ruffling through the papers some more. "We've had travellers through here in years past, and we always make a point of welcoming ye like you're our very own. We're all the Lord's children, after all."

And? What did this mean, exactly?

"We'd be delighted to have you here at Saint Malachy's."

I waited for the "but." *Sadly, we're too full at the minute.* Or, *It's just, the consumption epidemic. We're sort of quarantined . . . You understand.*

"The boys can start classes on Monday," he said.

Monday! After all them months and years of waiting, Monday was only three days away. Today was already Friday, and sure Friday was half over. It seemed impossibly quick.

"*Oh, thank you, Father!*" Brigid clapped her hands in front of her.

It was the first she'd spoke since we'd arrived, and I hoped it would be the last. She could still undo it. I willed everyone to be quiet and still and to barely move, in case the spell would break.

"I think you'll enjoy yourselves, boys. We've some wonderful pupils here at Saint Malachy's, and tremendous teachers," said Father Francis.

We nodded at him.

"The only question will be where to put you," he said, removing his glasses. "You're . . . What age are you, boys?"

"Twelve, Father," said Martin, and I added, "Me too, nearly. In a few weeks' time."

Father Francis nodded.

"And have you ever had any formal schooling before?" he asked, rubbing the heels of his hands into his eyes.

"Not formal schooling, no," Dad answered.

"But I read loads," I said.

"Loads?" Father Francis smiled.

I nodded.

"And what's your favorite book, then?"

"*The Hobbit*," I said, without thinking, and then I cringed, in case I was supposed to have said the Bible.

But Father Francis only nodded and said it was a fine choice.

"I'm afraid we may have to put you in second class," he said then, thinking. "That's the Communion class, but the children are much younger than you. Mostly around eight years of age."

Martin made a grimace like a monster, fleeting, but enough that Father Francis caught it. "Would you mind that very much?"

"No, Father," I answered quickly, even though it sounded horrible. "Not at all."

But Martin hadn't managed to fix his face, and Father Francis noticed.

"I don't suppose it's ideal," he said, leaning his elbows onto his desk. "Martin, did you know that before Pope Pius the Tenth, nobody received the Eucharist much before the age you are now?"

"No, sir," Martin said.

"It's true. So fifty years ago, you'd have been right on time." He chuckled.

"So we're not very late, after all?" I asked.

"Well," Father Francis said. "It all depends how you look at it, but there's no reason to worry. You can make the Communion and the penance, and perhaps even your confirmation all at once. It'll be grand."

Then it was quiet for a long moment, while the priest was thinking what to do with us, and I could hear the wind whistling in his nose hairs while he breathed. He flicked through some files on his desk.

"I think," he announced at last, "that you'd be best suited to stick with the second class." He frowned at Martin. "I know it's not what you'd like best," he said. "But I can't very well put you in sixth class, with the other confirmation candidates. You're just too young, and you'd be too far behind."

I could feel Martin clenching up beside me, and my insides was doing it, too.

"And I don't think we can just plunk you in with the other children your own age, because you need the religious instruction, to prepare you for the sacraments," he explained. "You boys are both small for your age. The other children mightn't even know you're much older. Right?"

"Yes, Father." We nodded.

He stood up and we followed his lead, standing carefully out of our chairs. I held the breath in my lungs, like water locked up behind a dam. It wasn't perfect, but I didn't care. After all them years of rejection, we was finally going to school. I would've started in baby infants if I had to.

"You can sort out the paperwork with Sister Helena, there," he said. "We'll need copies of the boys' baptismal certificates, of course, and then we're all set."

Dad's mouth opened a fraction, and a dart of worry passed acrosst his face.

"Of course, Father," Brigid was saying, shaking his hand like she was pumping water from a well. "That's no problem at all. We'll get them organized, Father."

But Dad looked startled, and his face had gone a bit whitish.

FIVE

Do you know the way sometimes, you don't realize you have a headache until it goes? And then after, you can feel your shoulders slip, and your breath loosen, and that absence-of-pain, that pure comfort, settles 'round you like a hot bath? That's what I felt like after we got into Saint Malachy's. Like I didn't know how awful black my mood had got, how miserable sad I was, until I was lended that sliver of redemption. It lifted me.

When we got back to camp, Dad got his tools out, and I went to help him. He gripped a sheet of tin on an anvil between his knees and turned it constantly with one hand, while he clutched a hammer in the other. Tapping.

There wasn't no careful way to bring up what I wanted to talk about, so I just launched right in. "Was me and Martin not baptized together?" I asked him.

"No," he said.

He wasn't browned off at me for telling the priest about my mam, which was a nice surprise. In fact, he seemed strangely lifted hisself. Maybe it was just relief.

"How come?" I asked.

"You just wasn't," he said. "They wasn't travelling with us that time."

He held the rivets in his lip, and he'd pull them out one at a time to tap them into place. I lined up the others on my leg and would hand them to him in fives when his mouth came up empty, pluck them up from my knee and count them out.

"Was it just you and me then?" I asked.

Dad hummed, which I guessed was a yes-answer. Brigid had gave Sister Hedgehog the name of the parish where Martin was baptized, so's she could write away for the baptismal cert. But Dad told her he'd send away for mine hisself, that the priest was an old friend, and he was overdue writing him anyway.

"So who's your old priest friend?" I asked.

"Jeez, you're awful nosey, Christy," Dad said.

"Well?" I said. "You never told me you had some old priest friend who baptized me."

A small spider slung herself beneath the corner of the wagon, weaving her brief home beneath ours. I watched her drop and spin.

"There's plenty of things I never told you," he answered. "I'd be hoarse, talking, if I tried to tell you all my life."

Dad dropped the hammer into the dirt and came to sit beside me on the back steps of the wagon. He sat on the middle step with his feet on the ground, and I sat on the highest step, above him. He lifted his beaker of water and took a gulp.

"What if they call us *tinkers*?" I asked. "In school."

I'd collected the signs after Grandda's funeral, from the doors of the public houses. NO ITINERANTS SERVED, read the nicer one. The others just said NO TINKERS. In between the *T* and the *I* on one of them, I added my own *H* with a bit of coal, so now the sign read NO THINKERS.

"So what if they do?" he said. He stood up and stretched before bending back to his hammering.

"Maybe I'll smack 'em in the mouth," I said.

Dad paused long enough to look up at me. "You do and I'll smack you in the mouth," he said.

I shook my head. "You never stand up to them," I mumbled.

Dad made an aggravated sigh. "You can't go fighting over every single thing," he said. "You have to learn to pick your battles, Christy. Otherwise you won't have no energy left for the important things."

"But that is an important thing," I said.

"It's just a word, for Christ's sake," he said. "It doesn't mean nothing."

I listened to the hammer striking the white tin, which curled between his legs, slowly taking the shape of a bucket.

"It's just a sound." Dad rapped the hammer against the tin. "There you are," he said. "The sound of a tinker—that's all it means."

I listened to the *tink tink* as the tin responded to the hammer. It seemed unlikely that such a harmless sound could be responsible for that word and its sneer: *Tinker*. Dad held the hammer out to me, centered one of the rivets over the place that was to be its home.

"Run that in for me there, Christy."

"Me?" I said.

Dad shook his head but answered, "Yes. You."

I stood up and spilled my lapful of rivets right into the grass, but Dad was in a patient humor, and he waited while I collected them up again. The hammer was heavier than I expected. To see Dad lift it, you'd think it was weightless, but I had to carry its heft with both my fists.

"Easy there, bucko," Dad said. "Just give it a good whack. No need to murder the thing."

I planted my feet wide, swung the hammer down. I missed the rivet and made a nice dimple in the smooth tin an inch north of my target.

"One more try, not so wild," he said. "You don't have to force it in. It wants to go in. You just encourage it in there, Christy."

I centered the hammer and swung again, lighter now, one eye closed and the other fixed on the rivet. I struck it with the flat of the hammer, and it slipped neatly into the tin—shone out at me like a teary eyeball.

"Now," Dad said, taking the hammer and pointing it at me. "You're not a tinker."

I shook my head. "I know," I said. "It's not our word."

I sat back down on the step and collected the rivets back into my hands.

"That's right," he said. "You're a *Pavee*, a traveller. They only call us that because they don't understand our ways, so they need to explain us in *their* words. You let them have it. It's nothing to us."

Dad was bent over the bucket again and, after a minute, he started to hum a little tune. It was one Grandda'd used to play on his fiddle, and I knew the words, but I wasn't going singing it just then. Instead I interrupted him.

"But how come that is, Dad?" I said. "That they don't understand our ways, like? It's not like we's that complicated."

Dad kept humming for a moment, but then he paused. "I guess it would be difficult," Dad said, "to see the appeal of our life, if you hadn't tried it yourself, like."

"It seems pretty great to me." I shrugged.

"That's because it's what you're used to," Dad said. "But if you was used to a house, instead, you mightn't even know what you was missing. The hearty, outdoor freedom of this life, to go where you want to go. To wake up every morning and be your own boss— that's a mad, big difference between *Pavees* and buffers."

"But what about doctors?" I said. "And people like that?"

"Well, yeah," Dad said. "I mean, some of them is their own bosses, like doctors. But most of them work for other people, like in shops or pubs or factories or newspapers. And worst of all is being a farmer—them farmers is just practically slaves, like, to the seasons, the land, to their animals, even. It's an awful hard life they have. But sure, they probably think the same about us. That we've an awful hard life, like, and they can't imagine why we'd choose it. But I wouldn't want no other life than our own one."

"Me neither."

"Sure even a king in a castle must get awful bored," he added. "Sleeping closed inside them same four walls every night. I'd take the open *tober* any day, over that."

He went back to his humming for a while, and I did sing along, but only for a minute. I reached into my pocket and felt the warm corner of the photograph.

"Dad?" I said.

"Hmm?"

"Do you miss Grandda?"

"I do, of course," he said.

"Me, too."

He went back to humming.

"I got a message from him."

He stopped humming. I knew it was a risk, telling him, but something moved me to do it.

"I did," I said. "And I'll show it to you, but you have to promise not to say I'm soft in the head."

Dad sat up straight and waited.

"Promise?" I said.

He made no reply.

"Well, okay," I said, and I reached into my pocket and drew the newsprint photograph out. "It came to me when the wagon went on fire."

"How d'ya mean it *came* to you?" he said even before he looked at it.

"Just like I said. It came to me."

"What, it grew legs and walked up and said, *How do ya do, Christy? I'm a message from your grandda.*"

I glared at him. "No," I said. "It was blowing around and I caught it."

"Well, then," he said, and when he leaned in for a look, his face cracked open.

I thought his heart would fall out of his mouth.

"Jesus," he said without thinking. "It's your mother."

The hammer landed in a puff of dust at his feet. He took the photograph from me, peering at it carefully, his face a mask of tenderness I didn't recognize.

"Where did you get this?" he whispered. It was shaking in his hands.

"My mother?"

That didn't make no sense. I searched his face. Dad looked away from me, turned so's I couldn't see him. He knew that his face was like a placard, advertising his thoughts.

"How?" I said. Well—she was wearing my chain. But. "Who's that with her?" I asked. "She . . ." But I'd so many questions, I didn't even know what to ask first.

"Who is the baby?" I said. "Did she have another baby, before me? Before . . . Who is that man with her?"

But I was only looking at Dad's back, and he was stitching the story up, locking it up inside him, closing it away. When he turned back to me, it wasn't even on his face no more.

"How should I know?" he said, handing the picture back to me carelessly. "I never seen him before."

WITH THE BENEFIT OF DISTANCE now, I can say I was remarkably calm. I just didn't understand, couldn't take it all in, the discoveries in that photograph. My mother's teeth: white like a string of pearls. It seems obvious now, but how could I imagine then, that my mother mightn't have been a traveller? How could I even begin to imagine such a thing?

Nobody ever talked to me about her, only Grandda, before he died—very secretively, when nobody else was around. She was a real beauty, he said, and she'd hair like a red tornado, its color so deep it was nearly purple, twisting all the way down to the backs of her knees. Her eyelashes was so long they was known to cause a breeze 'round her part of the country when she blinked, he said. And when she walked in the fields, the crops would go bending down in front of her, in an aspect of adoration. Even the cows would warble after her when she went by.

Before that day, I'd always been able to close my eyes and imagine her, so clearly I could nearly tangle myself up in that purple hair and breathe her in. I could nearly smell her on my skin, like the summer scent of dandelion wine. But now that comfort was gone. In one careless moment, that mother I'd built for myself out of Grandda's memories was snatched and shattered, replaced by a flat gray woman in a newsprint photograph. There was no violent storm of hair, brewing and pitching around her head in the breeze and tumble from her eyelashes. Instead, here in black and white was the woman I'd killed, smiling out at me with her perfect teeth, with a baby on her hip. I felt dizzy. I searched that baby's face, the round cheeks and clear, bright eyes. I tried to recognize them features. I groped along my own chin and cheekbones, to try and feel if they was the same. But how could that baby be me? *How?* Hadn't my mammy bled to death, pushing me into the world? Oh God, I was woozy with them questions. I shook my head to try and clear it so's I could think, but I couldn't make no sense of nothing. I wondered was it possible to miss somebody who was never around to begin with. Seven shared minutes of breath in this world.

Seven minutes.

———

"DID YOU WASH YOUR TEETH?" Dad asked me the next morning, after a breakfast of nothing because we'd no food in the camp.

"Yeah." I nodded.

He was toweling off his neck, and his face was bare. I knew there was no point in tormenting him more about the photograph. I'd tried all evening yesterday and got nowhere. He wouldn't tell me nothing until he was ready, or until I figured out some way to trick him into it. Last night, I'd studied the photograph for hours, to see could I get to *feel* anything about it, that a woman like that could be my mother. But she may as well have been *An Taoiseach* of Ireland, for all I felt for her. She was back in my pocket.

It was Saturday, and I'd hitched Jack up to the small cart, like Dad told me, and we climbed in, for to head into town. He handed me a wrapped and bundled parcel with an envelope tucked in under the string. The envelope said "Father Jonas Stapleton—Holy Ghost Parish House, Rathnaveen" in Dad's sharp, leaning hand and blue ink.

"Is that the priest who baptized me?"

"That's him," Dad said.

"Father John-iss Stapleton," I read aloud.

"Joan-iss," Dad corrected me. "It's an O, like in bone."

"Or home," I said.

Dad had been teaching me to read since forever, but sometimes I still got words wrong. I clambered up beside him in the cart.

"What're you going sending him?" I asked. I thought the parcel was for him.

"Nothing," Dad answered. "Only the letter—to get your baptismal cert."

"Then who's this for?" I plucked at the twine on the wrapped parcel.

"Not for you anyway," Dad said.

I fiddled at the corner of the brown paper for a peek.

"Leave it," Dad warned.

"Where're we going?" I asked.

"You'll see," Dad said. "It's a surprise."

Sometimes Dad's surprises was shite. Like: "*Surprise!* Them buffers hadn't no need of the tinware, so I sold them your shoes instead." I tried for a hint.

"Is there bacon there?"

Dad rolled his eyes at me, but then he said, "Listen, there's something we need to discuss."

I glanced at him. Maybe he'd changed his mind, and he would tell me about my mother now.

"You know the wagon fire," he said.

I cringed. Not the photograph, of course. Not my mother. I didn't want to talk about the feckin' wagon fire. I didn't even want to think about it—that I was the one to blame. Even though it was Martin who'd sprinkled the petrol, like a priest showering holy water on the congregation. It was Martin with the nerve to light the match. But I was the one who'd talked him into it. I was the one who always had to pick at things: to pull a thread loose from the hem of a jumper until all that was left was two sleeves and a tangle of kinked yarn. I couldn't never leave well enough alone. So maybe Dad knew. Maybe he'd sussed it, that it was all my fault. And now the interrogation would begin, and I'd crack straightaway, because that's the sort of egg I was. I was a cracker.

"The photograph you found," Dad said.

That startled me.

"What?"

"I know the wagon fire didn't happen the way it was meant to," Dad said. "And that was a very bad thing Martin did. And not just for what happened to your grandfather. But also, you know, he stole something very precious from your granny by doing that. He took that ceremony from her. It was hers to do, to say goodbye. But he done it, and even though he had no right, it's done."

I nodded, but I couldn't see what none of that had to do with the photograph of my mother.

"But everything belonging to your grandfather was burnt, and that at least is as it should be," he said. "Except that photograph. It should've burnt up as well."

My stomach swooped. "But it didn't," I said.

"No, it didn't."

"So maybe it wasn't meant to burn up," I said. "Maybe Grandda meant for me to have it."

Dad looked at me as if to say I should know better than that.

"Christy, holding on to that photograph is like keeping your grandfather captive," he said. "It's not fair on him."

I could feel my nostrils flair. "Not fair on *him*?" I asked. "What about me? It's *my* mother in that photograph. And you still won't even tell me nothing about her."

Dad set his jaw at a hard angle, and I could see a vein in his neck. "This is nothing to do with your mother," he said.

"It's feckin' everything to do with my mother," I said, getting angry. "Grandda wanted me to know her. He's the only one. He's the only one who cared about that. You never feckin' cared. You still don't care."

"That's enough, Christy."

"It's not enough," I said. "Grandda wanted me to have it, and—"

"You have to burn it," Dad interrupted me.

"*What?*"

"You heard me."

"No way," I said.

"It's not a request, Christy."

I shook my head. "You only want me to burn it because it's my mother's picture, and you don't want me to know nothing about her. Because you want to keep her all to yourself," I said.

He didn't respond. I needed something sharper to say, to hurt him the way I wanted to.

"I hate you," I tried.

Dad flicked Jack's reins. "Of course you do," he said, and then he yawned.

———

I SEETHED THE REST OF the way into town, but my mood couldn't infect the weather, and the sky seemed to lift a bit as we went. The heavy clouds looked higher in the sky by the time we got into the town, rolling down High Street. The butcher's boy was out sweeping the front of his store, and there was a delivery van parked at the bakery; its back doors stood open so's we could see the goods inside. It minded me of Jesus showing us the sacred heart—the same sort of suffering, the same colors. On the top racks was the goodies, the baked tarts, dripping over with lumped cherries and icing sugars, the cakes and puddings, the sweet, shiny pies. The jelly rolls. The crème puffs. Then below was the breads: browns, khakis, whites and off-whites, in bigs, littles, and mediums. Lumpy or round. Squat or lean. Flour and good grains. I was so hungry. You could smell them, still warm from their buttery ovens. Still sleepy. Like prey.

I heard a boy's voice hissing out, "Smelly tinkers!" and then laughter, but I couldn't tell which window or alley it came from. I spat into the road. Dad pulled Jack in beside the open-backed van, and I hopped down to tie him up. Dad lifted the parcel off my seat and climbed down after me. He turned then, and headed off. I was meant to follow him, but the back door of the van was stood open beside me, not three feet away. Just one little roll or a scone. Just a nibble, to fill the gap. I reached.

"*Hey!*"

The feckin' butcher's boy. It wasn't even his shop. It's not like I was pinching lamb chops.

"Hey, you, get away from there," he said.

I looked up at him and didn't say a word. He swatted at my feet with his broom. He was only maybe three years older than me. He had pimples on his meat-fed face.

"Go on," he said. "Away off."

I stood my ground, wondered if I could snatch one anyway and then leg it. But Dad was standing waiting for me a few doors down. He knew I was hungry, and he wouldn't have stopped me pinching a scone to keep my stomach from back-talking. But he wouldn't stop your man sweeping me into the road neither. He just waited to see what would happen.

I left the mean, pimple-butcher alone. He'd never knew a day's hunger in all his life. Never even skipped a snack, I'd say, by the size of him.

Dad was stood under the simplest sign in the whole row of shops, a rough wooden job with painted red letters: BOOK SHOP, and then again in Irish, beneath: SIOPA LEABHAR. We wiped our feet twice on the thick straw mat as we went in.

"Come in, come in, friends," said the woman behind the till, in a voice that rang around the book-filled room. "Come in outta that weather."

I didn't know what weather she was on about, but you got the impression she said this exact thing to every soul who jingled the bell over her shop door, and that she'd usually follow it up with "The wind is howling out there," or maybe "There's no end of that sun beating down on you—sure you'd be dead of heatstroke," depending on the day.

So in we went, as we was bid, and I noted the way the knotty wood planks of the floor was polished and squeaking. And I noted the dark hewn beams of the ceiling, the way the lights dangling down from them beams shone onto the colorful spines of the books—hundreds and hundreds of books. I ran my fingers along their fat and skinny bindings. I breathed them. I whispered them.

You could smell the coffee that the missus was brewing and drinking, sitting behind the till. She drank coffee instead of tea, so maybe she was a bit of an oddball. She folded down the page of the book she was reading, to mark her spot, and then set it down beside the till and left her coffee cup down on top of it. There was a berry-colored lipstick moon clinging to the rim. The thick smell of the coffee made me feel less hungry.

"Well, Christopher Hurley!" The missus stood up to greet Dad. "Back again, are ye? It's been a while."

"We are indeed, back again," Dad said. "Mrs. Hanley, this is my son, also Christopher."

I wanted to keep on with my mood, to punish Dad, but the missus smiled right at me.

"How do you do, Christopher?"

And something about her was so jolly that you couldn't be rough with her, not properly.

"Christy," I said. "Hiya."

She was lovely and round, but not in the same way Auntie Brigid was round—not with a baby growing in there every five minutes. And not even with a big, fat rump or hanging skin-bits or nothing. It was more just the impression that she was all round, soft slopes, and small, graceful arches. She was just a collection of these shapes, strung together in such a way that they added up to a body, and a face. She dressed like a nun—but one of them modern nuns who goes around in a skirt that covers her knees, and then a cardigan that's the same color of plum or blue or gray. She wasn't wearing glasses, but she looked like she should be, like her nose was a perch, waiting. Her eyes was small and brown, with hardly any eyelashes at all. And then her hair was white—as white as a winter sky, with only a couple of veins of silver swimming through it, and it was all collected at the back of her head in a giant bun that was the size of a second head. The hair looked older than the rest of her by a few decades.

She took Dad by the elbow, for to show him into the office behind the till, and I followed them into the neat little room. I knew why we was here. Dad had never brought me with him before, but I knew he did trades for books, that he was always on the lookout for people's used or unwanted books, so's he could swap for them, and then sell them in again to a dealer who might pay a nice packet for a rare one in good nick. In the office, there was one high window in the outside wall casting a cold light acrosst a tidy desk. A note pinned to the wall read, "Take, if you must, this little bag of dreams. Unloose the cord and they will wrap you 'round." In came the proprietor then, all keen bustle and business behind a healthy tummy, and the missus disappeared back into the front of the shop, her giant, white bun of hair following her.

Dad set the parcel down on the desk, and Mr. Hanley and I both watched while he untied the twine braces and let the paper fall open. Three books inside, naked and ready. Two leather covers and one cloth. They nearly shivered on the desk, exposed. But Mr. Hanley examined them with the abiding love of a book master. He touched them and smelled them, leafed gingerly through them, made ambiguous noises as he turned their trembling pages. Finally he grunted and removed his glasses.

"I know just the right collector for these," he said, folding his glasses and leaving them down on the desk. "He'll be delighted."

He was scribbling a sum on the corner of the unfolded brown paper. Dad leaned in for a look, and though I couldn't see what number was wrote there, I could tell from Dad's face that we'd be eating some fat rashers today, and maybe we'd have a drop of port even.

Dad stood up and stuck his hand out for to shake Mr. Hanley's one, without even trying to barter. Even if it was a fair price he got, I never understood why he wouldn't at least try to haggle, go for a few pennies more. But Dad always seemed content just to take what the buffers gave him. Him and Mr. Hanley went talking and slapping backs then, swapping news and money, and I slipped out of the office and back into the shop, for to explore.

The front room was all books, just nothing but books and more books, and the till, and the missus, and the steep and staggering smell of the coffee, and it nearly put you in mind of being inside in a wagon, because everything you needed was packed into the tight space, but orderly, tidy, neat. If it was a wagon, though, it would've had to've been the best wagon ever, with all them books inside.

I stood near the front of the shop and played a game with myself: if I could choose one book from each shelf, which book would I choose? I picked a paperback of *White Fang* for the wolf on the front cover, bearing his glowing teeth, but still hanging the ol' tongue out like a dog, friendly enough. Behind him, in the background, was tepees, which probably had Indians in 'em, and who didn't want to read about Indians? I selected *Lolita* for its circus-y title, and the fine-looking green silky box it came in. I reckoned a book that came in its own box must be very distinguished, like cigars.

"Not likely, mister," Dad said.

He musta been done with Mr. Hanley already, and he was folding our payday into his jacket pocket. I didn't even realize I had picked up the silky book-box, but I was holding it out in front of me like forbidden chocolates, and I didn't want to let it go. My fingers was clamped tight around it, but Dad took it off me and put it back on the shelf.

"Nothing wrong with your taste, anyway," he said. "Only the finest in the shop for you, ya whelp!"

Mrs. Hanley let out a little laugh, and the sound of it was the exact same as the bell over the door.

"That's all you need," she said, walking toward us. "Sure, *we're* not even supposed to have that one here. Still. Don't suppose it would do any harm, though. You don't *parlez vous* a bit of *Frances*?"

She winked at me, but I hadn't a clue what she was on about. She lifted the green box from where Dad had replaced it on the shelf. She dropped her voice to a loud whisper, even though we was the only ones in the shop.

"*It's banned, you know*," she said, and Dad raised his eyebrows.

"Oh, sure, that's the one!" he said. "About the ould fella and the young thing? I read about that in the newspaper."

"Shocking," Mrs. Hanley said, but she didn't look shocked in the least. She returned her voice to its normal melody and volume. "This is the Parisian edition—the only one we could get our hands on."

She admired the box in her arms, ran her fingers along the silk piping.

"Hmm," she said. "I think I'll just keep it with me behind the till. Safekeeping and that."

She patted the box in her arms, and then leaned down close to me so's her face was near, her hand on my shoulder. She smelled lovely. Very clean.

"Would you like to choose one out of the lending library?" she asked. "A bit more suitable for your age, perhaps? Or at least one that won't get you arrested?" She had a berry-colored lipstick smile.

"Thank you, missus," I said, without looking at Dad for permission. "That'd be class."

I pushed past him, and Mrs. Hanley steered me over to the lending-library section. She showed me which shelves I could pick from, and now the game was real. I really could leave the shop with one of these books—any book from these three shelves. Just one book. I took so long looking at them that Dad got exasperated and announced he was going to have a look at the paintings in back.

"Paintings?" I said, but I was only distracted for a moment.

"Don't be forever about it," he answered.

I ignored him. I had four books out now, stacked up like pillows, and I was trying to concentrate, to narrow them down. There was *The Adventures of Tom Bombadil*, which I knew I'd like because of *The Hobbit*. Plus, it had a sailing ship on the cover, and some really big fish. But the sail on the sailing ship was pink, so that more or less ruled that one out. I left *Charlotte's Web* aside just because. I don't know why. Maybe because she was a girl and I thought she might be dull, even though she appeared to have a pig, and also a sheep.

"I think you might really like *Charlotte's Web*," the missus warned, when she seen me putting it back on the shelf. "It's very popular in America."

This gave me pause. "America?" I said.

"Mm-hmm."

"D'you think Elvis read it?" I asked.

She slurped some coffee in through her teeth, and didn't laugh at me. She considered the question with seriousness. "Oh, that would be difficult to say, now," she said. "I don't know is Elvis really the reading sort."

So that left two. *The Adventures of Huckleberry Finn* looked class, and the kid on the cover was about my same age or maybe a bit older. Or just bigger, and anyway, he was wearing a straw hat. And he was barefoot. I figured we maybe had some things in common except for the hat. But in the end I chose *Gulliver's Travels*, a hardback cover, which made it feel a bit more substantial, somehow, than the others. I liked the extra weight of it in my arms. I liked that I could squeeze it with no fear of it buckling. It was bright red and all gilded with a hundred different golden curlicues and decorations. Spilled all over the cover, dripping down its edges, and even along the spine, there was puffy, raised, golden lines and swirls and letters. And smack in the middle of all them hundreds of curlicues, in a puffy, raised, golden halo of a circle, there was the puffy, raised, golden Gulliver. A traveller. It looked very academic and serious and dashing all at the same time. A proper book for a proper scholar.

"This one," I said, sliding the book up onto the counter at my shoulder-level.

"Ahh, a very fine choice," said the missus.

And then she took out her ledger book and wrote my name, Christopher Hurley, inside, along with the date, 17 February 1959. Then she gave me a small slip receipt on which was wrote, in squirrelly green-inked hand, "Enjoy this adventure, Friend! And then kindly return to Hanley's High Street Book Shop."

"Missus," I said to her then, leaning up on my tiptoes and dropping my voice as low as I could without trying to make her think I was whispering, "have you any old newspapers as well? I only need one page—any old page, it doesn't matter."

She was already leaning back, rummaging around on a low shelf beneath the counter. She wasn't even going to ask me what it was for. She drew out yesterday's *Irish Independent*.

"You can have the whole thing," she said, sliding it toward me. "I was only going to use it for kindling."

I glanced at the door to the back room, and hoped Dad would stay put for a minute longer.

"I only need a small bit," I said.

I flipped it open to a middle page and ripped off a large corner piece with a photograph on it, wincing at the noise it made in the quiet shop. Mrs. Hanley noticed my flinch, and she took into a fit of coughing to cover the sound. She did it for a disguise, I was sure of it, without even knowing me. She didn't care what I was up to; she just wanted to help me. I thanked her with a grin and folded my new, ragged newspage quickly into the back of the lended book.

"There you are now," she said loudly, pressing down on the book's cover to help conceal the newspaper inside.

Then she folded the rest of the evidence closed, and placed the *Independent* back beneath the counter.

"Thank you," I said, lifting the book.

I cleaved it to me like it was part of my anatomy. An arm, a leg. A pulsing, thumping, bloody red heart. With curlicues.

SIX

I found Dad in the back room gallery with his hands tucked behind his back and his hat hanging from his fingers. He was stood staring at a painting that had took him somewhere else, and it robbed the breath clean outta my chest when I seen it.

In a bleak and windy field, a single hungry house stood by the sea. Boulders surrounded the little house like a gang of yawning skulls. I could see only the backs of their heads, but I heard their desperate accusations; I felt their appetites. Hungry, ravenous, famished famine-heads. Openmouthed, starving. Grass green stains on their stony chins. I knew them; I knew every word for hunger.

Beyond the field, on the horizon, the colors of the sea and sky was reaching into one another tenderly, to beat each other up. Everything was bruised and punched in. All this violence and tenderness was captive inside a heavy gold frame, but its capture hadn't tamed it at all. Somehow, even on the clean white wall of the bookshop, it was still wild. It was like looking through the frame of a window into my own life, and it made me feel un-lonely, because I knew that, if people looked at this painting, they'd know what it was like for us.

I stood behind Dad as quietly as I could, and I stared. I watched. And I could nearly hear the click and hum of life in that house, hungry for us. And I could hear the fight of the wind at the rattly windows, and I could smell the turf fire burning low and sweet in the hearth. I could see Dad maybe snoring a bit, in a nice big-armed chair, with his shoes off and his toes stretched out toward the warmth. I could imagine the liveliness of Grandda's fiddle, the music warming the little room inside with the heat of joy and moving limbs. And then straightaway, my stomach filled up with the sorrow of remembering. Grandda's music was gone.

And then I felt more adrift, more alone, than I ever had in my life. I didn't understand what I felt for that house, why that painting should speak to me the way it did. I couldn't abide by houses. Couldn't never feel comfortable in them. Even when we visited them, I felt oppressed, confined in them, like the walls would smother and choke me. I couldn't breathe in a house. But there was a treacherous longing in me, all the same. And maybe in Dad beside me, staring at the house, too.

My confusion sharpened everything then, and I drank it all deep into me—the breadth of feeling in that painting. All my grief and yearning. I thought if I could soak it in, I might be able to make sense of it. I held the book acrosst my chest, pressed it hard into my rib cage, and hoped it would fill me up.

"Will we go?" Dad said, without taking his eyes off the painting.

I nodded, but I didn't look away neither. We stood there for three more minutes.

WHEN WE WAS LEAVING OUT through the front door, Dad stopped in at the till again, and I held my breath and didn't look at the missus, and just hoped to Jesus she wouldn't mention the newspaper. She was still slurping her coffee, but now she'd her nose stuck into the green, silk box-book, her eyes wide and greedy behind the pages. She folded her finger inside and half closed it when she seen us.

"See you next time," she said.

"You will indeed," Dad said. "Just—before we're away, I'm looking to post a letter. Have ye any single stamps for sale?"

"I have, of course," she said, and she nestled the book carefully back into its box before opening the drawer of the till and lifting an envelope out from inside.

"John Redmond or Arthur Guinness?" she asked.

"Oh, we'll take Guinness. Right, Christy?" Dad said.

I shrugged. Of course I wanted the Guinness, but I wasn't ready for making chat with him.

"Just the one?" she asked.

"That's it," Dad said.

She placed the small square of paper down on the counter between us. Mr. Guinness's head was pink on the stamp. I stayed holding my breath.

"Now," said the missus. "That'll be three p."

Dad put the coins into her hand and she dropped them back into the till drawer.

"Will I post it for you?" she asked.

Dad was licking the stamp, sticking it onto the corner of our important priest-letter.

"Oh, I'll take care of it," he said.

"It's no trouble," she said, pointing to a bundle of envelopes on the shelf behind her. "I've a whole stack of them to send off today myself. I'll save you the trip."

"Right then, so," Dad said. "Thanks very much." And he handed her the letter.

"Ah," she said. "No trouble at'all." She set it on top of her stack.

"*Slán leat,*" Dad said.

"*Slán abhaile!*" said the missus, and thanks to God, she already had her nose stuck back in the book.

I was home free. At the shops, we bought smokes and port, a newspaper, eggs, bread, butter (Dairygold), rashers, six potatoes, two apples, some Tayto crisps(!), a roll-pack of chocolate digestives, and—glory of all holy glories—a hefty, solid block of authentic Mitchelstown *cheese*. We would feast like we'd never feasted before. Jack couldn't go fast enough for me, I was that eager to get back to camp and devour the goods. I couldn't even stay mad at Dad, with all that food to distract me. My tummy made an eager groan.

"You've a certain Mr. Eliot to thank for all that," Dad said as I eyed the carrier-bags at my feet.

"Who's tha?" I said.

"George Eliot. He's your man wrote the book that paid for this feast," Dad said.

"What'd he have to say that was so important?" I asked.

Dad reached into the closest carrier-bag and tossed me a packet of the cheese-and-onion Taytos.

"I don't know, but he said it almost a hundred years ago in a limited first edition," he said. "So tonight, thanks to George, we eat like kings."

I ripped open the Taytos and paused for a moment to close my eyes and smell them before I started to shovel them in. They was cheese and onion flavor, the Taytos, and they really *was* like cheese and like onions. I didn't know how they did that—how they managed to get bits of potato to be so crunchy and to taste so like cheese and onions. It was a miracle. My mouth watered and watered, a gusher to flood them down and make room for more. I wondered if I should slow down and savor them, or if I could get another pack when these was gone because we had loads of them. I loved this town—nice priests, free books, excellent shopkeepers, Tayto crisps. What more could you want?

"Will we have to shift straightaway after me and Martin make the Communions?" I asked with my mouth full.

"We'll see," he said, which was always the answer whenever I asked when we was leaving, or where we was going next.

The shiny red book was clamped between my knees so's it wouldn't get dirty. I pointed to it with a salty, crumb-crusted finger.

"Do I have to give it back before we go?" I asked.

"No, Christy," Dad said. "Just whenever you're done with it. Or you might want to leave it back and get another one out instead, to bring with you on the *tober*, when you're finished with that one."

"But what about Mrs. Hanley?" I asked. "Does she know that whenever we go, we mightn't be back for months and months, like? She knows we's travellers, like?"

It was a question I wouldn't normally ask. Everyone seemed to know we was travellers, like it was branded into our skins somehow, written acrosst our foreheads. But Mrs. Hanley didn't treat us like travellers.

"She does, of course," Dad said. "And you heard her before we left. She said she'd see us next time."

"Yeah," I said, remembering. "She did."

Dad held out his hand to me, palm-up, waiting, and I poured some of the Taytos into it. He stuffed them into his mouth.

"And she lent it me anyway," I said.

"She did," Dad agreed.

"And she trusted I'd bring it back."

Dad nodded.

"That was dead nice of her," I said.

After that, I couldn't stop wondering about Mrs. Hanley—about what made her and her husband sell books and paintings. I wondered if they wrote their own books and painted their own paintings too, to sell, or if they only sold things other geniuses made. I thought maybe they was geniuses, both of them. Mr. Hanley—the way he handled them books, the way they spoke to him, and he could sense their worth just by feeling them and smelling them. And then the missus, just the way she spoke *into* you, somehow, instead of the way most people only talk *to* you, or the worse ones talk *at* you. I thought maybe the Hanleys was able to read books without even opening them—that they could just hold a book and absorb its stories through their fingertips. I got the feeling I could ask the missus all sorts of questions, and she would know the answers, and she would even tell them to me.

BACK AT CAMP, I UNHITCHED Jack from the cart, and he gave me a grateful nudge like he always did. Then I went over him with the dandy brush, til he was so content he practically purred.

"Now, just a drop or two of water," I said. "And you're good as new."

After I was finished my chores and my tea, I scrambled up into the climbing tree, which was thick and low-boughed enough that I could bring *Gulliver* up with me. I liked the change of scenery, the steep angles, the secrecy of it. I cracked open the book, and straightaway I knew I'd made the right choice. Sometimes I think you can tell just by the smell of the paper, different in every book—some pages sweet and damp, and others sharp, bitter. *Gulliver* smelled like an ocean journey, full of seaweed. Or barnacles maybe. I'd never smelt barnacles. Delicious. I turned every page slowly and read each word I could find, even the ones that wasn't part of the story and said things that didn't make no sense, like J.M. Dent & Co. 1909. I wanted to savor it, even though it was slow enough going anyway, because there was a lot of bigger words than I expected. Soon enough though, Gulliver went off in a big ship called *Antelope*, and I had a good feeling he was warming up for adventures. Then it got too dark to read, even after I turned the pages so's the firelight was showing on them. So I reached into my pocket and took out Grandda's newsprint photograph.

My mother. I looked at her face again, the shadow of her hand acrosst her eyes, and I wished for Grandda. The photo was beginning to soften a bit, from living in my pocket. The book would be a much better spot for it, so I closed it inside, along with the torn page from *The Independent*, which I shaped and trimmed until it was the same size as the other. Then I wedged the book against the tree trunk and spied on the camp below.

"Finty, did you know you're growing a bald spot there?" I called down to him. "It's spreading right acrosst the back of your head."

"Feck off," he said.

"Fintan!" Brigid said.

"I'm only telling the truth," I said. "It's about this big." I made an *O* with one hand. "I thought you should know," I said.

"Very kind of you to report," he said.

"It has freckles, too."

"You can see all that from up there?" he said.

I nodded. "I can see to Connemara from here."

"You may see the close side of my knuckles if you're not careful."

"It's nothing a hat won't fix," I said, and then he leapt for me and tried to grab my dangling leg for to pull me down.

I snatched *Gulliver* and clambered up to the next limb just in time, but he told me he could wait me out, and I had to come down out of the tree sometime.

"Why don't you play me some music?" I called down to him. "I'm gonna be up here ages. I need some entertainment."

"Martin, bring me the tin whistles, and then hie up this tree and kick your cousin back down to me," Finty said.

Martin brought him the whistles and then Dad came with his bodhrán and the port, and pretty soon Finty forgot about the bald spot or revenging me in the tree, and I was able to sit quite happily and dangle my feet low again. It wasn't the same without Grandda's fiddle, but the music was class anyway. It was that time of evening when you can't tell if the sky is purple or blue, and then it deepens to black before you have the chance to decide. Suddenly the firelight brightened and lurched. Then it was night.

There was a licking wind, and I smelled a shower twisting up behind it, but the cruel damp was lessened by the fire and the music. The night and the weather was pushed back from the edges of the camp just by the force of my family. I clutched *Gulliver* to my chest and fell backwards off the tree branch, hung there by my knees. My medal slipped out from under my shirt and hung over one eye so I was like an upside-down pirate. I swung and let the cool spot of gold bang softly against my forehead.

The others went off to bed early, but me and Dad lingered 'round the fire. I knew what he was waiting for, but I stalled. I acted like I forgot all about burning the photograph. Instead, I held my medal up by the chain and watched it glowing orange in the wheeling night-light. It had belonged to me for longer than I could remember. Some of my earliest memories was sitting on my hands on the back step of the wagon, and rocking side to side to side, watching that medal sparkle and swing from its chain 'round my neck. I used to torture Dad for the story, even after I knew it off by heart. He hadn't told it to me in ages.

"Was he a traveller, Dad?" I asked, looking up from the spinning medal and into his shadowy, firelit face. "Saint Christopher?"

"Not exactly," Dad said. "He was more of a helper to travellers." He'd tell you a story every time like he was telling it for the first time.

"Saint Christopher was a big, strong lad." He went rubbing the skin of his bodhrán with one hand while he talked. "And there was a powerful stream in his neck of the woods that nobody was able to forge, only hisself. So he used to hang around there, by the edge of the stream. And whenever anybody happened along that needed a hand, well, he'd lift them acrosst the stream to the other side."

"So that's what he's at in the picture?" I asked. "Helping a traveller cross the stream?"

"Not just any traveller, Christy," Dad continued. "That's Jesus, the Christ Child. See his halo, there?"

It was a very authentic-looking halo.

"Well, Jesus came upon Saint Christopher there one day and asked him for a lift acrosst. And Christopher says, 'Sure, hop on,' thinking by the looks of him that the child was only small, and would be an easy passenger. But as Christopher carried Jesus acrosst, the child got heavier and heavier until Christopher could barely stand up under his weight.

"'Why is it you're after getting so heavy there, big fella?' Saint Christopher asked. And Jesus explained to him that he was carrying the weight of all the world's sins on his back. And anyway, Saint Christopher struggled on, and seen Jesus safely acrosst the water. Nearly broke his back in the process, but he'd do the same for any traveller who asked him. He watches over us, Christy. And you're lucky enough to bear his name," he finished.

It was my oldest story in the world, but suddenly it was new again, because now I shared it with my mother. In the photograph, she wore Saint Christopher, my saint, 'round her neck. It was like a whole chapter had been ripped from a familiar old book, and I'd never even knew that chapter was missing until Grandda'd sent me her photo.

"Have you got that photograph there, son?" Dad asked.

I shook my head. "How come my mother doesn't look like a *Pavee*?" I asked. "She musta been a traveller, Dad, right?"

He wouldn't answer me. But she wore a Saint Christopher medal, like mine.

"Is that really her, in the photo?" I said.

"It's time," he said instead, like he was having a different conversation altogether.

"You can't," I said. "Dad, you can't make me burn it without giving me something else in return. I don't have nothing else of her."

Dad played a few beats on his bodhrán and stared into the fire, thinking.

"Have you any other photographs of her?" I asked.

Dad shook his head.

"Then let me keep this one," I said. "Grandda would want that, for me. Wouldn't he, Dad?"

He went on staring into the fire, shaking his head.

"He would, you know," I said. "Grandda sent it to me."

I stared at him, at the way the firelight skipped into all the shadows of his face.

"It's not fair," I said.

"There's nothing ever fair, Christy."

"You should at least tell me about her," I said.

Dad covered his mouth with his hand, and I watched him, the turns his face took when he was thinking.

"Are you still browned off at me?" I asked then. "For killing her? Is that why you never tell me nothing about her?"

"Ah, no, son, no," he said. "Don't ever think that."

"Well, what am I supposed to think?"

Dad took a deep breath. "Just that it's"—his voice caught and staggered like the firelight— "it's hard. You know, to talk about her. I know I should, for you—you deserve to know more about her. But for me, remembering only hurts."

He moved his hand from the bodhrán to his chest. "It's . . . I'm happy, now," he said. "We're happy, aren't we? I don't like going back, in my mind, to them times. There's no point ever dwelling on pain like that. It'd kill you, if you let it."

I reached inside *Gulliver* and drew the photograph out. I stared at my mother's face, her windy riot of curls. I stared at the stranger-baby and stranger-man, too. I was jealous of them, whoever they was. I hated them, because they was *with* her, and she was smiling.

I squared my shoulders and took a deep breath, like Granny might've done on Grandda's burial day, if Martin had gave her the chance. I took a step toward the fire and reached.

"Hang on," Dad said. "Let's see it."

I turned and held the photo at arm's length, for him to see. Grandda's ghost was still in it then, protecting it, guiding it. It shivered in my fingers. Dad's eyes fixed on my mother, and his face welled up with memories.

He nodded. "Go on then, son."

I took a deep breath, and turned my back to Dad, so's I was between him and the fire. One quick sleight of hand, that's all it would take. I knelt down and crossed my hands, I blessed myself, and when I stood, I tossed Missus Hanley's *Independent* newspage right into the bowl of the fire. It sparked and was gone in seconds. Grandda's photo was warm and safe, tucked into the loose lining of my coat sleeve.

"Now," Dad said. "That's done."

I gave him my gloomiest smile.

"You did the right thing, Christy," he said.

"I know."

THE NEXT MORNING WAS SUNDAY. Up the stone chapel steps we went, and I nodded at marble Mary with her outstretched arms beside the door. The sky was the same color as her veil: mineral white with slushy rain. I always thought Mary did the outstretched-arms bit especially for me, as a motherless boy. I always loved the freshness of the holy water wells inside the church doors, and I tried to dunk as much of my hand as I could. Dad yanked my ear because I was trailing holy water all over the floor, up the aisle to the pew.

"You're like Hansel leaving a trail of holy water." He made his voice like a shout and whisper at the same time. "And who'd want to find you, anyway?"

But I rubbed it 'round my knuckles and felt consecrated. Inside, the church was lit only by candles and the watery winter light that

struggled through the heavy windows. Shadows staggered into the
corners, and I could smell the odors of the damp and huddled people in their woolen coats. We kneeled in and lined up, and we took
up one whole pew in the church, my family did, and for a moment
I felt like a spoke in a wagon wheel, fitted in tight and solid where I
belonged, moving and unmoving, both.

"So we's stopping here for the whole of Lent, and then we'll make
our Communion at Easter time, right?" Martin said.

"Yeah, that's what the priest said," I whispered.

I kept my eyes glued to the floor, to the dirty mosaic tiles.

"So how long is Lent, then?" he asked.

"I think it's forty days," I said.

"Forty days!" he whispered loudly in the pew beside me. "Have
we ever stopped that long anywhere before?"

I shook my head and kept my eyes closed beside him. "Only the
couple of times when we was really little and we stayed in the spike
in the bad winters. Not since then," I said. Then I went moving my
lips a bit, for to make him think I was praying so's he'd shut up.

"Oh," he said. "Then what's the longest since that?"

He was so thick sometimes. He could count as well as I could.
Well. Okay, maybe he couldn't.

"I donno, Martin," I said as quietly as I could. "Maybe a fortnight. Maybe a couple days longer than that."

He was quiet, and I figured maybe he was nodding beside me so
I chanced a peek at him. He was kneeling too, but his arse was resting on the pew behind, and he'd only one elbow on the prayer rail,
chin in hand. I snapped my eyes shut again and tried to shift my
body away from him. I bumped Granny on the other side, and she
opened one eye at me.

"Sorry, Granny," I said, and she closed the eye again.

"How much longer is forty days than a fortnight?" Martin asked
then.

I tried to ignore him, but he asked again. "How much longer . . ."

"I don't know, Martin!" I said.

I could hear him make a gulping swallowy sound and as always, I relented.

"Forty days is maybe about three fortnights."

"Jesus, three fortnights!" he said out loud.

The whole pew of grown-ups and two pews in front and behind opened their eyes to glare at us. I whipped mine shut. Martin turned on his other elbow to whinge at his mam.

"Maaaaaaaaam, how come we never had to stay that long before, when Kevin or Eileen or Joseph or Michael had *their* ones?" Martin started, but he caught a glimpse of his mother's face and he wised up.

Finty and Brigid had loads of older childer, but all of them was married off and gone, so now Martin was the oldest, and Brigid expected him to be an example for John Paul and Maureen. Or at least she had, before the wagon fire. I was afraid that might've made her nearly give up on him, so it was something of a relief to see the way she glared at him. Her jaw was working up a storm. Martin lifted his arse off the pew behind, planted both elbows on the prayer rail, and closed his eyes. Maybe he even prayed. Auntie Brigid could have that sort of effect on you.

AFTER WE CHANGED OUT OF our church clothes, me and Martin went out working, stealing plastic buckets. By rights I should've hated them plastic buckets because they was starting to overthrow our tin ones. People wasn't buying so much tinware off us no more. But the plastic was so shocking, in mad, bright colors: blinding reds and blues and greens. They wasn't content just to glow the field and sky colors back at you, the way our tin ones did. Their plastic mouths was perfect O shapes, and so strong that if you stood one upside down, you could jump on it without making a dent. We seen them lined up outside the walls of the farmhouses, like garish little flags to warn us there mightn't be a good welcome in that place for us.

Dad said he didn't care. He said I was going learning the trades regardless, so's I could be a self-sufficient man of means. And I had to admit, it was class the way Dad could take a pile of scrap and make shapes out of the bits and pieces. Not just buckets, but bowls and beakers and whistles and kettles and all manner of useful vessels. And it was class the way they'd shine out beside the fire, all fierce orange and blue reeling reflections, waiting to be gathered up and sold into the houses.

So me and Martin went 'round to all the houses and we pinched the plastic buckets, but we was always careful to take just one or two of them. We never stole the whole lot, in case the farmer would cop on. But if you only took a couple of them, he'd think he only misplaced them. And then after a couple days, we'd go back 'round to all them same houses to sell them our tin ones. It was good business, even though sometimes it backfired. Sometimes, them buffers would accuse us of disappearing their plastic buckets anyway, no matter how careful we was, and they'd scream after us and run us off. But most of them farmers didn't bother with that, because they needed the buckets, or maybe also because they felt a bit sorry for us.

I wasn't much of a salesman, because I found Dad's buckets hard to part with, the same as them scrap heaps and tarps we left behind, the same as them driftwood rifles. I didn't like them getting sold off, into the service of strangers. I suspected they wouldn't shine out as brightly beside the fires of their new owners as they did the nights Dad fashioned them and brought them into being out of nothingness.

But anyway, that's how it was we was out stealing buckets on the morning we discovered Finnuala Whippet. I called her that because I'd no way to know what her real name would be, and it stood to reason that a girl with plaits folded tightly down her back, and small, round, pinched-looking glasses would be called Finnuala Whippet.

The first time we seen her, we done it by looking through the window of her house. She was about the same age as us, and perched on top of a well-shined piano bench, plunking out notes she had to squint to read, her head tipped back in a painful-looking posture. Her skinny legs dangled beneath her in dark tights, and she stretched her right foot forward in a vain effort to reach one of the pedals now and again. It was such an awkward motion she made of it, I was afraid she would slip right off if she kept it up, which seemed un-likely, given the stink of the music she made. Her vigor was surpris-ing though—it didn't seem to match the package it came in. She was like a man who rather enjoys the odor of his own farts, and she kept at it with apparent pleasure, while Martin and I cringed beneath her drawing room window.

"I bet she's called Finnuala Whippet," I whispered to Martin, and he giggled beside me.

"Yeah," he said. "And I bet she calls her parents mummsy and poppsy-poo."

Finnuala Whippet's was these parts' Big House. A solid, humor-less structure known to every Irish county—a hulking giant that grows like a trembling pimple on the crest of each town's highest hill. In houses like these, roasted lamb dinners came wearing small white booties, prepared that way by servants. We'd seen them. On summer days, we'd smelt them through stood-open windows, heady and succulent in their paper clothes. We'd slavered on thrown-open window sashes, smeared our faces with longing, licked the tangy, varnished wood of the window frames, wishing. Dreaming. To taste them dinners. But they was chewed and swallowed heedless in front of us, behind the hum and swell of voices with sore-thumb accents. The food was an afterthought, a sideline to conversation.

I wondered if Finnuala Whippet had a snotty voice, if she left lakes of gravy around her plate when she was done eating. But for some reason, I found myself giving her the benefit of the doubt. She'd sop up the leftover gravy with some bread, I decided. She'd lick her fingers. There was something undernourished about her. I believed she might even suck on the pit of a plum until it went dry and cracked in her mouth, scratchy against her tongue.

Martin and me was always scoping out the Big Houses wherever we went because they was the most fun, the most dramatic, the most imaginary. If you was going spying on people and concocting a house for yourself, you may as well spy on rich people, build the most ridiculous imaginary house available. So we'd peeped in similar windows before, but never had we spied a Finnuala Whippet sort. She took us by surprise.

We was hid from the back garden by a crowd of bushes, and we could've stayed secret where we was for quite some time if Finnuala Whippet would only amuse Martin in some way. A cartwheel would've done nicely, with a flashing hint of the knickers under them dark tights. But instead, she hammered away dutifully, practicing, butchering, and Martin grew impatient.

"For the love of Jesus," he whispered, slumping down beneath the window and covering his ears with both hands. "Christy, she is *rotten*. Will we go?"

But I was transfixed. Not just by her, but the house. The massive, imposing, daunting, magnificent, awful house. This room alone was big enough to hold maybe three wagons and a scatter of shelter tents. At one end of the long room was a roasty fire piled high with sweet-smelling turf. A small cluster of cushy chairs and one settee gathered close 'round the fire. On the far right-hand chair, a newspaper was abandoned. The wall behind Finnuala Whippet was lined with gilded frames, serious faces. But the third wall was lined, hardwood floor to fancy-molded ceiling, with glorious, glorious books. Their leather spines shone into the room like a thousand tiny beacons.

What would it be like, to live in a house like that, with all them books to read? The house was big enough, you mightn't even feel trapped in it, you mightn't feel suffocated. You might even manage to get comfortable, to kick off your shoes, to stretch out by the fire and read to your heart's content.

"Chriiiiiiiiiiiiiii-steeeeeeeeeeeeeeeee," Martin whinged.

He was always there to interrupt my fantasies.

"Go on, then, if you want to go!" I said. "Do you need me to do everything with you? You're like a pup!"

Martin pretended to ignore me. He leaned forward onto his knees, and parted some branches of the bush to look at the next farmhouse below. He pulled me down beside him to have a look: a standard thatched-roof cottage with two cows and a few chickens in the side yard. Outstandingly boring.

"Will we go down?" Martin said.

"I'm not," I said, and then turning, spotted a compromise.

"Martin, look," I said, and pointed him toward a small patch of mint that was growing wild and rampant there, in under the bushes.

"Ahhh—brilliant!" he said. "We'll have great smokes out of this!"

And he set to, plucking it cleanly and tossing it into the top of our filched buckets, careful not to rub the telltale stain into his palms. I returned to my post, without taking notice of the silence that had fallen over the room inside. When I peeked in, there was no sign of Finnuala Whippet. The piano was lifeless, its top still gaping open, propped up on its toothpick-arm. The sheet music was left on the stand like a panting tongue. I chanced poking my head a bit higher.

"Where's Finnuala Whistlebottom got off to?" Martin asked, without looking up from his harvest.

"Finnuala Whippet," I corrected him.

"Hah?"

"She's called Finnuala Whippet. Not Finnuala Whistlebottom."

At this, he paused. "Christy, does it really matter what your fake girlfriend's fake name is, ya gobshite? Where's she got to?"

"She's not my girlfriend," I said.

"'Course she is," he said. "The fanciest bird in town is always your girlfriend."

I kicked him.

"In your head, anyway," he said, kicking me back.

"I don't see her," I said. "She must've had enough of the caterwauling."

Martin laughed, but just at that instant, the scrunchy face with the pinched glasses popped up on the other side of the glass only inches away from my own.

"Ahhh–HA!" she said, through the closed window.

I started and fell backward, landing on Martin, who made an eruption of the mint.

He hadn't noticed her, and he was still trying to keep his voice down. "What's the matter with you, ya bollix? Would ya get off me?" he said in an angry whisper.

He squirmed and flailed, and I roiled on top of him, but my eyes stayed fixed on the eyes behind the glasses, behind the glass. She was smiling at me now, and laughing. Her skin was so clear you could nearly see through it, to the veins and the bones inside. A moment passed and there was a grown-up voice behind her, calling to her through the cavernous room.

"Darling, why aren't you practicing? Sweetheart, what are you doing at that window?"

My heart thumped as I registered the tones of the clipped and educated accent. It was like topiary. And still she looked into my eyes. I mouthed "Don't tell," and then prayed she wouldn't.

Our stolen buckets and harvest of stolen mint was in plain sight of the window above. I clamped my hand over Martin's mouth before I slipped off him and pinned him against the wall beside me. I glued the two of us in there as skinny as I could, while Finnuala Whippet swiveled her large head on her small body in the space just above us.

"Nothing, Mammy," she answered in a singsong that was far sweeter than the notes she was able to coax from the piano.

I heard her clacking her patent-leather shoes rapidly acrosst the gleaming floorboards.

"I think Rex got out—I think I heard him outside," she said.

We left them plastic buckets and we legged it.

SEVEN

"We'll be stopping here a good long while, hah, Dad?" I asked that night, as we was walking Jack down the road to put him into the field for the night.

Usually it was me and Martin's job to look after the horses—to find them food and lodgings wherever we was camped—but this time, since we was gonna be here for a while, Dad and Finty had made arrangements with a couple of the country families. The horses had to be properly grazed, and the farmers properly compensated, if we expected our welcome to last. It was a great worry off my shoulders, anyways, knowing Jack was safe and well fed. It was no secret that browned-off farmers was forever shooting at *Pavee* horses—the nicer ones shot over their heads as a warning, just to clear them off the land. But the angry ones wasn't above shooting a horse dead, just to teach a lesson. The gardaí discouraged that, but the law was clear: we was trespassing on private land. A farmer was rarely punished for shooting a *Pavee* horse. So it was nice to know that I needn't worry about Jack, as long as we was in this town.

Finty and Martin had put their pony in early tonight, and now Dad was showing me the place—Jack's new digs.

"What'll we do for food and that, while we's here?" I asked.

"Ah, just the same as we usually do," Dad said. "We'll get by."

"But it's not the same as we usually do," I said. "We never stop so long in one place—you always say it, about wearing out our welcome. About how we have to follow the work, to keep moving, for to make a living."

"Never worry, Christy," Dad said. "We'll sort it out. Finty and I will sort it out. The school will help, and the nuns."

"But what if they don't? What if they get tired of us?"

I was worried that, if it got tough, Dad would just yank us out of the school and pack us back onto the *tober*. It was so long coming, getting into that school. I wanted to make sure there wasn't nothing could wreck it now.

"If we have to, Finty and I will travel 'round a bit," Dad said. "And we'll send food and money back. We'll manage it. Okay?"

"Okay," I said.

Tomorrow was our first day of school, and I was awful excited, nervous. My stomach was in bits.

"Did you ever go into a school, Dad?" I asked. "You must've done, when you was younger."

"I must've?"

"To learn to read so good."

"Ah," Dad nodded. "Sure I was born reading."

"Sure," I said. "Nobody ever taught you nothing."

"Never."

"So what was it like, then?" I asked. "The school?"

"You know," Dad said. "It was grand."

Not really the wellspring of information I'd been hoping for.

"But I mean, *how was it*?" I said. "Was it difficult, like? Or, you know . . . scary?"

"I spoze it was," Dad admitted. "A bit scary. But I never really gave it no thought, I was that glad to be in it."

"Was it a boarding school?"

"Oh no," Dad said. "Just your ordinary Christian Brothers Academy."

"So where did you stay?" I asked. "Did Granny and Grandda stop with you, while you was in the school?"

"No, I stayed in the rectory with the priests—it was too long for them, with all my brothers and sisters to support. There was still . . ." He stopped to think. "I don't know, at least six? Five or six, or thereabouts, still living with your granny and grandda, so they couldn't stop with me. But there was a maid's room off the kitchen in the rectory, with a cot and a stove and a little round window, and I stayed in there. And didn't the priest apologize to me about the state of the place because the tile had been peeled up off the floor and never replaced. Sure I thought it was the Taj Mahal. It was warm."

Jack spotted some clover at the edge of the road and stopped for a snack. I let him eat for a minute before I urged him along.

"You know what was the oddest thing," Dad said, standing still in the dark road, so's he could light a fag. Cigarettes helped Dad remember things. He'd start a smoke and his eyes would squint up, and soon he'd have all sorts of things to talk about.

"I thought I'd love sleeping on my own in a bed, and nobody to go kicking at my head in their sleep," he said. "But that cot was a good three foot off the ground and I had an awful fear I'd fall out of it in the night and break my neck. So the first week, I pulled all the sheets and blankets down off it and slept on the floor." He took another drag of the cigarette.

"How long was you there for?" I asked.

"Same as you," he said. "Just for Lent, like, til I got my Communion. Your granny and grandda came back in time for that, for the big day, to collect me."

It was damp out tonight—not raining, but so misty that my hair was leaking onto my forehead. I wondered how come Dad's cigarette didn't fizzle and droop.

"But I got used to it eventually," he said. "And you know, priests is never done eating—them priests could eat for Ireland. And every time they was fed, I was fed. There was days I thought I'd be sick if I seen another spud."

I couldn't imagine.

"Hie, Jack," I said, tugging the leather of his rein when he tried to stop again.

Jack made a sneezing sound, which he often did when Dad went smoking too near him. He snorted and sneezed until Dad had to go waving the smoke away from his big nostrils, and then Jack just licked his lips and carried on. It was like a comedy routine, even though Dad said he didn't see what was so funny about it.

"And how 'bout the lessons, Dad? Was it hard to catch on, like?"

"You're not worried about that, are you?" Dad said, waving his hand in front of Jack's disapproving face. "You've got the lessons well in hand, Christy. Sure you can read as good as any of them childer, I'd say."

"No," I said. "I know."

Jack sneezed again, and Dad switched the cigarette to his outside hand.

"I'm not so good at the maths and that, though," I said.

"Ah, never worry," Dad said. "You'll be far better off than I was. Sure the second day I was in the class, I put my hand up for to ask a question and the brother teaching ignored me entirely. I had my arm up so long I felt the blood drained out of it and I had to hold it up with my other hand."

Jack snorted again and Dad shouted, "Oh for fuck's sake, horse!" at him and then threw his fag down and tamped it out with his boot. Then he went back to his story like nothing funny had happened.

"Finally I had to interrupt him because he was moving along

to the next lesson. And I says to him, 'Excuse me, Brother,' I says, 'but could you go over that last bit again because I didn't quite manage to follow it.' And d'ya know what he said to me, Christy?"

"What?"

"He said nothing. He opened the drawer in the front of his desk and drew out a fresh piece of clean paper and a pen and inkwell. He stood up from his desk then and fixed his eyes on me, walked slowly, slowly, slowly to where he'd sat me in the back row. Then he settled the clean, fresh paper in front of me and slammed down the ink bottle so hard I feared it would shatter. A few drops of black ink flew out of it and sprayed my knuckles. One landed on his face, just beneath his eye like a tear.

"'I will not hold up the entire class for the sake of a filthy little tinker,' he said. Then he straightened hisself up and gestured to the ink bottle between us. 'Why don't you draw some nice pictures until the real students are finished with their lecture?'"

"Janey Mack!" I said.

"Yeah," Dad said.

"That was pretty feckin' horrible of him," I said.

"Mind your language."

"But it was!" I said.

"It was, yeah," Dad agreed.

"So what'd you do?"

"What could I do?" Dad said. "I was stuck there for the time being, til my parents came back, like it or not."

"Did you draw pictures, then?" I said.

"I did not," Dad answered. "Sure, he only made me want to try harder."

I SPLASHED FRESH-PUMPED WATER ONTO my face and through my hair, down over my ears and the back of my neck. It was Monday morning, the first day of my life as a student. I couldn't wait to get to the school, to sit myself into a tidy desk with a shiny wooden top. My body was all bounce and motion, my excitement was locomotive. Father Francis had managed to get the supplies we'd need from the Sisters of Mercy: two pencils, two jotters, and one rubber between us, which we'd share. Martin's pencil already had gnaw-marks in it. "So we won't get 'em mixed up," he said, as the yellow paint flaked on his bottom lip. I put all the supplies into my rucksack, along with *Gulliver*.

We was early getting into the schoolyard, and we'd to line up outside with three bigger lads, a few years older than us, who was already waiting. I felt like Bilbo at the very beginning, standing on his neatly groomed little hobbit feet in the doorway of Underhill all them years ago, smoking his pipe and waiting for his life to begin.

One of the boys in front of us stood out of the queue and gave us the hairy eyeball with his whole face. I thought I'd have to rein Martin in to keep him from fighting, but when I turned 'round, he'd his head tipped back and was examining the sky with uncommon curiosity. It was a gray morning and the sky was blank. Martin took half a shuffle-step back so's he was standing nearly behind me.

"You lot's tinkers, is it?" the tallest of the three said. I waited for Martin to answer. Nothing. "Travellers." I tipped my chin, corrected myself. "*Pavees*."

The boy nodded and turned back to the others.

"Paaaaaa-veeeeees," he sang, in a high-pitched squawk.

He sounded like a parrot me and Martin had seen one time in a pub in Tipp town. I wondered if there was something the matter with him, to make hisself sound like a bird, but the other boys laughed, and then they all went on talking like me and Martin wasn't even there.

"I'm giving up sweeties for Lent," the tall boy said, and his voice was normal again. "Except for bickies. Bickies don't count."

"I'm giving up my mother's cooking," said another one, and they all laughed again.

I unflung my rucksack from my shoulder and pretended to rummage around inside. I pulled out my empty blue jotter and flipped through it. Still no words inside. I put it back. Then I felt around for my mother's photograph inside *Gulliver,* for Grandda's warmth that'd gone into it. I thought it might calm me, give me strength. Me and Martin was both clean and smelled good and had our hair combed and stuck back with Brylcreem like Elvis. How could they tell we was travellers? I wondered. How could they *always* tell? I reshouldered the rucksack. It was awful the way we was finally in school, and Grandda wasn't around to help, to give us pointers.

Two girls appeared then, about our own age, and identical in size and shape, but one with black hair and one with blond. Martin sprouted a big, stupid grin onto his face. We didn't know no girls, really, except for a couple of cousins we never seen much of, and then Finnuala Whippet.

"What about her?" Martin asked, dropping his smile.

"Who?"

"Finnuala Whippet," he said

"Oh, nothing." I'd said that out loud? "I, um, I was just wondering would she come here. Would she be in the same school, like."

Martin grinned again and raised his eyebrows. "Well," he said. "You seen the size of her house. It seems unlikely. She probably goes to some big, fancy boarding school somewhere."

"Well, if she's off at boarding school, then what was she doing at home yesterday playing piano?" I countered.

Martin shrugged. "I suppose you could maybe ask somebody about your girlfriend," he suggested then. "Oh, hang on a second. That's right—you don't know *her name.*"

I hit him a thump in the chest.

"I'm only saying it could hinder the romance a bit." He laughed.

He was right, of course; I was an eegit. My face was gone red, and I hoped nobody seen.

Sister Hedgehog turned up then, to unlock the big front door. I wanted it to creak loudly when it swung open, to herald my arrival, but it didn't so much as squeak on its well-oiled hinge. In we went then, single file: girls first, and then the other three boys, and then Martin, and last, me. Inside the door was a big black barrel and, as they passed it, each of the other students dropped in one, two lumps of turf for helping heat the school building. *Thump-thump.* Sister Hedgehog had already agreed to waive the turf-fee for myself and Martin (owing to our "financial situation"), but still, I was wishing for the ability to make that hollow thump sound in the barrel as we passed it. The absence-of-thump was louder than the five double-thumps before us, and the boys in front turned 'round to snigger at us.

Sister Hedgehog directed us to our classroom (third door on the left) and we marched down that echoing hall like men on the plank. I was glad to see the other childer turning into different classrooms than our one.

The school was way bigger than I'd expected. The country schools we'd seen before had one or two classrooms at most—all the childers of differing ages gathered in together, into the one or two rooms, with just the one or two teachers. But this school had five classrooms that I counted, a small library, a gymnasium, a court-yard, and then Father Francis's office and his little lobby where Sister Hedgehog lived. It was practically a whole town itself inside the walls of that school.

Then it was me and Martin in our matching navy jumpers, stand-ing in the empty classroom, leaning against the wall by the door, relieved to be alone again. We stood, staring at them empty desks, bolted together in pairs and lined up in neat rows, until the childer started to filter in. They found their desks and slouched into them. A couple of them didn't notice us at all. Others pointed and stared. Whispered. They was smaller than us, all of them, eight-year-olds. Like tiny martians. Most of them was missing their front teeth. I started to feel bigger and bigger, like Alice in Wonderland after she eats the cake.

But then the last to land was a big fat fella, taller than me by maybe an inch, and he nodded and gave us a thick smile as he passed. An aroma of beefy sweat trailed him.

And then Sister Phillipa was there, our teacher, mountainous in her black robes. I counted three chins, but reckoned she was hiding more under the habit. She stood us at the front of the class, and I felt small again.

"Class, I want you to welcome our two newest pupils," she was saying. "Martin and Christopher Hurley."

Beside me, Martin did something horrifying, like a small bow, or almost a curtsy.

"*Hello, Martin and Chrith-topher*," said the gap-toothed eight-year-olds in chorus.

And then Sister Phillipa herded us to an empty double desk, only halfway to the back, nearest the windows. And before I knew it, the hours passed in a whipsnap. Suddenly it was dinnertime. When Martin and me stepped out into the schoolyard at midday, and him jabbering away nine to the dozen, I couldn't remember nothing of the smell of the floor wax, or the feel of the jotter and pen under my slightly shaking fist, or the tickle of all them eight-year-old eyes traipsing up and down my goose-pimpled neck. I could only fix on Martin's face in the rain-soaked daylight courtyard, scrunched up on one side and red in the cheeks from excitement, his hair tossed up like a salad in the wind.

IN THE TENT THAT NIGHT, Dad slept, and I sat up with *Gulliver*, but I couldn't concentrate on the story. I kept flipping to the back of the book to stare at my mother. I made sure to keep the book tipped away from my dad, in case he popped an eye open, he wouldn't see it there, the unburned photograph, my gift from Grandda.

I could still feel the warmth of his ghost in the paper. I brought it up to nose my, and instead of fire then, I could smell him. I swear, I could smell Grandda. For just a moment, it was like he was there in the tent with us, and all the heat of him, and the smell of him, like earth and tobacco and clean sweat. I started, and looked 'round me, to make sure he wasn't there. He hadn't sneaked into the tent. He was still dead. But I could feel him, in my pulse, somehow.

"Help me," I asked him. "Help me do good at school, Grandda."

I darkened the lamp then, but I fell asleep with my hand tucked inside the book, silkying Grandda's ghost.

The next day I was prepared. I knew what to expect; I'd be better able to concentrate. It was only a crowd of eight-year-olds, anyway. Why should I care what they'd think? Maybe it woulda been worse, if the kids was the same age as us. Harder, anyway. Scarier. Me and Martin knew not to be so early, so there wasn't nobody walking in with us, to hear when we didn't thump the turf into the barrel. I coughed anyway, as we passed it, to cover up the sound that wasn't there. It was shadowy in the corridors, even though there was broad windows at either end of the long hall, and the classroom doors was left open as well. Martin was looking into his jotter while he walked. We'd done sums yesterday, in maths, and he wanted me to go over them with him. I was hesitating because I didn't want him to suss out that I wasn't as good at the numbers as I was at the words. He was walking slow beside me, engrossed in his jotter.

"I'm good up to here," he said, pausing to point at the second row of numbers in his list.

I stopped too, and glanced over at his figures, surprised at how neat they was, that he'd been able to copy them down at all. He'd never even held a pencil before, except for sometimes when he'd draw, and then the time last summer when I'd taught him to write his name. It had taken the better part of a sunny afternoon, and Martin had wanted to go swimming instead, but I'd insisted.

"You're really trying to learn them," I said.

"I may's well, now we're here." He shrugged.

I thought he'd just be killing time til he could get his Communion. I hadn't expected him to be actually interested. I reached across him and flipped to the next page. He'd wrote nothing down for the reading lesson. Martin flipped it back.

"I didn't ask for help with that," he said.

I looked at him.

"Christy, be serious," he said. "When am I ever going to need reading? At least with the maths, if I learn them good, I can make sure Dad gets a fair price when we go trading the scrap."

"But—" I started, and he cut me off.

"You're a *traveller*, Christy. Nobody's ever giving you a job at a desk, in an office, with a typewriter. In fact, they wouldn't give you a start as a gravedigger, and it's useless trying. Nobody cares if you can read and write. Cop on."

He pushed the jotter under my nose, but I pushed it back.

"I don't need nobody to give me a start," I said. "I'm going to be a veterinarian, so I'll be my own boss. Like Grandda."

"Grandda didn't need reading for that," Martin said.

Damn.

"But he wasn't official," I said.

"Who cares about official—he knew *everything*," Martin said, pointing back to his list. "Are you going helping me with this or not?"

We started walking again, and a square of light from one of the open classroom doorways fell acrosst us then as we argued. Beyond the tricky, double-digit numbers and the pale blue paper, beyond the square of light we was passing through, beyond the yawning gulf between me and Martin, I seen her. All yellow ribbons and crooked teeth and dopey, angelic smile. Finnuala Whippet.

"Hah?" Martin said.

But I couldn't answer him. My mouth was still open when the corner of my too-big, inherited shoe caught some wicked joint in the floor, and I was thrown forward. I lunged for Martin to break my fall, but I missed him. And then my jotter went flying (there was a terrible sound of the cover ripping itself loose from the pages) and down I went until *smack* went my nose against Finnuala Whippet's open classroom door. Then dust. Floor wax. Pain. The ooze of something salty and damp in my throat. Stars.

I was still for only a moment before attempting to right myself. But as I rocked onto my knees, my sharpened pencil punctured first the lining of my trousers pocket, and next, the skin of my thigh. I squealed. I'm sure I squealed, though I don't remember, to be honest, but I'm sure I made a sound something like a piglet, something distinctively un-Elvis-like. With tears in my eyes, I reached into my pocket to loosen the pencil point from where the lead lodged into my skin. In those last moments before I became fully aware of the searing pain in my leg and my face, before the tingles made the sensational leap to throbbing, quickening agony, before I recognized the appreciation of my audience, I lifted my head and watched the bright red drops of blood splatter their blossoms onto the remains of my ruined jotter.

SISTER HEDGEHOG MIGHT'VE BEEN A nurse before she was a nun or a hedgehog, she took that gooda care of me. She had magic potions in her bottom drawer. She had me roll up the leg of my trousers, all the way up above my knee and right up over my thigh, so she could examine the damage. She said it would've been easier just to pull the trousers down a small bit, but there wasn't no way I was going losing my pants in front of a nun. She used some tweezers and then a needle to remove the shard of lead that was lodged into my skin, but there was an angry red ring around it now. She pulled out the first of her potions: a brown, opaque bottle with some thick, red liquid that stained my thigh and made me shriek like a girl (in my head, and also possibly out loud).

Sister Hedgehog had a second bottle in her hand now, wrapped in paper. It held a golden juice that she poured into a tablespoon and then into my mouth, twice "to help manage the pain." A few minutes after I swallowed it, it made a lovely, insulating kind of dizziness in me, like the times I had gulped some of Dad's poitín when he wasn't looking. Finally, Sister Hedgehog applied pressure and then a cold milk bottle to my nose and both eye sockets "to discourage bleeding and inflammation." She was holding the milk bottle for me, against me. The drink she'd gave me made me see one and a half of her, overlapping. By the time the milk bottle began to warm, I was pronounced fit to return to class.

"Thank you, Sister," I said, and I scuttled out the door, pulling it closed behind me.

I leaned my back against it and stood there breathing and dizzy for at least three minutes. Maybe fifteen. I still had the doorknob in my hand, and I twisted it without turning around. I backed into Sister Hedgehog's office, and she looked up at me. She was likely startled, but I couldn't see much of her face, from the dizzy drink she'd gave me.

"Christopher?" she said.

I nodded.

"Are you all right?" she said.

And I tried to nod again, but I shook my head instead. And my lips turned hard against each other, and my chin grew dimpled, and Sister Hedgehog pushed her chair back away from her desk and moved toward me with her arms stretched out. I shook my head harder and then everything was blurrier again, for the tears that was coming. I threw my floppy, hand-me-down shoes over each other and reached out for her, collapsed my weight against her tiny, sturdy frame. I wrapped my arms in around her waist and I blubbered.

"Shhh shhh shhhh," she said.

Like Grandda's initials.

"Shh shhh, it's okay. It's all right."

She didn't ask why I was crying, so I didn't explain how humiliated I was, how overwhelmed. How much I missed Grandda. She pressed her strong, tiny arm around my shoulders and folded her hand through my hair and she mothered me. She *mothered* me. I cried so hard that my nose started to bleed again, and still she didn't let go. She mopped up the blood with the immaculate sleeve of her habit, and she rocked me in her arms, and for just a few moments, I felt like I belonged to her. Her hands on me. My chin and my neck folded into her arms. Just like a normal boy with his mam.

I don't know how long I cried, but it was long enough to last for three crescendos, long enough for me to recognize the gratitude I should feel that Father Francis hadn't wandered in. When I was finally, finally finished, I cried some more. And Sister Hedgehog caught all the tears and the blood and the snot and the hiccups, gathered them all up in her enormous, cavernous sleeves.

Then, head-pounding exhaustion. My nose and ears was muddied with the echoes of all that weeping, and my joints felt wet-sand heavy and weedy. Sister Hedgehog propped me into her very own chair and told me to wait while she called for Martin to bring me home.

"You'll be right as rain in the morning," she said.

I loved her.

EIGHT

"Tomato Spud," Martin dubbed me, because my nose was as bulbous and red as a potato, covered in tomato sauce. "Tom Spud" for short.

I was laid out on the ground beside the early campfire like a lamed soldier on the battlefield, and Auntie Brigid had rolled her eyes and tutted and called me a "big wee baby." But then she'd helped me get comfortable while she'd steamed a rag for me to wrap 'round my forehead, for to draw the swelling out.

"How's it look from in there, Tom Spud?" Martin said.

He lifted the corner of my steamed rag and peeked under at me. I cracked a lid and looked up at him with distaste. He was sitting beside me on an upturned pail.

"I mean, is things different-colored now, like because the two eyes is all black and purple and that?"

"Only your face," I answered him.

He snorted. "Class," he said. "I'd love a shiner like that."

I tucked the corner of the rag back 'round my forehead and let go a sigh. "I could boot you one," I muttered.

His own face was barely healed from his tangle with Granny, after the wagon fire. But Martin didn't want to think about that, and he was pretty good at switching off his brain when it suited him. I wished I could do that now and again. Martin was quiet for a minute, but I didn't take that to mean much. He'd only be picking a scab or something.

"You wanna hear what Beano said in the class this morning?" he said.

Beneath the rag, I opened my eyes. I began to crease my forehead into a frown, but the pain was too much, so I went slack-faced again. Without me beside him, to shield and bolster him in class, Martin had made up an imaginary friend—Beano, from the comics I read to him sometimes. For a moment, I was actually worried.

"Em," I said carefully, "Martin. Beano isn't *real*."

"Not *that* Beano," Martin said, snorting again, louder this time, and slapping his thigh into the bargain. "Not Beano from the comics." He laughed so hard he actually made a sound like *HAR HAR*.

"Well, what other Beano is there?" I asked.

"Beano in the class, ya big eegit. You know, the giant, black-haired kid."

But I didn't know. I didn't know none of their names. To me they was all just a pale-faced, sweaty-palmed, meat-scented assortment of the same kid. They lived in houses with mothers and fathers and brothers and sisters, and fireplaces and little holy water wells hanging inside the doors, within spitting distance of wherever the sacred hearts was on display. They was eight-year-olds. They was insiders. They walked through all kinds of doorways many times per day, and they usually did so without falling over theirselves and smashing their faces to bits. This was what I knew about them.

"Oh, right," I said. "*Beano*."

I could still taste the sour sludge of snot and blood in my throat. I hocked up and rolled over to spit, and when I did, I could feel my heartbeat in behind my eyes.

"Yeah. So Beano's sister is in the class as well, even though she's two years smaller, because he was held back a couple of times."

"So he's near our age?" I asked.

"Closer, anyways—I think he's ten or eleven," he said. "And so the sister is the real brains in the family—like you, Christy—and so we was doing readings, and it was a real tough one, and Kathleen— that's the sister's name, Kathleen—she got called on for to do the reading. And she stood up and she read the thing out as clear and as perfect! And when she was done and it was all quiet again, Sister Phillipa said, 'Very nicely done, Kathleen.' And Beano got so excited, he slapped the book down on the desk and he shouted, 'Fair fucks to ya, Kathleen!' And everybody in the class was all gasps and horrors, and Beano didn't move a muscle, only kept on grinning, he was that proud of the sister. He didn't even know he'd done wrong!"

I found this story very hard to believe, from beginning to end. I sat up to look Martin in the face, to see was he putting me on. Even *we* knew better than to shout fair fucks to anybody in front of a nun. My skepticism was such that it distracted me, and the pain was a little less, retreating to a dull, clockwork throb acrosst the bridge of my nose. It clicked when I pushed on it.

"Ah, come on now," I said to Martin. "How could he not know?"

Martin shrugged and plucked at the grass. "He just didn't," he said.

"Honestly?" I said.

Martin nodded. "It was fucking hilarious," he said.

I tried to picture it. "And what happened him?"

"Well, the Blob came racing down the back . . ."

"The Blob?" I said.

"Yeah."

I stared at him, waiting for him to explain who the Blob was.

"Oh," he said, "yeah, that's what they call Sister Phillipa behind her back. You know, because she's so massive."

"No way," I said.

Martin nodded again. How had I missed all of this? I felt like we was the two different halves of Pinocchio—I was the fake one, the wooden one with the clumsy strings and all the longing. Martin was the real boy. Bastard. He was always the real boy. I took a deep breath through the pain in my face.

"So what did the Blob do?" I asked.

"She came racing, thundering down the back of the class, where Beano was sitting in the second last row, and I donno where the ruler came out of, but she snapped it acrosst Beano's desk and that was the thing, finally, that cracked his smile."

"You mean he was *still* smiling?" I said. Unbelievable.

"Up to then," Martin answered. "And then, 'What did you say?' the Blob shouted at Beano. And Beano scratched his head, like he couldn't think what he'd said. And I thought for sure he was only playing dumb, but then—he remembered! And he *answered* her."

"He did not," I said.

"He did."

"You're lying," l said.

"Not a bit of it," he said. "'Oh, I was just saying fair fucks to my sister for doing so well in the reading, Sister,' he says to her, and the Blob was so shocked I thought she'd drop. But she steadied herself and told him to stick out his knuckles. And she hollered at him, that she'd have none of that filthy language in her classroom, and he should be ashamed of hisself, speaking to his sister that way, and all the time she shouted, she was clouting him acrosst the backs of the hands with that ruler. Slicing it through the air and bearing it down like the guillotine. And all the class winced except for Beano, and he only looked a bit sadly at his sister, like as if he'd maybe embarrassed her."

"Did he?" I asked. "Embarrass her?"

"I don't think so," he said. "She gave him the thumbs-up, after, and his big, cracked smile wasn't long coming back."

My kinda woman. "Man dear," I said. "That is some story, Martin."

"Right?"

"But *how* could he not know?" I said.

Martin shook his head again. I wondered if he was thinking the same shameful thing as me. If he was wondering if Beano and Kathleen was travellers, too.

"How come he's called Beano?" I said.

"I think all he eats is beans," Martin answered.

Well, he couldn't be a traveller, then. A traveller would eat anything he'd the chance to eat. We was quiet for a few minutes then, thinking it all over. It made me feel better, that there was somebody even worse-fitting than me. Maybe I wouldn't be the laughingstock when I returned tomorrow. Maybe I could redeem myself and nobody would even remember. Maybe Finnuala Whippet hadn't seen me fall at all, and I could start over, get to where Martin was.

"I think you're wrong, Martin," I said.

He shrugged. "I might be," he said. "Maybe he eats other things, too, and beans is just the staple."

"No," I said. "About the reading and writing."

Martin took up a stick and started drawing things in the dirt between his feet. He didn't answer me.

"I'm only saying there's a value in it," I said.

He dropped the stick. "I just don't see what's so great about it," he said. "It seems like you wanna be like them."

My face went hot in a flash, and I leaned over to pick up Martin's stick. I horsed it into the fire. "I do not," I said.

But I couldn't say no more than that, then. I couldn't defend myself properly, because in truth, maybe he had a point. I didn't know why I was so different from Martin. Why I couldn't be more like him, more comfortable in my skin, more confident and contented. I didn't understand none of it. I hated how Martin could always see the parts of me that I didn't want to look at. He stretched his arms up over his head and yawned.

"D'you know what we need?" I said to him, while we both watched his stick burn up in the fire.

"What's that, Tom Spud?" Martin asked.

"We need the sods of turf."

Whatever other differences there might be between us, I knew Martin wanted to make that double-thump in the morning barrel as bad as I did.

"Any ideas?" he said.

"We'll just have to find some."

"THE TRICK IS NOT TO be too greedy," I said to Martin. "To spread it around, like. Only a sod or two at most from each house."

Martin nodded beside me and I could see the white breath coming out of him in plumes. It stayed fairly dark out in the mornings this time of year, but it would be getting light soon enough.

"And we've to find a house where's no smoke from the chimney. To be sure they's still asleep inside," he said.

My turn to nod. "Good thinkin'," I said. "And no dogs."

We was aiming for the country houses, on the farthest edges of the town, where the sheds would be removed a bit out the back, where we'd a better chance of getting in and out unseen. But country-house dogs was mad. Not like *Pavee* dogs who was friendly and wandering and tongue-lolling. And not even like town dogs or city dogs, who was happy enough most times for a welcome rub, because they was usually looking for scraps. Country dogs was territorial and slathering and loud, with bloodshot eyes and human characteristics in their faces. If they caught you in the shed with your hand on master's turf, well, you'd get it then.

"Turf! Turf! Turf!" would go the alarm-bark and the next thing you'd be spending the morning in the garda station.

"No dogs," Martin repeated. "Right."

We was both quiet then, crouched down in the long-grass, eyeing up a small bungalow, close to the road.

"I'll go," I said. "And you keep watch."

"Right," Martin answered.

I stood, and we both caught sight of my too-big shoes, remembered my accident yesterday. Most of the swelling had went down in my face, but I still had a leftover headache.

"Right," Martin said, rising to take my place as the front-man.

That was a great thing about Martin—no matter how different we was, there was some times we could leapfrog each other's thoughts. We never had to waste time arguing about the details.

"So just whistle if you see a light go on," he said.

"Will you go right up the drive, or look for a gap in the tree line and then double back?" I asked.

He paused with his arms folded in front, studied the scene with his mouth screwed up. The ragged woolen sleeves of his coat was too long, and he'd pulled his hands inside, to warm his curled fingers. He took turns blowing up the two sleeves now.

"I think I'll just boot it up the drive and hope for the best," he answered.

I nodded, plucked up a thick blade of grass, and made ready my whistle. He took a couple of deep breaths, and then off he went like a jackrabbit into the ebbing dark.

Ten seconds later he was back, and already out of breath.

"What?" I said.

"How do we know if they've dogs?" he asked.

We both looked back at the house. The field beyond was starting to lighten 'round the edges. The sun would be coming soon. We didn't have time to be careful.

"If you get bit, there's dogs," I said.

"Right."

MARTIN WAS GONE FOR DONKEY's years. I chewed my whistle blade of broad-grass and waited while the sun heaved itself into the mid-horizon. I was passing time counting the crowd of dogs milling about the place, sniffing, pissing, yawning. So far, I'd counted three, but I couldn't be sure if the border collie I'd seen twice was the same dog or two different ones. I'd chanced the whistle four times before Martin said *boo* in my ear and scared the shite out of me almost literally.

"Where the hell have you been?" I said, and wished it hadn't come out sounding so exactly like Auntie Brigid.

Martin didn't seem to notice. He was grinning ear to ear. I could see the weight of the turf sods folded into his jumper.

"C'mon," he said. "We'll be late for school."

He hopped over the ridge of the ditch and was on his way before I had time to grab my rucksack and scramble to my feet. When we was down the road a bit, Martin opened the gap of his jumper to show me the spoils. Six fine, cakey-looking lumps of chocolaty turf. Six! So much for not getting greedy. I didn't care.

"Brilliant!" I said, and reached in to haul three of them out for myself.

All I wanted in the world was to time our arrival at school with the busiest moment. To have the largest possible audience when I scarfed them turf sods into the barrel with the most resounding of double-thumps. I pictured Finnuala Whippet's impressed face when she'd observe the strength of my walloping thumps. I didn't even want to know what'd kept Martin, or how he'd managed to avoid the dogs.

The dogs. One of them was following us—a border collie. He'd hopped the wall into the lane, and he was trotting after us, down the *tober*. Usually them country-house dogs wouldn't leave their line; they'd chase you right to the edge of their property, like they knew, like they'd been down to the courthouse and seen the property survey, and they'd chase you right to the edge of their land. But not beyond.

This fella was different. Interested. He didn't have a foaming tooth in his head, no tattletale barks out of him. He just came for the *craic*, to sniff us out. Martin glanced back at the house.

"Go on, *shoo*," he said to the collie.

The dog sat down at our feet, and I couldn't help laughing at Martin. He never inherited Grandda's way with animals the way I did. He didn't know how to talk to them.

"Hie on home now, little fella," I tried, leaning down to him.

He didn't show his teeth, so I gave him a push on the rump. He licked my wrist.

"Go on, now," I tried again, in a sterner tone.

He flopped down and gave me his belly. He tucked his chin close to his chest.

Martin was eyeing the house nervously. "Come on, Christy, we've got to go. There's no time for this."

But the dog wasn't bothered. I rubbed his chest, and he laid there in the dirt, as happy as Larry. His tail was going mad, beating up a small cloud of dust around him.

"Come on, Christy," Martin said. "I'm going."

"I know, I know," I said, and I stood to follow him. I wasn't missing my moment of triumph with the turf for nobody. Not even this dirty little furball.

"Go on!" I shouted. I snapped. I stomped my heel. I growled at him, but he only gave me his paw.

"Feckit," I said then. "I guess he's coming to school."

And off we went, because we'd no other choice, really. We could hardly stand arguing with a dog all day.

"What'll you call him?" Martin said.

"Who?"

"The Prince of Wales," he said. "Who d'ya feckin' think? The dog, ya eegit."

I glanced back at the collie. "How 'bout Fidel?" I whistled, and the dog came bounding up to my side, licked my hand.

Martin looked skeptical.

"For *fidelity*," I explained.

Still confused.

"It means *loyalty*."

Martin did his best to give me a dirty look.

"I think you should call him Scabbo," he said.

THINGS WAS SHITE LATELY: FIRST Grandda, and then the thing with my mam, too. I mean she wasn't no deader, now that she'd good teeth and a polka-dot dress, but somehow that photograph changed everything. It sunk me, that thin slice of knowledge. My dad was a bollix who wouldn't tell me nothing about nothing. And to top it all off, my first two days of school had been a total failure. I'd no fantasies left to float me through the day. But the turf sods got me a new outlook, like remembering that feeling when Father Francis said we could come to the school. That soaring flight-feeling in my stomach.

"How'ya, Mary?" I said to our Blessed Mother as we passed her, for such was my disposition, and also because I always greeted Mary, though usually not out loud, whenever I seen her.

She made no answer, but I winked at her all the same. I felt like Bing Crosby in *High Society*, which me and Martin seen in the pictures the time we spent Christmas in Dublin. Afterwards we mooched on Ha'penny Bridge for two days, doing jazz-hands and singing "Who Wants to Be a Millionaire?" (Martin: "I don't!") and made more money than we ever seen before. We was millionaires for about a week.

There was a few lads waiting already, when we landed, and they
was all lined up with their turf under their arms. I tried to hold
mine like they was holding their ones, tucked in so's not to seem too
proud of 'em. We'd stashed the two extras under some leaves in the
ditch about two hundred paces east of the schoolyard, so's we'd
have them for tomorrow.

No girls had showed up yet—it was only young fellas waiting. I
whistled "Who Wants to Be a Millionaire?" and Martin sang "I
don't" under his breath, but I don't even think he knew he was doing
it. I was hawkeyed for Finnuala Whippet, but trying to act casual. I
hoped to God and Mary she'd show up before Sister Hedgehog came
to open the doors.

Fidel sat behind me, already on his best behavior. He was as still
and unblinking as Mary herself—no wagging or panting or sniffing
out of him. He was like me in the wagon, trying to make hisself invisible, but the trick wasn't working. I noticed some of the other lads
noticing him, but nobody said nothing to us, almost like we was the
invisible ones. I whistled louder and faster, in an effort to keep up
my mood.

Beano was the next to land, with his sister Kathleen in tow, and
I knew it was him even before Martin said, "How'ya, Beano," because he just looked like the sort of fella who'd be called Beano. I
recognized him from our first day. He was hard to forget: big and
sweaty and shapeless, with hands like two ham hocks sticking out
the arms of his tight red jumper. His black hair was matted acrosst
his forehead in what might've been an effort at personal grooming.
He even looked to *smell* like beans.

"Well, Martin," he said, and I noticed he was carrying his sister's
turf for her. "Christy." He nodded at me.

I looked back at him with my mouth open, surprised he knew
my name. His smile was as broad and as ready as his belly, and it
made him better-looking. Well. Less ugly.

"He's changing the name to Tomato Spud," Martin said to Beano, pointing at me. "On account of the nose."

Beano laughed and slapped me hard on the shoulder, sending a slice of fresh pain through my face.

"Tom Spud for short," Martin said, and Beano answered, "Well then, Tom."

I smiled at him and stepped aside to make room for the sister, who I could tell straightaway was a weirdo. She never said hello; she just dropped down on one knee and squeezed between us, went groping at the dog. I didn't want her drawing attention to him, in case we'd get in trouble for having him there, but there was no stopping her. She was pretty, in a plasticized sort of way, like the multicolored buckets. She'd shiny brown hair and a large, round, solitary freckle over one eyebrow that looked like the start of a thought bubble in the comics.

"Kathleen, right?" I said.

She smiled up at me and shielded her eyes. She had a scab on her chin that was just enough to save her looking prissy.

"What's his name?" she said, and her voice was husky and warm, like gravy—more like a boy's than an eight-year-old girl's voice.

"Fidel," I said.

She turned her eager attentions back to Fidel.

"Amy!" she said then.

Man dear, she was odd.

"No, *Fidel*," I corrected her. "For fidelity. Because he's so loyal."

She looked back at me and smiled. She could get away with being weird, I guess, because she'd dimples you'd fall into, when she got a bit bigger and her teeth grew back.

"No, *Amy*," she corrected me right back, and pointed past me, to where Finnuala Whippet was marching through the schoolyard gates.

Amy. My heartbeat paused, while that name racketed around

inside my head. Amy. And I don't know why, but I got the feeling that if I said that name out loud, or even *thought* it with my lips, it would be like bad magic. It would cast a spell, or break a spell, and I would waken, and all the terrors at the edges of my life would rush in like water through a broke dam. This fragile big-house girl, with her dark plaits and skinny legs. She was Finnuala Whippet, not Amy. She was my invention, my imagined-girl. And I needed her to stay Finnuala Whippet, sweet and pliant. At least until I felt stronger in myself. I squeezed my eyes shut, sucked in a hard puff of air. She was still Finnuala Whippet. She was.

"Hiya, Kathleen, hiya, Beano," she sang, and my palms sprang damp like two sponges, and the stomach dropped clean into my trousers.

She walked right up to us and bent down to join Kathleen in smothering Fidel. Lucky bastard country-house dog. My heart had kicked in again, and I wondered if she could hear it clattering around in my chest. I looked down at the top of her head and didn't move a muscle. The part of her hair was so straight it didn't seem real, and the two plaits hung down beside her face like a second set of ears.

"D'ya know Martin and his cousin Christy?" Kathleen said.

I didn't have time to be offended that Martin got top billing, because Finnuala Whippet stood up and stomped her heel and pushed her sliding glasses back up onto the bridge of her small nose.

"We've met," she said, winking at me and pinching me on the elbow.

Even through my jacket and jumper, I felt the elbow start to sweat. Sweaty *elbows*, for crying out loud. She took a deep bow then, and stuck out her hand to me.

"Though not *formally*," she said. "I'm Amy."

Finnuala Whippet was stood in front of me with her hand out, and I had no choice but to shake it. I juggled my turf sods and then wiped my hand on the seat of my trousers, in hopes she wouldn't notice how sweaty it was.

"Hiya," I said, and I could've fallen right over. "I'm Christy."

I didn't want to let go of her hand, but she was already turning to Martin. He wasn't laughing at me, but I could tell he was struggling with it. She turned back to me before I could even catch my breath.

"How's the face?" she asked.

She *had* seen, then. Feck. I touched my nose, self-conscious. "Not bad," I lied.

She nodded. "And d'you mind, may I ask why the two of you gentlemen were crawling around in my garden last week?" she said, looking at Martin and then back to me.

As changes of subject go, she might've done better for me, but I was grateful. And anyways, she could've talked about snot-crust and maggots, and it wouldn't've mattered, because her voice was like the bells on Jack's harness. I wanted to hear her laugh, like she had when she discovered us under her window.

"Fidel wandered off," I lied again. "We was looking for him." I pointed at the collie and she scrunched up her nose.

"Funny," she said, narrowing her eyes right into me. "My dog Rex is a hunter, and he usually barks when there's another animal about. He was quiet as a church mouse."

Shite. Detective Whippet was on the case. I felt naked, but she was smiling at me, teasing me, and then Sister Hedgehog was there, and the girls was ushered in first, and I shoved to get near the front, so she'd hear when I belted my turf into the barrel. But she was already halfway up the corridor when I whacked them sods in as loud as I could. *THUMP. THUMP.* And I could feel the echo resound right down to the marrow of my shoulder bones. I watched her back and shoulders for as long as I dared, only taking glances down at my too-big shoes so's I wouldn't trip.

The Blob made to skip me during readings, in case I couldn't do it. I thought of Dad's terrible story about the Christian Brother and the drawing, but I put my hand up anyway and told Sister I wanted to read. Her nod was skeptical, but I read it out perfectly, and Beano gave me a hearty and silent thumbs-up. Kathleen looked impressed, too.

NINE

All the other students was away home as quick as they could after school, hopping to change their clothes so's they could go out and play football. But Martin and me knew there was work waiting us in the camp, so we dragged our feet.

"Beano's good *craic*, hah?" he asked me.

We was the only ones left in the darkening hallway, and there was a dead leaf scuttering through the front door.

"Seems all right," I said, tucking my two thumbs into the shoulder straps of my rucksack.

"You don't like him," Martin said.

"I don't even know him," I said. "And you don't either, Mister Fast-Friends. You're only after meeting him." I knew how I sounded. I tried to wish the jealousy out of my voice.

"I know why," Martin said.

"Why what?"

"Why you don't like him."

"Oh, do you?" I asked.

He was quiet for a second, waiting for me to ask the why of it, but I wasn't going to. He could wait all day.

"You don't like him because he's like us," he finally said.

I tried to swallow, but I choked a little on my spit. "What?" I said, coughing. "He's nothing like us. And anyway, I *like* us, ya big retard, so what sort of an explanation is that?"

"He's *just* like us," Martin went on. "Everybody thinks he's odd."

What a stupid theory. "What's your point?" I said.

"Since when do I have to have a point?"

I felt my face going hot and I had to take a deep breath. "Anyway, his sister's a right weirdo, too," I said.

"Well!" came a voice behind us.

We was nearly to the front door, but we turned to greet Father Francis, who was leaning in the doorframe of Sister Hedgehog's little office.

"And how are Saint Malachy's two newest academics getting on?" he said.

"Very well, Father," I answered him.

"I heard you had a bit of bother there yesterday." He gestured to my face.

"I did, Father, but it's much better now," I said, trying to cover the worst of the bruising with my hand.

"And how are the studies coming along?"

"Very well, Father, thank you," I said.

"And, Martin?"

"Hard, Father," Martin said. "But good."

"Now!" said Father Francis. "Perseverance!"

"Yes, Father," we both said.

"Well, Martin, you can tell your mother that your baptismal certificate arrived today and everything looks to be in order."

"Grand." Martin nodded.

"And, Christopher?" he said.

He put his hand on my shoulder and walked with us toward the front door. I couldn't remember a time a priest had ever put his hand on my shoulder.

"Sister Helena tells me your father is sending away for yours himself?" he asked.

"That's right, Father," I said. "We posted the letter off last week."

"Very good," he said. "It's coming locally?"

We stopped at the front door and turned to face him.

"From Rathnaveen, Father."

He frowned.

"In County Tipperary, Father," I said.

"Ah, so."

He smiled. "So long as it's not coming from America or England or somewhere," he said. "We'll need to make sure it arrives in plenty of time before the Communions."

"Yes, Father," I said. "I've never been to America or England, for to get baptized."

"Guatemala?" he asked.

Martin snorted.

"No, sir, Father," I said.

"Nairobi?"

I shook my head.

"And you call yourselves travellers?" he said. "Sure, you're just the same as the rest of us."

Martin beamed next to me, and I have to admit, my mouth was probably hanging open a small bit as well.

"I don't suppose County Tipperary is such a long way after all," said Father Francis.

"No, Father."

"So I'm sure it'll be here in plenty of time."

"Yes, Father."

"I certainly hope so, anyway, Christopher," he said. "'Twould be an awful shame for Martin to have to make his Communion without you."

They both laughed again and I tried to join them, but I felt something I hadn't known was there before that moment, something like a shuddering gargoyle curling up in my stomach.

I TOLD MARTIN I'D A message to do for Dad and I'd see him back in the camp. First I went to the post office, and Fidel waited outside.

"Anything for Hurleys?" I asked at the counter.

The postman didn't look up from his ledger. "No," he said.

I drummed my fingers on the countertop. "Are you sure?" I asked again. "It's really important, mister. Could you just check?"

The postman sighed heavily at me and set his pen down on the page. He rubbed his eyes beneath his glasses. "Listen," he said. "I've been doing this job for thirty-three years. I know the names of every man, woman, and child in this parish, and most of their birthdays. I don't know any Hurleys, so I can only assume that you are visiting itinerants with no fixed address?"

I withdrew my hand from the counter.

"Is that correct?" he said.

"Yessir," I answered quietly.

"Do you belong to the Hurleys who are stopping on the Long Mile Road?"

"Yessir," I said again.

"Well, it's like I said," he finished, retrieving his pen from the ledger. "There's nothing here for you."

I nodded at him and turned to go. But I stopped at the door and held it open in front of me. "We're expecting a letter," I said. "For my dad, Christopher Hurley. I'll call back again tomorrow."

He grunted a response and I let the door slam behind me.

At the bookshop, the missus was sitting in her usual spot when I jingled the bell over the door and went in.

"Come in, come in," she said to me. "Get outta that weather, Christopher, come in!"

So I was right about her weather-greetings. "Hiya, missus," I said, wiping my feet on the mat inside the door.

She left her book down on the counter and clapped her hands, rubbed them together, so's I felt like I was bringing the weather with me into the shop and making her cold, like the breeze rode in on my shoulders. She wouldn't last a day on the *tober*.

"Well," she said, hugging herself and smiling at me. "We're not finished with *Gulliver* already, are we?"

"No, missus," I said. "Not yet."

She had a smudge of the berry-colored lipstick on her front tooth.

"I just wanted to check if you'd had a chance to post that letter last week," I said.

"I did, of course," she said. "I posted it that very afternoon."

"Right, so," I said. "I figured. It's just it's very important and we haven't had word back yet . . . I wanted to make sure."

"No harm in following up," she said.

"No, exactly," I said.

"It'll be good news, I'm sure," she said.

"Sorry?"

"Whatever it is you're awaiting word on," she said. "A love letter, is it? I suspect. You've written your fevered adorations and now you're awaiting the verdict, like Romeo waiting for Juliet."

I shook my head at her. The bell over the door jingled again and a woman came in shepherding her two young childer along in front of her, one boy, one girl. They both had shiny blond hair, but apart from that they looked awful glum, and there was no chat outta them, only big, frowny mouths. Their mother wore a long, swinging coat with a belt, and glossy stockings. A hat was pinned in among her smoothed-down curls.

"Come in, come in!" said the missus. "Come in, and how are you keeping, Mrs. Mulligan?"

"Ah, we're very well, very well indeed, aren't we, children?" she said.

"Yes, Mammy," said the two glum-gobs.

I stepped to the side of the counter to make room for them, to sink into the scenery until they was finished. The boy was staring me out of it. He'd eyes like two saucers full of milk, like they might spill. I tried smiling at him, but it was no use. The mother looked over to see what he was looking at, and when she seen me there, she reached over and pulled her son away from me by the elbow.

"Shoo!" she said. "We're not buying any of your little trinkets and we've no handouts for you, so you may's well go on now. Shoo!" Like she was talking to a dog. She waved her hand at me.

"I don't speak dog," I said, but not loud enough for her to hear. I don't even know did I move my lips.

"Ah, now," said the missus. "Now, Mrs. Mulligan. Christopher's not harming anyone there. He's not trying to sell you anything at'all at'all, sure you're not, Christopher? He's a customer."

"Christopher?" said Mrs. Mulligan.

"Our little friend here," said the missus. "He's a great one for the fine works of literature. Loves to read! Don't you, Christopher?"

I stared at the boy, whose saucer-eyes was getting even bigger and milkier by the minute. His mammy was trying to tuck him behind her, on the other side where he couldn't stare at me, where he couldn't catch whatever disease she thought I had.

"BOO!" I said, and he jumped quick behind his mammy like a flea.

"What can I do for you today, Mrs. Mulligan?" said the missus.

But Mrs. Mulligan was too distracted. "We'll go," she said. "We'll come back another time." And she was turning, and gathering, and pushing her glummy childer toward the door.

"Ah, he's only a child, Theresa," said the missus. "He's not harming anything!"

But Theresa Mulligan was herding herself gone. The bell over the door jingled again, and the blond heads bobbled through and away.

It was awful quiet after they left, and still I stood sunk off to the side, and I didn't know what to say to the missus after they left, and I didn't know if I should apologize for saying "BOO" to the milk-eyed boy.

The missus perched herself back up on her stool. She pressed her lips together, and I figured she was thinking what to say, what pep talk to give me. The nice buffers was always making excuses for the mean ones, like if they was nice enough, they'd be able to explain it in a way I'd understand—why that woman had just talked to me like I was a dog. With mange.

"I suppose, really it's more Yeats waiting for Maud Gonne," she said, "than Romeo waiting for Juliet. Or at least I *hope* it is. It wouldn't do to have you spilling your guts all over my shop. I'm only after waxing the floors."

She wasn't even embarrassed about Mrs. Mulligan. She wasn't even embarrassed about me. No excuses, no reprimands. No discussion. She lifted her coffee cup and took a slurp.

"Ahhh, I love a good romance," she said. "A good love story— there's nothing better. I'm sure she'll write her devotion soon. Any day now, any day!"

I laughed at her—I couldn't help it, I laughed. "No way," I said. "That's disgusting."

"Disgusting?" she said. "Disgusting!" She sniffed, pretending to be appalled.

"Well, I suppose maybe you're a bit young for it after all," she said. "But you'll change your tune soon enough."

I thought of Finnuala Whippet and wondered if she was right. I would be twelve soon, and a lot of *Pavees* got married around fifteen or sixteen. There was no question I was starting to sense some rumblings. But I'd enough problems at the moment without going all squishy over some girl. Mrs. Hanley leaned back on her stool and held her coffee cup with both hands.

"It's a letter from the priest who baptized me—I need it to make my Communion," I explained, even though she didn't ask. "And I'm awful nervous I won't get it."

She leaned her elbows on the counter between us. "Why wouldn't you get it?" she did ask then.

I shrugged. "Donno," I said. "Only we never got this far before. Never been allowed to actually go into the school and do the classes. I didn't know we was gonna need copies of the paperwork, ya see, and my cousin Martin got his one already, but mine's meant to be coming in the post."

I'd an awful habit of blurting out my whole life story to people, Dad always said. But the missus didn't seem to mind.

"Never worry," she said. "I'm sure it'll be here in no time at all. It probably took them a couple of days to get it organized on the other end, is all. It'll turn up soon."

I took a deep breath and nodded my head. "Thanks," I said.

"No problem. Come back and visit anytime," she said. "You can get another book out when you're finished with *Gulliver*."

"Class."

"Right-oh," she said.

She was lifting her book again, so I took that as my signal to get scooting. I headed toward the door, but I turned on my heel before I got there and went back to the counter. She was smiling at me over the top of her book.

"Sorry, missus," I said. "Just one more thing."

"Mmm-hmm?"

"It's just."

She looked at me, waited.

"Just . . . well, say you had a bit of a newspaper article, and you wanted to figure out more about it," I said. "Would you know how to go about a thing like that?"

She closed the book again. "Only thing better than a love story," she said, rubbing her hands together. "A good mystery!"

"I guess so."

"Well, to begin with, I suppose you'd want to examine the article quite closely, to see what sort of clues you could extract from it."

"What like?" I asked.

"Oh, like maybe a date," she said. "Or the name of the newspaper, or the reporter who wrote the story."

"Right." I nodded.

"Nowadays, lots of the newspapers keep very detailed archives," she explained. "So that you could go back and look up the complete text of the article, if you had enough clues."

My mother's photograph was just inside *Gulliver*, in my rucksack. I could take it out right here. I could unfold it and spread it out on the counter and she could help me examine it. She could help me. I could feel my mother's presence there, trying to climb up my back, scramble out the top of the rucksack. She wanted me to discover her, just like Grandda did. Maybe their ghosts was working together now, for a reunion with me. I could feel it, like holy magnetism.

But then the bell over the door jingled again, and this time it was a young man in a suit and a hat. I could see Fidel's patient face outside the gap of the door, as it swung shut again. The man carried a briefcase and a raincoat.

"Good afternoon!" he called acrosst to the missus.

"Come in, come in," she said. "George! So good to see you. Come in outta that weather."

She stood up behind the till, and came 'round the end of the counter toward him. George paused at a section of biographies.

"All done with Mussolini," he said. "Ready for someone with a bit more panache. Who's next?"

She stood beside him now, and together they discussed the options. I headed for the door.

"See y'again, missus," I said.

"Good day, Christopher!"

And the bell over the door jingled me out.

WHEN WE GOT HOME, FIDEL introduced hisself into the camp by lifting his leg in the direction of Brigid's clean washing.

"Go'way, you filthy beast!" she screamed.

And that moment really clinched our devotion to each other. After tea, I gave him a bath and decided he didn't belong to that farm where we'd found him at all. He hadn't been cared for—not even a small bit, the way they do on the farms. He was more stray than working dog, and his ribs was lean beneath his tangled fur. It took me the better part of an hour to get him brushed out, but I was patient and so was he. I burned fourteen ticks off him, and he tried to go eating the bloated purple ones that fell off him like moldy berries. His feet was in decent shape, but I used Dad's nippers and rasp to file down his toenails anyway.

"Ah, isn't he lovely?" Dad said, only half sarcastically, while Fidel flexed and strutted after. "He'll win best in show at Crufts."

Dad and Finty was working on a pile of scrap they'd scrounged during the day. I grinned. Fidel would need a few good feeds before he'd be perfect, but he was a different dog altogether from the one who'd followed us home.

"Not too shabby, hey, Fidel?" I said, scratching the white spot on his clean head.

"He'd want to be lovely after all that mollycoddling," Martin grumbled.

He was only cross because he'd had to organize the scrap on his own. I got up to help him finish so's he wouldn't whinge. We made one pile for small motors and an old radiator (which we would disguise as cast iron by filling it with heavy sand before it went to trade) and then another pile of old pots and pans and kettles and that. Dad and Finty was drinking port from their beakers, and Martin tried to sneak a drop. Brigid caught him and sent him off to bed early.

Jack and Fidel sniffed at each other casually, like two old fellas who don't like each other much, but have to be social because they drink in the same local. Fidel came along when me and Jack walked down to the field to find our low spot in the wall.

"It's a pity you don't get to feast like we do," I said to Jack, leaning into his rump to urge him over. "No Taytos or cheese or chocolate bickies for horses, hey?"

His rough tail swished my face in the darkness, and for the nine millionth time, I remembered the night of his birth, how close he'd come to never being. How Grandda had saved him—for me, I thought, because he knew I'd need him. He knew Jack would grow big and strong, and he'd become my best mate.

"Just night-grass for you," I said, looking over the wall to where he was already grazing. "But I guess that's what you like."

I climbed up to sit on the wall, and Fidel hopped up, too. I set *Gulliver* down beside me, and rubbed Fidel. He was still damp from the bath.

"So how do you like it, Jack?" I said. "Coming back to the same spot every night? Good grass, room enough to roam, no watching over your shoulder for angry farmers with shotguns."

Jack went on munching.

"A travelling horse could do worse for hisself, you know."

I could just make out the flashing pink of his tongue finding sweet grass in the darkness. Maybe it was yummy.

"You couldn't never've been a farm horse, sure you couldn't?"

Jack snuffled. I jumped down from the wall and went to lean against him. I plucked a lump of grass, but he didn't wait for me to give it to him. He grabbed it outta my hand.

"Ah, ya big tulip," I said, but it never failed to surprise me, how gentle he was, how soft his big lips against my fingers.

I leaned my forehead against his nose. Fidel eyed us quietly from his perch for a moment, then disappeared down the back of the wall. We listened to him walking back to camp on his own.

"Good man, Jack," I said, clapping him roughly on the back.

Jack went on licking and chewing, but he watched me the whole time—he never took his eye off me. I'd always knew from that first night in the glowy barn that Jack was one of them rare horses who understood people-talk. Me and Grandda had talked him into surviving; we'd *convinced* him that living was worth the struggle.

"You miss him, too, don't you?" I asked, twisting my hand through his mane.

I untangled my fingers, then raked them through the coarseness of his hair.

"That reminds me," I said. "I want to ask you about something."

Not like I was crazy or nothing. Not like I really thought he'd tell me his opinion. Not in *words*, like. But I went to the wall and flipped *Gulliver* open, pulled out the newsprint photograph.

"It's my mother," I said, holding it out so's he could see.

Jack looked at the photo, took a step forward, and tried to taste it. I pulled it away in the nick of time.

"Whooooa," I said. "Not for eating."

I patted his nose, held the photograph at a safe distance now, in the other hand.

"D'you remember your own mother, Jack?" I asked, turning back to look at him. "She died, too, when you was born. Same as me."

I smiled at him, so's he wouldn't feel bad.

"Grandda made sure I got this picture," I said. "I just know he did. But now I have it, it's like a dead end, and that makes me nearly sick to my stomach. Because lookit her, Jack. She ain't like nothing . . . well, like nothing I ever seen."

It was a full moon out, and that rarity of things—a cloudless

Irish night sky. The moonlight fell acrosst my mother, standing with that man and baby, in the photograph. There was a spreading crease in the newsprint now, right down the photograph's middle, and it was about to detach itself into two separate pieces. The man's body and head on the left piece, and then the man's arm, my mother, and the baby on the right piece. I had permanently severed them, one from the other, for the convenience of a fold.

"Oh, quit being so dramatic, Christy," I said out loud to myself. Jack snorted.

"I know what you're thinking, Jack," I said. "But it's not me, that baby. It can't be. Because she died when I was born. So it must be . . . somebody else. I donno who the feck it is."

Mrs. Hanley had said she would look for clues, clues. Any words I could find might help. The photo had been clipped out of the newspaper—not torn. Carefully clipped, and none of the words had been saved with it. I didn't know how I was meant to find any clues from that. I shook my head, bit my lip.

"If Dad wasn't such a gobshite, he'd just tell me," I said. "He definitely knows more than he's letting on."

Jack chewed his grass loudly. Then he burped.

"Well, you are really not helpful," I told him.

I folded the newspaper back along its familiar crease, made to tuck it back inside *Gulliver*, and then I seen. I don't know how I'd missed it so many times before. How many times had I looked at it, by then? I studied that photograph whenever I was alone, but never once had I taken note of what was on the back side. I'd never cared. A Bewley's advertisement, I saw then—nothing much. But above that, in the upper left corner, was the number sixteen. One-six. So this was page sixteen of whatever newspaper it'd come out of. Which would make its flip side either fifteen or seventeen, right? Well, if I wasn't as proud of myself then, at that moment. I felt like both Hardy brothers rolled into one. Sherlock! I studied the rest of the page now, really studied it. I couldn't make much out of it, but there was a local ad—just the top bit of a local ad, for Cummins Plumbing Supplies in O'Briensbridge.

"Well, maybe this is something," I said. "Whattaya reckon, Jack? An ad for a plumber's in O'Briensbridge."

I knew that village—we passed through there regularly. Dad called it a perfect medium-village. Medium-size, medium-pretty, medium-generous.

I looked Jack in the eye. "How many newspapers can there be in a village like that? Not more than a one, surely?"

Jack went back to rooting in the grass but then stopped to look at me as I swung my two legs back over again to the road side of the wall. I think he'd been hoping I'd stay, but I had some thinking to do. Plus, *Gulliver* was waiting.

"G'night, Jack," I said.

I tried to stay in the shadows when I came back into the camp, like a proper sleuth. Or a cat burglar. Yeah, a cat burglar. Sometimes I liked to pretend I was a character from a book or the cinema—a spy or a detective or an Indian. So tonight I was a cat burglar and, if I could make it into the shelter tent without being seen, I would win the crown jewels.

I crept around the back of the camp, in behind the wagons, holding my breath. I slipped into the tent, folded myself in behind the flap, and then peeped back out at the fire. Dad and Finty was more at the port than the scrap, and Fidel was there between them, his chin resting on Dad's shoe. He wagged when he seen me, but he didn't get up. The jewels was mine.

Gulliver. I breathed again and felt around in the dark for the lamp and matches. I lit the wick and now the tent was an orange bubble of firelight, nestled cozy and low to the ground. The wattles was bending their ribs above me in graceful arches, bearing up their canvas skins. I took off my wellies and pulled the blankets up over me, opened the book carefully accrosst my two knees, to the page where I'd left off. I ran my fingers over the letters while I read, so's I could soak them in through my fingertips, too. Just like Missus Hanley, the mad genius.

Then I had this thought, which was enough to distract me from the book for just a minute: maybe Missus Hanley's giant, white bun actually *was a second head*. Maybe the hair was just a disguise for the area where she kept her second brain. You'd need two brains at least, to fit in all the worlds of books she had in her shop. I couldn't wait til I'd have a chance to get back to her, to tell her about the clue I'd discovered. O'Briensbridge. It seemed like a big one.

I don't know how long I read, but when I wakened up, the book was folded closed beside my head, so's it was the first thing I seen when I opened my eyes in the morning: cheerful red, golden spangles. Dad must've put it there when he came in and seen me sleeping over it.

Shit. The photograph. If Dad lifted the book, he might've found it, unburned. I sat up quick, panicked. I was alone in the tent. I listened for Dad, and when I didn't hear nobody outside, I opened the book to the back cover. My mother was still safe inside.

TEN

We wasn't long getting into a rhythm with the town and the school, so that soon the days began to blend and fly. On Saturday morning, Dad and Finty rode out a couple of towns over for the day, to trade with some fresh faces. It wasn't easy for them to keep in work for so long in the one place, to stretch out their welcome and keep us fed when they couldn't move along at their own pace. So they'd have to start doing daytrips now, overnight trips, the odd time, to keep working. Granny had gone off to the Monster House for to buy swag. So it was just Brigid and us childer. No school, no Finnuala Whippet. The long, slow day stretched out in front of us, empty as a bread box.

Martin found two lemonade bottles, Lord knows where, and tied them together in an X with a bit of twine. Apparently, they was a steering wheel of some description. He pulled his imaginary car up outside our wagon and hit the brakes. I was sitting on the back step with *Gulliver*.

"Hop in," Martin said, holding the steering wheel out in front of him. One of the bottles wasn't quite empty. It dripped.

"Where ya for?" I asked him.

"Oh, just thought I'd tool around for a bit in my new automobile."

He squeezed the invisible horn, made a wooogah sound.

"Nice one," I said. "What kind is it?"

"It's a Rolls-Royce," he said. "A convertible, so you don't even have to open the door. You can just jump in the roof. New model. Called the Mart-O-Matic. C'mon."

"I'm not getting in that thing," I said.

"Suit yourself, then."

And he peeled off. He'd be back, I knew. And I'd jump into the passenger seat, and we'd tool around together, honking at people, running over babies. Maybe we'd pick up a couple of birds. Because it was Saturday and there was nothing else to do.

After a while, Auntie Brigid announced we was heading out mooching, and I was never so happy to hear it. I had to get outta the Rolls. I slammed the door, kicked the invisible tires.

"You'll dent it!" Martin said. "Careful!"

"Get yourselves ready," Brigid said, walking 'round to the back of the wagon to plait her hair. "We'll head off now, in a few minutes."

"Do we have to come, Mam?" Martin whinged.

He was parking his steering wheel under the steps of his wagon for safekeeping. The clouds was peaky in the sky, and I had a feeling they'd lift their skirts and run before afternoon. There was two magpies in the climbing tree. Martin could feel it, too, the promise of coming sunshine, and he wanted to stay playing instead of going off mooching. Auntie Brigid didn't answer him. Instead she sat the baby Maureen on her knee and spoke to her while she rubbed her pink baby-feet with dirt.

"What is that brother of yours like?" she said. "If there was work in the bed, he'd be asleep on the floor!"

The baby was just beginning to sprout two white, half-moon slivers of teeth out her top gums, and she showed them off when she smiled. I hoped they'd straighten out when they dropped down into her face a bit more.

I didn't mind going mooching with Brigid at all. She had a gift for it—that's what everybody said. I'd never tell her, of course, but I sort of admired her for it. You could learn things from her if you paid attention, and the mooching was getting to be more and more important all the time, for *Pavees*.

It used to be, when I was real little, we'd hardly ever have to mooch—only the odd time—because Dad and Finty and Grandda was always able to get loads of work down the farms at different times of year, planting or harvesting. That was before all them farmers went out and bought theirselves tractors and bailers and combine harvesters. And all the farmers knew Grandda, and used to call for him instead of a doctor, if ever there was a breech birth or a sick heifer. He could heal nearly any animal, and the farmers respected him. It wasn't so long ago. Just a few years back, I remembered.

There was still plenty of buffers buying tinware off us then, or they'd pay us to mend their old pots and kettles. We could even sew up cracks in their plates for 'em. That was a secret only *Pavees* knew how to do, and the thing'd look brand-new afterwards, and you couldn't even tell where the crack had been. The buffers bought loads of swag then too, because none of them had cars, so they'd be delighted when they'd see us coming. We was a travelling shop, you see, a welcomed sight. A relief from their isolation. We could always swap them a comb or a thimble, maybe a pair of scissors. They'd give us food or a few bob for whatever they needed. Sometimes we'd run messages from town to town for them, because they couldn't move like we could. Back then, before cars and tractors and telephones, they needed us.

But not no more. Now we had to mooch, to make up the difference, and Brigid was good at it. It was mad the way you hardly ever heard a peep out of her when Dad and Finty was around. But when she was out on her own, chatting the ladies, she was all charm and wit, whispered fortunes and confidences—a different woman altogether.

Every travelling woman had her own approach, and Brigid's was to make sure we was good and dirty, even though we might've already had a wash in the morning. It was great *craic*. We'd be so dirty we was like a troupe of circus clowns, and I couldn't help wondering how thick could them buffers be, that this worked on 'em. The dirtier you was, the sorrier they felt for you, and the more food or money they'd give you then. You'd've thought they'd only offer you a clod of soap and some water. But no. They thought food or a few bob would help us clean ourselves up.

Brigid seemed ten years older when she went out mooching, and she wasn't no spring chicken to begin with. She was over forty now, so everybody reckoned that Maureen was probably her last wean. She would strap the baby onto her front, and then hunch over a small bit, or develop something of a gammy leg, for to show off the hardship that was setting so roughly on top of her. If she hadn't been a *Pavee*, she woulda been famous in the cinema.

"Christy, you'll not get a button looking like that, and you know it," she scolded me when she seen me waiting to go. "You're too clean by half for a child with a face as battered as your'n. You'd have this baby starving of hunger."

She made a clucking noise at me with her tongue. It was true that my bruised-up face was healing rather nicely, but I hadn't even washed that morning. My hair was still waking up, and I had morning breath, sweetened with lingering tea. I couldn't help it if my natural exuberance and cleanliness shined through all that. A *mudbath* wouldn't make me as dirty as Martin. She was holding me up to impossible standards.

"We can't all be scholars and gentlemen," she said, tipping her head back so's to look down at me more effectively.

"And we can't all be livestock either," I said, looking at Martin.

Maureen (who was in no danger of starving, mind, and who was the most spoilt and petted of all Brigid's childer, in the high hopes that she was the last) was tucked into a blanket slung acrosst Brigid's front, with her fat little arms and legs splaying out. It made Brigid look like she was growing a bad spud in there, budding eyes and roots. But four-year-old John Paul was the real ticket. The buffers loved him: Golden curls. Dimples. Filth. Giant, clear-blue eyes peering out of a dirt-brown face.

"That's my good boy, John Paul." Brigid reached for him. "Come to Mammy."

I imagined he had bugs on him somewhere. I pictured a whole army of them, ants and ticks and earwigs, marching under the collar of his shirt, hiking through the forest of curls, forging into the caverns of his ears.

Martin just looked like his normal self. He had a stain of something sticky acrosst his chin. Maybe juice, but I donno where he woulda got juice from.

Up the lane we went then, our dirty dust brigade. The buffers mighta looked out their windows and seen the cloud, mistaked us for bad weather coming. A storm rolling down the road, all thunder and bare feet. We headed away outta the town—out toward the country lanes, to the houses Brigid hadn't visited yet. Fidel followed us for a while, but he soon lost interest and went off on his own. He was fairly independent that way. Like a real *Pavee* dog, he always came back to us in the evenings. We wasn't long turning inside the gate of a house. There was a suck calf with its mother penned in along the side of the house. The mother mooed at us.

It was a large cottage, huddled close to the ground by its slanting, gray-shingled roof—no thatching of wild field rushes overhead for these modern buffers. The windows was set deep into thick-walled pockets, and somebody had hung empty window boxes, wishing for the brightness of flowers. Maybe Brigid could sell them some of her paper ones. The whole operation looked to've been newly washed with lime, so's it fairly glowed in the ragged yard.

"*Dia duit!*" Brigid called out the usual greeting in her northern accent.

"*Dias Maire duit!*" came the answer in country-Irish before the tidy little woman came into the light of her own doorway. "And who've we here, now?"

It was quiet around the house—no childer about, no husband to be seen. But there was tire tracks in the dirt of the road. They'd be back. Brigid shielded her eyes with one hand, and dangled the swag basket loose on her arm. The woman mightn't buy nothing off her, but you still had to pretend she might. It was bad form to beg outright, without offering something in return. A thimble, a tooth-brush, a song.

"We've just a few bits and pieces for sale, missus," Brigid ventured. "And if you've any old rags around the place, we'd be happy to take them off ye."

The woman was wiping her hands on her apron and squinting out. She looked healthy and well fed. Brigid wouldn't offer to read her palm or her tea leaves unless she hinted a curiosity first.

"Come in anyway," the woman said. "We'll see what we can find for yous."

She stepped back into her doorway and herded us through like chickens. Livestock after all. She smiled at John Paul as he came marching through and almost—but not quite—patted his head. The main room was small but immaculate. The thick stone walls of the house felt even thicker once you was inside them. The hearth looked freshly swept, and there was a neat fire tucked into it, just glowing warmly without giving too much hot breath into the room.

Above the door we'd come in, the Man Hisself was up on the cross, watching the proceedings of the household.

Martin and me sat down on a wooden bench beside the table. Brigid took a chair, and the little country woman drew hers up beside. The woman sat straight and proud—a buffer in every bone of her spine, right the way out to her fingers and toes. But she was shy at the same time, her hands folded neatly in front of her, her ankles crossed beneath her chair. She wore soft house shoes, and I tried to remember had I ever seen Brigid's ankles before. The *Pavee* women wore their skirts so long, you'd never see their legs. You wouldn't even see a suggestion of a leg. I liked the way the buffer ladies dressed their legs like apparatus. Loose skirts, short enough to accommodate farm chores. Practical wellies on their working feet. They didn't hide nothing. It was all business.

John Paul was puttering around the room as if he owned the place, sticking his runny nose and his hands into everything. I yawned, to try to get some extra air in. I always had to breathe a bit deeper in a house, to work more at filling my lungs. I watched how the woman breathed, and wondered if maybe their lungs was shaped different from ours, on the inside. It seemed easy for her.

"Are they all yours?" the woman asked.

She said it like there was a hundred of us.

"All except Christy," Brigid said, pointing to me. "He's my nephew."

John Paul examined everything like an auctioneer. He touched things, stroked things, smelled things, shook and rattled things, peered inside and behind things. Left a trail of muck fingerprints everywhere he looked. Nobody minded him. Over his head, out of the reach of his sticky hands, three pieces of dustless porcelain was yellowing with age on the mantelpiece: a swan, a white horseshoe covered in clover, and a very thin, pale lady holding what maybe used to be an umbrella. She still clung tightly to the handle, but the stem was cracked off just above her head. The country woman saw me staring at the fractured figurine.

"Ah, now, we'd better get her fixed before it rains, hah?" she said, laughing.

But I felt her wishing I hadn't noticed. I felt her thinking that having a mantelpiece with a cracked figurine was better than having no mantelpiece at all. She bristled and turned back to Auntie Brigid.

"Taking him in as well, are ye?" the woman asked while I chewed on the inside of my cheek. "Have ye not enough with your own to look after? My goodness!"

I stared at her bare ankles. They suddenly looked a little obscene. Fat and naked.

"Well, his mam died in childbirth," Martin explained.

I looked at him and wished death upon him and all of his children. His children's children. The woman blessed herself predictably and came over to lay her callused hand on my forehead.

"Ah, God love you," she said. "No wonder he's a bit out of sorts."

I kicked Martin's foot hard under the bench. The woman's hand smelled of tobacco and something sour, and I wished to Mary and Joseph and all the saints that she'd take it off of my head. I wondered how somebody so house-proud could walk around heedless to the smell of something dead up her sleeve. And they thought we was dirty. I gave a small cough but willed myself to be still. I knew there'd be biscuits, and probably some eggs to take away with us as well. Maybe even some rashers if the woman was kept in good spirits. There was nobody better than our Brigid at working up a good lather of sympathy, given half the chance. I didn't want to ruin it by getting browned off or puking on the clean, clean floor. But I needed some air, and bad. I was dizzy with the feeling of it, with the need yawning up in me.

I looked to the open doorway, the high sun beginning to shine out faintly in the late winter yard. My legs was twitching to go. I reached so's my arm was hidden beneath the crook of Brigid's elbow, and pinched Maureen's fat little baby-leg. She squealed and flailed her arms. The woman took her hand off me and turned to the baby to check out the fuss. I gulped a deep breath of relief while Auntie Brigid opened the blanket so the woman could have a look. Brigid shot me a warning glance over the top of the woman's head.

"Why don't yourself and Martin take young John Paul out in the yard there now, and have a look at the suck calf?" Brigid suggested. "Let me and the missus talk awhile."

I was up off the bench and out into the garden before she could finish the thought.

"Yeah, Mammy!" John Paul answered. "Suck calf!"

John Paul skittered out the door behind me and was straight over to the fence where the cattle was kept. The cow was chewing her cud. She gave us the lazy once-over, decided we was no threat to her little fella, and went back to her morning meal.

"Why is it called a *suck calf*?" John Paul asked.

He was standing beside me, his four-year-old arms draped over the lower rail of the fence. He and the baby calf studied each other with equal curiosity.

"Call him over—I'll show you," I said.

I stretched my arms over my head and let my body unfold outside the walls of the house. I took deep breaths, to cleanse out the scent of the woman's manky hand on my skin. John Paul made a kissing noise toward the calf and rubbed his fingers together. The suck calf sniffed his way toward the fence line in a zigzag pattern, cautiously approaching John Paul's outstretched arm.

"Give him a small bit of grass," I said.

John Paul bent down and plucked a single fresh blade. He held it out to the calf, who sniffed again and came closer. John Paul stared into the calf's big eye and wiggled the blade. The calf showed his tongue and went for the grass. John Paul's tiny fist disappeared inside the calf's mouth and an instant later his wrist, his elbow. John Paul was shoulder deep down the suck calf's throat and the animal was slurping with all its might. John Paul shrieked and tried to pry the sucking head off of his vanished arm.

"Get it off me!" he screamed. "He's eating me!"

But the disappointed calf had already realized that John Paul wasn't an udder, and was losing interest. He gave one last, powerful glug before freeing the arm. John Paul stumbled back and fell on his rump, holding his slimy arm aloft. He made a cross little frown and planted both of his hands into the dirt to pick hisself up. He pushed me into the fence and reached up to wipe the suck-residue off on my shirt. I let him.

"That's why it's called a *suck* calf." I laughed.

"Not funny," John Paul answered, but he was smiling now and going for a piece of grass to give the calf another go.

Martin sauntered out behind us then and plucked a strong blade of grass from beside the fence post. He tucked it between his two thumbs, puffed out his cheeks, and blew. A loud honk sounded out acrosst the yard, startling the calf, who trotted back to join his mother. John Paul jumped up and down and clapped his chubby little hands together.

"Show me, show me!" he shrieked.

"Get a big, broad one," Martin said.

He stooped over to help his brother select the right bit of grass for honking, and over the top of his back, I seen the rusty red lorry turn in to the gate of the lane, kicking up dust behind its wide tires.

"Daddy's home," I said.

Martin stood and turned to look at the lorry that was rolling toward us. The buffer fella scrunched on the brake and the lorry spluttered to a stop. He got out, slammed the door of the cab. There was two boys in the front as well, and they scrambled out the far side. The father was lifting their carrier bags out from the back of the little lorry, and handing them to his sons.

"Well, boys," he said to us.

"How'ya, mister," Martin said.

But I couldn't say nothing because I seen the boy who was taking the carrier bag from his dad now, and he was grinning at us, and he was the tall boy from school. The one who made hisself like a parrot when he said *Pavees*.

"Bring these in to your mother," the dad said, and he turned and headed for the shed at the side of the house.

He'd pretend to be feeding his chickens or repairing a bit of machinery or something, but really he'd just be keeping an eye on us til we left, seeing we didn't steal nothing. I wanted to tell him he didn't have to bother because I didn't want nothing of his, but I wouldn't've been believable. The tall boy went inside the door of his house with his little brother, and I could see him dropping the carrier bags on the table beside his mother. He was saying something to her, I couldn't hear what.

"That's your one from school," I said to Martin. "The parroty bastard. 'Member him?"

Martin nodded, and now I couldn't see where the boy had got to, but a minute later he was back in the doorway of his house. He came out into the yard and closed the door behind him. He was carrying something in his arms. A hideous orange color, like barf after carrots.

"My mam said to give you this," he said, handing me the pile of orange wool.

I unfolded it and let it hang from my hands: the ugliest jumper I'd ever clapped eyes on. Why would they even make wool this color? It had dark brown stains in the armpits and a cloud of clotted white along one side that was God-knows-what.

"It doesn't fit me no more," he said. "But I'm sure it'll be lovely on you. It's a right tinker's jumper anyway."

He was grinning again, and I'd a sudden urge to make a gap in his slick line of teeth. I handed the jumper to John Paul.

"Thanks," I said. "We was running short on toilet roll, all right."

He stepped back and folded his arms acrosst his chest. He wasn't stupid; he stepped back.

"Beggars can't be choosers," he said.

I opened my mouth, but couldn't think of a single word. Not even "fuck."

"I like your suck calf," John Paul filled in for me. "What's his name?"

"He doesn't have a name," the boy said. "His name's Dinner."

John Paul made a face at him. "He doesn't have a name or his name's Dinner?" he said. "It can't be both."

"Jesus, you're each as thick as the next," the boy said, but he was backed away even more now, toward his house. "No wonder you're homeless."

I felt violent then. I saw myself rushing him, tackling him, grabbing his ears like they was handles, and bashing his skull against his mother's spotless doorstep. John Paul was giggling.

"We isn't homeless, ya big eegit." He giggled. "Who told you that?" John Paul held the orange jumper by the two sleeves, and was twisting it into a jump rope. "Christy, how come your ears is going all red?" John Paul asked.

"Shut up, John Paul," I said.

"Shut up, John Paul," the tall boy echoed. "His ears is red because you lot are a crowd of dirty, begging tinkers."

John Paul closed his mouth with a snap. He caught it, suddenly, the clang of hatred in the air.

"Well, you are a loathsome child," Brigid hissed.

The hair on my arms stood up. Jesus, I was awful glad to see her standing there in the doorway, the baby Maureen still strapped acrosst her chest. Her fury calmed me, somehow, reminded me how much we stood to lose here, by losing our tempers. I didn't want to get kicked outta school, to get run outta town. I wanted to stay. The tall boy turned to look at Brigid, and the satisfaction leaked off his face, but his ears didn't go red. His mother was stood behind Brigid in the doorway, her mouth hanging open a small bit.

"Patrick!" she said stupidly.

But that was it. Not much of a telling off. Patrick wasn't smart enough to make up that sorta speech on his own, you could tell. He was only repeating things he'd heard. Parroty bastard. The father was stood off down the side of the house a bit, in his shed, pretending not to hear nothing.

"We'll skip the tea, missus," Brigid said. "Thank you for your hospitality."

She started to protest, but Brigid was already halfway acrosst the yard, brushing past Patrick the Parrot.

"He doesn't mean any harm," the woman said.

Brigid turned to face her. "Does he not?" she said.

"You know children . . ."

"The divil take him!" Brigid interrupted. "May the divil take this house and all that's in it!"

The woman gasped, paling at once, and Brigid turned again toward the road. The buffers hated a good curse; that was one thing they was really afeared of us for, the curses. They thought tinkers was bad magic. I made a clawing gesture at the house, to fix the hex in her memory. And then Martin and me went belting out through the gate, but John Paul dawdled, confused. He still had the puke-orange jumper twisted in his hands.

"We're going," Brigid said, trying to get back to her mammy-voice, taking him by the hand.

She strangled the rage out of her voice, but her cheeks was white instead of pink, and there was nothing to be done about that. Behind us, the woman dunked her hand into the holy water well beside the door and started sprinkling it all around her. She grabbed her parrot-son by the arm and yanked him inside to douse him. He started to whinge.

"Get in!" she snapped, and slammed the door.

I couldn't make no sense of why my ears had went red like that, standing in Patrick's yard. Mostly it just felt like fury. I wished I had a ring, like Bilbo, that'd make me invisible. I'd tramp into that shingle-roofed cottage and I'd haunt them all, the bastards. I'd crack their porcelain lady off at the head.

Dad always said there was no shame in the mooching, that we should think of it like a challenge, a matching of wits. Anyways, we didn't choose to do it. We had to do it. We was happier working—we would always choose that first. To work, or to sell. But when that work was drying up all over the place, and when them buffers was stingier all the time about buying our swag and our tinware, what else could we do? It wasn't our fault if they felt guilty, if they felt sorry for us. Or if they was prone to flattery and charm. It wasn't our fault if they insisted on pressing food and coins into Brigid's waiting hand.

Patrick thought he was better than us because of them walls and windows, because he slept nights with a roof pushing down over his dreams. But his family wasn't rich. His mammy probably couldn't even read. His dad probably took handouts hisself, when times was lean on the farm. They wasn't no better than us. In fact, they was stupider. At least we knew what we was.

So why, then? Why did I still feel hot in my cheeks and hard in my knuckles? Why did I feel like the blood would bubble in my veins?

When we got back to camp, I'd to find something to distract me from my wicked mood. So I stole one of the lemonade bottles out of the Rolls-Royce Mart-O-Matic, and lopped the bottom off, for to make a magnifying glass. I knew Martin would be deranged if he

found out, but I couldn't help that. I had work to do, sleuthing. I was
tired of waiting for Dad to soften up and tell me about my mam. My
beautiful mam, way prettier than Patrick's thick, homely, mingin'
mother.

I went into the tent, and took out the photo, studied it again. The
graceful way my mother stood, her back straight and strong as a
birch tree, her bow lips, her dazzling teeth, her windy, sideways
curls. She was beautiful. Whole. Even flat on paper, she didn't look
flattened like Auntie Brigid, her body used up by all them babies.
She was unbroken, sturdy. I couldn't believe she was mine.

I found a twig that had the right wishbone fingers then, and I
wedged the bottom of the lemonade bottle in there, bound it up with
a bit of twine. Then, back to the tent, and I ripped one page out of my
jotter and tore it into a dozen smaller pieces, bound them together
with some more twine for to write down clues in. On the front, I
wrote "CLUES." And then a gust of a breeze came in through the
tent flap and made a whizzing sound against the canvas.

"Grandda?" I whispered.

Because it felt like him, for some reason, that draft acrosst my
neck. Like he was there again, to encourage me. His hand on my
shoulder. That gust flipped through the blank pages of CLUES.

"I haven't found nothing yet," I said. "I'm only getting started.
Can't you help me? Who can I ask? Who can I ask, now?"

And then the wind whipped right out of the tent, through the
flap, kicking CLUES along in front of it. I chased it down and then
started my interviews straightaway. It was tricky going, because I
had to interview everybody without them knowing they was being
interviewed. Dad and Finty was still away, so I started with Granny,
who was just back from the Monster House.

"Granny, do you remember my mam much?" I asked.

She shook her head and tutted. Always the same, whenever I
asked her.

"Oh, 'twas awful sad," she said. "Awful sad about her." She

glanced at me, put her hand under my chin. "You musn't mind it too much," she said. "You're lucky to have all this family anyway."

Granny was minding Maureen, and I made like I was helping, even though really I was performing my investigations. After a moment, I tried again.

"Did you or Grandda ever buy much newspapers?"

She looked at me strangely. "Sure what would I do with buying newspapers?" she said. "Wasting my money on that? That's your father's practice, not mine."

I hadn't planned out my questions that carefully. "I donno," I said to Granny. "You could maybe sell them in again, to the houses."

There wasn't much to minding Maureen, really. She was sitting out the back of their wagon playing with the blocks Finty had whittled for her. She'd stack them on top of each other, three-high, and knock them over. Then she'd do it again. Granny looked at Maureen, who was stretching for the third block, which had tumbled beyond her reach.

"There you are now, love," she said to the baby, dismissing my question completely.

Maureen squealed and placed the block on top of her tower. Then she knocked it over again.

"Granny, do you know the way all of Grandda's things got burnt up in the wagon fire?" I tried again, a different tack.

This time she only answered me with a sorrowful sound in her chest and a slow, dipping movement of her shoulders.

"I know it wasn't the way it was meant to happen," I said.

"No," she answered.

"So what would happen if, because of all that, because there wasn't time to get it organized properly . . . what would happen if we found out later that we missed a spot?" I asked. "Like just say you found something of Grandda's that didn't burn up in the fire?"

I wondered if I could show her the picture. Granny closed her eyes and blessed herself, moving her lips silently. When she was done praying, she leaned in to peer at me closely, and her eye was like a magnifying glass itself.

"There'd be no question of that, Christy," she said. "Whatever it was, we'd have to burn it up, and quickly. And then we'd have to leave that place again behind us."

Leave! Jesus God, she would make us leave, if she knew! Dammit. My hopes sunk. Granny wouldn't help me; I couldn't show her the picture. There was nobody I could trust.

"Why are you asking these questions?" she said. "Did you find something, child?"

She called every one of us "child" when we was in trouble.

"No, Granny, no," I said, staring quickly down at my knuckles. "Nothing like that. I was only curious."

She nodded slowly, but she was still staring at me, and I was unsettled.

"D'ya know how many newspapers is published in O'Briens-bridge?" I asked, changing the subject again.

She looked at me with sort of a confused scowl. "No," she said. "How many?"

"I donno," I said. "I was asking you."

Granny shook her head at me. "Never mind that," she said, and then she sent me off to fetch water to clean up Maureen, who'd just pooped all up her back to her neck.

After I brought the water back, I went into the tent, opened CLUES, and wrote down my discoveries on the first page. Then I got out my magnifying glass and tried to read it back, but the glass made the words curl up and I only knew what they said because I was just after writing 'em.

My interviews with Brigid and Martin produced similar results, so that after the whole afternoon, all that was wrote inside CLUES was this:

Bewley's advertisement
Page 15 or Page 17
Cummins Plumbing Supplies in O'Briensbridge
O'Briensbridge is southwest of here some ways
Newspapers in O'Briensbridge: ?

Maybe I'd have better luck with Dad and Finty, but that would have to wait until tomorrow, because it was dark enough now, we knew they wouldn't come back until morning.

Granny and Brigid built the fire up hotter and brighter whenever the men was away, and I didn't know was that because they liked the extra bite of it, to keep them feeling safe, or was it just because there was nobody around to nag them for wasting fuel. It was nice when they didn't come back, though—just for the change that was in it. The camp felt specially merry for the first time, really, since Grandda'd died. Granny was singing out hoarse in the solid night, and the lilt of her voice without pipe or drum behind it was something brutal and beautiful. Like the wind howling over wet sea cliffs. She sang about weavers and cobblers and soldiers, and that was fine. But then she sang a mournful love song in crooked Irish, and I could hear Grandda's absence in the crags of her split voice, and I could feel the way she missed him, the hollows she was left with. And I felt like one of them grief-thieves then, with my sorrow and my hot photograph. I ached from all the sound of it.

ELEVEN

Dad and Finty came back the next morning, in time for the late Mass. Martin and me was just debating what to do with the puke-orange jumper when they arrived, but in the end, we just threw it in the fire. Dad always said it was no use antagonizing people, and that trouble would find you well enough without you going looking for it. But then, Dad probably would've taken that puke-orange jumper with gratitude. He'd have tipped his hat and pleased them buffers with his thankfulness, because he never stood up to nobody. It was just as well we never had a looking glass, because I didn't reckon Dad could look hisself in the eye, not even for the space of a shave.

The next day, I kept an eye out for Parroty Patrick at school, because I'd planned all sorts of pretend things to say to him, to do to him. Black eyes, fat lips, bloody noses, my knuckles white against the gripped skin of his neck. My wellie digging into his stomach. I dreamed of snots I would hock into his face, fantastic indignities involving underwear and whimpering. But when I seen him, I just sneered at him and he didn't respond at all. And that was worse, in a way, than anything. Like I didn't even exist.

When the Blob came in, she told us we'd be taking extra religious instructions for the remaining weeks of Lent in order to prepare for our holy Communions. First was the Ten Commandments. We all got our jotters out while Sister explained how important this was.

"The most vital thing you've learned thus far in your short lives," the Blob said. And then she began to give them to us. She started with, "Number one: Have no other gods before me. Thou shalt not worship false idols."

Sister explained that this meant God wanted us to only love Him, and not to love no other gods, which seemed like just pure common sense to me. Sure, who else was there except God?

But Beano's hand went up, and he struggled for a while with some questions about there being Jesus plus God plus the Holy Ghost. Sister explained to him that they was all the one God, and that was all well and good.

But then as she was about to go on to number two, the hand went up again and "What about the Virgin Mother, then, Sister?" he said. And Sister looked a bit flummoxed and said that, no, the Virgin Mary was a saint, to be sure, and certainly the holiest woman who ever lived, but she wasn't the same as God. I didn't really want to admit that Beano's question made so much sense, but it did seem a bit odd that Jesus and the Holy Ghost was God, but Mary wasn't, especially when there was a whole prayer that was said all the time just to Mary. It was even called the *Hail Mary*. It was Granny's favorite prayer.

Beano said that was grand, but then, up went the hand again before Sister could move on to the next one and he says, "But how can she be the mother of God if she's not God herself?" And I had to admit that maybe he wasn't so thick as he let on. But Sister was so exhausted, she lost her patience and says to him that he'd used up all his questions for the day and we still had nine more Commandments to go.

So then she gave us the next one. "Thou shalt not take the Lord's name in vain."

Now this one we'd heard before, and not in church, but because Brigid was always saying it to Finty as a reminder. We knew it meant you wasn't never supposed to use God's name or Jesus' name lightly, and most especially never when you was angry or cursing. It seemed like a pretty hard one because you'd have to stop and remember it whenever you was in the middle of a temper and was just shouting things out accidentally.

I glanced over at Martin to see was he worried, but I doubted it. Martin never worried about nothing unless I convinced him to. I tried to remember Grandda's talking, and I couldn't ever remember him taking the Lord's name in vain, but I said a quick prayer that went: *Dear Lord God, please look after Grandda, and forgive him if he ever took your name in vain because I'm sure he didn't mean it if he did.*

But Sister was on to the next one. "Remember the Sabbath and keep it holy."

I didn't even know what the Sabbath was, never mind remembering it or keeping it holy. But then Sister told us that "Sabbath" was only a fancy word for "Sunday." And in this Commandment, God was only telling us to remember to go to Mass on Sundays, which was grand because Granny always made sure we was in Mass every week, no matter where we was halting. It was also true that no matter what sort of welcome we ever got in a town, we was always welcomed in the church. Or maybe that's putting it too nicely, but I should say we was never turned away from a church. Plus, some churches in the bigger towns had hymnals in the pews for reading, and the windows was all lovely colors, and the ceilings was high enough you never felt you was being smothered. In the bigger churches, you'd hardly even know you was inside, and sometimes you'd get the feeling you was in a big, tall forest or something instead. Going to Mass every week was an easy one—I didn't even mind it.

Then she gave us the next one. "Honor thy father and thy mother."

I wrote it down, and I could nearly feel the pulse of my mother's photograph, folded into the back page of *Gulliver*, and tucked inside the rucksack hanging from the back of my chair. Honor her, I thought. Maybe that's what I was doing, by trying to find out about her life.

A few hands went up around the room. Kathleen was first, and she wanted to know, what if your father and your mother asked you to do two different things. Sister told her that, in that instance, she should simply ask them to clarify. Then another young fella asked what if your mammy asked you to do something bad, what should you do? Follow the Commandment, or honor the mammy? Sister gave him a look that would've curdled fresh milk, and told him to stop being ridiculous, that his mother would never ask him to do something bad. And then, much to my horror, I noticed that Martin's hand was up.

"What if you don't have a mother to honor?" he asked, when Sister called on him.

I took my breath into me sharp and held it there. Why did he ask that?

Sister responded in a softer, more thoughtful voice than I'd heard her use before. "I think," she said to Martin, a look of gentle concern crossing her fleshy face, "if you haven't a mother to honor, then you should do your best to always behave in a way that you know would make her proud. You should honor her *memory*."

I stared at Martin, his face creased and intense. Why did he always have the courage I didn't? Damn him. She's *my* dead mother, I thought, not yours.

"What if you don't have even that, though, Sister?" he said. "What if you can't properly honor her memory because what if you don't remember her at all?"

My heartbeat stuttered. What did he know about it, the bollix? How dare he? He didn't know nothing at all. I had plenty to remember about my mam. I had all them memories Grandda'd gave me, them stories about her near-purple hair and her powerful, long eyelashes. And now I had her picture, too. Her face and her smile, her slender hand.

"In that case, Mr. Hurley," Sister was saying, heaving her misplaced sympathy on Martin, like he was a spud she was loading with butter, "you should be especially careful to honor your father, and whatever other adults are in your life for to give you guidance and supervision. And you should know that, by doing that, you will make your mother proud."

"Thank you, Sister." Martin nodded.

I rolled my eyes. She leaned down into our shared desk, so's her habit draped itself acrosst my arm and made my pencil drag on the page. The jagged pencil trail was blurry under my fixed gaze. Sister patted Martin's hand beside me. Not my hand. Martin's.

But then, when she turned, he winked at me, and I knew that he was only trying to help. He never thought things through before he said them or did them. He'd more balls than brains, Martin. He was still a bollix, but maybe it wasn't really his fault.

Sister returned to the front of the room and read out the next one. "Thou shalt not murder."

That one was simple enough, if I could manage to not kill Martin.

"Thou shalt not commit adultery."

This one was hazy, even after Sister explained it. It had something to do with marriage, but I made a note in my jotter to look up the word "adultery" in Dad's dictionary when we got back to camp.

And then she hit us with the doozy. "Thou shalt not steal."

What? Hang on, really? I lifted my pencil and stuck the end of it into my mouth, bit down hard. I wouldn't take my eyes off the page. I'd written the number down—seven—but nothing after it. Maybe if I refused to write, it wouldn't be real. *Thou shalt not steal.* I could see the pointy end of the pencil sticking out of my mouth, and it was trembling.

I mean, I'd always knew that stealing was sorta wrong, but this seemed to leave very little room for interpretation. No gray area to speak of. Like what about how Brigid said it was fine to take a doll, if a child left that doll outside the house in the rain, for that was a sign that the doll wasn't nothing special to the child, and it wouldn't be missed. Or the way you could sometimes take apples out of an orchard if your stomach was well and truly empty, and you'd nothing else to eat. How could them things be wrong? Was that just a difference between stealing and taking? Maybe stealing was wrong, but taking was okay.

I looked over at Martin, but he was leaned so far over his jotter, he was about to fall in. Finally I wrote the words "Thou shalt not steal," and then looked down at them throbbing on the page. They looked heated, angry. I'd wrote them so hard that the pencil made an impression all the way through to the next page, and the next one after that. I started to write it a second time, but I heard my pencil lead snap.

All around the room, I felt like people was glancing at us, and for an instant, I imagined having a rager of an outburst. I would turn purple with wrath, and I'd pop my bolted desk loose from the floor, and I'd throw it across the room. And I'd scream: *What the fuck do ye know about stealing? Did ye ever go to bed hungry, ye crowd of righteous wankers?*

But it was only a daydream, and nobody was looking at us after all. They wasn't asking questions. They'd took it in their stride, like ceilings and pillows and cheese. And quickety-split, they was on to the next one.

"Martin, give me your pencil," I whispered.

"Why would you think we was all going to hell?" he asked quietly. "What did the teacher say that worried you?"

I looked down at my plate; it was still full. I wished Grandda was here, for talking to instead. But he wasn't. I felt like God was letting us down, and I was angry. And in truth, I *was* afraid. For Grandda, for everybody. I didn't have nobody else to talk to about it, only Dad.

"Thou shalt not steal," I finally said. "That's one of the Commandments. That stealing is, like, an *official* sin."

Dad opened his mouth and then closed it. He was trying to think what to say. "But surely you knew that already?" he asked.

"What?" I said.

"Surely you knew that stealing was a sin."

I hadn't eaten a bit, but suddenly, I thought I'd puke again. "How would I know that?" I said.

"Sure, I've always told you stealing was wrong, haven't I?"

"Told me? Yes," I said. "You told me. And then you also told me to steal the plastic buckets, and sometimes you told me to steal eggs from a henhouse. And one time you even told me to steal a goat—d'you remember that one? Because no one was minding him?"

My voice was rising, and Dad eyed Brigid's back, bent to the washing, to see was she listening. I didn't care. I wanted him to feel the way I'd felt in class. Forsaken. Damned.

Dad took a deep breath and licked his lips. I was staring right at him. I'd never felt so defiant. I thought I might throw my whole plate of food 'round his head.

"You'll not speak to your father that way," he said. He looked back at me, dead in the eye, and his voice had a strength I'd forgotten. I'd nearly forgot him, in all my grief and my anger—the man I'd grew up with, the sheer might of him. The thrashing he'd give me if I lost myself enough to stand up to him fully, if I really dared throw my plate of food over his head. He spoke quietly, but the steel in his voice was unmistakable.

He scowled at me.

"Trade me your pencil!" I said again.

He wasn't using his one anyway. He wasn't even writing them down. He flicked it over to me.

I could barely hear her as she went on. "Thou shalt not bear false witness against thy neighbor."

This one didn't make no sense neither. We didn't have no neighbors.

"Thou shalt not covet thy neighbor's wife."

Sister was talking, but I wasn't hardly listening no more. These rules wasn't made for us. Even God had us as outsiders. It wasn't fair. I'd always felt like church was a safe place, where I could talk to God, and He didn't expect me to be nobody only who I was. Who *He* made me. Now I felt betrayed, angry.

"Thou shalt not covet thy neighbor's house."

And now Sister explained that we shouldn't even *want* things, especially houses, that belonged to other people. For fuck's sake. I couldn't never live in a house, I knew that—I felt bound to the point of suffocation just walking into one. But could it really be a sin, just longing for something?

"Covet," Sister explained. "It means to desire, to yearn for, to crave."

I thought of the hungry-house-by-the-sea painting in the bookshop. I thought of Finnuala Whippet's house. I thought of Patrick's clean house with the suck calf and the mother cow and the yellowed porcelain lady with the broken umbrella and, if I was being honest, if I really looked inside myself bravely: I wanted all of them. I wanted all them stupid, suffocating houses. I wanted falling-down, ramshackle houses and grand, pristine estate houses and city row houses and beach cottages. I wanted shacks and igloos and hobbit holes. I coveted every last one of them.

After that, I couldn't even feel angry no more. All I could feel was ruined.

———

ON THE WAY HOME, I puked into the ditch while Martin waited. He didn't say nothing.

"Do you think we's going to hell, all of us?" I asked him, leaned over with my hands on my knees.

"No way," he said. "Not a chance."

He was always so sure of things, so positive. And anyway, Martin didn't have to imagine what hell might be like. He'd already filled up Grandda's coffin with rocks. I felt sick again, but I dry-heaved. My stomach was empty.

"Maybe we don't need the turf no more," I said after I mopped up my chin. "Maybe we've made our point and all."

"You're going to let some nun tell you what's right and wrong, Christy?" he said.

"Who else is going to tell us, sure?" I shrugged. "D'you not believe her, then? D'you not believe in none of it?"

It was a lovely, orangey, cold-sunset of a day, and we started to walk again.

"I do," he said. "I mean, I believe in Jesus and all that. But we isn't eight years old like the rest of 'em, Christy. They boil it down so's childer can understand, but it's just guidelines, like. Suggestions."

"That's not what the Blob said."

"She's hardly going to say that, Christy, is she? Use your head."

But my head felt like cotton wool. I couldn't make no sense of nothing.

"It just seems so unfair," I said. "Even Granny steals a spud, or an egg, when she has to." I felt like I was dragging my stomach through the road behind me.

"You worry too much, Christy," Martin said.

If I could give half my worries to him, maybe we'd both be normal.

"Think about it: how could the rules be the same for travellers," he said with sublime insight, "when nothing else is?"

"SO HOW ARE YOU GETTING on in school?" Dad asked that evening. He was just finished his tea and was picking his teeth and warming his boots beside the fire.

"Grand," I said.

"What are the studies like?"

"A lock of shite, really," I said.

I was still browned off about the Commandments, and Dad was in my bad books anyway. He knew why. He thought he could make all my questions go away just by burning up my mother's photograph. But they only got stronger in me. Dad didn't know how I'd tricked him, that the photo was still safe, my prized possession. My gift from Grandda. I wouldn't never let him take it from me.

"A lock of shite?" he said. "They're teaching you lovely language, anyway."

I shrugged.

"We learnt the Ten Commandments today," Martin said. "And Christy got an awful fright, thinking we was all going to hell."

"Feck off, I did not get a fright."

"He puked in the ditch," Martin announced. Bastard.

Dad ran a hand up the back of his head, and he looked at me. I did my best to deflect his sympathy. I didn't want it.

"What had you worried, son?" he said.

"Nothing."

"Nothing?"

"Nope."

"Okay," he said.

But then, after Martin was finished his tea, and Auntie Brigid was collecting the things for the washing up, he tried again.

"You shouldn't never steal for greed or for badness," he said. "Not ever. I always taught you that. There shouldn't be no hurtfulness in the thing. D'you understand me?"

"Yes."

"Hmm?"

"Yessir."

He leaned back, and I couldn't tell what he was feeling. Maybe relief that I'd backed down. That the moment was past, and the balance restored. Maybe I was relieved, too, a little bit.

"You know, sometimes people don't always appreciate what they have, Christy," he said. "And we would have a greater need of a thing. Like food. Now God wouldn't have us starving, son, just because we's travellers."

He looked at my plate. "So eat," he said.

I lifted my spoon, shoveled in a mouthful of lukewarm beans. I managed to swallow them down.

"And anyway, that's what confession is for," he said.

"How d'ya mean?" I took another bite of my beans.

"Because sometimes, it is unavoidable," he said. "For travellers, anyway. Like if your cousin Maureen was hungry, and there was no other way, Granny might steal her an egg, hah?"

I nodded.

"And then Granny would have to go to confession and do a penance," he said. "So's God would know she was sorry, but she'd no other choice."

"But why should it be wrong in the first place?" I said. "If there isn't nothing we can do about it?"

Dad shook his head. "I don't know, son. It's just the way it is."

"So I guess God doesn't like travellers neither," I said. "Because surely He woulda taken that into account, when He was making the rules, like. If He cared."

Dad sighed. "Now I think you're just being difficult," he said.

But I wasn't. I mean, maybe I was, being difficult, like. But I really thought that now. That maybe God wasn't no different from nobody else. Maybe He didn't like us neither, and maybe Dad was just too cowed to see it.

"So what about the one about the houses, then?" I said.

I didn't really mean to say it, to reveal that much. I was only trying to prove my point, but now I had to explain myself. Dad looked at me strangely.

"The what about the houses?" he said, completely confused.

I hesitated, then decided it was too late for that. "The Commandment about the houses," I said.

Feck it. I'd come this far, I may as well go the whole hog. I leaned up, retrieved my jotter from where I'd stashed it under my arse-cheek, and then flipped to the page where I'd wrote the Commandments. I handed it to Dad.

"Number ten," I said.

His eyes flicked down the list, and then the breath went outta him like wind outta sails. His eyes leeched into my face. "Christy," he said, and his voice was so sad it sluiced the anger clean outta me. "Christy, you don't want nobody's house, sure you don't? Why would you be worried about that one?"

I couldn't answer him. I felt all flooded and muddled. I looked at my feet.

Dad leaned forward with his elbows on his two bent knees, dropped his voice to a whisper. "Do you want a house, Christy?" he said. He even touched my forehead, just brushed it, with his finger.

I bit my lip and nodded my head. An elephant-sized betrayal. Way worse than what God did to travellers.

"Oh," Dad said, and there was depths of sorrow in that syllable.

That was maybe the lowest I ever felt. What would Grandda think of me, if he knew? I felt like a traitor, a liar. A fraud. Dad's face was so sad I had to look away from him.

"Eat your tea," he said, still looking at my list.

I couldn't.

He was quiet. Then he said at last, "You know, it clearly says your *neighbor's* house. So whose house is it, exactly, you're after coveting?"

"Everybody's," I admitted as quietly as I could. There was no use trying to keep secrets at that stage. The damage was done.

"Everybody's?" Dad said.

I nodded again.

He lifted his chin and swallowed, covered his mouth with his hand. His face was awful. "Brigid's?" he finally asked. His jawline was tense, his lips tight while he spoke.

"Well, no," I said quietly.

"Why not?" he said.

"Sure, Brigid doesn't have a house. She's the same as us."

"Granny's, then?" he asked, waving acrosst the camp.

"No." I shook my head.

Even though her wagon was brand-new, only got three days ago, I didn't want it off her. I was very happy with our own one.

"Well," Dad said then. "Isn't Brigid and Granny your neighbors?"

I nodded.

"And have you other neighbors I don't know about?"

I shook my head.

"So, really, you just want *a* house," he said. "Any old house would do. It's not that you want a specific house that belongs to your neighbor."

"Well, no," I said, slowly conceding. "Not exactly."

"And it's not as if you'd like to boot your neighbors out of their homes so's you could have them all for your greedy little self."

"No." I really didn't.

"Well, then," Dad said, closing the jotter and handing it back to me. "I don't see a problem."

I nodded, but he wasn't looking at me. He was looking into the fire.

"Okay," I said.

And I felt something creeping over me, relief mingled with something else. I was glad I'd told him, and I even felt grateful to him a little, because he'd managed to bring me back from a dark place. But as he stood and brushed his hands against his trousers, I had the feeling I'd taken something very big from him. Like he'd seen I was missing a leg, so he'd lopped his own one off and gave it to me.

TWELVE

After school the next day, me and Martin went into the town and stole a load of turf from a wheelbarrow that was setting outside the back door of the butcher shop. I didn't feel bad about it, and I didn't worry about it. That's what I told myself.

We buried the turf in the road-ditch near school, and then went back to the butcher shop, right in the front door this time. Martin went up to the counter and asked the butcher had he anything left-over for tea, and had he any need of repairs about the place, because we was stopping in the town for a while. Your man told us our daddy had already been in to see him, and had fixed him up with a new kettle.

The whole time they was chatting, the young pimple-butcher was wiping his hands on his blood-stained apron and looking at me with his lip curled up. He was the same one who'd chased me away from that warm, lonely scone that first morning. I stuck my tongue out at him, secretly, so's the real butcher wouldn't see. Then I opened my palms and smeared them onto the glass case, peered down in-side and walked the length of it, pretending to examine the meat-cuts inside. Pimples McButcherpants would have to wipe down my fingerprints after we was away. I did a second pass for good measure. The real butcher was still chatting away to Martin, wrapping something up to take home to our mammy, he said. A fat, round pig's head for a stew. It looked very disgusting, seeping blood and muck through its newsprint wrapper, but I thought that was very good of him all the same, especially after we nicked a load of his turf.

"Thanks, mister," Martin said, heaving the head up onto his shoulder, beside his own one.

The pig's head was slightly bigger. And then on our way back to camp, I had an ill-conceived moment of enormous generosity: I brang Martin into the bookshop.

THE MISSUS WAS STANDING ON her head when we came in, so's all we could see was her two shoes sticking up in the air behind the till. They was a pair of black lace-up jobs with thick heels on them like you'd expect. But I guess she heard the bell over the door go, because her legs started to fall over like *timmmberrr*, and then one of the shoes caught the handle of her coffee cup, but it didn't tip like she did. It only sloshed in place. And then her face popped up behind the counter and it was all red, but not from embarrassment, but just from all the blood going gushing up there from the head-standing. Her white bun was still perfect behind her—more like a hat than hair.

"Come in, come in, friends!" she said. "Come in outta that weather!"

Martin looked behind him, to see if a storm had cropped up outside. It hadn't, of course. The missus disappeared for another second, plomped a book up onto the counter, and then dragged herself into standing right-side-up. She smoothed her hair down (it still didn't move), and settled herself on her stool. She took a loud slurp from her coffee cup and made an "ahh" sound.

"Hiya, missus!" I said.

"Well, hallo, Christopher!" she chimed.

The pig's head was heavy, and Martin was carrying it with both hands, but Mrs. Hanley didn't say nothing when he hauled it up onto the counter beside us. We should've left it outside, I guess, but I never thought nothing of it til I seen it sitting there between us. Even through its newsprint wrapper, I could feel its dead eye sockets watching us. I could feel its tongue lolling, and I was afraid it might open its dead mouth with a great grunt and snarl, "You tinkers, get out of this bookshop at once! You little tinkers don't belong in a place like this!" I took a step away from the head, tried to distance myself. Two flies had followed us in, and they was stuck to that head like apostles. Mrs. Hanley was blinking at the two of us like she never even noticed the head.

"And who would this be, now?" She smiled at Martin.

"Oh, it's just a pig's head we got outta the butcher's for tea," Martin answered, staring her out of it.

He pushed the pig's head a little closer to the missus and the flies followed. He was trying to force her to look at it, to acknowledge it. But she wouldn't. She went on smiling at him some more. She even laughed.

"I meant yourself," she said. "Mister . . ."

Martin didn't answer.

"Mr. Pig," I said, when he wouldn't. "You can call him Mr. Pig."

She blew steam off the top of her cup while she thought this over. I knew she wouldn't address Martin or the head as "Mr. Pig." She was too nice a lady for that. And she still hadn't clapped a single eyeball onto that pig's head, despite the fact that one of the two orbiting flies was now dive-bombing her coffee. Martin turned his back to us and pretended to examine some of the nearby bookshelves.

"What about I call him Mr. Darcy?" the missus suggested.

"Mr. Who?"

"My name is *Martin*," he finally said.

If she wondered why he was being so rude to her, she never let on. She didn't even seem to notice.

"Well, how do you do, Martin?" she replied. "Would you like to choose a book from our lending library?"

She indicated the three shelves he was eyeballing.

"No," he said. "I don't read." He said it like it was a choice.

If I hadn't known it when Martin heaved that pig's head up onto the counter, I knew it for certain now—bringing him here was a terrible idea. He would never understand the sanctity of a place like this. And even worse, I could tell straightaway what Martin thought of the missus, how he'd made up his mind about her already. That she was the worst kind of buffer—the kind who wants to *improve* you. Them ones is worse even than the ones who look down their noses at you. As far as Martin was concerned he'd met the missus a hundred times before, in a hundred different shops. What I couldn't figure out, though, was how the head-standing hadn't tipped him off that she was different. I think all them books was making him nervous, like they was knocking him blind instead of making him see. He had a look on his face like he was smelling something bad, but I knew it was the books (and not the pig's head) that was making him make the face.

"Did your correspondence arrive?" she asked, turning her attentions to me again.

The priest letter! I felt my stomach swoop with remembering.

"No, missus." I shook my head. "Not yet."

What was keeping it anyway? The baptism cert should've got here by now.

"Ah, well," she said. "Any day now, any day." She smiled.

"We'd better get on," I said, and Mrs. Hanley nodded at me.

God bless her. She acted like it was normal to call in for a visit and then to leave thirty seconds later. She acted like that pig's head was nothing out of the ordinary.

"Come back anytime!" she said. "And yourself as well, Martin."

Martin rolled his eyes at her and hoisted the pig's head back onto his shoulder.

"Oh!" she said then, as we was headed for the door. "What about the mystery? Any new clues crop up?"

I cringed. I had thought it over, but decided not to tell Martin nothing about the photograph. It was too risky for anybody to know, especially a loose cannon like him. And besides, I wanted to keep my mammy all to myself. I shook my head at the missus.

"Clues?" I said. "No." I tried to make my face blank, like I didn't know what she was talking about, and she copped on straightaway, winked at me.

"Sorry, sorry!" she said, waving her hands. "It was Christy *Daly* who's working on a mystery. I had ye mixed up there for a minute, would you believe it? Oh, where is my head!"

"Check the floor," Martin muttered. "Maybe you left it down there."

I smiled at her, hard. Martin was already out the door.

I'll be back, I mouthed, without making no noise come outta my mouth.

She winked again, and waved, as I followed Martin out.

On the road home, Martin said to me, "Is she a mental patient, or what?"

I looked at him like I didn't know what he meant.

"All them books've made her doolally," he said, and he made a loopy gesture 'round the pig's head with his finger.

"She is not," I said.

Martin laughed at me. He didn't even have to make an argument—we'd caught her standing on her head, after all. Maybe she was doolally.

"She's just good *craic*," I said. "And anyways, it's not just books they sell. They've got paintings, too, out the back. And there's this one and it's this house by the sea, and it's . . . well, it's hard to describe. But you should see it. When you look at it, it's like the house is nearly a person. Like a haunted person, with big, droopy eyes for windows. Like it's nearly *hungry*. You know?"

Martin did not know. "The house is hungry," he said.

It sounded stupid when he said it.

"Yeah. Well. Yeah. Like, it just makes you feel things," I said.

"Like it makes you feel hungry?" He was smirking at me.

I wanted to punch his face in. "Forget it," I said. "I should never've took you there."

He was quiet for a minute. "You'd wanna mind yourself with all them books, Christy," he said then. "I thought they was harmless enough, but you might be catching a bit of the doolally yourself."

AFTER WE SEEN HOW EASY it was, me and Martin started taking turns sometimes, getting the turf. It got to be a bit of a competition, to see who could get the most when it was their turn. And we stopped telling each other where we'd got it from, so's we could each keep our best stockpiles for secret.

That's why it felt like he was baiting me that Wednesday morning, when we was grubbing the turf outta the ditch and he clapped his hands together and says, "Thank you, Mrs. Hanley!"

I stopped in my leaf-digging. "What did you say?" I asked.

Martin lumped two of the sods under his arm and said, "Wha?"

"Thank you, *who*?" I said, standing up.

"You know, your one. From the shop with the books. And the *hungry house* painting," Martin said, but he said it with a cartoon sarcasm in his voice.

I should never have took him there. Never. My fault.

"The house might be hungry, but the missus sure isn't." He laughed.

I stared at him and didn't move. Maybe only my jaw moved, or maybe my tongue inside, where I was trying to swallow what he'd just said.

"Can you believe she leaves them sods right by the door like that? In that open basket, like as if she's advertising 'em?"

Martin was pretending not to notice my disgust, that I'd stopped and stood up to stare at him. He was trying to press two sods of turf into my hand now, but I was looking at them like as if they was Mrs. Hanley's severed limbs. I couldn't take them, couldn't hold them. They tumbled back into the ditch, and I cocked back and swung for Martin, clattered him hard on the side of the head. Then again from the other side, I caught him straight on the ear to send him ringing, hit him so hard my knuckles smarted.

He dropped his turf and folded hisself into my stomach, and just like that, I was up in the air, my feet off the ground, Martin's shoulder beneath me, sending me flying. And now we was both on the ground, me on my back, and Martin trying to get up on his knees above me, scrambling. His fingers digging into my arm. We was both breathing hard, and struggling, struggling. He was going to win. I wrenched my wrist from his grip and sent it flying again—I caught him a glance in the nose this time, but his knee was on my other elbow, and all the weight of him was on that knee, and I thought I might have to scream uncle. Or maybe I could still bite him to get him off. My free arm was still swinging. He slapped me hard acrosst the face—once, twice, three times, and I could feel my eye tearing up, could taste the slightest tang of something wrong in my mouth. I jammed my knee up and managed to graze him just in the back of the ballsack. He groaned and rolled off me.

Then it was only the sound of our breath, heavy and fresh.

I tried to sort it out in my head, what had happened. How it happened. Martin was balled up, clutching his groin beside me in the dirt. Our breathing was starting to catch and slow, steady. Martin's still had a moan attached to it.

"She's been nice to me," I whispered. My face was wet.

"Am I bleeding?" I said, rolling toward Martin, who was beginning to unclench beside me. The daylight was all over his face.

"No." He shook his head and took another deep breath. "But I could try again if ya want."

He grinned, and I wiped my face. Tears or sweat.

"You're all right," I said, sitting up.

I spit, to see if any pink came out. I'd leaves stuck all over me, and Martin was trying to sit up, too. I gave him my hand, and he pulled hisself up, rested his elbows on his knees.

"Never in the ballsack, Christy, what's wrong with you?"

"I was desperate." I shrugged.

The turf was around us. We'd rolled in it.

"You shouldn't've," I said. "You shouldn't've stole from her."

Martin dropped his hand down between his legs to check was he still all there.

"Will we leave them, then?" he said quietly. "Will we go without, just for today?" And he wasn't messing. He was as serious as a horse with a gammy leg. He'd never apologize, but he didn't have to.

"What do you think?" he said.

I licked my teeth. I tried to summon my courage, but I couldn't find it.

"Don't be daft," I said, grabbing up two of the sods and handing them to him. "They's here now. No use wasting 'em."

I'D HAVE TO FIND A way to face Mrs. Hanley again, so I told myself that she wouldn't even miss the turf. That she didn't need it enough to note it was gone. After school, I told Martin to feck off on his own, and myself and Fidel trotted down into the town. I could see through the front window of the bookshop that the missus was busy with a customer, so I waited til I heard the bell over the door jingle, and then I caught it while it was still open and scooted myself inside.

"Hiya, missus!" I said.

She was just settling herself back onto her stool behind the till. "Christopher!" she said.

Maybe I was getting to be such a regular that she didn't have to pass remark on the weather no more.

"Lovely day, lovely day, hmm?" she said.

Maybe not.

"You can feel the spring coming in—the first hints of it coming," she said.

"Lovely." I nodded.

"I'm afraid I nearly wrecked your mystery the other day, did I?"

"Oh no," I said. "Never worry, missus."

"Did he interrogate you much, after you were away?"

"Nope," I said. "Martin isn't much for the curiosity. I don't even think he noticed."

"Well!" she said. "*Phew!* Such a relief! I was afraid I'd ruined everything."

She leaned over, drummed her hands on the counter between us. "Sooooooo?" she said then. "You *do* have something new, haven't you? A clue?"

I wriggled out of my rucksack and set it up on the counter between us. I unzipped it and handed her *Clues*.

"I knew it!" she said, clapping.

I reached into the rucksack a second time, and felt around in the back page of *Gulliver* to find my mother's photograph. Mrs. Hanley was nodding and making mmm-hmmm noises while she read *Clues*, and when she was done, I took a deep breath, a leap of faith, and handed her the folded newsprint photograph. She opened it carefully, like it had teeth.

"So this is the mystery," she said, peering at the photograph.

She reached under the counter then and drew out a *real magnifying glass*. I tried not to gasp. She held it up to her face, and her brown eye was gigantic behind it. She studied the photo from top to bottom while I eyed the door, nervous somebody would come in.

"Very interesting," she said.

"She's my mother," I said, and even though I was whispering, my words fell into the quiet room like stones into a pond.

They rippled out til I could see them on Missus Hanley's face. She knew the weight of them words; she took them serious. I opened the neck of my jumper, drew out my medal, and held it out to her. I let the chain make a line from my neck to the counter, while the missus held the medal in her hand.

"You have her medallion," she said. "It's such an unusual piece. Beautiful. I've never seen anything quite like it."

It felt like evidence. Even though she seemed to believe me, I wanted her to know for sure that I was telling the truth. The woman in the picture *was* my mother, even with her earrings and her fine polka-dot dress. The medal was proof. The missus turned it over in her hand to examine it more closely. She spun the golden and silver rings from their post while Saint Christopher stood still inside them.

"So what is it you need to find out?" she asked.

She never let nothing shock her. I really liked that about her, the way she never looked surprised or skeptical. It would be easy to just tell her everything. Well, almost everything. She didn't need to know about Grandda and the coffin-rocks.

"Well," I said. "When my grandda died, just a few weeks ago, I found the photograph. He . . . he sort of left it to me."

She nodded, so I went on.

"And I didn't know who it was, in the picture, but I noticed straightaway that she was wearing my medal."

"You didn't know your mother?" she asked.

"I never seen her before."

"Oh, Christy," she said, and her voice was all smushed up, but I plowed ahead anyway.

"She died when I was born."

The missus put her hand on her heart.

"And I showed it to my dad, and I asked him who it was, in the picture, and I don't think he even meant to say it, but he told me it was my mammy."

She nodded again.

"But I don't know who the other people is, and my dad won't tell me. He said he doesn't know who they is, but I don't believe him."

She wrinkled her forehead. "But why would he lie about that?" she asked.

"I donno." I shook my head. "But sure, how could he not know? He must know."

She took a deep breath into her and then took a long time breathing it out again. "She's very beautiful," she said, still looking at my mother's picture.

I beamed. "She is, isn't she?"

"What else do you know about her?"

I tried to think, but there was so little.

"Do you know where she's from?" she asked.

I shook my head. "I always thought she was a traveller," I said, and again my words felt heavy in the room.

Because it was beginning to seem obvious then that she wasn't a traveller, that she couldn't be. I really had to face that truth, but it still felt impossible, somehow. The missus pointed at the baby.

"Well, let's start here," she said. "Could this be your brother or sister?"

"No, it's only me," I said. "I was their first baby, their only baby, and then she died."

"Okay," she said. "So maybe it's a niece or nephew? And that could be her brother she's with?"

I shrugged again.

"Is there anyone else in your family you can ask?"

"No," I said. "Dad thinks I burned the photo. He made me burn it, because it was Grandda's. And if anybody found out I still had it, I'd be in awful trouble."

She looked at me, drummed her fingers against the countertop for a long moment. "Okay," she said then, nodding firmly. "I'll help. I will try and help you."

I grinned and rocked up onto my toes. "Thank you, missus!" I said.

"But we have to have an agreement first," she said.

I nodded. Anything.

"There's obviously some reason your father didn't wish to discuss this with you," she said, gesturing at the photograph.

I looked down, but she leaned in closer again, waited for me to lift my eyes back to hers. She tucked my medal back into my hand and didn't let go.

"Information is the most powerful and dangerous commodity of all, Mr. Hurley," she said to me. "So whatever information we unearth—it's your responsibility. Okay?"

We was both holding my medal now, between us. Her fingers was wrapped around mine.

"Yes, of course," I said carelessly.

"And you'll manage it carefully, this information?" she pressed.

"Yes," I said. "I promise."

She nodded cautiously, and then opened *Clues* again, to reread my list inside. I watched her.

"So that's everything I found out from examining the back side of the photograph," I said, leaning up on my tiptoes so's I could look at the list with her. "And from asking questions of my family. They wasn't much help, though."

She nodded and frowned.

"See the advertisement there, for the plumbers?" I flipped the photograph over onto its back side so she could see it. "They're in

O'Briensbridge," I said. "So I figured maybe the newspaper is from there."

"I don't know of any newspapers in O'Briensbridge." She wrinkled her nose. "It'd more likely be Nenagh. Or even Limerick—they might've advertised in one of the Limerick papers."

Sleuthing was full of wrong turns. I was awful glad of the missus.

"Right," I said. "So."

She stood and scooted her stool over toward the edge of the counter.

"Sit up there, Christy," she said then.

I glanced at the door and then climbed up onto her stool, the seat still warm where she'd sat. She was at the telephone, draping the wire acrosst the counter. She set the heavy-looking contraption between us, and it landed on the counter with a jingly clunk. She lifted the handle-piece and held it at an angle, so's we could both hear, even though I didn't know who we was meant to be ringing. I'd never rang nobody before. And nobody'd ever rang me. She stuck her finger in one of the number-holes and twisted it 'round. It clicked back and then there was a woman's voice on the line.

"Operator," the voice said, and I nearly fell off my stool, from the loudness of it. She sounded like she was right there under the counter.

"Good afternoon, Loretta, it's Margaret Hanley here," said the missus.

"How'ya, Margaret?" Loretta the Operator answered through the telephone. "How's business? Good, I hope?"

"Very good, very good, thanks to God," the missus said. "And how's your mother keeping?"

"Ah, she's feeling much better, Margaret, thanks for asking," said Loretta.

"Ah, good," said the missus. "Tell her I was asking."

"I will, of course," said Loretta.

"Loretta," said the missus then, "could you connect me to a line for Cummins Plumbing Supplies in O'Briensbridge? I'm afraid I don't have the telephone number."

I stared at the missus. This was some real sleuthing right here. The magnifying glass should've tipped me off. I glanced at the ad on the back of the photograph again. There was no number on it, all right—the ad had been snipped in half.

"I will, of course," Loretta said. "Just give me one minute there."

And then there was quiet, and I was nearly afraid we'd lost her, but the missus just smiled at me, and in a minute Loretta came back.

"Hold the line," she said.

And then there was a ringing noise, and after a couple moments, there was a man's voice.

"Hello!" he said.

"Hello!" Missus Hanley answered. "Is this the line for Cummins Plumbing Supplies in O'Briensbridge?"

"It is, indeed," the man's voice said. "This is Seamus Cummins."

"Ah, lovely," said Missus Hanley, and then she looked at me, like as if to ask did I want to talk to him.

I shook my head frantically, and pushed the handle-piece closer to her. She nodded at me and patted my hand.

"I've a funny old question for you, and I wonder if you could help me," she said then. "My name is Margaret Hanley, and I've come across a bit of a newspaper clipping in my bookstore."

She paused to see would Mr. Cummins make any reply. When he didn't, she went on. "There's an advertisement for your shop on the back of the page, you see, and I'm trying to track down the original source of the article."

There was a crackly noise on the line, and I wondered if Mr. Cummins had a beard, because it sounded like sandpaper was scratching against the phone. He mumbled something we couldn't hear.

"I'm sorry?" Missus Hanley said, and then she sealed the earpiece against her head, stuck a finger in her free ear, so's she could hear him better.

Now I couldn't hear him at all; only a murmur of him leaked out of Missus Hanley's ear-phone seal.

"Well, that's all right," she said.

Murmur.

"Oh, but you *did* place one, then?" she said. "It doesn't matter how long ago it was."

Murmur.

Missus Hanley nodded, reached under the counter and uncapped a green pen, then grabbed my hand, twisted it so's it was facing palm-up. "LIMERICK LEADER," she wrote. And then, "December, 1947." Right there on my damp hand in green letters.

"Mmm-hmm," she said. "Gotcha, right. Just for the Christmas season. Your first year in business. Makes sense, yes. Mmm-hmm, mmm-hmm."

Murmur murmur murmur.

"And you must've done very well," she said. "Here you are, still with the thriving business all these years later."

Murmur murmur murmur.

"Ah, very good." She laughed, giving me the thumbs-up. "Yes, thank you very much, Mr. Cummins. Ah, that's all right. Yes, you too. Thank you, thank you!"

She hung up and I looked at the green letters seeping into my skin.

"The *Limerick Leader*?" I said.

"That's the one," she said, and she was already lifting the earpiece to get Loretta back on the line.

The call to the *Limerick Leader* took a lot longer, but Missus Hanley was patient. She told them roundabout the date we was interested in, and she explained that the article in question must've been on page fifteen or seventeen, since the advertisement was on page sixteen. She got up to lock the door in the middle of the call, in case any late customers wandered in. By the time I left the bookstore that evening, she'd gotten us a promise. The *Limerick Leader* had tracked down the article. Yes, they'd tracked it down. And yes, they would send it along in short order, they said. We could expect it to arrive sometime in the next week, they said.

"Yes, I'll be happy to remit payment on return," she said into the phone. "Thanks so much."

And she hung up. My heart was hopping outta my mouth as she walked me to the door and opened the lock for to see me out. I was that sweaty and nervous and excited, the green letters on my palm had melted into one thick, gloppy smudge. I didn't know how to thank her. It had got dark outside, and she'd the lights in the shop turned on, so's I could see our reflections in the glass of the windows, all surrounded by the colors of books.

"Thanks, missus," I said.

It wasn't enough, but it was all I had.

THIRTEEN

Fidel was still waiting for me, and the two of us ran all the way down High Street, giddy in the dusk. I felt like cartwheeling, and Fidel did leaping dance moves 'round my ankles as we ran. We was too late for the post office. The lights was still on inside, so I tried banging on the door, but the grumpy postman looked at me over the tops of his glasses and pointed to the sign on the door. His voice carried, warped, through the glass.

"I'm sure you can't read that, but it says we're *closed*."

I stuck my tongue out at him, but I was too cheerful to mean it. I banged on the door with the flat of my hand.

"*I'll see you again tomorrow, mister!*" I shouted through the glass.

Then I pressed my lips against the windowpane and blew my cheeks up like a fish balloon, but he only looked at me with a long gob. There wasn't nothing could make him laugh.

"Maybe he's got arthritis," I said to Fidel. "Or a wicked wife. Or a limp. Ooh, a postman with a limp. That would be rough, hah?"

The sweat was drying against my neck in the winter wind. Myself and Fidel bounded down the Long Mile Road toward home.

—————

EVERY DAY AFTER SCHOOL, I went to that post office, til I got to be like a hemorrhoid on the backside of that already grouchy postman. Every day, I asked him, "Anything for Hurleys, mister?" and every day, he came up with the grumpiest way he could find to tell me "no."

On Friday, the Blob made an announcement:

"Now, children, we've a special treat this afternoon," she said. "We'll be working on an art project."

She made a long pause to give this information time to sink in, and there was a whisper of excitement that ran among the eight-year-olds. When there was quiet again, she went on.

"We'll all be making cards for Mother's Day!" She beamed.

Martin made to put his hand up and I kicked him hard beneath our shared desk til he put it down again. Mother's Day! Good God, what new horror was this? The Blob explained a bit of the history to us, how it had been sort of an old-fashioned holiday a couple centuries ago, mostly so's servants could get a nice weekend away from work to head home and visit the old mammy, but that it had nearly died out before the war, until the Americans came all over Europe and more or less revived the tradition.

"Feckin' Americans," I said quietly.

Why did they always have to go reviving everything? Martin looked at me distastefully, which I knew was probably because any curse on the Americans was really a blaspheme against Elvis. He shook his head at me slowly.

"So we'll all make some lovely cards for the mammies," the Blob said, in a tone that was nothing short of gleeful. "And won't they be *delighted* when you bring them home!"

She clapped her hands in front of her in a gesture of tremendous satisfaction. I could feel Martin looking at me from the side, and I willed him to look away before I'd be forced to clock him in the head. I took a deep breath and made a quick decision: I would just make the stupid card. It was no big deal. I didn't need a mother to give a card to on some made-up, American holiday. It didn't matter.

On the Blob's desk, there was three stacks of different-colored papers for us to choose from, and then there was real wax crayons and charcoal chalks that the Blob encouraged us to use at will, to create whatever we wanted. I chose the purple paper, which was stupid, since my mam would never see it anyway, on account of her deadness. Martin was excused from the card-making because of the Blob's misconception that he was the one with the dead mam. Instead, he drew a tractor and a bunch of apple trees. I cast an eye around me to see what the eight-year-olds was doing, who was making cards for real mammies who was less dead. I didn't care. I could throw the thing out on the way back to camp, or burn it or something.

But when the hour had went by, I looked down at the purple paper and seen the red wax love-heart I had drew, with the smoky charcoal letters M-A-M-M-Y, and I knew my plan was in danger. Inside, I'd drew three fishes, a dog (Fidel), Jack, and then me and Dad's wagon. I wrote a very stupid message to my deceased (which is a nicer word for dead) mother, and it said, "To Mammy from your son Christy. I miss you." And I hated it. It was so stupid. And yet, for some reason, I tucked it carefully into the back page of *Gulliver*, alongside her photograph, for safekeeping.

FATHER FRANCIS STOPPED ME IN the hall.

"Christopher!" he said. "Saint Malachy's newest star pupil!"

I smiled. Star pupil, just like I'd planned it. I had even managed to make some pretty good progress at the maths. I stood up a little straighter.

"Excuse us for a moment, Martin?" Father Francis said.

My heart skidded and thumped.

"Sure," Martin said. "See ya at home, Christy."

And he was out the door like a shot. I tried to breathe through my nose, but it felt like I was breathing through my stomach instead.

"It's about your baptismal certificate," Father Francis said.

Oh no. Tears sprang up behind my eyes.

"I've been to the post office every day, Father," I said. "I don't know what more I can do, except maybe we should write away for it again because it hasn't arrived yet, and—"

"Your father dropped it in this morning," he said, interrupting my panic.

Oh. I clamped shut my mouth. I hadn't known; of course I hadn't. I was afraid to look up at him. Something was wrong. Dear Jesus, please don't let nothing be wrong.

"Everything looks fine," he said.

I could count my heartbeats in my throat. Why didn't I feel relieved?

"Okay," I said.

"Okay?" Father Francis smiled at me. "So you can stop your worrying. You'll be taking your First Holy Eucharist with the rest of your classmates."

"Oh Jesus God," I breathed. "Thank you!"

I was so relieved I had to blink to keep a tear ball from rolling down my face. Father Francis clapped me on the back.

"Now," he said. "When I was your age, I was a real worrywart myself."

I finally looked up at him, his bald head gleaming in the pale light of the open doorway, his black dress swishing beneath him, even when he stood still. He'd never been my age, I thought.

"You have to learn to have *faith*," he said. "And everything will turn out all right in the end, see?"

"Yes, Father," I said.

"Now"—he squeezed my shoulder—"tell your father thank you for dropping it 'round. There was no need for the special delivery—he could've sent it with you."

"I guess he's a bit of a worrywart, too," I said, even though I knew that wasn't true.

The truth was I didn't know why he'd dropped it 'round hisself, why he hadn't just gave it to me. He hadn't even mentioned that it had arrived, even though he knew I was sick, waiting. It was odd—like he was trying to keep it from me.

"We'll see you tomorrow, Christopher," Father Francis said, and he swished his skirts in the doorway, turned to head back to his office.

"Father?" I said.

He paused with his hand on the doorjamb.

"Does it have pictures on it?" I asked.

"The baptismal certificate?" he asked.

I nodded.

"Photographs, like?"

"No, son. Just words."

"Oh," I said.

"Study hard tonight, son." He was turning to go again.

"I never seen it before, is all," I said.

He turned back around. He smiled at me with his lips closed. "Would you like to see it?" he asked. "Is that what you're asking?"

I hadn't meant to ask that. Or maybe I had. "Yes, Father," I said.

"Come on, then."

He held out his hand toward me, ushered me through the doorway, through the little room where Sister Hedgehog lived, past the desk where she'd saved me. She wasn't home. Down the little corridor we went, then—me and Father Francis—through the second door and onto the thick, queer carpet—midnight blue, and soft and deep as the Shannon. My feet sunk into it. Father Francis moved

ahead of me, around past the ball-map on its stand, and started sorting through some papers on his desk.

"Ah, here we are, now," he said, finding the one.

He lifted it out from its stack of family papers, and handed it
toward me. My baptismal certificate. I had a sudden, weird notion
that I shouldn't take it from him. That it would burn me, or it'd be so
heavy I wouldn't be able to hold it, that it would break my two arms
clean off, from the weight of it. So strange. A thin, flimsy bit of paper
in his hand. I could see the light shining through it, could see the
stark silhouettes of its printed ghost-words on the other side. Father
Francis was reaching it out to me. I sat down in the chair opposite
Father Francis's desk. I didn't mean to, but I did. Sat down with a
thud, without even looking behind me first, to see was there a chair
there to catch me.

"Are you all right, Christopher?" Father Francis said.

I didn't look at him, but I nodded, stared down at the precious
document in my wobbly hands. There was a cross at the top—very
like the one from Grandda's Mass card, with the stripes coming out
of it. But here there was a dove, too, with a branch in her beak, under
one arm of the cross. Under the other arm was a candle, lit with
flame. I don't know why, but I was almost afraid to look past that, to
move my eyes away from the pictures and onto the words.

CERTIFICATE OF BAPTISM, it said, in big letters acrosst the top.
And then beneath that, a line, where somebody had wrote *William
Christopher Hurley* in a messy scrawl. My stomach swooped. Wil-
liam? Who was William? They'd sent the wrong one! No, wait. Be-
neath that again, was more words and lines, like this: Born on the
_____ day of May, 1947. Child of Christopher Hurley and Nora
Angela Cleary was baptized in the name of the Father, and of the
Son, and of the Holy Ghost, by Reverend Father Jonas Stapleton at
Holy Ghost Catholic Church, Rathnaveen, in the County of Tiobraid
Arann, Eire on this, the 16th day of December, 1947. Godparents:
Fintan Hurley and Millicent Cleary.

Father Jonas Stapleton had signed his name at the bottom. This *was* the right baptismal cert. William was *me*.

"Nora," is what I said out loud.

Father Francis sat down in his chair acrosst from me. He folded his hands quietly in front of him, and his eyeglasses glinted in the dim light. "Take your time there, Christy," he said.

I don't think he'd ever called me Christy before. It made me nervous—the informality of it, and the clash of it with the name on this paper in front of me. But I fixed on my mam's name instead.

"Nora Angela Cleary," I whispered.

It was beautiful. My hands was trembling. Father Francis opened his desk drawer and reached in, drew out a box of matches. He took the glass off his lamp and struck a match, cupped his hand 'round the flame, lit the wick inside. He blew the match out and dropped it into a bin beside him, replaced the lantern-glass over the flame. I hadn't realized how dark it'd got until he put the light on.

I'd never knew my mother's name.

I TOOK MY TIME GOING home. I needed to sort it all out in my head, to think it through. My name, William. It was like a halting foreign language I couldn't speak. Like a brogue—that was the Irish word for shoe, really: *bróg*. It was what the English said about how we talked . . . like we had a shoe in our mouth, and that's how I felt, suddenly. That name, William, was like a hobnail boot on my tongue.

And then Nora Angela Cleary, my mother's name, all grace and light. I would've thought that learning her name might make her more real to me, might give me something new to add to those seven minutes we shared, as she lay dying. Those minutes I tried and tried to remember. Did she hold me first? Did I open my eyes to her? Did I try and suckle, and did I hear, then, pressed up warm against her breast, when the blood ran out of her, when her heartbeat slowed and then stopped? Did she have time to love me?

Nora Cleary. She felt farther away than ever. I'd never met nobody called Cleary before. Maybe she hailed from somewhere far-off, some remote Northern clan. Maybe they was from the islands, Inis Something. Maybe I had the salt-sea air and white island rocks, too, in the blood of my veins. And I guess my mam had a sister, maybe, or a cousin. Millicent. Auntie Millie. How come I'd never heard nothing about her? And come to think of it, what about the rest of my mam's family? It was like they never existed. Like after she died, they'd all died, and it was only me and Dad who was left.

And then there was my godfather, Fintan Hurley. Dad said they wasn't travelling with us that time, so then how come Finty was my godfather? And why had they waited so god-awful long to baptize me? I counted out the months on my fingers: May, June, July, August, September, October, November, December. Eight! Eight whole months of mortal danger. I crossed myself and said a prayer of thanks to Jesus that I hadn't died before eight months of age. I would've ended up in Limbo! How could they do that to me? I'd never knew Dad to be so reckless—eight months without a Christening was way worse than being late for your Communion. It was startling, shocking. Wild. I couldn't breathe.

I had to breathe. Deep breaths. Maybe Mrs. Hanley had rubbed off on me, because my hands had memorized every word on that page. They'd leaked right into me like holy water, like new fingerprints. I had a whole new truth, a new name. And my mam, too— she had a name.

"Nora." I said it out loud again.

And I tried to imagine her all in a cloud of purple curls, like I used to when Grandda would whisper her to me. That other mam, that realer mam, before the photograph. I tried to get back to her long, wind-whipped purple tresses, tumbling all the way down her back to her knees. I closed my eyes and winced and whispered, and finally, up she loomed—all windy eyelashes and long, slender limbs. Pale fingers. Warm cheeks. I couldn't see her face.

I decided I couldn't ask Dad about it. Something about this place, this moment, ever since the fire, the photograph. It all felt like tripping through a minefield. If you'd asked me then, I couldn't have said why it felt that way. But now I think it was Grandda, warning me, trying to prepare me for the shock that would come. He made me sense that there was a sharp peril on the edges of things, waiting, and that feeling made me vigilant, careful. One wrong step, one whispered word, could wreak havoc on all my young world. So even when I learned that my name was William, I tiptoed.

That night I had the heavy impression of something menacing me in the dark, and I couldn't sleep. I thought every moon-shadow crossing the tent flap was a bogeyman. Dad snored beside me.

"I wish Grandda was still alive," I whispered into the darkness.

Every night that weekend, for all three nights, I dreamed the following dream: I was half Bing Crosby and half Elvis. I wore a tuxedo and a snarl, and stood beside a piano in a debonair fashion, tapping my foot and swirling something brown in a fancy glass while Finnuala Whippet played Tchaikovsky like she was the man hisself. The music was so beautiful and haunting that purple smoke crept out from beneath the piano keys and curled around Finnuala Whippet until it was a thick cloud around her.

When I blew into the cloud, my breath was purple, too. I blew harder, and when the purple smoke cleared, it was my mother, and she played on without noticing me until I whispered, "Mammy." And then her hands stopped in their playing, and hovered for a moment over the keyboard until she turned and stretched them out to me. She swept me up and under her storm of hair, and folded me into her like she'd never let me go, and I could feel the softness of her eyelashes on my face and the jutting length of her collarbone against my chin, and I burrowed into her like a baby kangaroo. I held on to

her til my fingers ached from the effort of it, and when it was time
to waken, I fought and fought to stay asleep.

ON MONDAY THERE WAS MAYHEM in the schoolyard.

"It's like cattle day at Puck Fair," Martin said as we made our
way into the heaving crowd.

It was midday, and we bumped into Beano straightaway, the
trademark grin stuck firmly to his face.

"Amy's having a birthday party!" he said, waving a piece of card
in his hand.

Finnuala Whippet.

Was having.

A birthday party.

I caught my breath, tried to catch a gawk at the invite, but Beano
shoved it carelessly into his pocket and rubbed his hands together.

"*Everybody's* going," Beano said, and I took him to mean *almost*
everybody.

My stomach gave a heave and a tumble, and I turned to look for
Fidel, mostly to give my face something to do. He usually met us
straight out the door, but today the place was bunged with childer.
Usually half the school ran home at midday, so their mammies could
stuff them up with food before afternoon classes, but today nobody'd
went home for their dinners. Everyone was mobbed into the schoolyard instead, clamoring excitement, hoping for their invitations. I
was sickened with possibility and fear. I wanted to bolt, like Jack
when he took a fright.

"She's invited the *whole school*," Beano said.

I looked at him. "That can't be right," I said. "Can it? The whole
school?"

Even that wanker, Patrick? Even me? And now I took a closer
look around, and it was true I couldn't see a single invitationless

hand. Not a one. Well, hang on. There was a couple: myself, and then Martin. Feck.

"How would she know not to miss nobody?" I said.

"Her mammy got the enrollment list from Father Francis, and she's invited everybody on it," Beano explained.

Shite. Surely we wasn't on no enrollment list.

"How do you know all this?" I said.

"Our mammies are friendly," he said. "My mam gives them piano lessons."

"Your mother teaches Amy piano?" Martin asked.

I cringed, remembering her playing.

"She teaches them both," Beano said. "Amy and her mammy."

"Her mother, too?" I said.

Whose mother took piano lessons?

"Yeah, she said she wanted to learn." Beano shrugged. "But Amy's far better than her."

My mouth dropped open. The mother was *worse*?

"The mammy can't carry a tune," Beano whispered loudly.

The crowd was thinning, and the smug bastards was all sauntering off with their invitations. I hated myself for even wanting to go to her stupid party. And then, through the thinning throng, Kathleen could be seen on tiptoe, waving over to us. I looked at Beano, to be sure it wasn't him she wanted. The crowd dispersed even more.

There she was, Kathleen. Standing beside Finnuala Whippet, holding a cardboard shoe box in front of her.

"Martin," Kathleen called, in her husky boy-voice. "C'mere!"

Martin slapped my arm again and trotted over. I followed him, of course. What else could I do?

Finnuala Whippet's plaits was hanging into the shoe box, obscuring the view. But she popped her head up fast and nearly hit me in the chin.

I took a quick step back. She was brandishing two crisp, white, folded note cards. She reached past Martin to hand me mine first.

In that instant, my heart burst into a new state of being; it was the size of a fish in my chest, a salmon maybe, or at least a herring, and as floppy and wet, and as slippery. It was all I could do not to reach acrosst that shoe box, take Finnuala Whippet's pale cheeks in my two hands, and snog the face off her.

She smiled at me. I'm sure she handed Martin his without even looking at him.

"That's all of them." Finnuala Whippet smiled at me again. "And you *must* bring Fidel. He and Rex will have their own little party."

She bent to give Fidel a little pat, and I'd an awful urge to lick the part of her hair, right down her scalp between the two plaits. And then I thought that surely that was a disgusting kind of urge to have, and there must be something very wrong with me.

There was hardly anybody left outside, because the break was over. I let Martin go ahead with Kathleen and Beano, and I dropped back to wait for Finnuala Whippet, who always seemed to have difficulty tearing herself away from Fidel, even though she was gonna be late for class. I wanted to be next to her. I hadn't a clue what to say, but I wanted to try and maybe accidentally rub my forearm alongside hers while we walked.

"That was very good of you," I said. "To invite us."

She looked a little confused. "Don't be silly," she said simply. "I invited everybody."

I looked at the cover of my folded note card. It said "Master Hurley" in meticulous black script, and I could scarcely believe that Master Hurley was me. I wouldn't open it until later, when I could savor it like it was a ham.

"I know. But it's just, when you invite *everybody*," I said. "Well, sometimes, you know, Martin and me. We's not always *everybody*."

She looked over at me quickly, suddenly, the same jerky head movement that'd nearly cost me my chin earlier. And then, in the

single greatest moment of my life, Finnuala Whippet reached over
and squeezed my hand.

"Christy, you're not looking well," Dad said, over tea. "What's
the matter with ya?"

What was the matter with me was that my name was William
and I barely even cared about that, because Finnuala Whippet had
squeezed my hand, and I was going to her birthday party, and that
had wiped me cleaner, even, than a new name. I was so excited I'd
nearly forgot to call in to the missus that afternoon to see if our
newspaper article had arrived from the *Limerick Leader*. My thoughts
was all twisted up in her, in Finnuala Whippet, and my stomach felt
funny the whole time, like even when I wasn't thinking about her,
my intestines was.

"How d'ya mean?" I said, chewing.

"You're not yourself at'all, at'all," Dad said. "It's like you've delirium tremors or something."

"What's that?" I said.

"Delirium tremors?" Dad asked.

"Yeah."

"Oh, it's what your uncle Michael gets every time he takes the
pledge and goes off the drink for a while," he said, and then he pan-
tomimed Uncle Michael having a big, ghastly face on him and going
into a dose of the shakes.

I laughed at him and took another big bite.

"Are you coming down with something, maybe?" Granny asked,
laying the back of her hand acrosst my cheek. "You're all flushed in
the face."

I felt myself redden deeper, a hotness spreading over my cheeks.
Martin looked over at me and rolled his eyes. He stuck his finger in
his open mouth like he was goin' ta make hisself puke. He knew
what was wrong with me: I couldn't stop thinking about Finnuala

Whippet, how her fingers felt when she twisted her soft, white hand around mine. I stammered something.

"Yep," Dad said. "That's the tremors."

And he went shaking again, the tongue poking out the side of his face, and this time he shook so hard that he went arse-over-bucket, and it was lucky he'd finished his tea already or it would've been everywhere. And now he was on the ground, the bucket tipped over beside him and his boots in the air while he shuddered and trembled. Fidel was over to him like a shot, to cure him with mouth-licks, which did the trick straightaway, and Dad came out of his episode, spitting and wiping down his chin.

"Ah, ya filthy mutt," he said, scratching Fidel on the back of the head. He let go a spit.

"I'm grand," I said after that. "I just . . ."

Granny leaned forward with the pipe clenched between her teeth and her eyes pinned to my face. Dad was sitting cross-legged now and dusting hisself off from the spasms.

"Just what, child? Speak up," Granny said.

"I just. I . . ."

Granny was nodding at me impatiently. I thought of Finnuala Whippet's perfect invitation, my name written clean acrosst the front.

"I like it here," I said finally.

And the words felt monumental, like a dam finally giving burst to an itchy, tormenting leak.

"Arrah, yeah," Granny said. "It's a grand little town."

IT WAS A CLOUDY NIGHT, and that dark in the tent that the white of Finnuala Whippet's invitation didn't even make a faint glow in front of me. I checked the rhythm of Dad's breathing, rolled over onto all fours, and felt my way toward the mouth of the tent, careful not to crease the note card as I went. Outside, I could make out a dim square of light when I held the invitation up in front of my face.

I felt my way toward the darkened skeleton of the fire and with a few careful manipulations, I coaxed it back to a wary, glowing half-life. I saved out a skinned log, stretched back, and propped my head onto the warming wood. There was a good chill out, but my body stayed cozy in along the fire. I placed the note card on my chest where I could watch the words "Master Hurley" rise and fall with my breath in the growing firelight.

It was good to be alone in the quiet dark, with my bare toes pointing into the moonless, starless sky. I would do this more, I thought. I would steal these moments of hush, when I could be all alone in the world, where no one else's thoughts of me walked, only my own. Here by this fire, on this night, I wasn't a tinker, or the new kid who broke his face on the second day of school, or the half-child of a mysterious, long-gone, newspaper mammy in a polka-dot dress. I wasn't punctured with questions, twisted with worry. Here I was barely even Christy Hurley. Or even William Christopher Hurley, whoever he was. Here I could be nameless, invisible.

Outside my bubble of firelight, the world was pitched in a deep, black tar, and that darkness muffled even the quiet sounds of sleep. The breathing, the dreaming, the farting and rolling over, the kicking at a wayward blanket wrapped around an ankle—all of it was blotted out by the thickness of the dark. In a field not too far away, the night's only sound carried to me acrosst the breeze: the trace of a tinkle from Jack's little bell. He was done eating by now and would be asleep standing up, close by to the fence where I'd pushed him in before bed. I smiled thinking of Jack standing wait-ing me, his big eyes rolling in behind his closed lids, dreaming his horsey dreams. Maybe Jack dreamed of purple humans. I closed my eyes, too, then, and with the breeze, I felt that if I lifted my arms and let it take me, I would fly.

Then slowly, very slowly, handling it only by the edges so's not to smudge it with my damp nerves, I lifted the note card from my chest and I opened it. I allowed my eyes to drip and dribble along every word. I let the black loops and swoops and curls run together into my brain, and make me dizzy.

> *Master Hurley,*
> *The honor of your presence is requested*
> *This Saturday, the fourteenth day of March,*
> *Nineteen hundred and fifty-nine*
> *At one o'clock in the afternoon*
> *For a celebration!*
> *To commemorate the eleventh birthday of*
> *Miss Amy Margaret Whitherspoon.*

I felt the warmth of excitement come spreading over me, and for a moment, I was so happy I thought my willy might let go a small spring of piss—the sort that can leak out from pure contentment. I had to read it again. This was some real Cinderella-going-to-the-ball type carry-on. And then straightaway I felt like a bit of a mong for feeling like Cinderella. I bit my lip and drilled it into my head that I should never, ever make that Cinderella crack out loud. Under no circumstances, and especially never in fronta Martin. And then I read the invitation over and over again. Maybe fifty times.

That night I had the dream about Finnuala Whippet and my mammy again, except this time, it wasn't just the smoke was purple. Everything—the piano, the hardwood floors, the stacks of leather-bound books, the Elvis-and-Bing-style suit I was wearing, the fancy drink I was drinking—all of it was differing shades of purple. Finnuala Whippet even had lilac eyes in behind her plum-colored glasses.

FOURTEEN

When I wakened, it was nearly dawn coming to the edges of the sky, but it was still quiet in the camp. I heard Jack's bell and knew I'd to rescue him out of the field before dawn came fully, and revealed him to the angry, fist-shaking farmer whose crops he was munching. But then I remembered where we was, that we was welcomed here. That Jack was safe here. And that was such an unfamiliar feeling to me, that I had to try it on, like a hat, and I had to work at getting accustomed to it. The fish-heartbeat in me quickened as I sat up, and I felt wide-awake to the world in a way I hadn't been yesterday. The corners and colors and edges of things had a new sharpness to them, a new distinction, even in the foggy predawn. I think that feeling was joy.

I slipped into the tent and hid my invitation, then took my time going down the road to Jack, following the clink and tingle of his bell. When I found him, I stepped one, two bare feet up onto the cold wall, soggy with moss. He let me climb on.

"I am not Cinderella," I whispered into Jack's ear.

We jumped the fence and trotted bareback into the camp. You couldn't beat the smile off me with a hammer.

WHEN GRANNY HEARD ABOUT THE party, she managed some tricky negotiations in town for some new clothes. I was a bit worried when she arrived in camp, smiling her toothless smile and shaking the paper-wrapped goods at us, but I had to hand it to her. She really came through with the duds: two spanking new cowboy shirts for myself and Martin, and man dear, was they good ones. They wasn't even the same color. Martin's one was blue with tartan around the shoulders, and mine was red with white piping along the seams and some curlicues down the back (very like the ones on the front of *Gulliver's Travels*). Both had pearlized snaps to close them at the front and the cuffs. It was the first new shirt I ever remembered having, as in it wasn't only new-to-me, but it hadn't never belonged to nobody else before me, neither. I didn't even try it on, in case I'd wreck it.

I was sure Saturday would never come. Something would happen. I would get hit by a howling train or a runaway heifer before then. Or I would catch consumption and die on Thursday. Or maybe I would survive on my deathbed just long enough for Martin to return from the party and tell me all about it before I would cough up my last bloody tumor and expire.

So when the morning finally did arrive, growing colder with the daylight instead of warming up, I bathed Fidel first, forced Martin's comb over most of him (breaking off seven of the teeth in the process—explain that one to Auntie Brigid, no thank you). Then I washed myself twice in the freezing pump water, from ears to bollix and back again. I manhandled my hair for the better part of a half hour, til it performed a decent ducktail. And then I trembled while I snapped up them pearlized snaps, like they was bombs made of eggshells. I stepped my feet in front of each other like the earth was a trembling quicksand that would swallow me up with one wrong step. I pulled at my cuffs, tucked in the shirttail, and it was perfect, the way it fit me. From the center of my gut, all the way to the tips of my scrupulously slicked-back hair, I quivered like a plucked bow-string off Grandda's fiddle.

I hummed the whole morning, and then tried to distract my-self by reading about Gulliver, who had managed to get hisself into a real spot of bother with some tiny men in Lilliput, but even that wasn't enough to occupy me long. I sat straight and stiff in my cowboy shirt, afraid I would crease it or stain it. And when the hour rolled finally on to noon, I said to Martin maybe we should head up.

"Dad, what time is it?" he said to Finty, who paused in his ham-mering to pull his old-fashioned watch out of his pocket by the bit of twine it hung on.

Martin hated to be early for things. He didn't like waiting.

"Just gone twelve," Finty answered.

Martin turned to look at me, and he couldn't hide his apprecia-tion. He gave a low whistle, which caused a bit of excitement in Fidel.

"Very dapper," he admitted. "I'll get mine on."

And he scuttled off to leave me a few extra minutes' preening. Granny clapped her hands together and rocked back on her haunches when she seen us all kitted out. She dangled John Paul from her knee.

"You're like two film stars!" she said, pointing at us, and then she called over to Auntie Brigid, "Would ye lookit the two film stars!"

We debated whether or not to take Jack, in order for to make a proper entrance, but the debate was short-lived because, we had to admit, Jack wasn't exactly in a condition to be improving the bra-vado of our arrival. Even after all that, we was still a bit early, so we had to loop around the town twice before we went up, and I couldn't manage a single sentence to Martin the whole time, which was just as well because he was talking away like an auctioneer and when I didn't answer him, he'd just turn and address hisself to Fidel instead.

I was worried about what the other boys would be wearing, especially that bastard Patrick. But when we stopped in front of the bookshop to examine ourselves in the glass, I didn't reckon you could do much better. We took our jackets off for a look, and I wished I had some denims to go with my new cowboy shirt instead of the old gray flannel trousers, but all in all, it was a better job than I'd expected. I seen Martin's reflection beside me, about an inch taller, slightly broader acrosst the shoulders, but no question my hair was doing a better job. He didn't have my patience.

There was a quick *BONG BONG BONG* sort of a sound, and the glass we was looking into vibrated, and who was in behind the window only Mrs. Hanley, holding her coffee cup in one hand and waving like a flag on a windy day with the other. Her smile showed all her teeth and gums. I waved back. Martin stepped away from the glass. She moved to the door and cracked it open, so's not to let in too much of the cold air. I was struggling back into my coat.

"Well, don't you lads look *handsome!*" she said.

I smiled back at her and wondered if my own gums showed as much. I checked them quickly in the glass and closed my lips.

"Thank you, missus," I said.

"Ah, now," she said. "The girls are in for some trouble!"

She folded her one arm inside the other and took a sip of the coffee. Martin was taking his time with the toggles on his coat.

"Are we off to a party, then?" she asked. "The two cowboys?"

"Yes, missus," I said, pointing out the end of the town and up the hill. "Up at Finnua . . . I mean, up at the Whitherspoons'. It's Amy's birthday."

It was the first time I'd called her Amy, and she sounded like somebody else.

"Oh, how exciting!" she said. "And a lovely day for it, too."

I could see my breath in the cold, and there was a bone-dampening chill, but still and all, I couldn't disagree with her.

"Well, you boys have a good time and don't go breaking too many hearts!"

"Thank you, missus," I said, and I was pleased to hear Martin chime in behind me.

She closed the door and we set off, but before we got too far, I heard the bell jingle again, and I turned to see the door swung open and Mrs. Hanley popping her head through.

"I nearly forgot!" she said. "Christopher, I've something for you to take to your father."

She was waving an envelope in her hand. Martin stayed where he was while I ran back to her. She dropped her voice as she handed me the letter.

"For Mr. Christopher Hurley from the *Limerick Leader.* Oh, now I suppose that could be for you—not for your father after all." She winked. "My mistake."

I grinned at her. "Did you read it?" I asked.

"I did not," she answered solemnly. "It's all yours, when you're ready for it."

"Thanks, missus," I said.

She took a step back inside the door, but I grabbed her free hand. "Missus?" I said.

"Yes, Christopher?"

I glanced behind to make sure Martin wasn't looking. "Really. Thank you," I said again.

This envelope might hold the answer to everything. It would surely tell me who my mother was—at least a little bit about her and the other people in the photograph, in her life. Me and Martin had botched Grandda's goodbye, but here was his final wish for me, fulfilled. Even in his passing, he'd gave me a gift. He'd wanted me to know about my mam. I leaned in and hugged the missus quick around the middle. She patted my hair, kissed me on top of the head.

"Ah, you're such a lovely gossoon," she said. Then she shooed me off. "You'll be late for your party."

I let go of her. "See ya, missus."

"Come back and visit as soon as you can," she said. "I'm dying to know how the mystery ends!"

I tried not to skip because Martin always said skipping was for girls, but I felt like skipping. So instead I sort of trotted. Like Jack. A manly horse-gait. Martin and Fidel was dreaming in the bakery window. I slipped the envelope into the inside pocket of my jacket, where I could almost feel it creaking and groaning, straining against the fixed rhythm of my heartbeat.

"What's all that about?" Martin asked.

"I donno—something for Dad," I said, sniffing. "You know, he does trades with Mr. Hanley."

Martin nodded, and I hoped he hadn't noted my sniff. One time he told me I always sniffed when I lied. I sniffed again for good measure, in case he'd caught the first one and thought it was a lie-sniff. If I sniffed again a few times, maybe he'd think it was only the cold or whatever. I sniffed. Martin looked at me sideways but didn't say nothing. We could see Finnuala Whippet's house down the end of the town, balanced up on its hill, alone, and spreading its lawns out around it like skirts. Somebody was already there, spider-sized, walking up the drive toward the house. I bounced. Martin was walking on his tiptoes, as excited as me, but better at hiding it.

We'd walked this way before, just a few weeks earlier. We'd hopped the wall and approached the house from the side, in stealth. We'd dashed up the hill and into the hedges unseen, like a pair of sprites. How much things had changed since that first day.

This time Martin boldly swung open the front gate. Fidel stepped through first and I followed, my heart racing and rolling in my chest.

This was it. I would take a heart attack at the foot of the hill—that would put me in my place.

The gate squeaked and clanged as we closed it behind us, and I cringed on instinct, in case anybody would come racing down the hill to throw us out. In case there'd been a mistake and we wasn't invited, of course we wasn't, and who did we think we was, and would we please very kindly leave on the double before we'd offend the little hostess and her guests.

I held my breath as Martin went ahead, and I watched the house at the crest of the hill for signs of unwelcomeness. None appeared.

EVEN THOUGH I'D PEERED THROUGH these windows before, even though I'd memorized it and imagined it and dreamed it a thousand times since, everything about the house surprised me, beginning with Finnuala Whippet's mother.

She answered the door herself, dressed in tweed trousers and a button-down shirt like as if she was a very lovely-smelling little man. Despite the man-clothes, she managed to be more feminine than any woman I'd ever clapped eyes on. She had a very glossy mouth that was like a perfect red love-heart, and all the different parts of her seem to point up. Her eyebrows, her dimples, her nose. All the other bits. Her hair was dark, like Finnuala Whippet's, and it curled around her head in effortless perfection. She was like a lady from a magazine, but she was standing in front of us in 3-D, without so much as a fat maid to protect her.

"Hello, boys!" she sang, as she swung the door wide, and it was the voice we'd heard before, through the window, polished to a high sheen, but friendly nonetheless. "Do come in!"

I told Fidel to sit, and he grumbled, but plomped hisself down outside the door.

"Oh no! Bring him in! Everyone's welcome!" she said.

"Inside the house, missus?" I asked.

"Of course!" she said. "This must be Fidel. Amy mentioned that Rex was having company as well."

She winked at Martin as she said it and he went flush to his toes, so I stepped in behind him, in order for to catch him in case he should fall over.

"The two fellas are having their party in the kitchen," she explained, and then she called the previously invisible maid to escort Fidel to the kitchen.

I took a moment to thank God that the two fellas who was having their party in the kitchen wasn't us.

"I'm Maxine," said Finnuala Whippet's mammy, giving the front door a hefty shove with her arse, and slamming it back into its sturdy frame.

Maxine. How exotic. How American. I'd never met nobody with an X in their name before. With her back against the door, she stuck her petite hand out and I noticed that her nails was done up in a shiny red lacquer. So this was where Finnuala Whippet had picked up her funny handshaking habits.

"Now, which one of you is Christy?" She smiled and arched her wiggly eyebrows at me.

I felt naked again, like I did when her daughter teased me, and my neck went hot. How did she know my name?

"I am," I said. "I'm Christy." I shook her hand with my awfully sweaty one.

"Lovely to meet you, finally," she said, and she put her free hand over the top of my knuckles, so's her two hands was hugging mine.

Lovely to meet me *finally*? There was a distinct lump in my throat, and I prayed she'd turn her attentions to Martin because I would surely die if I had to perform one more word with her. Martin was looking at me with his mouth hanging open, as astonished as I was, apparently. She turned to him then, and I breathed for what may've been the first time since we'd stepped inside.

"So you must be Martin, then."

"Yes, missus," Martin answered.

"Please, there's no *missus* here," Maxine said, shaking her glorious head. "Mrs. Whitherspoon is my mother-in-law, not me." She smiled at her own joke, but had better manners than to laugh. "You must call me Maxine."

"Right, so," Martin answered, but he couldn't bring hisself to add the *Maxine*.

She started walking, so Martin and I followed her, feeling the thick carpet squelch beneath us.

"Amy's just finishing getting herself ready in her boudoir, upstairs," she said to us over her shoulder. "So you boys can wait in the drawing room with the other guests. Make yourselves at home."

She pulled open a wood-paneled pocket door and revealed the very room we'd peeked into from the outside, that first day we seen Finnuala Whippet. I wasn't mad about the idea of going in through that inside door, of Maxine shutting us so tightly into the house, where we wouldn't even be able to see the front door. And upstairs there was a whole 'nother level, I knew, whole rooms and rooms of furniture up there, hovering over our heads. What was to keep it all from crashing down on top of us? I felt the walls straining from the weight of it.

"I'll just take your jackets," Maxine said.

And that was it. I had to leave, or go inside. Those was my choices. So I made sure my envelope was tucked well into my pocket, and then I peeled off my jacket. I pulled my sleeves down over my wristbones, touched my ducktail to make sure everything was in place, and then I pressed my hands into my stomach, to try and quell the storm that was pitching around in there. I filled up my lungs as best I could, and then I stepped inside.

Martin stepped over the threshold behind me, and I heard the sharp intake of his breath. The room smelled of woodsmoke, not turf, and indeed there was actual logs crackling orange on the glowy fire. The hardwood floors was even shinier up close, and I could just make out my red, curlicued reflection beneath me. The half a dozen huge windows stretched from floor to ceiling, and the cold sunlight gushed through. You could easily jump outta one of them windows if you had to—you wouldn't even have to bend.

Beano was already enthroned in one of the chairs beside the fire, and Martin made a beeline for him. He was dressed in short pants and wellies, which was ridiculous considering the cold, but he had on a striped party shirt beneath a flannel blazer, both of which fitted him nicely and made him look a bit slimmer than his usual self.

There was four other kids already there: a girl from one of the baby classes in a frilly party dress, who was sitting on her own and looking nervous, and then three freckle-faced brothers, who I recognized. The middle one was in our class—an eight-year-old. They was all wearing coonskin caps that I'd only ever seen drawings of, but which I knew was meant to be all the rage over in America and England. The youngest brother looked plainly uncomfortable in his, and he kept knocking it sideways to get a good scratch underneath. But the other two looked class, like real hearty pilgrims, and I thought of asking one of them could I try it on, but I was afraid they'd say no, and anyway I didn't wanna wreck my ducktail.

I had a good gander about the rest of the room and noted the covered tables that hadn't been there at our last visit. Behind these tables, standing up flawlessly on their shelves, was the armies of books, like a whole company of pint-sized soldiers. They stood rigid and proud with their dark leather shields pressed out in front of them, protecting theirselves til somebody would come along and pull one down to do battle. Their spines was all in dark leathers—greens and browns and reds and blacks, and most of them had gold lettering on them that made them gleam with promise. They looked richer, somehow, than most of the treasures Mrs. Hanley sold and traded and lended in her little two-room shop. I had to peel my eyes away from them.

The piano had been closed and its keys covered, a rug draped over its back so that it nearly took on the appearance of an old *Pavee*—a granny, hunched over and covered for warmth. Three items was stacked there on its back, wrapped in brightly colored papers with ribbons trailing off them. I stared at them ribbons, curled and dangling down in festive colors. They looked like nooses.

But I knew what they was: birthday presents. People had brought Finnuala Whippet birthday presents, of course they had. I felt my cowboy shoulders drop, my nose fill up with snot. I bit my lip, swallowed my breath.

Like most *Pavees*, me and Martin both knew roundabout when we was born—a year, a month, even. But travellers didn't have *birthdays* the way buffers did. Neither one of us had ever gave or got a birthday present in all our lives. But when I stood there, staring at them in their piano-topping splendor, they felt like a truth I'd knew all my life. The sweat that had been staying on the palms of my hands sprung at once to my forehead, my armpits, my toes, my ballsack. I darted over to Martin on the settee.

"Martin," I said urgently, while the smallest freckle-faced brother leaned over the back of Beano's chair and started twitching the tail of his cap in front of Beano's face for badness.

Martin was watching for a reaction from Beano, who was as undisturbed as ever, his wide smile unflinching. He leaned up on one arse-cheek and let go a silent and smelly warning in the boy's direction. Martin snorted and I elbowed him to attention.

"Martin!" I hissed again.

"Wha?" He finally looked at me, annoyed.

I put my hand up to cover my mouth, so nobody else would hear. "There's *presents*," I whispered, nodding my head toward the piano.

Martin's gaze followed the direction of my head-jerk, and a look of confusion spread acrosst his face. "For us?" he said.

I had to take a deep breath. "No, not for *us*, ya dickhead," I seethed. "For *Finnuala Whippet*."

"And?" He shrugged.

"And we haven't got one," I said in mounting desperation.

Martin cracked a smile at me. "What do you care, Romeo?" he said.

I glared at him.

"It's lovely to meet you *finally*," he mimicked Maxine and then licked and pursed his lips at me.

He really wasn't bothered. In that moment, I could have killed him. With my bare hands around his throat and not so much as a thought toward the eternal damnation of my soul, or Auntie Brigid's wailing grief, I could've knuckled down and strangled the life out of him no problem.

"Somebody's been talking 'bout yoooouuuu," he taunted.

I nearly wanted to warn him how close he was to bringing permanent mutilation upon his body, but then I glanced over and Beano was smiling acrosst at us. He'd heard the last bit.

"She does," Beano agreed. "She definitely fancies you." He was nodding and smiling.

It was all too much.

"Martin, would you shut your face for two seconds and listen to what I'm telling you?" I said, louder than I meant to.

My words knocked the good-natured grin from Beano's doughy face. I wished for a similar effect on Martin, but that was like wishing for a fish to jump outta the sea and land on your plate, fully cooked and drenched in butter.

"Wouldja ever catch yourself on?" Martin said then. "Quit being such a baby. She'll never even take no notice."

Beano was looking at me with real concern. He seemed to be weighing whether or not to get involved. He leaned forward, tried to drop his voice like mine. "What is it?" he said in a loud whisper. "What's the matter?"

I leaned in to meet him. "We didn't know about the presents," I confessed as quietly as I could.

He looked back at me blankly, confused. "Didn't know?" he said. "How d'ya mean?"

I felt the anger in me again, but only for a moment. Beano was simple. He wasn't tryinna rise me. He didn't understand. I looked around to make sure nobody else was minding us. "We've never been to a birthday party before," I whispered. "We didn't know we was supposed to bring presents."

Painfully slowly, the penny dropped and Beano nodded his head. He leaned back in his chair. He nodded some more and stared at us intently. "Really?" he said then.

I clenched and unclenched my jaw. "Really," I said.

He nodded some more. Then he said, baffled, "But how couldja not know, like?"

"It's like he told ya," Martin explained. "We've never been to a birthday party before."

Beano continued nodding. "But what about your own ones?" he asked then.

I had to hand it to Beano. At least he paused and really thought his questions through before he came out with them. He was maddening, but at least he was mindful—and he never gave up tryinna piece things together. I wouldn't've liked to live in his head for a day.

"We never had our own ones," I said.

"Never had your own birthday parties?" he said loudly.

"No," I answered.

He was really perplexed. The struggle of concentration in his face was enough to make me feel constipated just from looking at him. "So whatta ye do on your birthdays, then?" he asked. "I mean, I only ever had a real party once when I was six and Auntie Claire was visiting from Dublin, but apart from that, at least Mammy always has an old present or two for us, on the birthdays, and a special dinner. Would ye not know about the presents from your own mammies? Or did ye maybe think that only the mammies had to get presents, then?" His nodding grew more excited, as he felt he was beginning to put it together.

"No, Beano," Martin explained. "We don't have birthdays."

The nodding ceased at once, and I thought Beano would just keel over and die altogether, in his efforts to get his head around that one. He had a real heroics about him for not giving up though, and Martin, too, for the patience to explain it all. I just wanted it over quick, so's we could get back to the point. We didn't have a feckin' present.

"Don't have birthdays . . ." Beano was saying. He looked shattered.

"What I mean is, travellers don't always know when their birthdays *is*," Martin said. "Because we don't always be born in hospitals or have birth certificates and that. And we don't be mindful of calendars and dates the way ye do in school. So we don't wind up celebrating the birthdays with parties and presents, like."

Beano started to nod again, more cautiously this time.

"Plus, you know, every day is like a party when you're travelling," Martin said.

Beano's grin came back to him then, good-oh.

"Out on the *tober*, sleeping under the stars, always with a bit of music in the camp and the freedom of the road ahead. Who needs presents to lug around with you when the whole world is like a gift, waiting to be unwrapped?"

I rolled my eyes. Martin did have a great faculty for this kind of shite-talking, which I sometimes appreciated, but this was really not the time.

"I'll tell ya who," I interrupted. "Finnuala Whippet, that's who!"

Martin and Beano both looked over at me as if they'd forgot I was there.

"Who?" Beano asked.

"Amy," Martin answered.

"It's her birthday, and we've showed up here empty-handed like a couple of tramps," I went on, in my panic. "And it's all very well and good that every day's a party in Martin-land, but we need to find us a feckin' present already!"

"Good God, would you ever relax?" Martin said. "You're such a total spa. There'll be so many people and presents here, she won't even notice."

Beano nodded at this too, and we was all quiet for a minute. I just wasn't convinced.

"Then, on the other hand," Beano said, leaning in again, "if she really fancies Christy the way she seems to, she'll be looking for his present especially." He pushed back into his chair, pleased with the point he'd made.

I clutched at my stomach and tried to think what to do. I shouldn't be here. I had lucked my way into this house, into this party. Finnuala Whippet maybe even fancied me. It was too good to be true, and the moment it was beginning, it was all about to come crashing down around my head like upstairs furniture.

And that was the moment Patrick walked in, lugging a present so big, he could scarcely be seen behind it.

"Fuck," I said.

Even if by some miracle, it managed to slip the attention of Finnuala Whippet, Patrick would note it and he'd report it: no present from the dirty tinker camp. He glanced in our direction and gave his customary smirk, then struggled over to the piano, where he placed his huge present on the floor because it was too big to set on top with the others. Maxine was thanking him now, telling him he really shouldn't have, and he was smiling at her. He stood up then and straightened hisself, and even though he was only maybe a year older than us, he was already a hair taller than Maxine. He ran his hand through his dark, wavy hair.

My fish-heart was in my stomach, and my stomach was in my shoes. I eyed the windows, but couldn't see no real way out. Maybe we should just leave now, head back out the front door before the party started. Maybe I should fake a seizure. Delirium tremors.

I was, after all, an imposter. I didn't belong in this shirt, on this settee, with my flawless ducktail and pearlized snaps. I belonged with Dad and Martin and Granny and Jack, on the *tober*, which was better than this old wood-smelling room anyway. No matter how high the ceiling was, it wasn't the sky. I only belonged here long enough for a mooch or a swap or a mend of a kettle. Maybe long enough to sweep out the chimney for them, to earn a few bob. I wondered how my cowboy shirt would fare with the woodsmoke soot. Escape. I had to plan our escape.

Maxine dashed out to answer the door again, then arrived back with a half a dozen more kids, clutching shapes neatly creased into folded papers, shining ribbons draped over their fingers. Dutifully, they marched to the piano to unload their presents.

Patrick slouched onto the settee facing us and did his bird-voice again. "*Pa-Vees!*" One of his mates was there already, and when they laughed, I imagined slamming Patrick's head into the piano—opening its top, and sticking his head in there, and then yanking out the toothpick-arm til it fell right down and smashed his head like a nut. I bet it would make a real racket, smashing a head in a piano. A real jangly gong-song.

Maybe I could steal a present from somebody. Scratch out the name and pretend it was from me. But every present was wrapped, so what if I got a really horrible and frilly one, like a baby doll or a pink, ruffled dress or something? And what about the kid who'd actually brought that present? Wouldn't they squawk? I scrutinized the piano and tried to think, but my head was pounding. Feck.

"Would you catch hold of yourself?" I heard Martin's quiet voice in my ear. "You've muttered *feck* about ten times."

This was a genuine surprise. I hadn't known I was saying it out loud.

"You're scaring the locals."

Patrick smirked acrosst at us.

Feck.

And then I heard Beano's voice, breaking through the cloud of my dread, inserting itself into my thoughts.

"Christy," he said.

The loud whisper again.

"Christy!"

I'm sure I gave him an awful face. I was trying to think. "What?" I said irritably.

"You can have mine," he said.

"Your what?" I said.

"My present," he said.

Thump thump. I stared at Beano and he stared back at me. Martin folded his arms acrosst his chest in front of him.

"What'd you get her?" I said.

Beano screwed up his face like he was trying to remember. "A book," he said triumphantly.

I nodded, thinking. A book. That was good, very good. "What book?" I asked.

Beano made a grimace, and leaned back to study the ceiling. "Oh," he said. "What book, what book?" He rubbed his fingers against his teeth. "Oh!" he said. "I remember!"

I leaned forward.

"Hands Christanderson," he announced.

Never heard of it. "Okay." I nodded my head. "Okay."

Martin smacked me on the chest. "Christy!" he said. "Are you sure you don't mind, Beano?"

Since when had Martin sprouted manners?

"Sure I don't care," Beano said. "My sister brought a present as well. We'll just share her one. We'll fix the cards."

"That's awful good of you, Beano," Martin said.

I breathed and Martin glared at me.

"Thanks, Beano," I said, breathing again to steady myself.

Patrick was watching us with narrowed eyes, like he was waiting, just waiting. Like a chicken hawk—any excuse to pounce.

"Really," I said then, finally letting that feeling of sweet relief sweep over me. "Jeez, Beano, you're a lifesaver. Thank you."

He smiled his big, fat smile.

FIFTEEN

A parade of suit-clad fellas came through then, carrying platters and buckets and bowls of food and drink. The suit from my dreams, I realized, was what the help was wearing. They went single file to the empty tables, and loaded them down with mountains of ham and chicken and all kinds of creamy-looking salads and shiny breads. There was whole plates of nothing but biscuits and chocolates, and whole other plates of Tayto crisps, heaped into bright, foil-wrapped pyramids. One table was just nothing but rows and rows of minerals in small glass bottles of every color.

Oh Lord Jesus, the smell. I could already taste it, all of it. Swallow it down me, just from the scents of it. The ham, the bread. Butter. Salt. Cheese. The suited fellas spun into the room in clockwork choreography, and left things down on tables before spinning out again. It was all staged and directed by Maxine, who watched cheerfully while the final platter of sausages found its home on the table.

My stomach gave a loud rumble and my mouth watered like a pump. I'd never seen so much food in all my life. It was like being in a hotel restaurant and ordering the *everything*. And then Maxine seemed to remember something, and she gave a little snap to herself, and she scurried from the room, reappearing a couple of moments later with a steaming bowl.

"For you, Fergal," she sang, waving over at Beano.

Fergal? He gave her the thumbs-up and his trademark grin widened. "Ah, thanks, Maxine," he said. "You're very good."

"Beans," he explained, turning back to us. "She always has them special for me." As if he lunched here every Saturday, after his polo match. He smacked his lips.

I was still watching him when the now-full room grew quiet of a sudden, and everyone turned toward the door.

"*Amy!*" Maxine cried. "Don't you look *beautiful!*"

I steeled myself for the vision before I turned to look at her. Finnuala Whippet placed a saddle-shoed toe into the hardwood room, and I think I may have gasped. Thank God, whatever sound I made was lost in the general murmur.

"Your girlfriend looks well," Martin said.

"She's not my girlfriend," I grumbled.

Finnuala Whippet wore a pale blue poodle skirt with white socks, folded down on theirselves and sagging around her skinny ankles. She had a white, button-down top with short sleeves, like Maxine's, that was tucked in tight around her middle. Her dark hair wasn't in her usual trademark plaits, but all swept back from her face in an American-style ponytail. She'd a shiny, blue satin ribbon tied 'round her head, and her skin didn't look as see-through as usual. She pushed her glasses up on her little nose. She looked like a girl Elvis would fancy. Or okay, maybe more like a girl who would fancy Elvis. But she looked American, anyway, almost like a *teenager*. She looked like *Amy Whitherspoon*.

Maxine was at the gramophone now, and the volume was down low, but she turned it up and somebody was singing rock 'n' roll music. There was a swarm of girls around Finnuala Whippet now, and she disappeared in the crowd, but I kept my eyes glued to the sliver of blue ribbon I could still see, so's I wouldn't lose her. All the other boys was frozen stiff but the girls was swinging into action. The room was pulsing and still all at once—mayhem and still life. The commotion gave me hope.

All was madness for a while, and then a more-organized madness, with Maxine commanding us to "Eat, eat! Everybody eat!" and then, total chaos. I queued up, along with Martin and Beano, on one side of the heaping table, and someone handed me a plate. My plan was to watch the other plates, ahead and behind me, so's mine wouldn't grow too outrageous. But when I actually got stuck into it, I couldn't help myself.

The butters was arranged to look like small little roses, and I took eight of them, even though I only had the one roll because I didn't want to waste too much room on breads. I heaped on the roasted beef and the ham first, and then the cheeses (of which there was about five different colors), and then the salads, til the plate was actually in danger of toppling. There almost wasn't room for the sausages, but I managed to perch two of them on top of one of the salads. Martin (and a few others I noticed) did the same.

Beano's plate was covered from edge to edge with a fine layer of beans—just the one layer—like a lumpy film acrosst the plate. It was a bit shocking, actually, and I wondered would he go back for six or eight servings, and if not, how did he get to be that size, if that was all he ever ate. I was so engrossed in the food that I lost track of the blue satin ribbon, so I didn't turn around, at first, when there was a tap on my cowboy-shoulder. But then I heard her voice.

"Christy," and I spun so fast that one of the sausages went flying off my plate.

She had to jump her saddle shoes back to avoid the missile. I made a face, but she only laughed. I reached over and picked up the sausage. I wanted to put it back on my plate, but I had an idea, somehow, that it mightn't be the done thing. So I had the sausage in my hand, and she pointed to it.

"You gonna eat that?" She laughed.

I looked at the sausage and didn't know what to say. I sure as hell wanted to eat it. I was holding it in my fist.

"Happy birthday," I said instead, because that's what I'd heard other people saying.

"Thank you," she said, taking the sausage from me delicately, with two fingers, and hiding it behind a bowl on the table.

I watched it go. Mournfully. She took my napkin and wiped her two fingers on it, then handed it back. I was wondering how I could manage to get another sausage, when she reached toward me and flattened my collars down. The back of her hand brushed against my jaw and I could smell her, through all the fog of the meats and the butter, I could smell her, and she was bopping her head to the music and her skinny ankles was moving. She was dancing without realizing it, and my God but I could've sworn she was about to throw me in the back of her Cadillac and take me down to the local drive-in movies. I felt about nine million miles away from wagons and tents and wellies and fires. She smelled like fresh oranges, and I was sure, in that moment, that I would never have to go back. That I would grow comfortable in this Big House. That this party would last forever, and we would all become American teenagers here, with as many sausages as we could eat, and we would all turn blond and smooth-skinned with white teeth and rhythm.

"Great threads," she said, pulling back from me.

All I wanted in the world was for her to put her hands back on my collars, to brush against my jaw again. She was singing along to the rock-'n'-roll music, and I wished I could venture some comment, but my education about rock 'n' roll was limited to what Martin and me seen in the magazines we pored over in shops until the shopkeepers kicked us out, or whenever we was in a real big town with a cinema, and we managed to sneak in. All the Americans sounded like variously watered-down versions of Elvis to me—slick and foreign and larger than life. But, of course, Finnuala Whippet, with a

mother called *Maxine* who wore trousers and probably owned a television, would be an expert in all things American. She wore her
poodle skirt like a pro. She was tucking the ends of the blue satin
ribbon in behind the ears of her glasses.

"These things keep coming out," she said.

"You look," I started, and didn't know how to finish. "You look
nice."

Great, Christy. Way to sweep her off her feet. Every girl wants to
look "nice."

She smiled at me. She did look nice. *Real* nice.

"D'ya wanta see where Rex and Fidel are having their party?"
she asked.

I looked down at my plate and then back to her, and there was no
question, really. But I was sick at the thought of leaving the food
down, and I knew if I took my eyes off it, it'd be gone when I got
back. I wondered could I bring it with me without spilling it. Maybe
I could eat it on the way. I hadn't got a fork yet. She took my free
hand.

"C'mon," she said, and she was leading me toward the door.

Me and her and my plate full of food was going to be alone
together.

IN THE KITCHEN, FINNUALA WHIPPET took my plate from me and left
it on a high counter, which was surrounded by three stools. She
pulled one of them out and climbed up on it, one leg over one side,
the other over the other side. She had to fluff out the poodle skirt
from in between once she got herself settled.

The poodle was staring at me with its single beady eye. I climbed
up onto the next stool beside her because I figured that's what I was
meant to do. There was a door in the kitchen, leading out into the
back garden, and one of the maids opened it a crack, for to let out
some of the heat off the cooker. I was so relieved to see that tall sliver

of daylight, like God put it there for me as a favor, so's I'd be able to think and breathe. I looked at my heaping plate and wondered if it'd be too much to ask God for a fork, as well.

I'd hoped we'd be alone in the kitchen, but the big maid from earlier was there, along with two younger maids, both with cheeks a deep pink color. The big maid was issuing orders to the littler, pink-cheeked ones, and they was hopping to it. One of them brought us over a pair of forks and left them down on the counter. Hallelujah!

The fellas in the dream-suits was there too, standing waiting instructions. There was only two of them, I realized, and I wondered how they'd seemed to be a dozen when they was twirling through the party room with their platters and buckets and bowls. The big, solid kitchen table was cluttered with the remnants of the food preparation—splattered with flour and then littered with crusts and wrappers and a rolling pin and all manner of unrecognizable tools and gadgets. There was eight chairs around the table.

"Have you no brothers or sisters?" I asked Finnuala Whippet, because I just realized I hadn't seen none.

"No," she said. "Just me. Daddy wanted a whole army of us, but Mammy couldn't have any more after me, which suits her just fine, she says."

So Finnuala Whippet had a daddy. Of course, she *would* have one. I don't know why this should come as a surprise to me. I just never really considered it before, and come to think of it, he was nowhere to be seen neither, not even today, on his daughter's eleventh birthday.

"I'm not a boy," she said then, and I almost laughed, but I caught her face in time, and I seen how sad she looked when she said it—how far down the corners of her mouth turned.

"No," I said, and wasn't sure what else to add.

She definitely wasn't a boy.

"Daddy wanted a boy," she explained. "He wanted a whole load of boys, actually. But one at the very least, a son." She forced a quick smile.

"I wore blue, though! Next best thing." She smoothed her hands over her lovely blue skirt.

I couldn't believe the easy way she talked about her sadness. It wasn't just the ponytail and the shoes—she really *was* like an American. Not that I'd ever met a real American before, but in the pictures, they was always on about things normal people would never say out loud. I imagined Finnuala Whippet slept with her curtains thrown wide open because she wouldn't have no problem with people looking in on her, snoring in her nightdress and drooling on her pillow.

"I don't have none neither," I said, to try to make her feel better. "Brothers and sisters."

She handed me one of the forks, and took the other one up in her own hand. I hoped she wasn't going to share my food. She had plenty of her own food, after all. And then I remembered that, in fact, it *was* her food, all of it, and that I should really try and be more gracious. She took a nibble off one of the salads on her side of the plate. I stared at her. At least it was only salad.

"Your mammy couldn't have any more either?" she asked.

I took my first bite and felt my mouth spring full of the flavors of it. Sharp and tangy. Oh.

"No." I shook my head. And then for some reason I can't imagine, I also said, "I don't have a mammy."

"How d'ya mean?" she said, but she didn't really seem all that concerned. She was going in for another bite of salad.

I decided to fill my mouth up with roast beef so that I couldn't answer her, and also so she wouldn't get to it first and eat it out from under me. I stuck so much in there I could barely chew.

"Everyone has a mammy. You can't be born without a mammy," she reasoned. "Did she run off to be a film star or something?"

I shook my head.

"That's it, isn't it?" she said, giggling and elbowing me in the ribs. "She went off to Hollywood and now she's Maureen O'Hara, isn't she?"

I felt my cheeks going hot. She was taking the mickey outta me. Here I was, all gussied up, all hopeful, and she was making fun of me. I looked down at my cowboy sleeves and felt like an amadán. She probably believed my mother was a dirt-down bedraggled drunk in a gutter somewhere. Maureen O'Hara. I stabbed my fork into the remaining sausage.

"No, she's not Maureen O'Bleedin'Hara," I said. "She's dead, if you must know. And it was me killed her."

I was a little shocked at myself, but I couldn't help it. I was hardly going sitting here in her big, stupid house and let her rip the back outta me. I tried to make my face careless while I chewed. So I'd been wrong about her. So what? I didn't care. I looked at her mouth hanging open. I took another bite of my skewered sausage.

"I—I didn't mean . . ." she said.

"That it would be ridiculous for Maureen O'Hara to have a tinker for a son?" I finished the sentence for her.

"Christy, no," she said. "I promise you, I didn't mean that. I was only messing."

Her eyes was welled up, and I told myself that if she let go a tear, I would slap her in the face and then I would storm out. I put my fork down.

"I'm sorry, Christy," she said.

Fuck sake, what was wrong with me at all? I looked at her face again—there wasn't no malice there. Jesus, I needed to relax or I was gonna wreck everything. I cleared my throat.

"I know," I said. "I know, I'm sorry. Me too."

She had a way of making me feel like there wasn't maids and fellas in suits standing all around us. She squeezed my knee in a tickly way, like Dad sometimes did, only she wasn't as strong as him, so it was different. I squirmed on my stool and felt hot right up the back of my neck. I could smell the oranges again.

"I wasn't making fun," she said again. "I promise, I didn't mean that. I'm sorry about your mammy."

She was biting her lip. Eager. I could see it was important to her that I believed her.

I nodded. "I know," I said again. "She died when I was born, seven minutes after I was born."

I could feel my shoulders lifting, my chest expanding. My breath carried the words free of my mouth, and I could feel the expelled weight of them. They'd been with me for so many years, I'd never realized how heavy they was. I'd never told them to nobody before—not freely and gently. Not just because I wanted to. I wondered if this was how Jack felt whenever we took the yoke off him. I sat up straighter on my stool and breathed. Maybe I could show her my mother's picture, show her how beautiful she was. Maureen O'Hara was nothing.

A filthy dog came ambling into the kitchen then, beating the side of Finnuala Whippet's poodle skirt with its tail. It couldn't be Rex—it just couldn't be. Rex the hunter'd be groomed within an inch of his life. He'd have a sheen off his coat, trimmed toenails, a moist and healthy pink tongue, clear eyes, and a splash of cologne.

"There's Rex!" Finnuala Whippet said with terrific affection, and bent down from her stool to give him a rub behind the ears.

Good Lord, but Rex was shook-looking. He was scraggly, with patchy fur and a couple of bald spots that was oozing something pinkish and lumpy. He moved with a slow caution, like he was rid-dled with arthritis, and every step was a struggle. His eyes had a film acrosst them, and the tongue hung crooked out the side of his mouth. He panted heavy and his breath was like mothballs. He made Fidel look like the Elvis of the dog world.

Rex licked Finnuala Whippet's face, and when she sat up again, she had a tongue-print acrosst one lens of her steamed-up glasses.

Fidel wandered in behind, but kept his distance, sitting and watching with a look of unmistakable disdain acrosst his face. If he could've spoken at that moment he would've told me that he'd never forgive me for this.

"D'ya not miss her?" Finnuala Whippet asked, and for a moment I was confused.

She took off her glasses and wiped them on her poodle skirt. They'd made little red dents in the sides of her nose, and her eyes struggled without them.

"My mammy?" I said.

"Yeah."

"I guess." I shrugged. "I never knew her."

We ate side by side for a few moments then, in silence, and I was surprised by how quiet it actually was, given the number of other people in the room. I could hear myself chewing. Just as in the party room, the girls was aflutter with activity around us, and the fellas was stock-still, like statues. The big maid was issuing her orders without even opening her mouth. The other two flitted around her, reading her hand signals and her face.

"My family moves around a lot, too," Finnuala Whippet said. "We've only lived here a year."

The plate was starting to look empty. I could eat a whole lot more.

Finnuala Whippet dangled her fork out, and Rex leaned up to give it an enthusiastic going-over. When he was done, she took one last lick of it herself, and I didn't know whether to be impressed or disgusted. Fidel watched the exchange, practically rolled his eyes, and then threw hisself down on the floor with a yawn.

"So I guess we've a lot in common," she said. "With all the moving, and being only-children, and that."

For a second I thought she was taking the piss again. I looked into her face and she pushed her glasses back up her nose.

"I guess so," I said skeptically. "D'ye have a television?"

She looked at me strangely and shook her head. "What would we do with a television?" she said.

"Look at it?" I shrugged.

She shook her head again. "We listen to the wireless," she answered. "Maxine loves Radio Luxembourg."

"D'you always call her Maxine?" I asked.

"No way," she said, laughing. "Everybody else calls her Maxine. I call her Mammy."

"Well, she's not really all that *mammy*ish, is she?"

"She is so," Finnuala Whippet sniffed defensively.

"I only meant," I said, "you know. She's not hefty or tired-looking. And she doesn't have no lines on her face. And she wears *trousers*."

"Well, yes," she said then. "I suppose she is quite *glamorous*, isn't she?"

Finnuala Whippet sucked in her cheeks and batted her eyelashes at me. I laughed. Finnuala Whippet was swinging her spindly legs from the stool beneath her, and Rex was watching closely, hoping for another lick of food.

"Thank you, Mary," Finnuala Whippet called suddenly, and I realized she was talking to the big maid, who only nodded in response.

Finnuala Whippet was scooting her bottom over to the edge of her stool and she was dropping down now, to stand up. There was nothing left on the plate except four of the little roses of butter. I wanted to take them with me.

"Will we go back?" she said.

And I didn't want to, but I said, "Sure" because it was her birthday party and I reckoned she'd be missed eventually, so I hopped off my stool to join her.

"Finnuala," I said, and she looked at me like I was crazy.

"Amy," I tried again.

"Who's Finnuala?" she interrupted.

"Em," I said. "You are."

Her eyebrows arched up over the tops of her glasses.

"I mean, that's what Martin and me called you before we knew your proper name," I said. "Finnuala Whippet."

Holy God, was nothing sacred? Was there nothing I wouldn't tell this girl? She laughed out loud and clapped her hands in front of her.

"Finnuala Whippet," she howled. "That's the best one I ever heard!" She was laughing so hard she was bent double over her big blue skirt. "D'ya hear that, Rex?" she said. "You can call me Finnuala Whippet from now on."

And now she was reaching up under her glasses to wipe the tears that had collected at the corners of her eyes. I was laughing too—I couldn't help it. Finnuala Whippet flounced over to the kitchen door and pushed it open. She was still laughing, but she managed to get hold of herself. I followed her through the swinging door, and the hallway beyond was darkened and quiet, like a cave. The door swung shut behind us. No one else was there. I looked at her baggy white socks and her saddle shoes on the plush carpet in front of me. She was walking fast. I lunged for her hand in the dimness and the calm. I caught her fingers in mine. She spun around to face me.

"Amy," I said, and we was standing as close together as I had ever stood to anybody.

I wasn't dreaming. She wasn't purple. My eyes was open, and I was holding her hand in mine. The scent of oranges was so strong I thought I might swoon.

"Amy, I never told nobody about my mammy before," I said quietly. "I mean, not like that."

I could hear a tick-swish, tick-swish, and I couldn't tell what that sound was. I didn't think it was my heart. I was a couple inches taller than her, and her face was tipped back, looking up at me. She nearly glowed.

"I won't tell anyone," she whispered, and she was that close I could feel her breath on my face when she said it.

I believed her. And then, neither one of us breathed. We didn't move. We was suspended. And then there was a loud GONG so close to my ear, I near jumped out of my skin. A grandfather clock, the tick-swish. I was clutching my chest, it'd scared me that bad. Finnuala Whippet giggled at me and the clock gonged a second time.

"It's gone two o'clock already!" she said. "You're missing the whole party!" And she spun on her shoe and started to drag me down the hall.

"Amy," I said again, and this time she turned around and looked at me impatiently.

"Maxine is going to think we ran off together," she said, and she waggled her eyebrows at me in the same way her mother had earlier.

I flushed. "Just one more thing," I said.

She nodded and I took a deep breath. I squeezed my eyes shut.

"I didn't bring a present," I said. I kept my eyes shut. I didn't want to look at her. I didn't want to see her disappointment.

"I didn't know," I said. "I've never been to a party like this before, and Beano's awfully good, and he said we could give you his one, so Patrick wouldn't eat us alive, but really, it's not from us, and I didn't even pick it out or nothing, but I will—I'll get you something, and—"

"Oh!" She interrupted me. "I don't care at all."

And I opened my eyes just in time to see her stretching up toward me.

Slow, slow. Slow.

Tingles.

Loose joints. Dampness and movement. Softness. Stiffness. Her lips. They barely touched me, brushed me. Slow. And then: spinning. Goose pimples. Music—I swear I heard a pipe organ. Oh. Shadowy, daytime stars. Stars! And that mad, rushy, dizzy, powerful scent of peeling, stripping oranges. Naked of their skins.

———

AFTER THAT, THERE WAS THE largest cake I ever seen (and the only cake I ever tasted), with pink icing and two different choices of ice cream. (I had both.) Then there was a dance contest, which was a flop because none of the boys wanted to ask none of the girls to dance.

Finnuala Whippet caught my eye while everyone was standing around awkwardly waiting for it to be over, and I prayed very fervently that she wouldn't ask me to dance. I had a feeling that a girl who went around shaking hands with boys and then kissing them at her birthday party wouldn't think twice about asking for a dance, but she only winked at me and looked away, which was a tremendous relief. From the safety of my chair beside Beano, I could replay our kiss in my mind, privately, without nobody noticing. Over and over. Beano didn't want his cake, but Martin made him take a slice anyway, and then the two of us split it. It was the most beautiful thing I'd ever ate, and if I hadn't had to share it with Martin, I would've made it last hours.

Then there was Pin-the-Tail-on-the-Donkey, musical chairs, something called "hot potato," and finally, Maxine dragged the piano bench out into the center of the room, and her daughter sat down on it obediently. She folded her two legs beneath her and they disappeared inside the poodle skirt. Then began the endless stream of presents, which Maxine would lift from the piano and admire, before passing them along to her daughter.

There was two Hula-Hoops, a skipping rope with yellow handles, a record by Cliff Richard, loads of dolls and a couple of jumpers, a signed photograph of Elvis that Kathleen had sent away for (and everyone was mad impressed with), a set of colored pencils, a wooden kaleidoscope, a 100-piece jigsaw puzzle of Buckingham Palace, and a sparkling pair of red and white roller skates which Maxine insisted was "from your father." It was like a bleedin' toy factory had been hijacked and delivered wholesale to the Whippet residence. Our borrowed book-gift came and went with very little remark.

The gigantic present from Patrick was last. It was an ornate doll-house with shutters on the windows and tiny people inside doing various things. A tiny girl sat at the tiny piano. Her tiny dad smoked a tiny pipe and read a tiny newspaper.

"Would you look at that!" Maxine gushed.

I tried not to notice how much Finnuala Whippet loved it.

"What does the newspaper say?" Maxine said, and Finnuala Whippet picked up the tiny dad and his paper.

He stayed sitting down, with his leg crossed over at the knee, even after getting picked up by the head.

"It says the war is over!" Finnuala Whippet said.

Everybody laughed and then clapped for Patrick's present.

"Oh, Patrick—you're too good," Maxine said. "You must thank your mother for us."

I felt sick to my stomach. But Finnuala Whippet was looking at me, steadying me.

"Say thank you to Patrick," Maxine instructed her daughter, and for the first time, I caught something in that cultured voice that wasn't covered with a coat of varnish, something raw.

She glanced from her daughter to the smug and shiny Patrick, his dark hair flopping over his forehead. Why couldn't he at least be ugly, the bastard.

"Thank you. Patrick," Finnuala Whippet finally said.

But not like she meant it.

DAD AND FINTY BUILT A great campfire that night, and then Martin filled everybody up with stories of the party. The food, the music. He skipped the best parts though—never told them about the books, or Finnuala Whippet's saddle shoes. I kept my own stories private, and afterwards, while Dad and Finty played music and Granny and Brigid sang, I went off dreaming in my head all over again.

With all that excitement the camp was late going to bed, but still, I was wide-awake, wide-awake. I'd never sleep again, maybe. How could you sleep when you'd a kiss like that to ponder? I tried to brush my fingers acrosst my lips in the dark—in the same way Finnuala Whippet's lips had done—but there wasn't no sparks. I couldn't smell no oranges. I gave up and rolled over to give Dad a good shove to try and shake the snores out of him, but he only went going louder.

And then I remembered with a start: the envelope tucked into my jacket pocket. Jesus God, how could I forget a thing like that? I was on my feet without even thinking, and then I stopped frozen and had a good cautious listen to make sure all the camp was as sleeping as Dad. Silence.

I took the lantern with me, and Dad stirred when the handle made a little clink as I lifted it, but then he spluttered and snored again. I slipped out through the tent flap and then battened it back down behind me so's Dad wouldn't catch a draft and waken.

I crept out of the tent and over to the wagon. Fidel seen me and lifted his head. Either he was too tired after the party, or he was still annoyed. He dropped his head back onto his front paws and closed his eyes. I hopped into the wagon and went straight to the press, opened the latch, swung the door on its rusty hinge. My coat was hanging inside. I reached in, felt for the paper jammed into the pocket, and drew it out.

I put the jacket on me, and then followed the sound of Jack's bell down the road, found our low spot in the wall, and set the dark lantern up beside me. This moment was too big to endure alone, and Jack was trustworthy. He could share my secret. I lit the wick, and then I could see him—only a few feet away in the new light. He blinked at me, stepped toward me.

I lifted the envelope in my shaking hands. Mr. Guinness's pink head was on the stamp in the corner, and the postmark said "Luimneach." My name was in authentic typeface on the front. It looked real official.

And there was time, even then, to turn back, to change everything that would happen. There was still time. I could've fed the sealed envelope to Jack. I could've stood up on the wall and let the wind whip it out of my hand and off into the night-fields. I could have prayed for guidance. Instead, I took a deep breath and ripped the envelope open along one end.

"Well, Grandda," I said. "Here we go. Here we go, Jack."

The answers I'd been waiting for. My mammy-mystery solved. The paper slid out of its wrapper and into my hand. My mother with her graceful hand cocked against the light of the sun. But I immediately noticed things I hadn't seen before. The severe man beside her, smiling, trying, his hand clamped like a padlock on her slender elbow. That round and jolly baby on her hip. In the new copy, they was all cleaner, crisper. My headline was as clear as the one in the tiny dollhouse newspaper.

"KIDNAPPED!" the headline said. "Local Boy Missing; Itinerants Suspected."

Itinerants was what newspapermen called travellers because it was meant to be nicer than calling us tinkers, but Dad said it was worse. He said it made us sound like hobos, which I didn't really mind because a hobo seemed something like a clown, but Dad said it was an abusive term altogether. I read on.

Under the photograph, the caption said, "Mr. and Mrs. William and Nora Keaton of Ballycinneide. Their son William has been missing since Tuesday night."

William.

William.

Nora.

I read it again. I tried to breathe. Jack stepped toward me like as if to catch me.

Then,

> William Keaton, aged eight and a half months, went miss-ing from his Ballycinneide home Tuesday night. Local garda are struggling to piece together the mystery of what happened, after receiving conflicting reports from the boy's parents.

William. Aged eight and a half months.

> According to Garda Finnerty, it was Mr. William Keaton, the boy's father, who first reported the child missing at approximately four a.m. on Wednesday. But when guards questioned the mother about the abduction, Mrs. Nora Keaton claimed that the child was gone visiting in a neighboring village with her sister. Those claims are now believed to be the product of Mrs. Keaton's confusion after the ordeal. Mrs. Keaton's sister, Ms. Millicent Cleary, who is a schoolteacher in Rathnaveen, confirmed that she does not have custody of the child.

Millicent Cleary. From my birth certificate—my godmother.

> "Please God, we'll find young William safe, and he'll be returned home to be reunited with his mother, where he belongs," Ms. Cleary added.
>
> Upon further investigation, it seems the guards are concentrating their investigation on a group of itinerants who had recently been halting in the area. There appears to be some evidence that the abductor was among those itinerants, and further that he was personally known to

the Keaton family. Guards declined to comment further at this stage of the investigation.

"Our top priority is to get the boy William home safely," Garda Finnerty said. "We can worry about appointing blame later."

I leaned against Jack. Leaned my whole weight against him like he was a ladle and I was the soup. I felt like the soup.

"It's me," I whispered. "Oh my God, Jack."

And my mouth fell open and I couldn't make another sound after that, or even a breath. Jack buoyed me up as best he could, so that I didn't fall over dead in the road. His heart beat for me, and his lungs breathed for me, and somehow the warmth in his neck and his face kept the worst chill of that shock from invading me and killing me clean dead on the spot.

After some time, when I was able to muster the courage, I looked at the photograph again. It was shaking, so I had to pin it down against the wall with my finger. I breathed my liquid breath and tried to spill it out of my mouth, but it wouldn't budge. Instead, at long last, tears.

My mammy smiled at me from the page. She shielded herself from the sun, and it was *me* on her hip. I was that baby, reaching for her. All my life, I'd been reaching for her.

SIXTEEN

I don't remember how I got there, but there I was, flying through the air of our tent like a crane, landing with an awful, brutal collapse of all my weight on Dad, as heavy as I could make myself. I wanted to be like a boulder, and crush him. But instead, I was straddling him like he was a horse, and my hands was at his throat, and his eyes was open, and he gasped, but even though it wasn't a fair fight, he still won.

And he pried my smaller fingers off his neck, and he grabbed my two wrists, so now I was writhing and flailing on top of him, but useless. I couldn't move. I struggled, and he threw me off him, pinned me down into the tick with one arm. He slapped me hard acrosst the face, and I was crying, but not from the slap.

"What the fuck are you playing at?" he shouted, and his hand was in the air, and I knew he would hit me again, but I didn't care.

"*You're not my father!*" I screamed, and then I spit in his face.

I actually spit in his face. And I thought that woulda brought a shower of slaps down on me, and a couple of fists into the bargain, but Dad just sighed and let his head slump back. He knew better than to let me up. I squirmed beneath the weight of his arm, and he rubbed his still-waking face with his free hand. He wiped my spit off him.

"What are you talking about, Christy?" he said tiredly.

"This," I said, and I waved the newspaper in his face.

Dad glanced at it in the dark and shook his head. "This again?" he said. There was confusion in his features, like he'd seen a ghost. "I thought you burned that," he said, blinking. He rolled onto his back and lifted his arm off me.

"Well, I didn't."

And maybe it was the defiance of my tone that gave him pause and dread, instead of anger.

"I see that," he said, slowly. "But what is it about that damn photograph that has you so worked up?"

I sat up and shoved the newspage closer to his face. "This isn't the same one as before," I said. "It's a new one, with the story attached. I sent away for it. Read it."

He took it from me reluctantly, held it between his fingers. "Where's the lamp?" he said, feeling around for where he'd left it before bed.

"It's here," I said, and I crawled toward the tent flap to retrieve it.

I lit the wick, and the tent glowed up with light. Dad blinked his nighttime eyes against it. He sat up and looked at the newspage. His hand shook, too, in the quiet. Then he let it drop to the ground between us.

"So what?" he said. "This is nothing. A misunderstanding . . ."

"*Stop it!*" I screamed at him. "*Just stop it. I know everything!*"

"Would ya whisht, will ya, you'll waken the whole camp," he said.

"I don't care if I wake the whole fucking county," I said, pounding my hands against the tick. "Enough! You may tell me the truth!"

"What truth!" Dad said, exasperated.

"My truth!"

My hands was balled up into fists, and I was afraid I'd launch myself all over again.

"Where is my mother?" I picked up the newspage again and stabbed a finger against her face in the photograph. "Where is she?"

Dad shook his head. "She's gone, son. And I know it must be hard for you, growing up without her. But haven't I done all right for the two of us? Amn't I enough?"

I stared at him, but he wouldn't meet my eye.

"You let me believe I killed her."

I felt fierce violent with all this new truth welling up in me. Dad sighed.

"How could you do that to me?" I said. "Seven minutes—all my life, that's what I believed. That I only had seven minutes of my mother's love. That she *died* for me to be born."

He couldn't look at me. "I don't know what you want from me, Christy."

I drew my knees up in front of me, propped my elbows there, and let my head drop into my hands. My voice was a hollow squeak in the tent. A mouse.

"I seen my baptismal cert," I said softly.

Dad took a sharp breath, and the sound of it was like the blade of a dagger unsheathed.

"I seen it. Father Francis showed it to me. My name is William. Finty is my godfather. Millicent Cleary is my godmother, my mother's sister."

I scanned the article for the part with her name. I read it aloud.

"Mrs. Keaton's sister, Ms. Millicent Cleary, who is a schoolteacher in Rathnaveen," I said. "That's her. Millicent Cleary, my godmother.

And this . . ." I turned the photograph around to face him and pointed to the happy little baby. "This is me. William Christopher *Keaton*. This is me, with my *mother*, who was supposed to be dead the day I was born. Here she is holding me, eight months old."

Dad covered his face with both hands.

"You can't pretend no more," I said.

He shuddered. "Oh, Christy." His shoulders trembled, and he hid his eyes behind his hands. "I'm so sorry." His voice was wet with guilt. "Oh, Jesus, son."

"Don't call me that," I said. "I'm not your son." I felt my lips turning to stone, my whole face hardening. "You have to tell me the truth now," I said. "You have to tell me everything."

And then there was silence for a few minutes. Or a mostly-silence, where it's only the sounds of breaths and tears and terrors, and long-held truths yielding and giving way, leaving only a chalky, ghostly powder behind them. I was wholly eroded then; I was dirt falling into the ocean.

"Tell me," I said again.

Dad sat up, shook hisself up, and turned the lantern down. I folded my legs beneath me and set the newspage on my knee. He faced me, so's our knees was touching. He reached over and took my hands in his big, rough ones, but I took them back. Then he took a deep breath of preparation, and I thought he might exhale my whole life's truth in one big breath of hours.

"Okay," he said. "Okay."

And finally he looked at me, and his eyes searched my face, groped into my own eyes, but I don't know what he was looking for there. Maybe he was hunting for the seeds of forgiveness, to see if it would be possible, after all this.

"Your mother," he said. "She . . . I . . . I loved her, very much. Very much."

He'd been lying to me for so long, I could tell he didn't know where to start, how to tell this truth.

"Just tell me if it's true, what the article says," I asked. "Did you take me from her? Did you steal me?"

Dad's eyes was damp, and he breathed with his mouth open. "Not like that, son," he said quietly. "Not like they said. Sure you was already mine. You was *mine*."

"But I was hers." I pointed to my mother.

Dad nodded and his lips trembled. "You was," he said. "That's true. But I just, I couldn't leave you there. I couldn't survive without you. I couldn't *breathe* without you. Jesus, Christy, you was this helpless little thing. You was so beautiful. My boy."

He stroked my cheek and his tenderness shocked me. It was so confusing, to see him like this. My gruff, fearless father, reduced to pleading.

I felt a surge of angry joy. "But maybe I can't breathe without her," I said.

He winced.

"Maybe that's what's wrong with me, the way I cramp up walking into a house, but can't never stop thinking that I need one," I said. "Did you never think about that? That it might fuck me up, thinking I'd killed her?"

"I'm sorry." Dad shook his head.

And for the first time in my life, I realized what a stupid, futile thing that was to say. "Yeah," I said, slipping the newspage into my pocket.

I crouched and moved over to the flap of the tent.

"Me too."

THE COLD AIR WAS GOOD for me. It washed my lungs clean of this new grief, and that's what I needed it to do. I needed some time, before I could face Dad, before I could listen to whatever he had to say for hisself. It felt like all my life had been sitting up on a high shelf, and suddenly that shelf had come loose from the wall. When the shelf crashed down, my life slid off, upside down. Everything was a jumbled mess, and I couldn't even think how to start cleaning it up again.

I swung myself up into the climbing tree and then rolled over so's I was hugging the branch. I pressed my face into the rough bark and remembered the way Dad's callused fingers had felt against my cheek. I could hear him weeping in the tent, the selfish bastard. Muffled sobs. Great heaving, shuddering racks of strange tears. I wondered if my mammy had wept like that when she discovered me gone. When she looked into my crèche and seen the rumpled blankets, the soft absence. A ghost-baby. I pressed my face harder into the scratchy cracks of the aged wood. She might be out there somewhere.

"Grandda," I whispered, because I needed some extra guidance now, and nobody else felt real to me no more.

I reached into my pocket and felt the new newspage, but it was cold, empty. It was ghostless.

"Why?" I said, from the back of my throat.

But there was almost never any point in asking that.

After some time, Dad came out of the tent, drew hisself close to the fire, and built it up again. He'd one of our quilts draped 'round his shoulders, and in the budding firelight, I could see that his face was swollen, his raw eyelids was weary of tears. He almost didn't look like Dad. He didn't see me in the tree, so I stayed quiet there, and I watched him. He filled the kettle with water from a standing bucket and then drove the pothook into the ground over the fire for to make hisself a cup of tea. He sat on one of the lawn chairs until the tea was ready, and then he took two gulps before he collapsed into tears again. He dropped the cup onto the ground between his feet and used both hands to cover his face. He was a trembling heap.

I dropped down from the tree and went over to the fire. I sat in the empty chair beside him and waited, but he stayed bent over.

"Stop crying," I said, after a few minutes. "Why're you crying?"

I was angry that he should be the crying one, instead of me. I was jealous of them tears. I never even seen him cry when Grandda died, and now here he was falling apart just when I needed him most. But with my words, his shoulders went still, and I could see that he was wiping his face under the quilt.

Then he sat up to face me. "I don't want to lose you," he whispered.

I wished I could make some grand gesture of defiance, but I couldn't think of nothing that would hurt him the way I wanted to. He didn't want to lose me? After everything he'd stole from me? My mammy. How could he say such a thing?

"Never mind that," I said. "It's my turn. I want to know everything. You have to tell me."

Dad noticed his toppled teacup at his ankles, and seemed sort of embarrassed by it. He reached down to pick it up, filled it out of the kettle again, and handed it to me. I slurped and he cleared his throat. He stretched his feet out toward the fire and stared into the flames.

"Your mother was the most beautiful woman I ever seen." There was a catch in his throat, a body-reluctance to give up this story, but his face sagged with resolve. He knew he had to.

He glanced at me and then back to the fire. "I knew from the moment I clapped eyes on her that our destinies was intertwined."

And then he looked me in the eye, steady as you like, and finally I recognized him again, the hard man I'd knew all my life. His eyes could be like anchors when he was telling the truth. I welled up, but he went on ahead.

"Your grandda and a few of your uncles and us was stopping near her family house, you see." His voice was gathering strength.

"House," I said. "So she wasn't a *Pavee* at all?" I sat back in my lawn chair and tried to let the fullness of that truth finally drop over me.

"No, son, she wasn't a *Pavee*."

I mean, I guess I'd knew it ever since I first seen the photograph, but hearing my father say it out loud, well, that was something else. I shivered, and Dad leaned forward in his chair, unwrapped the blanket from his shoulders.

"She was a buffer," he said, flinging the blanket out like a wing, and then folding it 'round my ears.

There was crickets and night noises in the fields.

"I'm a buffer," I whispered, my words like water.

"You're not," Dad said, and his eyes flashed in the quickening firelight. "And she wasn't a normal buffer, anyway. She was differ-ent. Will I tell you about her?"

I nodded.

"Her father was a very wealthy landowner," Dad said. "And he'd gave us all a bit of work pulling beetroot. Myself and Finty, and your grandda, and your uncle Michael, too—that was before he went over to England. And there was a few other *Pavees* besides—he'd that much land, he'd to hire an army of us to keep up with it, and he telled us he'd keep us in work for the whole of the harvest season, if we was willing to stop that long. After the beets was in, we'd pull the leeks and radishes and cabbage and carrots, and then he'd even keep us on for cleaning and sorting and packing, preparing that autumn harvest to ship over to England. It was nearly two months' work if we wanted it, and a great decent wage, he offered."

He watched me while he talked, watched how his words fell acrosst my face, like Hansel leaving them bread crumbs in the forest.

"We wasn't used to halting that long in one place, Christy, but sure it was a lovely little township, and the work was grand, so we stayed. The beet was hopping out of the ground that season, and into the bag," he said, and he even smiled.

After all, Dad was a *seanchaí*, a great storyteller of the ancient tradition, and he wasn't going wrecking the greatest story of all my life just on account of our brokenheartedness. He would give it heaps.

"Sure I'd only to walk along the rows with my sack gapped open, and in them beetroots would jump—the size of heads. And not just any heads, mind. No, these was great large heads like the one your uncle Finty has setting on those two insufficient shoulders of his. The biggest, reddest crop of agitated beet I ever did see, Christy, and I practically running down the rows of the field to keep up with it leaping out of the ground."

I couldn't help seeping into the story, sinking, letting it take me. The anger was still in me, and something worse, some new and permanent feeling of betrayal. But for these moments, if I let them, my dad's words could rinse me clean of all that. I wanted the freshness of them words. My story.

"So I'd taken on the work in the high field myself—the field nearest the house—and I was nearing the end of the row. It was a chilly enough day, but I was in a full sweat from my work when your mother came stomping out the front door of that big house, and slammed it behind her with an authority that shook the very timbers of it. The ground itself was throbbing with her anger, and it pulsed acrosst the field to where I was stood. The beet heads was nervous and juggling theirselves in the bag, but your mam took no notice of none of it. I was flummoxed. And the anger just kept beating acrosst that field in a symphony of waves."

I pulled the newspage back out of my pocket and stared at her again.

"What was she wearing?" I asked. "Did she look like this then?"

I was greedy for a new image of her, to replace that broken, purple-haired one in my imagination, and this flat, gray one on the page. I wanted to see more of her now, her realness, in different colors and shadows.

"She wore a thin cotton blouse with a high neck," Dad said, "and with little, tiny buttons all spilt down the front of it. Them buttons was so delicate I wondered how they could contain her, powerful as she was. And a woolen skirt wrapped and folded around her legs like as if she was a present. She was shocking beautiful, son."

I closed my eyes and tried to dress her in the clothes my father described.

"She froze me, Christy, when I seen her there in the field. Her arms was folded acrosst the front of herself, and she stomped her heel as she let go a curse—a word I'd never heard from a lady before, nor never again after. It boomed out of her like the murderous blast of a cannon."

"What word was it?" I asked.

"Never mind that," Dad said.

"But was it at least a proper swear word, like? I mean like *shit* or *feck* or one of them? Or was it one of them ones that Auntie Brigid says are swear words but really isn't, like just putting the word *bleedin'* in front of something ordinary?"

Dad gave me a look. "She was hardly a reprobate, Christy," he said. "And besides that, you're fixing on the wrong point. Wasn't her face angrier than them words, anyway? *That's* the article, Christy— that's what I'm getting at: she had a fire in her. I was nearly afraid them lengthy eyelashes of hers would go right up in flames, if you could've seen what was blazing there."

"Oh," I said. "She'd long eyelashes?" That sorta detail was hard to see in the photograph.

"The longest in all Ireland," he said. "You'd trip over them."

Just like Grandda'd said. He'd always been trying to tell me the truth, and now, at last, he'd managed it. He'd made sure.

"It took her some time," Dad went on, "but she managed to compose herself before she returned inside the house. The waves of her fury tapered off. She doused the flame in her cheeks and her eyes. The beet finally settled itself and went limp in my bag. And what was left of her anger she simply folded up into a fist-sized piece, and exhaled into the afternoon breeze. It scattered on the wind and went to live among the crops, harmless or cancerous.

"When she turned toward the house to go, I realized: it was too late for me. In just those few moments, I was undone. She disappeared inside, and I dropped right down on my two knees in the field where I was, and I says to the good Lord that she was the only thing I'd ever wanted in all my life. For that was all it took for me to see that she was different to the rest of her people," he said. "She was like us—your uncles and aunties and me, she was like *our* women, like *our* people. She had a heart and a soul of freedom in her, and by God, she was a prisoner in that house. The front door was like a mouth that licked its lips and swallowed her up when she went inside. I half expected it to burp and sigh afterwards; that's how irretrievable she felt to me. Still, I was determined to emancipate her from that suffocating pile of brick.

"I didn't mention my feelings to no one, not even your uncle Finty," Dad explained, "because I knew what they'd say. 'Leave it alone, Christopher,' they'd've said to me. 'Her kind is nothing to do with us,'" Dad said, using a sensible voice that was meant to stand in as the whole of the family.

"It was a terrible situation altogether, Christy. I knew that if your grandparents found out, it'd bring a terrible shock and shame into the family. After all, it was no secret what her people thought of ours. They was nice people, kind. And her father was a good man. But they was buffers, you see, and very, very wealthy ones, at that. And what was worse . . ."

Dramatic pause.

"They was Protestants."

This may've shocked me if I'd learned it on its own, of course. But in the grand scheme of the evening's revelations, it felt like a nothing. Like a wart or a hiccup—hardly cause for astonishment.

"Somehow," Dad went on, "I just *knew* your mother wouldn't feel the way other buffers did. I knew she would reject the notions other people had of us, if only I could give her the chance. And then finally came the day when that chance appeared. And it was up to me to show her what kind of people we really was.

"That day, I seen your mam down the side of the road," he said. "Herself and the older sister had run their motorcar into a ditch with a flat tire. The like of which I'd never fixed before, of course, but I was anxious to impress your one. So up I went, before I could even think to stop myself, and asked if they'd be needing a hand. 'Well of course we do, you simpleton,' the sister said to me with her eyes all rolling around in her forehead. 'We're hardly standing here for the view.'"

The voice for the sister was great *craic*—mewling and rotten-toothed.

"Was that Millicent?" I said.

"That was her, all right," Dad said. "And your mam was disgusted with her, but she wouldn't redress her in front of me. Instead, she shut her up with one savage look, and the sister withered like a salted slug. Then, turning all her sweetness on me, your mother said, 'Why, thank you, Christopher, we'd be much obliged for your kindness.'

"My mouth must've dropped plumb open. She knew my name! I would've found a way to change my own *head* if she'd asked me. I'd manage the tire if I had to break both arms in the operation. So it wasn't a pretty affair, what with the two of them observing daintily while I scratched and sweated and calculated and heaved. But I was moderately sure they didn't know the difference anyway, between competence and a good performance. In the end, I wasn't entirely sure the wheel would stay affixed to the car, but I forgot my anxiety when your mother put her hand on my elbow."

He tipped his head back and looked at the night sky.

"All I could think of was her fingers on my skin," he said. "They branded me, Christy. They made me *hers*."

At that moment, I remembered who I was. The real me, Christy Hurley. Or whoever—maybe the name didn't even matter, because I was still the same boy, the one Finnuala Whippet had kissed. She'd branded me, too. Just a few hours ago I'd grasped her fingers in mine, and all my insides had swooped and soared. So maybe I could begin to understand then, what'd happened to Dad. How he'd let all of this happen.

"'Where're you for, then?' your mother asked me, and I told her I was heading into the town for to collect our dinners.

"'Nonsense,' she said. 'You'll eat dinner in the house with us.' And then she caught herself, softened the invitation. 'That is, if you'd be so kind as to join us.'"

The voice he gave my mother had a lovely soft sort of a melody to it.

"And d'ya know, Christy, when I looked into your mam's eyes that day on the roadside, the jack still dirty in my hand, and her sister standing not three feet away . . . d'ya know what I seen in behind them wild eyelashes of hers?"

"What?"

"I saw you, big fella. Plain as day, on your mother's face. She was as undone as I was."

There it was: my spark. My beginning.

"After that, your mother and I saw each other every chance we could get," Dad said. "We hid away together, ran away from the world."

"Where did ye run away to?"

"We went walking, out on the land," he said. "She knew every inch and fold of it, every blade of grass, every hole where you'd turn your ankle. Her family was there forever, so she reckoned she was born with a map of it printed on the insides of her eyelids. She knew every rock and sapling, every tumble of leaf. She even knew the winds."

"But didn't people talk about ye, out walking like that?" I said. "What did her family say?"

"We couldn't let nobody see us," he said. "For a while, we met in a glade in the wood, and we'd walk from there, where we was hidden. She knew all the secret places. But she'd a little greenhouse of her own as well, and nobody ever went inside there—she forbade them. She invited me, so in I'd go, and I'd sit and wait for her. There was vines and greens all twisting up the glass walls of that little shed, so's it was like her own secret garden. A warm, glowing, sunlit hollow."

"What was it for?"

"For raising orchids and lilies and spices," he said. "Things that wouldn't ordinarily grow in Ireland, in the damp."

"Spices?"

"Yep. Cloves, chicory, ginger, all sorts."

"So, did you help her with the spices?"

"Not really." Dad grinned. "I mostly just watched her, the way she tended them, the way they sprung up under her fingertips. She'd only to breathe on them, and they'd push up their heads, open their leaves, and stretch for the sun. You could hear them growing, that's how quiet it was inside. You could hear them drinking the water down, unfolding theirselves in the warmth."

"And that was all ye did in there?" I said. "Watched her grow lilies and cloves?"

Dad scrunched up his nose. "Well," he admitted. "That wasn't *all*."

"What else?"

He filled up his lungs with the fresh night air. "She taught me how to read."

My mouth dropped open. "*She* taught you?"

Dad nodded.

"My mother?"

"Yep."

I closed my mouth.

"I always thought you learned in school," I said. "When you was little."

"Nope. It was her," he said. "It was always her. I mean, I learned what I could in that school, but it was awful basic. Them priests wasn't interested in helping me. But your mother, she knew I was smart, that's what she said. She knew I'd pick it up quick, and I did. I was fast. She lended me books."

"What books?"

"Poetry, mostly, at first," he said. "Yeats, Tennyson, that sort of thing."

"But how did it start? Her teaching you?"

"It was simple. I came into the hothouse one day, and there she was, sitting on an upturned crate, her nose buried in the pages. I asked her what she was reading, and she just started talking, reading out loud, til she'd the whole story told to me."

"What story?"

"'Rappaccini's Daughter.'"

"Do I know that one?"

Dad scratched his chin. "Probably not," he said. "Leastways, I never read it to you."

"How does it go?"

"Well, believe it or not, it's the story of a young fella who falls in love with a beautiful girl in a secret garden."

"Just like you and her."

"Sort of," Dad said. "Except that in the story, the young lady has grew up in this dreadful garden, with these lethal flowers all panting their fatal fumes into her little mouth and nose from the time she was a baby. So as she grows, she becomes nearly like one of them flowers herself, like an exquisite, treacherous bloom. They's bewitched by each other, the two of them, and they fall in love, never mind that her breath is a deadly venom. Never mind that it infects him, bit by bit, each time they meet."

"What happens to him?" I asked. "Does he get sick?"

"Worse," Dad said. "He starts to become poisonous like her."

"But why don't they just leave, then?"

"Because she can't survive outside the garden," Dad said. "She needs the terrible scent of them blossoms to survive."

"So there's no place for them to be together," I said.

"No." Dad shook his head, and then we was both very quiet for a while.

"So what happens in the end?" I finally asked.

"Well," Dad said, taking a deep breath. "He tries to make her a potion, so's she can leave the garden and they can be together, but it doesn't work."

"She's still deadly, after?"

"No, son," Dad said. "There is no after. When she drinks it, she dies."

"Feck, Dad, that's a gruesome story."

"It is," he agreed with a laugh. "But sure, it sounded like paradise when your mother read it."

"So then what?"

"Then we started reading together nearly every day, and she said she couldn't believe how quick I was, to catch on." Dad smiled. "Soon I was reading to her, instead. Christina Rossetti was the first one—*The Goblin Market*."

"Oh, that one's class," I said.

"Your mother loved it, too," he said. "Her eyes was so bright when I read it, I could just about concentrate on the page. Her face was an awful distraction. She stood up to applaud after, she was that overjoyed. She leapt onto my knee."

Dad flushed. He had to shake hisself out from under that memory. My mother, on his knee, her red curls collapsed all over his shoulder, her soft white arms 'round his neck. The scent of her, in the hot stillness of that greenhouse, heady and powerful. Like a dangerous flower herself, all the vivid colors of her.

"It wasn't just her beauty that was rare," he said, but he was talking to hisself now. "Her mind was extraordinary. She'd have loved to be a traveller, to walk out into the wide world and have adventures—that's what she said. But she reckoned them spices and flowers was the next best thing—a way of bringing the exotic world home. She said she could lean over her moon orchid and close her eyes, and just the scent of it would send her spinning and tumbling acrosst the ocean to some tropical island, to some hidden jungle. And she could stay there, framed by giant, flapping palm leaves, with the caw-songs of huge, vibrant birds ringing in her ears, and the bursting sweetness of fruits she'd never tasted, ripening on her tongue."

I stared at Dad, and he was gone, too—off to that thick, dripping jungle with my mam.

"So she wanted to be a traveller?" I said, trying to bring him back.

"She did," he said. "In a way. And maybe that was why she took me serious. She respected us, the way we live. I never met another buffer like her, never met nobody like her."

He shook his head. "She was ahead of her time," he said.

"So what about me, then?" I asked. "Where did I come in?"

Dad winced, then shrugged. "Right between the dragonwort and the jasmine."

"Dad!" I said.

He laughed, and his tongue was sticking out the corner of his mouth. He was delighted with hisself, guilty with remembering, like the cat who ate the canary—thrilled and embarrassed in equal measure. It was mad, seeing him like that.

"Gross," I said, while he tried to collect hisself.

"In truth, I didn't know," he said, shaking his head. "I didn't know about you. I couldn't see no change in her. But she must've known. And I guess her taste for adventure washed away with the morning sickness."

Dad got up and walked over to the tent, went rummaging in behind the bread box, and drew out a hidden bottle. He unstoppered it and took a small swig, winced as he swallowed. Poitín. He brought it back and set it under his lawn chair.

"Your mam, she was a bold one," he said, sitting beside me again. "I really thought she might run. She might've leapt over the front wall of that big house like a spring lamb with her red hair flying out behind her against the green fields. She might've took to the *tober* with your old fella. God knows I wanted her to."

His eyes emptied theirselves out again; that dreamy look of joy fled from them until they was hollow, like two bottomless holes in his head.

"I'm not ashamed to tell you that I cried real salt and water when I left her, Christy," he said. "I waited outside her house for four hours that morning we pulled out of camp. The others went on ahead and I told them I'd follow, and I sat and I waited, hoping. For four bleedin' hours."

He shook his head, took another pull on the bottle.

"My hands was wet with my own tears when I finally flicked the reins and left. I turned to the road where I belonged, and it was the first time in all my life I truly hated the travelling, hated the life I was born into. I cursed your grandda, and all the granddas before him, for whoever it was first took out to the road, and left me bereft of my one true love. I wished it was in my power to give your mam an acceptable life for herself, to make her my wife. By God, it made for a cold and lonesome year, Christy—you've no idea. Even the summer was soggy with misery and sorrow. But as the seasons of the year passed, I seeded and fertilized and watered my despair til, the following spring, up poked a shiny green head of hope."

I closed my eyes and tried to see Dad a decade younger, his face all screwed up with a love like I'd never seen before. Not the sort of domestic, match-made, pot-scrubbing, food-sharing, child-rearing love that Finty might've had for Brigid one time. But a strange and wild passion, like in stories, in books, that could spur people to hike up their skirts and run leaping over gray stone walls, leaving their money-stuffed mattresses behind. I couldn't imagine it, but there was something about my dad that made him believe it was possible. I was the child of that possibility.

"I made up my mind to go back for her," he said. "And this time, I was determined. I'd not be leaving alone."

"So you really are my father, then," I said quietly.

Dad took another suck off the poitín, and gave me an odd, sort of sad, half smile.

"I am, of course."

SEVENTEEN

I wanted a gulp of the poitín. So I took one, and Dad didn't stop me. He watched me quietly while I struggled: Bilbo doing battle with the dragon. There was a great love one time, that crossed lives and boundaries, that defied all the usual rules and expectations, and my dad was a partner in it. A great love. And I was the outcome, the score: one-nil. My mam wasn't a *Pavee* and she mightn't even be dead. She might live in a house somewhere, a big house, like Finnuala Whippet's, with fierce red hair and ropes of eyelashes. While I lived here in this tent. Without her.

"I had to rescue you," Dad said quietly.

Rescue. A far better word than kidnap.

"Are you okay?" Dad asked.

I took another sup of the poitín in response.

"Will I go on?"

I nodded.

"Your grandda was trying to make a match for me," he said. "I was awful late for it—I was near twenty by then, but I managed to buy time til we came 'round again to your mother's homeplace."

I breathed against the burning in my throat.

"We stopped in at the same camp," Dad said, "pumped sweet water from the same rusty pump, loosed our horses into the same field. And what a homecoming it was, Christy—the very air seemed to quiver with joy. My arms and legs never knew such strength of purpose, I was so determined.

"The dust was hardly settled when I called to her house under the guise of looking for work. Man dear, how my heart thumped when I walked up that lane. The grass was high on either side, and it all seemed to ruffle as I went past, like it was whisking me up to her. A couple of the horses was out to pasture, and a fella I'd never seen before waved me over to the stables.

"'Is it work you're looking, friend?' he asked.

"'It would be, if ye've any going,' I answered.

"I was tryinna stay calm, like, or at least to sound calm. But I could hear my heartbeat in my ears, and it was like the devil's own bodhrán, Christy. I didn't know who your man was, you see, and I was in terrors. He was brushing a fine, tall-looking horse, who flared his nostrils at me when I leaned in to pat his muzzle. The fella paused in his work and took a glance over his shoulder toward the house before he spoke again.

"'You'd want to check with the missus,' he said, and then he dropped his voice low. 'The truth is, we need all the help we can get, but the new man of the house is stubborn; he's after letting go most of the staff. I'm only here a few weeks, myself.'

"My heart stopped, Christy. There was a new man of the house. And a missus. They'd sold and all, I just knew it. Well, my face must've taken the news even harder than my heart, because your man laid down the brush and stepped around the animal toward me.

"'Are ya right there?' he asked me. 'You look a bit ashen on it.'

"I shook my head. I couldn't answer him. He was a nice fella, and he put his hand on my shoulder to steady me. I was grateful for it. He wasn't a traveller, but he was kind.

"'Go on up to the house,' he said to me. 'Go to the side door of the kitchen and Kitty'll get you a drop of tea and that. You don't look well at'all, at'all.'

"I nodded then, and he turned me physically toward the house, bent my shoulder in the proper direction and gave me a nudge. The kitchen door was stood open to the sunny yard, and I walked through that doorway like a zombie, uninvited. Inside the door I stopped, and my eyes popped wide with relief. Sitting with her back to me, facing the kitchen fireplace, was your mother. Even before she turned her head, I knew her. By the graceful tilt of her neck, and the bundle of messy red curls. I knew from the breeze of her eyelashes in the airy room, and my mouth fell open so I could breathe her in. She heard my footsteps in the doorway, but she thought I was the housekeeper. 'Had they any nice chops for supper, Kitty?' she said, without turning.

"And I didn't know how to answer her. I closed my mouth and it fell open again. Your mother bent forward, clucking and cooing, and her hair tumbled acrosst her shoulder and that's when I seen one tiny little fist reaching up to tangle itself into that mass of curls."

Me, center stage. A bright-eyed baby boy, my little fingers tangled into my mammy's hair. I stared down at my knuckles in the firelight and tried to imagine my mother's red curls twisting around them.

"The animal instinct that struck me when I seen you there was like nothing I ever knew existed," Dad said, and then he waited for me to look up at him. "I was completely awash with the born knowledge that you was *my* little man. My bones sang with it, Christy. It all came at me in an instant, like there was a shift and a click in the universe, and afterwards, nothing was at all the same. My astonishment was too big to handle, too big to even register. But Bob's your uncle. There you was."

And now at long last, I was crying next to Dad, with quiet little rivers of tears just sliding down my face like they'd always been there, like they'd always be there from now on. Dad was crying too, some, but not like before. He let most of the tears be mine. He went on.

"When your mam laid eyes on me, her face was even more astonished than mine. We said nothing to each other for a full minute, or an hour maybe. We just stood staring at each other, openmouthed, drinking each other down. There was something strange about her, something a bit off—a grayness there I didn't recognize. Heartbreak in behind her eyes. Still, I didn't understand, when I finally rushed acrosst the room to take her in my arms, why she wouldn't accept me. She pushed me away. Stuck her two hands hard into my chest and shoved. I was overcome, Christy. I reached out for her again and she stiffened.

"'I'm a married woman now, Christopher,' she said, and she gathered her sleeves in close to her mothering hands."

Dad took a big gulp out of the bottle, and looked down at his own hands then. *"A married woman now,"* he repeated, like he was stuck in that phrase and didn't know how to move past it, even after all these years.

The words was like ghosts of theirselves.

"'The baby?' I finally asked her. My teeth was clenched so's I could hardly speak through them, Christy. I felt awful cold, of a sudden, and I was shaking, clattering. I could hear my bones knocking against each other, in under my skin. I thought I'd be sick.

"'My son,' she said.

"A solitary answer. A singular possessive. Now that I was up close to her, I could see it more clearly: all them months of catastrophe written in the lines of her face, like a film of ruin. I bent into your cradle then and seen my own features on your tiny, puckered infant's face. My God, how I loved you in that instant. It was like a thunderclap.

"'His name is Christopher,' your mam said, 'William Christopher,' and that was all the confirmation I needed. You was named after me, you see, in a last moment of boldness from your mother's waning courage.

"But there was footsteps then, the click and echo of a polished shoe on a polished floor, an abrupt and unwelcome rhythm approaching. A thin, slicked-back man was stepping down the long hallway toward the kitchen. He was a diagonal line, sloping away from me even as he approached—his shoulders and head only reluctantly keeping up with his precise, leading hips. His shoes appeared in the doorway before the rest of him. He locked eyes on me immediately, without so much as a glance toward your mother. She seemed to shrink into herself at the sight of him. There was an acrid smile stuck to his face, and I noticed that his teeth was too long for his mouth—like fangs they was."

In my mind's eye, I could see this man perfectly as my dad described him. He was crystallized—still and sneering. I could even smell him, and he stunk of something sweet gone off, like a caved-in pear soaked with linseed oil.

"What was I doing, Dad?" I asked. "While all this was going on?"

"You went sleeping in your cradle," Dad said. "Not so much as a peep out of ya. Your breath was reliable as the tide. And God love her, the rotations on your mother's face was so quick they was nearly imaginary. First panic, then defiance, then hatred, and finally resignation. She flipped through them like pages in a book, and then made toward setting herself in stone while I watched. She managed all of it before the fella even opened his fangs to speak.

"'Ah, we've no work for you now,'" Dad said, in the slicked-back man's voice. "'No work at all, I'm afraid.'"

I hated that man's voice, the way Dad whispered its perfect malice, the way it broke free of the story and hung itself up in the air, hovering over us like a sharpened blade. I swore I could remember it still—that voice—that I'd carried its echo in my ears all this time. It had a sort of diseased quality to it, so that even in Dad's whispered story, it oozed and seeped from the man's mouth like an open sore.

"His eyes trailed down my front as he leaned back and disapproved of me," Dad went on. "I stood looking at him, too astounded to respond, my mouth hanging open. I may's well've been a tonsil salesman." Dad chuckled at hisself, but the joke wasn't funny enough. Not tonight.

"It was just too much to take in at once. Here I was, after finding out I had a son, finding out about *you*," Dad said. "After finding out your mam had got stuck, and was gone off and married to some horrible, fang-riddled, slicked-back yokel, and him trying to rid me of the place all in the space of three minutes. I felt like swinging at him, but it was all a cloudy mess. It was all I could manage to keep my feet under me, to prevent my knees from buckling.

"'And if that will be all?' the man said, and he raised his stupid, slanting eyebrows into his forehead, waited for me to leave.

"I started to panic. I couldn't just walk away, couldn't turn and go whistling back down that lane, when my whole life was stuck in that breathless kitchen. I felt a gulf of terror rising, but I didn't have no words for this man. There wasn't nothing I could say that would make no sense. In desperation, I looked at your mother, silently begged her to intercede. I just knew she would. She would tell him something, anything—buy us a few moments alone together. At the very least, I knew she'd want some time with me, to explain. But her face stayed still and vacant, and my pause swelled into a moment, which expanded til it was a bloated cloud hanging over the whole of the village, casting shadows acrosst barrooms and shops and herds of grazing cattle. Still, I wasn't able to leave; I was rooted to the spot. Rooted! Some traveller, hey? I couldn't move. Your mother retreated to her armchair beside you."

I could see the armchair. I could see my mother's hands, fidgeting in the shadow of Dad's silence.

"I couldn't tell if it was exhaustion or stubbornness that landed her in that chair, but she was sat down and she wasn't moving," Dad went on.

"'Come away with me,' I said to her.

"Can you believe that, son? Bold and simple, right there in broad daylight, I said it, right in front of your man. It was the plainest appeal I could make, but it was all the world to me, and your mother knew that. It was my naked soul unfurled between us. For a moment her movements quickened. She snapped her head up, and her face was alive again, the face I had memorized and adored. Her eyes flashed with something terrified and brave and real. I took a step toward her, but the man moved into my path. He grabbed my wrist, and all of a sudden he was upright in a way he hadn't been upright before. His pelvis shifted and his head came forward and he was three inches taller than he'd seemed. His forehead gleamed, and I could see blue veins behind it. I was aware of his spindly grip on my arm, but the greater threat was in his eyes. An unusual kind of hatred lived there.

"'Are you mad?' he seethed. 'She's going nowhere with you, ya filthy tinker.'

"There was white pockets of spittle gathered at the corners of his mouth, and they freed theirselves onto my face.

"'You have no business here now,' he said. 'I know your kind, and I know you were welcomed here once. Well, no longer! Not while I'm man of this house. You'll do well to leave my wife and me in peace.'

"At the word 'wife,' he took a step back and shifted his grip to your mother's stooping shoulder. He tried to possess her with his hand. He was diagonal again, and his belt smiled out at me.

"'Go back to your horses and your dogs and your *own* women.

Go back to your *tint*,' he said, and he exaggerated the word, said *tent* the way we say it, Christy. He was mocking me. But there was a snarl and a hiss to his voice; he was more animal than man, and it was only sadness I felt for him.

"I didn't move. My mind ticked over slowly, methodically, like a waiting bomb. There was nothing more to lose, I realized.

"'He knows?' I asked your mam.

"She couldn't look at me, so I turned to him instead. At least he was capable of anger, of communication.

"'You know?' I asked him.

"His lips curled into a grimace.

"'You know about me? You know who I am?' I was shouting now, my voice rising to cover the thrumming of blood in my ears.

"'My dear boy, what are you talking about?' The man laughed. And I could see that he did know. 'You really are mad in the head altogether. Isn't he mad, darling?' He looked down at your mother, squeezed her unresponsive shoulder. She shifted in her seat and finally looked up at me. I could see some shame there, and a great deal of sorrow.

"'You'll wake the child,' she said.

"'My child,' I shouted. 'I'll wake my child!' I didn't care. I wanted to waken you, wanted to see the colors in your bright little eyes. The diagonal man forced a laugh that was like a croak, but it didn't hurt me. It was a coarse, deliberate sound, and it was pathetic.

"'Does that look like a tinker's child to you?' he asked, pointing.

"He bent then and hauled you up carelessly, pinching the fine silk folds of your dress between his fingers. His fingernails was too long as well, like his teeth, and he held you roughly with one hand under your arms, juggled you 'round and showed me the hem of your garment. He flung the end of it at me, but the material only flittered back down and settled lightly in around you like feathers and wings. The dress didn't share his fury, but that only fueled him.

"'Silks!' he spat. 'The silken tinker! They'll write songs about him! He'll be famous. HA! And the cradle?' His voice quieted now, with a strange and perverse new interest. 'Well, the cradle is an antique,' he explained, plopping you back into your créche.

"*Plop*," Dad said, and banged the back of his head lightly against the lawn chair behind him, to show how recklessly the man had tossed me back home.

"The rage that was in me then was a physical force I didn't know how to reckon with, Christy. I wasn't sure I'd be able to rein it in if it broke free of me; I was afraid I might kill him. My hands was shaping theirselves into cinder blocks on the ends of my arms."

I didn't think Dad would be able to kill a man, just out of pure rage, but in truth, I wasn't sure about nothing no more.

"It wasn't his words that rose me, Christy," Dad said. "Sure, they was only useless, peppery little things. But the way he handled you was beyond the pale. He didn't take no notice of *you* inside them silks. He didn't even mind how your little head rolled when he stuffed you back into that cradle, or how your eyes popped open to peer out at me. We stared at each other, you and me did.

"Blue," Dad said, smiling at me. "Your eyes was blue. I'd never been much of an authority on the ocean, Christy, but I reckoned maybe there was some resemblance there."

He leaned forward in his chair and reached for me, put his hand under my chin so's he could get a better look at my eyes.

"Yep," he said then. "Definitely oceanish."

I wasn't ready to forgive Dad, even a little bit. So I pulled my chin away, but I couldn't help imagining the whole expanse of the sea billowing around inside my head, showing its skin in my eyeballs.

"But that man didn't even notice you, Christy," he said, resting his hand back on the bottle. "He'd been living with you all them months—eight whole months—and I reckon he didn't even know you *had* eyes that opened and looked around you and seen things.

Your cradle was rocking from the swing arm and you was lolling back and over, back and over. He seen me watching you and he thought I was eyeing the crèche. It was some kinda fancy antique.

"'We inherited this piece from my dearly departed father-in-law,' he said, straightening hisself back to the diagonal.

"There was no pause in his voice at the words 'dearly departed.' He breezed past them.

"'Along with the rest of our fine home here. Of course, I've filled it with the heirloom treasures of my own family, and it's quite a home we've made between us.' He made a grand gesture, to indicate a fortune so big it was practically spilling out of every press and drawer in the place. 'The home where we will raise *our* son.'

"I stared at him and wondered what was going on in his head. Was he appealing to my good sense? Asking me to abandon you there because there was money in it? Or was he simply trying to make me feel small? I hadn't a notion how his mind worked. I hadn't a clue what he might be thinking, and it didn't matter anyway. Whatever he planned was lost on me. I looked to your mother again, and saw the enormity of her pain coming fully home to roost on her face. Her devastation was pure. On top of everything else, I realized, she must've lost her father.

"But the slicked-back man kept on: 'My son. A tinker.' He laughed, shaking his head. 'Of all the absurdities.' And that's when your mother couldn't take no more. She stood up—for you and for me, she stood up against the man she was married to. Her arms flew into the air around her head.

"'That's enough,' she cried. She looked a bit rickety standing there, but her voice was steady, sturdy. 'Christopher has been a friend to this family.'"

"Yeah, Mam!" I interrupted.

And then, sitting there at that fire beside Dad, I had this overwhelming moment of illogical hope: that she would tell the slicked-back man off, that she would even slap his face maybe, and then she'd run away with me and Dad. I know that wasn't how the story ended, but that's what I was hoping for, somehow.

"Yeah, Mam," Dad agreed. "Her voice had a volume that didn't invite debate," he went on, switching back to the sweetness of my mother's voice, growing louder:

"'This man worked for my father, God rest his soul. My father who laid *me* in this créche when *I* was a baby. Please,' she said to him, her voice going quieter now, 'just give us a moment. This is all a terrible misunderstanding.'

"His eyes narrowed and he fixed me with one last glare, but he didn't have no desire to tangle with your mam. He spun on his shined heel.

"'Disgusting,' he muttered at the three of us, as his hips led him clicking back down the hallway, deeper into the house."

I imagined my father, alone in the room with this beautiful woman. My mother. I imagined the two of them looking down, and me giving them back a gummy grin. I imagined what it must've felt like for me, back then, to belong so much to her. To belong so much. And I wished *that* was the feeling I'd been able to carry with me all these years, instead of that man's terrible sickly voice and all my clumsy fears. I tried to sink into the memory of it, of belonging.

"Your mother was silent as we listened to those footsteps slink deeper into the house," Dad said. "I searched her face for a glimpse of familiarity, but there was too much confusion.

"'How could you?' I asked her simply.

"I knew the question wasn't fair. She was grieving for her father, grieving for me. Grieving for everything she'd lost. And still she was standing up. She wouldn't let it pass.

"'How could *I*? *How could I*? How could I *not*?' she said. 'What choice did I have, Christopher? What would you have me do? Pack up my child and myself and go out roaming, out to raise him along the side of a road somewhere, in a ditch? I have sheep that live better than that!'"

I gasped. Dad tucked his lips inside his mouth for a moment. He blinked to clear his eyes.

"That time it was like she had smacked me clean acrosst the face, Christy," he said. "All the hours and days and weeks and months I had loved her. And there it was, in that moment. When it came down to it, what she really thought of me—what she thought of us. You started crying then—making an awful racket, and your face going red with it. I took a step back from her and crossed my arms in front of me, touched my own face to remind myself that it was all real, that it wasn't a bad dream. I felt like she'd actually stricken me.

"'You can't change him,' I said, and I pointed at you in the crib. 'You can't change who he is.'

"'I can try to give him a better life,' she said.

"'This?' I asked, waving my arms around. 'This is a better life? Why, because of silks and antique cradles? And this . . . this . . . this man is to pretend the part of father? Jesus, did you see the way he lifted him, like he was a sack of spuds?'

"I was horrified to find there was real tears on my face then. I wondered if your mother'd seen them, but she was too busy trying to calm you. I wiped them away quickly.

"'Come here to me,' I said, and I lifted you out of that swinging cradle, right out from under your mother's hands.

"You was heavier than I expected, and holding you in my arms was more substantial in every way. You stopped fussing when I lifted you, and you stared at me so much I thought you might open your mouth and tell me what was on your mind. Your eyes was as wide! You examined my face with your fingers. Your eyelashes fluttered and you let out a dedicated sigh. And then you was still, and I could feel your heartbeat against my arm.

"'Is it supposed to be going so fast?' I asked your mam. It was a bit alarming.

"'Is what supposed to be going so fast?'

"'His heartbeat,' I said.

"She smiled at me. Couldn't help herself. And that instant she was again the woman I loved.

"'Yes, it's supposed to go fast,' she said. 'He's only small, so it has to go that fast to keep up.'

"'Right.' I nodded, satisfied.

"And then there was a lovely moment of quiet among us. We was a little family there in that kitchen, all eyelashes and warm cheeks and heartbeats. She reached into my arms and smoothed your ruffled collar back from your face.

"'I had no choice,' she said simply, and I understood that to be probably true," Dad said. "She looked at the two of us together, and then looked into my face for a long moment before squeezing my elbow and returning to her chair. Her fingerprints still left a shocking impression of heat on my skin. She sat there for a moment and her eyes welled up, and her shoulders shook, the world shook. She buried her beautiful face in her hands, Christy. It was horrible to see. I was so helpless. But then, with a monumental effort, she stopped the unraveling dead—just like she had on that first day I'd seen her. She talked herself into composure by sheer force of will; she stitched up the fissures and the cracks the same way we stitch up holes in tin pots, Christy, or cracks in porcelain plates. They disappeared right in front of me and the next moment, it was like the whole thing'd been a figment of my imagination.

"'I have no choice,' she said, bringing us all wretchedly into the present tense. 'He's a good man, Christopher,' she told me—she actually managed to look me in the eye when she said that. 'And he loves me.' As if he was capable of love. All I could do was shake my head.

"Then she scooped you out of my arms with one clean motion. I looked down at my empty hands, and my shoulders felt light from the very sockets. I thought my arms might float away without the weight of you in them. You reached your tiny hands out toward me, and our arms hovered for each other as your mother carried you away."

Dad's hands was out in front of him now, between the two of us in the dimming firelight, and I reached out to touch a fingertip softly to his. And then I had the thought that maybe Dad had been reaching for her all these years as well. Just like me. Maybe he felt only half whole, too.

"I donno how the idea came to me, to rescue you," Dad went on. "I don't remember it being a sudden flash, or a long, ponderous decision. It was more like an inevitability: you couldn't stay in that place. So I waited til it was well dark, which wasn't too late, given the black wetness of the day. I left my pony and wagon in behind the house, under the cover of some dense trees, so's they would keep dry and ready. Then I crept toward the house and watched for the lights to go out. One by one, they did, and then it was quiet, all other sounds drowned by the sheets of rain casting theirselves at the eaves and glass windowpanes of that silent house. Through the bucketing downpour I strained to listen for signs of life from within. I couldn't hear no fighting between husband and wife. I couldn't hear nothing.

"After the last light was blackened, toward the back of the house I went, stealthy as a jungle cat in the night, and in through the kitchen door, closing it silently behind me to shut out the cry of the wind. I was dripping onto the warm, dry floor, and I cringed at the echo of every drop announcing my arrival. I peeled off my wet shirt and stood on it in the kitchen doorway to catch and muffle the drips. The house was dead quiet and I could hear the *tick tick* of an unseen clock. I wrung out the ends of my trousers over the discarded shirt and then rolled them up to my knees for to catch the renegade drops. I stepped off the island of my shirt and recognized the high squeak of my wet shoes on the polished slate floor. I'd have to lose them as well. Off they came, and then I was like a pale, damp shadow in the house, sniffing and feeling my way noiselessly toward you in the dark.

"I went up the staircase on all fours and didn't pause when a floorboard squeaked beneath me, trusting the lashing rain to disguise the small noises of my ascent. At the landing I turned left on instinct and found my way to you like tin to a magnet. Your blue eyes was open in the dark as if you'd been waiting me. You showed me your gums, and then sucked on your fist. I reckoned it was your way of promising to be quiet. I hoisted you up, ready for the weight of you this time, and tucked you neatly into your blanket the way I'd seen Brigid do. I tied you 'round my bare shoulders and you nestled in for the haul. We'd have to be quick-going.

"My eyes was adjusted to the dark, but my body felt clumsy inside the walls of the house. I felt my shoulders and thighs expanding, and for a moment I feared I would outgrow the nursery—I would wake the sleeping occupants of the house, as my arms and legs sprouted and lurched through every room like fast-growing strands of ivy. I looked down at your wide-open face, saw the glint of your own slobber on your fist in the scant, rain-discouraged moonlight, and I had to catch my breath. That was the most important moment of my life, Christy, and I had to get it exactly right. I had to achieve fast and flawless silence. There wouldn't be another chance. I turned and stole from the room."

Dad's voice was low and serious, and I was taken so deeply into the story that I was holding my breath so's not to make a sound, so's nobody would hear us and find us and rend us apart.

"I was like a ballerina, son, you want to've seen me," he said. "I hurdled misplaced shoes with silent grace and leapt acrosst the outstretched body of a sleeping cat without so much as causing a breeze on his whiskers. At the staircase I stepped into the air and the two of us glided down to the bottom without stepping a wet toe on a single squeaky step in between. We negotiated the long dark of the front hallway without sound or hesitation. And soon, I could see my puddle of shirt and shoes where I'd left them in through the kitchen doorway. Or. Not quite where I'd left them.

"My stomach dropped at the realization that my shoes had been moved closer to my shirt, one of them kicked over on its side. I stopped dead and, without turning around, began moving backwards down the hallway, groping my way back toward the front door at the foot of the steps. My hand clutched the doorknob and I heard a rusty click as I twisted it open. Your man came flying 'round the corner of that kitchen doorway wielding a cast iron fry pan in both hands. He wasn't diagonal now as he lunged toward us down the hallway, and I could see his long teeth bared in a silent scream.

"I stumbled out the door backwards and landed on my arse outside with a thump. But I somersaulted, tucked you inside the curl of my body—like we was a circus troupe, performing tricks. How easy it felt, like we'd done this all before, like this was the movement we was made for, the way we fitted together, seamless and simple. We was up again before I even registered the fall, and the two of us was off like a couple of jackrabbits through the wet fields. My bare heels made a thwapping sound at each step, with the effort to release theirselves from the ankle-deep mud, and bullets went flying by my head like wicked midges. I covered your head and slapped them away, except for the one that got me, here."

Dad leaned down and showed me the back of his earlobe: a small, crescent-shaped scar, the size of my pinky nail. My mouth was hanging open.

"You mean he really shot at us?" I said. "With bullets?"

Dad nodded, and I tried to picture him slapping them bullets out of the stormy sky, his callused hand swiping through the raindrops like a scythe. He went on. "The rain was dancing its way along the fields in long, twisting columns that reached their arms deep into the folds of the night sky and pulled the water down. I tugged the blanket up 'round your ears and I ran for our lives, Christy."

My own heart was racing now, and in it I could feel the gallop of our escape.

"I never chanced a look back until we reached the stables, but your man wasn't far enough behind for my liking. I unhitched my pony from the wagon with one hand, like only a traveller could do, and in a flash, the two of us was up on his back and galloping into the rain-soaked night. One more look back and your man was on his knees in the muck now, with his fists to the sky, and shouting after us. I finally heard the bellow he'd been saving, and it cleaved the air. I noticed a lamp flicker on in an upper window of the house, and I had to push any thoughts of your mother's grief clean outta my brain. I knew she would miss you something terrible, son. That you was the only joy she had left in that brokenhearted house. But there was too much sadness to leave you stuck there, smothered by plaster walls. Too much heaviness and not enough love. I knew I had to rescue you from that life that swallowed your mother's dreams. I knew it was in your bones to be on the road with your dad. And in that moment when I held you to me and we ran away together, I felt your little heart bump with the rhythm of the road, and I knew I'd done right by you."

EIGHTEEN

I fell asleep in the lawn chair. I didn't mean to, but I did, and I guess Dad fell asleep, too, because speaking the truth after a decade of lies is exhausting. But learning that truth, absorbing it into your headbox and tryinna make sense of it is even worse. It would be something akin to climbing Croagh Patrick without using your feet—that's how grueling it felt.

So in that deep and shattered flight of sleep, I dreamed of the boy William, in black and white and gray. And there wasn't nothing easy or dreamy about the dream at all. I dreamed of Mr. and Mrs. Keaton loving that bundled baby boy, and bouncing him on their knees and fondling him and cooing at him. In the dream, that's what Mr. William Keaton was like: regular white teeth, cooing, smitten. And they argued about whether to call the baby Willie or Liam, but it was a nice kind of an argument with smiles and wagging fingers, and no punches or even unspoken threats of punches. And the baby William was all smiles and squeaks and feets and hands in the air. And then it was dark and the mammy and the daddy Keaton was fast sleeping in their room with its four walls and its closed door, and I was standing over the baby William in his crèche. And the rain was lashing down at the windows outside, and a streak of lightning lit into the blackened room, and I could see the baby William with his moony blue eyes, wide and staring. His fat baby hands was up at his face and he couldn't stop them—he didn't know how to move them yet. And them fat little hands went swooping into his face like birds of prey, and his tiny, little finger stuck straight into his eye like a beak, and in one awful motion, he plucked his little eyeball out. His arms flailed out at me, and the lightning cracked again and I could see the eyeball stuck, perched onto the end of his little baby-bird beak-finger, and I could see the empty, plummy socket on his head and his mouth gaping open. Then I heard the faraway, curdled horror of a scream.

"*Nooooo!*" it shrieked, "William! *Nooooo!*"

And then my dad was shaking me awake.

"Christy!" he said. "Christy!"

And that was my name. *That* was my name. Christy. Named after the good Lord Hisself.

I was awake in the lawn chair, and it was the high sunshine of the day because that's how long me and Dad had slept. Dad. He was holding me, and I didn't fight him. He rocked me and shushed me and told me it was okay, Christy, and I let him do all that. And I tried to believe him.

I STARED AT MY HANDS and my feet. I stared at them and studied them, because they was still the same as yesterday, and that was something. I had the same wart on the pinky finger of my left hand, the same bumpy, green vein in the hollow of my wrist. My toes still curled just so, lined up in perfect symmetry against each other. They knew where they belonged.

It was Sunday and that meant going to Mass, never mind about nothing else. Never mind that the ground had dropped out from under me, and the sky'd fell down around my ears. Never mind.

Dad got dressed in silence, so I did too. Everything was different now, even the light, the grass. I was like Granny, all my past life gone up in smoke and flame. Even my name was burnt and blistered, unrecognizable. William.

"Christy, come on, we're going," Martin said, standing in the gap of the tent. "We'll be late."

In Mass I wanted to talk to God, but I didn't know if He'd recognize me. I couldn't think of nothing to say. So instead I pictured my life as a shattered plate, a fine piece of crockery broke and splintered into a thousand tiny pieces. And then I spent the hour collecting up all them bits of colored wreckage, and one by one, I placed them shards into the invisible hands of God. I hoped He would maybe glue them back together for me. He could stitch them up the way *Pavees* did, until the cracks was so well healed that nobody could see them at all.

After Mass, Dad took me fishing, which made everything worse, because he'd never took me fishing on my own before, and the gravity of that was like a sad confession. He knew he had to do something, and the fishing was all he had to give me. We stripped wattles off a tree and Dad tied some line onto them. He clapped a dragonfly dead and we used that for bait.

The river was quiet, rippling instead of rushing, and we found a cold, fresh pool, deep under the shade of a wych elm. We waded in off the bank, cast our hooked lines in among the rushes. I still had so many questions.

"Is that why you waited so long for to get me baptized?" I said. "Because that's how old I was when you took me?"

Dad was whipping and casting his line over his head like an old-time cowboy with a lasso. He always caught loads of mackerel, and sometimes even the odd salmon, so we had the net and bucket ready, waiting.

"That's right," he said. "That was my best guess of your age anyway."

I let my line go drooping in the rushes. The fish would have to walk into the bucket for me today.

"So the date on my baptism cert—my birth date," I said. "It was just a guess? You made it up?"

Dad's line made a regular whirring sound over our heads as he cast and recast it.

"Not really, son," he said. "I just did the calculations."

"How d'ya mean calculations? Like you could calculate from how big I was?"

"No, sure you can calculate the birth of a child as being forty weeks from . . ."

Phhhhhht—Dad's line went flinging out, flying out over our heads, and it landed with a tiny plop on the far side of the pool. He immediately started to rein it back in.

"Forty weeks from what?" I said.

"From when . . ." He faltered, towing his line back up. "From when I knew your mother."

"Oh," I said.

I hoisted my own line in and tossed it out again halfheartedly. It went limp straightaway and I watched it sink.

"And what about Saint Christopher?" I asked. "It belonged to her?"

"It did," he said. "It was my parting gift to her, that first time I left."

"You bought it for her?" I asked.

I clamped my fishing rod between my knees and pulled the medal out from under my collar. I flicked its gold and silver bands, sending them spinning.

"Jeez, Dad, it musta been awful dear."

"It cost me the entire wage her father paid me that harvest time," he said. "That was meant to be my pay for the whole winter, and I spent the lot of it on her. I hoped it would convince her to come with me. I wanted to show her that I was capable of providing her nice things. A life."

The sky had took on a goldish afternoon hue that made it feel warmer than it was. On any other day I woulda loved this moment with Dad.

"Saint Christopher protect us," I read the etching off the medal.

"That's right," Dad said. "I wanted her to feel safe enough to come with me. But she never did, she never did. So it ended up a parting gift."

"So how come I have it, then?" I asked.

"It was hanging on your lampshade that night I came to get you," he said. "I thought you should have something of her, so I took it with us."

I spun the medal again, and this time I looked at the back side of the center piece, the Saint Christopher disc. In it, I could see my tiny, warped reflection. My nose, huge and bulbous, and then my tiny chin and distorted eyes.

"So why did you christen me William?" I asked. That felt like the biggest betrayal of all. "That was his name," I said, thinking of the awful slicked-back man from the story.

"It was," Dad said. "And it was your name as well."

I cut my eyes at him.

"I wanted to keep the names your mother gave you," he said. "I felt like I owed her that much. She'd called you William Christopher, after both of us—him and me. So that's what we christened you."

"But why would she call me after him?" I said. "If he wasn't my father?"

Dad took a deep breath. "I don't know, Christopher," he exhaled. "Maybe it was her way of making amends. An olive branch."

I twisted my line around my finger and watched the tip go purple with blood.

"But we always knew you'd be called Christy," Dad said. "You've always been Christy."

He was trying to make his voice bright, to push some cheer into it.

"Why did she even marry him in the first place, if he was that awful?" I asked.

"She had to, Christy," Dad said.

I shook my head.

"Do you know what might've happened to you if that man hadn't married your mother?"

I turned and looked at him. I shrugged.

"Your mam got pregnant before she was married, Christy. That's an awful delicate state of affairs. I mean, it's true I would've married her in the morning. I felt she already *was* my wife. But she wasn't, not really." He'd stopped fishing and he looked at me, earnest. "They might've taken her away, to a convent, or worse maybe, to an asylum—they do that to lots of young women, you know, who fall pregnant. And then after the baby is born, they take it away from her and they put it in an orphanage."

I pulled the line tighter around my finger and watched the skin turn hard and yellow under its bite. I didn't want to look at him. Maybe that's where I belonged, an orphanage.

"You mightn't've had a mam or a dad, if that'd happened," he said.

Would that've been worse? At least I'd have known then. I wouldn't have spent my whole life getting lied to.

"You'd've been all alone in the world," he went on. "So that man, William. He might've been horrible, like, but in a way, he saved you. He saved your mother. It took me a lot of years to admit that, even to myself. But it's the truth."

Dad flicked the line back over his head and cast out again.

"So you just let him have her," I said. "Because he was some sorta phony hero."

Dad ignored this, but it wasn't so shocking really. It was right in line with my growing opinion: that my father was a coward, that he never stood up for nothing. Even the way he took me, his own son, sneaky in the middle of the night like a thief. Everything he ever did seemed to have shame melded into it. I almost didn't want to know no more. I wished I could stopper up all my questions, but I'd nothing to jam into them. I still needed answers.

"So then how was Millicent my godmother?" I asked.

"We had a proxy," Dad said.

"What's a proxy?"

"It means we had a substitute, since she obviously couldn't be there for the baptism," he said.

"But she lived there, Dad. Didn't she live there, where I got baptized, in Rathnaveen?"

"That was a wild coincidence," Dad said, shaking his head. "Rathnaveen was two or three villages over from Ballycinneide, and I didn't even know she was living there, that time. I didn't know til I read it last night in the article."

He sucked a bit of air in through his teeth. "Jesus, that was a close call, that," he said. "We went right by, under her nose. We only stopped there because that's where Father Jonas was, and I knew he'd baptize you for me."

A fish made a jump and a splash right beside me, but I just looked at it, watched the rings ripple out acrosst the smooth surface of the water til they reached my wellies and overtook me.

"We had to do your baptism in great secrecy," Dad said. "In great speed, and to get the road under us and get gone. Millicent was your absentee godmother because I knew that's what your mam would've wanted. I still felt I had to do right by her, even after everything that happened."

"So who was there?" I asked. "Who was the proxy?"

"Your auntie Brigid," Dad said.

"Auntie Brigid is my real godmother?"

Dad's line flew above us in graceful arcs and swipes.

"Everybody knew." I shook my head. "All this time, all of ye kept it from me."

My whole life was a sham, even my baptism. I tried to swallow, but I felt like there was a mackerel in my throat. Tears was passing over my face, trickling down my neck, in under the collar of my shirt. Saint Christopher was getting wet. I turned my back to Dad, cast my wilted line in the other direction.

"Does Martin know?" I asked.

"No, son. Martin could never have kept that from you. We didn't tell nobody. We never talked about it again, after—not once in all these years."

I looked at my reflection in the still water beneath me. "So it was you, and then Finty and Brigid as my godparents," I said. "And Granny and Grandda must've knew. But then what? Didn't Father Jonas ask about my mammy, where she was?"

"I think he misunderstood from the beginning," Dad said then. "Father Jonas knew me from years past, from doing my own Communion when I was a boy, and all our visits after that. So when we turned up on his parish doorstep, desperate in the middle of the night, he didn't ask no questions. I think he just presumed your mother was dead, and the most important thing to him was to claim your soul for the church—to get you christened. So I guess that's where it started. I needed a story, to protect us, and that seemed like the most believable one."

To protect us.

"I always tried to get people to come to the conclusion on their own, though," he said. "I never liked to say she was dead. I wouldn't like to say it. And I never liked to lie to a priest, especially."

Dad reeled in, and some fish had ate his bait but not his hook. He went looking for a new fly to string up, brushed the palm of one hand acrosst the tops of the rushes, searching.

"You never had no problem lying to me, though," I said to his back.

Things had changed that much in one day, now I could say that sort of thing to my father, and he couldn't even say nothing back. He turned to look at me, one hand on his hip.

"Seven minutes of breath in this world," I said. "That's what you told me." For years I'd lived with the weight of killing my mother. And it was all imaginary—my father's lies. "Why, Dad?" I said. "Why did you tell me that? Why seven minutes?"

There was a breeze now, sending little peaks acrosst the water, drying the tear-tracks on my neck. Dad looked like a big child, standing there among the rushes in his wellies, the fishing rod bowed in his hand.

"Because that was how long we was together as a family in that kitchen," he said. "More or less. I don't know, Christy, I guess I hoped you'd find some poetry in it."

I opened my fingers and let go my own rod, watched the wattle fall. It lay on top of the water for just an instant before it slipped under and disappeared. I turned and sloshed past him toward the bank.

"I'm going home."

EVERYBODY WAS AWAY WHEN I got back to camp. They'd probably stayed in the town after Mass for to do their shopping and their messages.

Fidel was on his own, stretched out by the fire. I sat down beside him and rubbed his head. He licked me.

Dad was along in a few minutes, and I could tell by the weight of the bucket, he'd caught something. He set it down by the fire and got his knife out for to gut the fish. Myself and Fidel watched him. The camp was uncommonly hushed and clear, like you could hear miles away.

"I want to say something to you." Dad paused, his voice cushioned by the cottony quiet. "I'm glad. I'm glad it all came out, like."

Fidel rolled onto his back so's I could scratch his belly. Dogs never lied. Fidel loved me the same as yesterday. One hind leg thumped the ground.

"I always knew I'd tell you someday," Dad was saying. "I'd hoped to do it in my own time, in my own way." He tried a smile, but it didn't work. "You deserved to know the truth."

"So what was you waiting on, then?" I asked.

"I guess I just wanted you to be old enough to take it all in," he said. "It's an awful heavy secret to drape on the shoulders of an eleven-year-old boy."

I didn't know if I believed him that he would've told me. It was hard to believe anything he said.

"So I'm supposed to believe you lied to me all my life just because you didn't want to burden me?"

Dad looked down at his shoes, but then flicked his eyes back up. "You'll believe whatever you have to," he said. "But that's the truth."

"And that's the only reason?" I said, searching 'round his face.

He was quiet for a moment, deciding. "Honestly?" he said.

I lifted my chin.

"There may've been another reason," he said. And then he cleared his throat, to make room for what he had to say. "I—" He stopped. "Maybe I thought you would leave." His voice was a hoarse whisper. "I thought you might want her instead," he admitted. "Instead of our life." He sat down in one of the lawn chairs, ran his tongue acrosst his top teeth.

"She—" I gulped. I'd saved this biggest question, because I wasn't sure I was ready for it. I held my breath. "Is she still alive?"

I was terrified of the answer, that she might be dead all over again. Or that she might be alive. Breathing. Laughing. Not wanting me.

"I don't know, son." Dad seemed to cave in a little, a hollow from the chest.

"D'you miss her?" I said.

He tucked his lips inside his mouth and nodded.

"Every day," he said. "Every single day of your life. I see you . . . I see her in you."

His eyes was soggy. He breathed one gasp, then a deep, shuddering breath after.

"Did you never think of going back for her?" I asked.

Dad drove his knife blade into the dirt between his feet. "Impossible," he said.

THE BOOKSHOP WAS CLOSED SUNDAYS, but I went anyway, just in case the missus might be there. I pressed my face up to the darkened glass of the window, and made a hood out of my hands so's I could see. The stacked spines of the books inside was like streaks of muted color, like long faces with closed eyes. She wasn't there, so I went to Finnuala Whippet's house instead, and knocked on the door. The maid, Mary, answered.

"Is Miss Amy in?" I asked, squinting up at her.

Mary raised her chins. "Miss Amy is gone out for the day with her mother," she sniffed. "She shan't be back until very late." She tried to make her voice fancy, but her accent was thick as the bog she was reared on.

"Would it be okay if I maybe left her a note?" I asked.

She looked at me blankly. "Come back tomorrow," she said, and she made to close the door on me.

I pushed my hand against it. "Sorry, missus!" I said, shoving my shoe into the doorjamb.

She opened it up again, but not as wide this time.

"I can't," I said. "I can't come back tomorrow."

She looked at me with arched eyebrows and made no reply.

"Please," I said. "I just want to leave her a note."

"And who do you suppose will write this note for you?" she finally asked. Of course—she couldn't write.

"Oh, I will," I said, too quickly.

She put one hand on her hip and looked at me like I was a liar. "*You* will?" she said.

I nodded, and tried to make my face lowly. I looked down at my toes.

"*You'll* write the note," Mary said again. She was daring me to say that I could do what she couldn't.

"I mean, it would be far better if you could help me," I said. "I can't write very good. But I could probably manage enough."

I stayed with my eyes glued to my shoes. Mary opened the door a bit wider and made a shooing gesture with her hand.

"I'm too busy for love notes," she said. "But there's a pen and paper at Miss Amy's desk in the parlor. Hers is the smaller rolltop on the right."

I breathed and followed her inside. We walked down the hall and she showed me into a room directly opposite the door where the party had been yesterday.

"Don't be all day about it," she said, before disappearing down the hall and into the kitchen.

The parlor was a cozy room, dominated by a big elephant of a desk right in the middle. There wasn't no papers on the desk, but there was a telephone and a lamp, and a pen that was disguised as a feather, and a big calendar with writing all over it. I went for a closer look. Yesterday was circled in red ink, and "MY BIRTHDAY!" was wrote in capital letters. Above that, in a smaller, more controlled black script, someone had wrote "Frankfurt." There was names of different cities on loads of the different calendar days: Geneva, Dublin, Brussels. Along the far wall of the room, two rolltop desks sat side by side.

I went to the smaller one and lifted its top. I caught the scent of oranges again, inside. And then, just for a moment, behind the oranges, I could smell myself, my family-scent: sweat and moss and tree bark and fire, mostly fire, and then earth and soil and damp leaves and wind. And then the oranges again, wafting up, the clean brightness of oranges, and they rinsed me away again. I sat down and placed my two hands flat on the desk for a moment to steady myself.

In front of me there was a neat stack of paper, and a jar with pens and pencils. I took a deep breath, drew one clean sheet of the heavy paper, and smoothed it out in front of me. I already knew what I wanted to say. I lifted a pencil and quickly wrote down these words:

Dear Amy,
I feel brave now, because of you.
xo

   Christy

I folded the note in half and left it sitting there on her desk. I rolled the top down, closing my words inside. At the door, I listened for Mary, and I heard her humming and banging pots beyond the kitchen door. I tiptoed acrosst the hallway and pulled back the pocket door. It rumbled in its track and I held my breath, in case Mary would hear and come legging it, but she was still humming away in the kitchen. I crept inside.

There wasn't a single remnant from yesterday's party. The food and drink was all cleared away, the gifts and wrapping papers bundled off, the piano opened again, waiting. I walked as softly as I could, aware of the echo of my footprints against the planks of the floor. At the wall of bookcases, I stood still, gazing up and down at the spines, not wholly sure what I was looking for until I seen it: ENCYCLOPAEDIA BRITANNICA ISLAND IRELAND MAP ATLAS.

I pulled the giant book down from its shelf and brought it over to the piano bench. I sat down and opened it acrosst my knees. It took me ages to figure out how to read it, how to use the index in the back to look up the right pages, the right maps. My throat was all tensed up with worry and hurry. I found the page, and I said a quick prayer in case what I was about to do was some very deep kind of unwritten sacrilege. And then I held my breath and closed my eyes. I ripped that page loose from its binding.

I didn't have time to feel sorry for the wounded book; it didn't bleed. I rolled up my prized page and slipped it down into the side of my wellie, pulled down the leg of my trousers to make sure it didn't show. Then I put the book back into its proper gap in the shelf. I knocked on the kitchen door and thanked Mary before I left.

BACK AT CAMP, I WAS restless and breathless. Jumpy.

"You're acting even weirder than usual," Martin said.

"Shut your pie hole," I said.

NINETEEN

Dad said it felt inevitable, the way he took me from my mam's house. That there wasn't really no decision in it, that it just happened. But before that night, I don't think I could've understood how that was, how sometimes even the biggest decisions slip right by you like as if they isn't decisions at all—like as if you're just riding a bobbing canoe on a mad, rushy river, and you just seen your oars get whipped outta your hands by the stronger grip of the river, and now you're watching them sink their narrow heads under the foamy slobber. You're watching them drift and drown. And then your canoe slides right over them—*calunk-unk!*—in the wicked water, and all you can do is hold on to the sides and say your prayers out loud.

God knows how many times I panicked in the nighttime road. I turned around that much, Jack was dizzy. But in the end, he was steady under me, and he felt sort of like an anchor, instead of oars. Like it couldn't be classed as running away so long as I was with Jack, because it's not running away if you bring your home with you. So in that way, I managed to tamp down all them panics and sweats that came on me every time I pictured Dad's face tomorrow morning, wakening up, wiping the sleep from his eyes. Stretching and yawning. The scent of Brigid's breakfast on the fire. I wondered how long it'd be before he noticed—we was gone.

Hours, I hoped—it could be hours and hours, so long as he didn't check on Jack straightaway. So long as he kept close 'round the camp in the morning, maybe working the tin. So long as Martin looked after Fidel, and kept his gob shut and went off to school like a normal Monday, like I made him swear to do. Please God. But I couldn't shake the fear that Dad would waken early—that he was wakening even now. Groping toward me in the empty dark, feeling the cool hollow of the tick where I should be, where he'd expect me to be. But I was gone.

It woulda been better if them panics had worked on me, if one of them times I turned us 'round in the road, we'd stayed turned around and we'd gave up, and we'd went sulking back to camp. Everything woulda been different if only we'd did that. But we didn't, we didn't. We went on, marking our hoofprints into the black dirt of the night road like we'd no choice, like it was all mapped out before us and there was no getting away from what would happen. It had to unfold this way.

This way, this way. The glowing white of the moonlight signposts, like the bone-fingers of faeries, pointing us, urging us. Ushering us. No, no, this way. Hurry! He's coming! He's behind you only a few miles, hurry! Birr to Roscrea. Roscrea to Templemore. Templemore to Thurles to Dundrum to Donaskeagh, oh. Hurry!

"Hie, Jack, hie!"

We stopped only once, and then just for a moment, at a blackened square in a sleeping town. I studied my map in the moonlight: where we was, how far we'd come, how far we'd yet to go. We went in at the fountain just long enough to dip our faces and swallow our fill. We left there with dripping chins, we crept, we crept until we reached the last house of the town, and then I curled over Jack, my knees tight to his neck and my arms around him. And he ran. This way, Jack, hurry!

I don't know what I expected—that it would take days or weeks or a dozen different moons before we found it, maybe. I never dreamed it would be so close—that all my life, she'd been this close. A half a night's gallop. To my mother.

Ballycinneide. The moon was sloping, glowing down over her yard when we arrived. It threw its light down onto the grass like a dress, like a bride, with a veil of darting silver clouds. We stayed at the end of the long drive for a few minutes, watching the house.

It was on a swell of ground, surrounded by gobs of working fields and some pasture as well, just like Dad had described. Maybe this was the very field where he'd stood with the beetroot, where he'd first seen her. There was a fence, but it looked too delicate to be functional. Yes, it was loose, easy. Jack knocked the quiet top-board into the grass with one hoof and we stepped over. We didn't even have to jump. I got down so he could eat. I stood behind him, patted his neck, but I wasn't tall enough to get a good look at the house over the back of him, so I stepped around. Four, five steps. I left my foot-shaped dents in the dewy grass behind me, and the moon shone into them, too. Silver grass for Jack to eat.

The house from Dad's story—Cleary House, it was called, which was what made it so easy to find. Too easy—like gravity, the way we came here. Me and Jack was an apple that fell out of a tree, and this was where we landed, in this field, looking up at the darkened windows of Cleary House, like two rows of deep black eyes. The front door looked permanent, shut. It was like a vault, this house, but still you got the impression that it could, with a great deal of effort, and only if you made it very angry, lift itself up off its manicured haunches and chase after you at a terrible pace. That it could overtake you and pin you down by the shirttail, and then it could carefully lower itself right back down, all the vast weight of its ancient rock-heaps and stones, bearing down on top of you, crushing you. Bursting your lungs like rotten grapes.

I shuddered.

"Come on, Jack," I said. "We'll make camp."

We went so far as the tree line, just a couple dozen paces into the tree line, and it wasn't much of a camp to make, between us. I didn't want to light a fire in case somebody seen us for trespassers and called for the guards, or worse, just went shooting at us to clear us off. It was only a couple hours til daylight, anyway. Jack could eat and doze. I would snooze, if I could quiet the hammering heartbeat in me long enough. Just there, acrosst that field—my mother was waiting. Beneath the shingled roof of the house there, just above the crest of the field, a canopy of watchful trees gathered close around her. Inside that gathering of leaves and limbs, she slept. Fitful or peaceful. I wondered if she could sense me here, on the edge of this field, her field, leaning my head against the trunk of a big tree in the dark. Moss for my pillow. Just a few hours now.

I DIDN'T EXPECT TO SLEEP—NOT really. Sleep was catching me off guard now. That's what newness does to you—it makes you believe you'll never sleep again, but instead you sleep like the dreaming dead. You sleep hard and deep.

This time, I dreamed of Finnuala Whippet with her plaits dipped in purple paint. I dreamed that I was watching her, in through her window, behind the bushes, clinging to her window frame when out of nowhere, I was swept up by a purple cyclone—my fingers seizing desperately onto the splintering wood of the window, my feet flying, caught in the sucking air behind me. I was ripped away from her, and I woke up pulling my own hair and gasping for breath, breath.

I opened my eyes, and the leaves of the big tree was dancing above me in the early breeze, the trace light of the pink morning sun sloping through. Sunlight. It was morning. Feck. I'd slept in.

"How d'ya sleep in on a tree root, Christy?" I said, and I sat up as quick as I could.

I was on my feet, crouched. I had to get my bearings. Where was I? Where was I? Which direction had we come in, now? It looked different without the angled light of the moon. Which . . . I turned around.

"Jack," I said.

Oh God. Jack. I whipped around again, but it was only my own two feet on the ground beneath me.

"Jack," I called, louder this time.

He'd never run off before—he was too smart a horse for that. But then, he was usually stuck into a field, where there was plenty of grass for him to eat, or else he was tied to the wagon, where everything around him was familiar. I'd heard stories of some horses going travelling miles and miles on their own to get back home again. But Jack was a travelling horse. His home was with me—it always had been, since the day he was born, and I took that burlap feed sack and rubbed him til he breathed. He would never leave me, right?

"Jack!"

I could see now, through the assembled trunks of trees, the rooftop of Cleary House, with its chimneys sticking out of its top like half a dozen thorny little crowns. I hoped Jack had gone the other direction, into the wood. That's what I wanted to have happened, so, for a moment, I made myself believe it.

"Please, God," I said, and I took a few steps that way.

Maybe I knew that was wrong. But I went faster, deeper into the wood. I was stubborn in my hope; I followed the path I wanted him to have took. Because if he'd gone the other way, it might've been a catastrophe. Somebody might have spotted him. I was trotting now, trying not to panic, trying not to think what might happen if an angry farmer found him before I did.

"Jack!" I called, not too loud, not too loud.

There was just a tinge of pink underfoot now, as the forest drank in the filtered light of the coming day. My bare toes beat into that pink dust and—where was my wellies, now? I'd left them behind me, by the tree. I must've. No time to bother.

I caught some real fear then, looking down at my naked toes. The sight of them woke me up somehow, because they was real—I wasn't dreaming. I turned then. Stopped still where I was, and turned. I had to face it, I had to be brave. He wasn't this way—I knew he wasn't. He would've gone into the field. Deeper into the field, higher into the field. For grass. Sweet breakfast. Jesus God, he would've gone toward the house.

I sprang. I leapt. I flew. Back, thundering through the trees that snapped around my head and face, back through the twigs that slapped and broke along my arms and legs. And now I was scream-ing, shouting my head off, and I didn't care who heard or seen me.

"JACK!"

I was fairly belting through the wood now. I knew he was in danger. The trees was hanging black above me, showing their green arms and fingers, their barks silvering around me, the inevitable broad light of the day was coming, coming. And I ran.

Jack.

And I think it was after I said his name, I heard it, but it might've been before, or it might've been even as the name crossed my lips again: Jack.

The gunshot.

It didn't sound like a bang or an echo or a ping or a piff or a crack or anything else that a gunshot is meant to sound like. Instead it was like the sound of my heart stopping, my breath leaving this life. It was like silence.

I nearly stopped in my path, but then I was moving faster than I'd ever moved, like as if my feet wasn't feet at all, but was hooves, like I had the power to move that fast. I was an animal streaking

toward the sound of my grief, and I couldn't even see the blurry
ground no more, moving under me.

Jack.

The trees broke above me then and I caught my heel on a stump,
and I tumbled out of the tree line and into the field, faster than a
rabbit, and I seen him.

"Jack!"

He was standing, he was still standing, thanks to God he was
standing, and he whipped his head toward me when he seen me
crashing through them leaves. And when he moved, he was ordinary and light-footed, and I gasped my relief out loud and I fell onto
my two knees to thank God. And then I could feel myself smiling,
grinning, the tears of relief spilling outta me, and then—click—
everything went sickening slow, and I heard the stretched gallop of
Jack's feet making their thumping approach. And then the gunshot.
The second gunshot. And Jack's feet left the ground.

And he fell and he fell and he fell.

And I couldn't hear nothing after that. I couldn't hear my own
feet under me as I leapt for him, and I couldn't hear the screams that
was coming outta me. I couldn't hear Jack as he struggled and kicked
the air and snorted and fought with that bullet in him.

Jack.

THERE WAS BLOOD ON ME. A lot of blood. It was black and sticky, and
had a sweet, sort of rusty odor to it. It was on my hands and my
shirt, dried to a crusty film. It was matted into my hair and nostrils.
It was smeared on my face.

Jack's blood, his careful insides. First, I'd tried to cover the bullet
hole in his neck with my hands, to stop the geyser-blood spurting
everywhere. Then I'd used my shirttail, then my hands again, but in
the end there was too much of it.

Jack died under my arms. I lay with him while he died. I stroked him along his big strong neck and I covered him over with my tears like a blanket, and in the end, I just held on to him and whispered to him that it was okay, Jack, it's okay.

Then there was footsteps, crunching over the morning grass, human footsteps, approaching. Jack gave me his last tremble, his last, loyal breath. All the years I'd spent worrying over him, terrified of this exact moment, and still, I never really thought it would happen. Life without Jack seemed impossible. I closed his eyes and then I sobbed into his mane, clung into him, tried to wish him back. I donno how long we stayed that way, the three of us. Jack, laying beneath me, holding me up. My face pressed into his hair, my fingers gripping him, refusing to let go. The silent murderer standing beyond, the shotgun still slung acrosst the front of him like a promise.

When I finally lifted my eyes to face him, it was like remembering a nightmare, the way that memory can gallop up on you in the broad daylight. He'd only been a gunshot before now. A sound. Now his eyes leeched into me like I knew him. This is what he looked like, the man who killed Jack: he was monstrous, with horns and fangs, and a face twisted up into a mask of pure wickedness.

But that's only what my grief saw. In truth, he was a regular-looking, clean-shaven man with a gun, and a hat shading the eyes of his rangy face. He looked like he might move toward me, but he hesitated. Finally, he slung the shotgun 'round to his back and he stepped toward me slowly.

"Come on, then," he said to me. "Let's get you cleaned up."

And I went with him because I didn't know what else to do. We walked acrosst the field, back toward the house. I was barefoot and covered in blood. I stood apart from him, a space of bald grass between us.

"You shot him," I said, though I still couldn't really believe it. "You killed Jack."

The sun was vomiting all over the sky. Jack was a heap of blood and bones in the sunny grass behind us. There was no breath left in him. He was dead, and Grandda was dead, and now I was really alone. I thought I'd fall down, that my legs would just wilt beneath me and I would die, too, of grief, right here in this field.

The man knocked his hat back from his forehead and wiped the sweat off his brow, then scrunched the hat back onto his head. The shotgun rattled on his back while he walked. I looked down, and even my toes had drips and daubs of Jack-blood acrosst them.

"Where are the rest of you?" he asked me. "The others? Your family?"

Instead of answering, I pointed ahead of us, over the crest of the hill, toward the towering chimneys of Cleary House. "You live there?" I asked him.

He nodded.

"You're William Keaton?" I said.

We was climbing the rise of ground now, nearing the top.

"I am." He nodded again.

And the way I deflated at that moment was like a bullet had ripped clean through me, too, and popped me like a balloon. But we was at the crest of the hill, and the house loomed up before us.

"So am I."

But he was already heading down the slope on the other side and he didn't hear the words, whipped out of my mouth and carried off, as they was, by the wind.

And then my mother. She came in and filled up my mind with her purple hair, and for a moment, she swept everything else clean outta me with her purple broom-hair, and I glanced back over my shoulder at the pasture below, behind us, where Jack lay lifeless in the sun. The shape of him at that distance was like a man lying wounded in the field. My hand flew to my earlobe, and I touched the back of it, remembered Dad's crescent scar, how he said he'd slapped the bullets out of the sky to protect me. I'd thought them bullets was only part of the tale, his embellishments. But just there, rattling against the shoulder blade of the man walking down the hill, was

perhaps the very same gun from that mythic night. I gaped at Jack's
twisted body and felt washed over with astonishment and regret.

"That's what Dad risked for me," I whispered onto the breeze, and
my mouth hung open, after. I turned and staggered down the hill.

Inside the open front door of the house, William Keaton unshoul-
dered his murderous shotgun, and leaned it against the wall in the
corner. It minded me of the way Grandda's fiddle stood in the corner
of his wagon on that other mournful day. I stood behind William
Keaton, bloody in his doorway, and I peered at that brutal gun. If I
wanted to, I could've walked over to it and picked it up, still warm.
I could've cocked its trigger and sought my revenge.

"Stay here," William Keaton said to me. He went down the hall
and disappeared through a swinging door at the end.

"And don't touch anything," his voice carried from beyond.

Then I was alone in the front hall of the house. This house that
could've been my house. I looked around me and tried to take that
in, tried to imagine myself in some fancy trousers with a pair of
braces, a red school blazer with some sort of a crest on the pocket. A
beanie on my head. Holding my mother's hand.

I might've been an expert at sliding down that very banister,
polishing it with my bum. I might've played here, on this carpet,
with loads of rich toys like Finnuala Whippet had. I might've hid
under this table, or knocked over this lamp and got a scolding. I
touched the soft yellow lampshade and left a bloody fingerprint on
it. I pulled my hand away. In this house, I might've read every book
I ever dreamed of, holding them acrosst my knees in bed, turning
the pages in the glowy lamplight. If Dad hadn't took me, I might've
known my mother's face in the softness of that light. I might've belonged to her instead. Everything would've been so different then.
I'd never have known Dad. Or Grandda. Or.

"Jack."

When I said his name out loud, I could see him falling again, in
my mind. I could see the blackness of him hanging stark and rugged

against the pink morning sky, his hooves scraping the air, his head crashing down into the dirt and the grass, and I had to blink very hard to remove the image of it. I stared at the port wine curtains hanging in the high front windows instead. They was tied back with broad silk sashes, tassled and fringed. And then there was a tiny gap of a gasp in the room—a colored little breath, a note of song, nearly. A surprised O sound. In purple.

My mother, on the stair. Her white hand, small and clean against the dark wood of the banister. She hovered above me like an angel. She shimmered, she was that clean. Her face glimmered down at me, all round and white. Her eyes, broad and blue, wide and staring. Long, long lashes. Her hair folded back off her face, its tangle of wild red curls barely contained by the green band that strapped them 'round. Her cheeks was a perfect pink, flushing deeper when she seen me, and her mouth was a round, perfectly round O.

"*William,*" she called.

"It's Christy," I said, staring up at her.

We stared at each other.

"*William!*" she said again, and the door swung on its hinge, and William Keaton appeared again from behind it, and then I understood—she was calling her husband.

And he bustled into the room, coming between us—my mother on the stair and me still standing muddied with grief in the front hall of her grand house. William Keaton handed me a damp and steaming towel, and his wife—my mother—took a tentative step down the stairs.

"William, who is this child?" she said to him. "What is he doing here? What happened to him?"

"Never mind, Nora," he said to her.

She came down two more steps and then stopped. I took the towel and rubbed it over my face til it was covered with sticky, brown blood. I wiped the damp cloth between my knuckles, and then stooped to get the glob on my foot as well. Jack's blood. William

Keaton went toward the steps, went up a few steps to meet his wife, and he dropped his voice so's I wouldn't hear, but I heard him anyway, and I watched them in the mirror.

"I shot his horse," he said to her.

Nora gasped and leaned away from William Keaton. Her white hand paused at her breast, and then went to cover her mouth. She shook her head the tiniest bit, but she didn't say nothing to her husband, who went on. "He's obviously a tinker, and he'd loosed his horse to graze into the bottom pasture," he said. "They were trespassing. They're *always* trespassing."

"But, William," Nora said sadly. She glanced at him and then turned her face away, so's all I could see was the line of her jaw, the back of her head, in the mirror. She wouldn't look at her husband.

"How many times would you have me warn them, Nora? It's not as if I enjoy shooting horses," he said. "But I've had enough of them taking advantage. I won't have them using our land for public grazing. I've given them ample warnings. I've even posted signs. At some point, a man has to defend his land, his home. It's a matter of honor."

He turned to look at me over his shoulder, impatient with his wife's silent compassion, exasperated that he should have to defend hisself in front of me. I pretended not to listen to the whispered, one-sided argument.

"We're not running a campground; we're not a soup kitchen," he said, but Nora was still quiet, a mournful, dignified quiet, I thought. She wouldn't look at him.

I went closer to the mirror on the wall and tried to wipe the rest of Jack's blood off me. There was a stain acrosst my neck. In the mirror, I saw William Keaton shake his head on the stair. He seemed determined to defend hisself to Nora, to win her over. But maybe he sensed it was a lost cause, that he'd took the wrong tack with her. He looked up at the side of her face where she stood, still one step above him, still dismayed.

"Still, I don't suppose I meant to kill the poor beast," he finally admitted. "Damn it all."

And a quick expression of remorse did cross his face then, but I thought it was more for Nora than for Jack. She turned and looked into his eyes for just a moment. She allowed him that brief grace of her gaze. And then she moved past him on the stairs. She touched his shoulder as she stepped by. And now she was moving toward me, and I was terrified, paralyzed.

"Would you like a bath?" she said to me, in the mirror. She stopped a few feet behind me and looked at my pained and filthy reflection. Her voice softened and dropped. "I'm so very sorry for your loss. So very sorry." She shook her head, her forehead creased in sympathy.

I couldn't speak. I stared at her face in the mirror above me.

"Where is your family?" she said, leaning toward me.

I took a deep breath. The towel wasn't so warm now. Its dampness grew chilly.

"Are you all alone?" She tried again. "What's your name?"

She was looking at me in the mirror; her hand was on my shoulder. I stared at her. I felt like I'd never been looked at before that moment. Here was my mammy, looking at me, muck-dirty in her gilded mirror.

"Christy," I said, but my voice fell out of my mouth like dust.

She nodded behind me, leaned to take the towel into her own clean hands. She didn't seem to mind if she'd get my dirt on her, on the fine white linen of her dress. I suddenly wished I was clean.

"William," I said then, my voice a little stronger now.

I was correcting myself, but she didn't understand.

"William Christopher Hurley," I said.

And this time the gasp that escaped into the room wasn't a small, pretty thing. It was deep, like the grunt of a feral boar. It came from the man on the stairs, and it echoed in the mouth of my mother. I pulled at the bloody collar of my shirt, drew my medal out from inside and showed it to her.

"My name is William Christopher Hurley," I said again, pressing my medal into her hand. "And you're Nora Keaton. You are my mother."

TWENTY

After that, William and Nora Keaton sat silently on the stairs for a long time. Nora had sat down with a thud after I'd told her she was my mother, and William sat three steps higher up than her. They didn't speak or look at each other. A few times, William tried his voice, but he could only manage one word at a time, and then he'd shake his head and fall silent again.

"How."

"Where."

Like that.

Finally, Nora Keaton stood up from her step and smoothed down the already-smooth linen of her dress. Her face was like a flickering lantern. I watched her very carefully. She crossed the space between us and came to stand beside me again. She stretched her hands out to me then, and it wasn't nothing at all like I'd imagined. She leaned down to me, near fell down in front of me, really—on her two knees—so we was looking eye to eye. And she had my dirty hands in her clean ones, and her face was so awfully pretty—God, she was like a saint, the way she looked, with her sparkly blue eyes and her

ginger eyebrows knotted up in her forehead. She'd tears coming
down her face, then, rolling down in big splashes of drops, and she
put her hand on my face, on my jaw, and that hand was so soft it
wasn't like a hand at all. And then she drew me into her, for to hold
me. And I wanted it to feel like it did in the piano-dream, where
I felt like a baby kangaroo, burrowing in, safe. But she called me
William.

"William."

I pushed away from her. "Christy," I said.

And she looked into my eyes, and she still had tears streaming
down, but all mine was spilt already. I was dry. She made a big
sniffle, and then she wiped her nose with the back of her soft, un-
spoiled hand, and she nodded her head.

"Christy," she repeated, and she tried out a smile, but it was a
broken one.

A MAID CALLED KITTY SHOWED me upstairs, which was strange because I'd never been up no stairs before, never more than a few anyway, into the back of a wagon. I had the impression there was an
awful lot of air beneath us, that we was hanging, suspended in this
heavy, floating room.

Kitty filled up the tub for me. I stood smeared with Jack's blood
in the stark, white room, and tried to make myself careful and delicate, so as not to be too heavy. She left a clean towel and some clothes
on a chair for me.

"Come down to the kitchen when you're finished," she said.

I nodded at her. She turned to go, but paused in the doorway. She
looked back at me.

"I'm sorry about what happened to your horse," she said.

"Jack."

"I'm sorry about Jack," she said. "Really, Master shouldn't've
done that. It was a wicked thing he done."

I nodded, but couldn't look her kindness in the face, in case I might cry again. She pulled the door shut behind her with a click, and left me alone to survey the bathroom. It was about the size of a wagon, and the heavy, iron tub stood in the middle of the room, steaming all with bubbles. There was colored pots and jars and tubes of goo all around the edges of the tub, and I picked them up one by one to smell them: cinnamon, apple, lavender. I could still get the scent of Jack's blood caked into the hair of my nostrils, so I dunked my hand under the hot bubbles, and brought it out wet to rinse my nose. Then I moved the towel and clothes off the chair where Kitty had left them, and I pushed the empty chair over against the door. There was a key in the keyhole, but I was too afraid to lock it in case I'd get stuck inside. I didn't want nobody barging in on me in the tub. I jammed the back of the chair under the doorknob, and then I backed away cautiously, counted to ten, and then stripped out of my stained clothes and sprang into the roasting bathwater as quick and light as I could.

The water sloshed out one side of the tub and then settled back around me. The heat of it was gorgeous on my skin, and no amount of grief or guilt could hinder that. I washed with every pot of goo, one at a time: a little blue goo for my left foot, a glob of red goo for the right, a smear of lemony-yellow goo for my face and my armpits, and then some chunky white goo for my arse and balls and the rest.

When I was done, I felt clean. Not just my skin and my hair and my ears, but also my insides. And then I thought how odd that was, the way a proper tragedy can cleanse you and make you new again. All my sins and terrors, all my anger at Dad, even the memory of burning Grandda in the wagon, all of it washed away. Vanished. One gunshot can do that.

Because when it came down to it, all them other worries had only been in my head, really. Grandda was already dead when we burned him. Dad still fed me and slept next to me, even after I found out about everything he done.

But with Jack, it was different, because I was the cause of what happened. Two hours ago, he was standing, eating breakfast. Waiting for me. Two hours ago, he was still that twin baby colt me and Grandda had saved. Shiny and black, grateful, smart. Motherless. Two hours ago, we still belonged to each other. And now he was dead, his blood spilled out of him in a murky stain acrosst the grass. Because of me. Because of the decisions I took.

How, Jesus, how would I tell Dad? He was so fond of Jack, singing to him and arguing with him and teasing him all the time. I had *wanted* to hurt Dad. But not like this, never like this. In that moment, I understood something new about the notion of family. Because that's who Jack was to me; he was my family. In my anger and confusion, I'd went chasing after a ghost—a mother who didn't even recognize me. I'd traded Jack's life for a fairy tale.

I cried into the tub water for only a moment's pardon, and then I climbed out of that bath because I didn't want to be alone with my thoughts for another minute. I heaved my dripping legs one at a time over the edge of the tub, and then I was standing on the piled towel in the middle of that big, echoey room, and I could hear the drip, drip, drip of myself, smattering onto the tiled floor beneath, the same way Dad had stood dripping in this house ten years before me. Drip drip drip. And then he'd stole me away.

I clutched the towel up 'round me, covered myself with its warmth. In Dad's story, William Keaton was mean and diagonal, villainous. He was evil. He shot bullets at us in the night-rain. And now William Keaton had murdered Jack. I felt sick in my stomach.

I unstoppered the tub and watched my dirty gray bathwater drain. Then I dressed quickly into the clean clothes Kitty'd left, pushed the chair away from the door, and padded barefoot down the stairs. I was grateful to come back down them steps, to feel the earth beneath the floor beneath my feet. I found William and Nora Keaton in the kitchen. Nora was seated on a small settee, and William stood with one arm draped over the mantel of the fireplace. On a low table between them was a plate of fresh sandwiches on a silver tray. Nora half stood out of her seat when she seen me, to wave me over.

"Come in, Christy," she said. "I've sandwiches made for you."

Kitty was tottering around at the sinks on the far side of the room, and something in me wanted to go to her instead, to her comfort and mildness. I glanced at her, but she wasn't looking at me. She was absorbed in her work. I made my way over toward the fireplace, toward the settee and the silver tray of food Kitty had prepared. There was a second settee facing the first, facing Nora, so I slouched into it, even though that meant having my back to the doorway. I twisted my body halfway in the seat, until I could sense the door from the corner of my eye.

I didn't take a sandwich straightaway. I was hungry, but I didn't want them to know I was hungry. I didn't know the why of it, but it felt like treachery, somehow, to admit hunger.

"Whose clothes are these?" I asked instead, pulling at the leg of the trousers that almost fit me.

They was only a bit loose around the waist. They was just slightly too long, to cover my naked toes. My mother glanced up at William Keaton.

"They're Henry's," she said.

I looked at her. "Who's Henry?" I asked.

She swallowed and leaned forward. "He's our son," she answered.

I sat back against the fluffy cushions behind me. "Oh," I said. I didn't know why I should feel betrayed. I didn't know why I shouldn't eat a sandwich.

"We had another son," Nora Keaton continued. "After."

I took a sandwich, fiddled with the crust.

"After you. After we lost you," she managed to say.

I took a bite. It was chicken, with butter and tomatoes. I chewed, and then repeated, "After you lost me."

"Yes," she said.

I tried to swallow the chicken, but my throat was awful dry. But I did swallow, and then I said, "How come?"

"Kitty, will you bring him a cup of tea, dear?" Nora Keaton called acrosst the room.

"How come you never came after me?" I said, and then I dogged into the sandwich again, the biggest bite I could fit into my mouth. "You never came looking for me. I wasn't even very far away."

I was talking with my mouth full. My mother's lips went small in her face—she pursed them. She cleared her throat, too, and then took a swallow from her own cup of tea in front of her.

Kitty crossed the room silently, and set the steaming cup down on the table in front of me. I stared at her face, hoping for a furtive smile, or a glance to give me strength, but she only turned and swept away again.

"I—" Nora Keaton said. "I did. I mean. We did. We . . . we looked, but . . . Ultimately, you know, after a great deal of sorrow and soul-searching, we eventually decided that maybe we shouldn't, you know." She was shaking her head. "We thought that maybe it was all for the best," she finished, clamped her hands together.

That was way harder to swallow than the chicken.

"For the best," I said. I blew on my tea and then slurped it. "So you didn't have no instinct for me, then?" I said after a minute. "Like to come and get me, no matter what?"

Nora Keaton's hand flew to her throat like a bird, like a white budgie, and her husband shifted his diagonal weight by the fireplace. He stood up a little straighter.

"Now, hear," William Keaton said, but my mother interrupted him.

"It's okay, William," she said, restraining him with a gesture of her hand. "Christy has a right to be angry. He has a right to ask me these things."

William Keaton leaned back again, against the wood of the mantel. We stared at each other while I ate his food.

"Of course I had an instinct for you," Nora Keaton said, and I turned back to face her. "I . . . I wasn't well, Christy. I don't know how to describe it. I wasn't myself then, after you were born. My father had died, I—I was so overwhelmed with grief. I wasn't sure I could manage. I was in an awful state, all the time."

"She cried for weeks!" William added.

"Really, weeks?" I said. "Wow. Sounds like you was really broke up over it."

I took another bite of my sandwich. I didn't know why it was going like this, why I felt so angry at them. I sorta hated them both, not just William, and it wasn't even just because of Jack. I hated them for their normalness. I hated them because they had a regular life here, and they had a son called Henry, who was a little bigger than me, even though he was younger. He was a little better-fed.

I hadn't come here to hate them, but here I was. Hating them. I had wanted to rush her, and call her mammy, and to really feel that—that she was my mammy. I looked acrosst at her, beautiful on the settee in front of me. So clean, angelic. Her hair violently red in the firelit, daytime room. She didn't feel like mammy to me. She felt like that cracked porcelain lady from Patrick's mantelpiece.

They was quiet, watching me chew. They didn't know what to say to me. I was a tinker in their house—that's how I felt; it was on William's face. Even clean after my bath, and in Henry's fine, laundered clothes.

"So where's Henry?" I asked, sticking my hand into his trousers pocket, pulling out Henry's lint.

"He's at school," my mother said.

"Boarding school?" I asked, studying the lint.

She nodded.

I flicked the lint into the fire and took another slurp of tea.

"Listen," William Keaton said then, but his voice was softer this time. He stepped away from the fireplace, clasped his hands behind his sloping back. "I don't imagine you'll be able to comprehend all of this. You're just a child, after all . . ."

I arched an eyebrow at him. He hadn't a notion what a child like me could understand. I might be smaller than his son, but I'd lived a dozen more lifetimes, at least.

"And a tinker." He gestured at me and shook his head. "But I don't suppose that's your fault, really—what you are, that you are feral like this, that you don't understand the ways of society."

He smiled at me, a vacant, seeping kind of a smile, and I caught my mother's grimace from the corner of my eye. She was embarrassed by his condescension, and that cringe felt like a glimmer of hope. William was pacing now, behind Nora's settee, his hands still clasped behind him, his head tipped back while he talked.

"But that was a very difficult time for your mother." He paused to look at me, then squeezed his wife's shoulder. For the first time, I was struck by how different he was from the man in Dad's story. He *was* diagonal, but not really in the way Dad seen him. There was something waitful about the way his body hung sloped on his bones. Something more wretched than wicked. He had hoped for my mother—you could see that in the way he looked at her; he was still trying to stir up her feelings for him. He had hoped for her and waited for her and, in the end, he'd won her, at least in part. My father's rival. He was haughty and thoughtless and unkind. He was hollow. But he seemed to want his wife, her goodness, the way a decrepit moth wants the luster of flame.

"Your mother longed for you; she wept for you. Even now, I catch her on occasion, with such a stark sadness on her face," he said, looking over at her. "She has always missed you. I thought she'd never get over it, even after she got pregnant with Henry. I was so angry when it happened, I wanted your father hanged for his vile crime. Such audacity he had, violating our home in that way. Such base thievery. I had taken you in, a boy who was nothing to me. That was

my decision, to make you my ward and charge, to raise you in priv-
ilege. That was my chosen act of charity for you, and your scoundrel
of a father had no right to take that from me. No right!" He pounded
his fist into his hand.

"William," my mother said sternly, and he paused in his pacing,
draped his arm back acrosst the mantelpiece. "I think I'd like to
speak with Christy alone for a few minutes, if you don't mind," she
said.

William glared at her, his face washed pale even in the firelight.
"That's hardly necessary," he said. "There are things the boy needs
to understand."

"And he will," she said gently. "In time. He has already had one
terrible shock today, and I think it's best if we take all of this rather
gradually."

William Keaton crossed his arms in front of him and leaned back
on his angled hips. My mother rose to him.

"Thank you, darling," she said softly, and I watched William's
features melt when she kissed him lightly on the cheek. "We won't
keep you any longer from attending your day's business." She
squeezed his forearm, and he shook hisself from the shoulders.

"Very well," he said, and then he lifted his chin, called acrosst
the room, "Kitty, serve tea in the library. I'll be at my ledgers."

He tried to face me before he left, but his eye wouldn't settle
on mine. He nodded at Nora instead, and then he was away. My
mother gave me a weak smile after the kitchen door swung shut
behind him.

"He's—" She shook her head. She was searching for something
to explain him, maybe something that wouldn't feel disloyal. She
settled on, "He's not very good with people."

I lifted another sandwich from the tray, and glanced over at
Kitty, who was busy with a second tray, preparing a steaming little
pot to follow William to the library.

"You know, William was very angry, when your father took you. Furious," she said. "And I—I just wanted you back so much. I grieved. God, I missed you, Christy. But I was never angry. And I feared for what would happen to your father if you were found. I knew you were safe with him. That you would be happy."

"Happy," I echoed.

I still felt invaded by William's hollowness. My mother bit her lip.

"I thought you was dead," I said.

She shook her head. "I never meant for you to think that. That wasn't part of the plan."

My mouth fell open. "Plan?" I said. *"Plan?"*

My mother flashed her eyes first at me, and then acrosst the room to where Kitty was lifting her burdened tray from the sideboard. Then she looked down at her folded hands, and waited silently for Kitty to bustle out through the swinging door. I took her cue, and waited.

"What plan?" I said, when Kitty was gone.

My mother sat forward on her seat, leaned as far acrosst the table as she could. The sleeve of her white linen dress was draped across an escaped tomato on the tray between us.

"For your father to rescue you," she whispered urgently. "To save you from this awful life."

The sandwich fell from my hand and landed noiselessly on my bare foot. "You knew he was coming for me?" I said.

My eyes must've been as wide as my mother's then. She locked hers on to mine, like they was buoys, like they could save me from drowning.

"I did," she whispered.

We stared at each other for a long, silent moment, while my eyes flooded up with the drowning.

"You let me go," I said then. "You just let me go, like I was nothing. I was your *baby*." My mother was shaking her head, but I went on. "And you just shrugged me off like a runaway dog. Ah well, he's gone, we'll just get another one."

"It wasn't like that," she said. "That's not fair."

"Nothing's fair in this life," I said. Didn't she know?

My mother covered her face and cried quietly until I was almost sorry. After some minutes, when she finally raised her face, it was puffy and swelled with tears.

"You have no idea," she said. "You have no idea how I ached for you. God, how I wanted you, Christy. But I wanted a *life* for you more. Freedom. Happiness. I knew your father could give you things I never could. I knew you would be miserable here, that your life would be bleak, that William would make every decision for you in life—your education, your marriage. I knew he would be terrible to you, even though he tried—he tried not to resent you. He would've ruined you. I know that I wasn't brave enough to go with you. But my God, Christy. Don't you dare imagine that I haven't suffered for it. I did it because I loved you."

She made a spectacular sniffle, and I thought she looked prettier, somehow, her face all red and blotchy. Imperfect.

"But Dad said he took me in secret," I said. "In the middle of the night."

My mother nodded. "I left the kitchen door open for him," she said.

"But William shot at Dad, at us," I said. "Didn't he? He could have killed us both."

"I was seized with terror when I heard the sound of those gunshots," she said. "I flew down the steps and out the door, and I tackled him in the mud. God, it could have gone so wrong."

She shook her head.

"But how . . ."

"He was reloading," my mother said. "And I wasn't strong

enough to wrench that gun from him. So I stood in front of him instead, weeping. I told him he'd have to shoot through me."

I pictured my mother in a nightdress, in the moonlight, soaked through to the bone, her red curls clinging wet to her neck and forehead.

"Did he suspect you?" I said.

"No," my mother said, shaking her head. "He knew I still loved your father. And he knew I was protecting you, that was all." My mother put her hand against her heart, like she could nearly feel that distant terror pounding there, still. "William would never guess I had anything to do with it—how could he? He'd have to look beyond his own impulses to even think of it."

"But why—why didn't Dad tell me all of this?" I said. "When it all came out, when the secret came out, he made it sound like he did it all on his own. He never told me you knew."

Now the tears coming down my mother's face was hushed and grateful.

"Would you have been able to forgive me, if he had?" she asked. "If you knew, would you still have come looking for me?"

I stared into the crackling fire, reached down and retrieved my fallen sandwich from where it'd landed on my foot. I tossed it into the flames. I was shaking my head.

"Maybe he knew that," she said. "Maybe he knew there were certain things you had to hear from me."

My head was swimming, trying to sort it all out, trying to make sense of everything.

"But look at you now, Christy," my mother said. "We were right, weren't we? Look at you. We did the right thing." She reached again, and the tomato clung to the lace of her sleeve. She lifted my chin with her fingers. "You're my dream come true."

I couldn't help it then, I sniffled, too. And then there was an almighty floodgate of tears that opened in me. A well of tears. A cracked egg. For Grandda, for Jack. For my imaginary purple-haired mammy. For Nora Keaton. For Dad. Cups and cups of tears.

"You're a perfect boy," my mother said, crossing from her settee to mine, wrapping her arms around me tight. "You're just as I imagined you could be."

She folded me in this time, and I let her. Even with her slender arms and tidy rib cage, even with her clean, soft hands and her tears, she did it right. I burrowed into the scent of her cinnamon-red hair like I would never let her go.

"It's okay," my mammy said. "You're all right, now. You're all right."

MY MOTHER AND I WALKED out alone together, like her and Dad did once. Just the two of us. "There's something I want to show you," she said to me.

And we walked down the lane of the house, and acrosst the road and over two fields. I was barefoot because my wellies was still in the forest, but I didn't mind. I was holding my mother's hand. The ground began to climb in front of us, and soon there was wild purple heather all around, and she worried about my feet.

"Never worry," I said. "I go barefoot all the time. I only ever wear shoes when it's cold."

She picked her way through that heather like she was an expert mountain goat, and it growing thick and brambly all around us. But she was sure-footed and quick, and I was mad impressed because Brigid or Granny would never've walked that way. There was something adventurous about her—that she'd go hiking up a steep hill among the heather, even in her fine, white linen dress, the green, silk band strapping down her wild, red curls.

"So you loved my dad?" I asked her.

She swallowed and blinked, nodded her head. "Very much," she whispered.

"Then how come?" I said. "How come you didn't go with him?"

"I just couldn't," she said, squeezing my hand. "I wasn't able. I was too trapped here, I couldn't see any way out. My father was desperate to see one of us married, Millicent or me, before he died. He wanted to bring a son-in-law into the family, someone who could manage the land. He'd have liked a son of his own, for the land to've kept to the Cleary name. He was a little old-fashioned that way, to make sure the land would stay in the family. I knew it would kill him if I went off with your dad. I couldn't let my father down." She looked around her, opened her arms to the fields. "We've been here eleven generations," she said. "Our family was here during the famine-times, even before that. We were never absentee landlords; we always took care of our tenants, our land. It's in my blood," she said. "The same way the road is in yours, in your father's. I know this place so well, it's like my family."

Like Jack.

"I've loved this land my whole life." She looked over at me and smiled. "But I could've done without all the trappings that came with it."

"What like?" I said.

"You know, being a lady of socie-teh," she said in a silly, fake-posh accent. "It's all a load of bollix, really."

I gasped at the oath, but she only smiled.

"Well, it *is*," she said, nudging me. "The ladies get all gussied up in their fine frocks and their powdered faces, and they gossip and preen, while their men drink brandy and grow fat. Where's the fun in that?"

"Sounds awful," I agreed.

"It could be worse," she said. "But it's not my cup of tea."

We came to a rock wall then, with barbed wire at the top, and I thought we was at an end for sure, but she hiked up her skirt and found a footing in the wall. She reached her hand down, to help me over.

"You go first," I said. "I'll manage."

So she hoisted herself up, and then I seen her pale and slender leg—her whole leg! Out in the sunshine like it was nothing. And she threw that leg up onto the top of the wall and stood there for a moment, stepped over the barbed wire and then hopped down on the other side. I followed her over, scrambling. "So how did it happen with Dad, then?" I asked. "Like when did you know you was in love with him?"

She cocked her hand up against the sun—just the same way as she did in the photograph—and my heart felt swampy and full.

"Oh, I don't know, really," she said. "It was quick, unexpected."

I got the sense she was picking her way among her words the same as she was picking her way among the heather—careful and steady.

"Unexpected, like, because he was a traveller?" I asked.

It was hard to imagine a girl like her, all scrubbed and fastened, with a parasol and bonnet, looking twice at my dad, even as handsome as he was.

"Well, yes," she admitted. "There was that. But more, I just wasn't looking for love. I was young and I was trying hard to be carefree. I was attached to this land and my books and my flowers and my family. I felt whole already. All my friends and cousins ran off to England, to get launched into London society, to hunt for husbands. Millicent liked the idea of that, but I just wasn't interested, not in the slightest. I wanted a different type of adventure. I wanted realness, something solid and stirring. I didn't want to be clucked and cooed over. I didn't even want to fall in love."

She was walking ahead of me now, the heather was that thick and close we could only walk single file, and we was climbing, really, instead of walking—using our hands as well as our feet.

"But I guess that's how it happens, most times," she said. "Love takes you unawares." She reached back and gave me her hand, helped heave me over a steep bit.

"But why Dad?" I asked. It still seemed so unlikely, so inexplicable. I wanted to understand.

She just shrugged. "I don't know," she said, and then she was quiet for a moment, maybe trying to puzzle it out herself. "You know, sometimes, when you fall in love with someone . . . what you're really falling in love with is the way they make you feel about yourself."

She glanced back to check on my progress, and then plowed ahead. "You might catch a glimpse of your reflection in your lover's eyeball," she said. "And think to yourself: *Good Lord, I'm ravishing!*"

We both laughed at that. I thought of Finnuala Whippet, how she made me feel, like I was normal, like I didn't have to try to be nothing, only who I already was. She thought we had things in common, that we was alike.

"And your father just made me feel so alive, so brilliant," she said. "He made me feel rare. I'd always felt myself sort of bookish and odd. Even when I had other suitors . . . I don't know. They'd only say I was pretty, and they'd treat me like I was a glass ornament or a china doll. They'd admire me, sure, but it always felt academic, practiced. But your father, he was so raw in his emotions, he was so real . . . he made me feel powerful, astonishing, like I was shot through with energy and life." She caught my eye then, and shrugged, like it was the simplest thing in the whole world.

"He woke me up to life," she said.

TWENTY-ONE

While we talked and walked, the heather cleared out from under us, and we was suddenly stood in a sunny clearing. The grass grew soft underfoot, and still the ground rose ahead of us, and we climbed the last bit of it til we came to two giant rocks perched beside each other, at the very top of the hill. The rocks was about twice my height, higher than my mother's head, too. I turned around and looked back the way we'd came. You could see the house from here, the road, the stables. The ruins of an old cashel in the distance. You could see a crowd of grooms gathered in a bent circle in the field around Jack's body. I guess they was preparing to move him. My mother disappeared into the gap between the two big rocks.

"Come in," she said, and I followed her into the shadows.

She sat down inside, cross-legged, with her back against one of the rocks. I made to sit down opposite her.

"No," she said. "Over here."

She patted the ground beside her, and I went to sit next to her, grateful of the cool rock-shadows after our sweaty climb. Her white hands seemed to glow in the dimness.

"Look," she said, and she pointed to the rock face above us

And there I saw it. A crooked love-heart, scratched deep into the surface of the stone. Inside, the letters W.C., and the date 1-5-47. I reached acrosst and traced the grooves with my fingertips.

"What is it?" I said.

"It's my memory-stone," she said. "For my baby. For you, William Christopher. And that's your birth date."

I gasped. I had an actual, specific birth date. A *birthday*, even. Like Finnuala Whippet. What my mother gave me in that moment felt like twelve whole years worth of music and cake and balloons and presents.

"It's a bit silly, I know," she said. "A bit childish, maybe." She breathed, straightened herself up. "But it helped," she said. "Something about the ceremony of it . . ." She traced her finger into the love-heart. "It helped me remember you."

I was quiet for a minute then, trying to take it all in. Trying to imagine her coming here, alone, all broke with grief, tearstained and hollow, scratching my initials into the hard rock. Over and over again til her pale hands was torn and bleeding.

"I was shocked by the grief," she said. "Even though I'd helped plan it, even though I *wanted* your father to take you, so you could be happy and free. So your life wouldn't turn out stunted, like mine. I never imagined the way that grief would gobble me up, after, when you were really gone. So many days, I regretted it. I wished I could take it back. I missed you so much, it was a physical pain, like my heart was split, and I was bleeding to death on the inside. But then there were other days I felt reassured, even beyond that hurt. I knew we'd made the right decision."

"Like when?" I asked.

"Well, like, whenever I saw the local travellers, here," she said. "I would take such joy in greeting them, in seeing their encampments. I loved the children. Children are *supposed* to be dirty. Did you know that?"

I gave her a doubtful look.

"They are," she said. "All children. Supposed to be like filthy savages. They're supposed to have dirt under their fingernails, and trails of stickiness across their chins, and grass and reeds and flowers all tangled through their hair. Henry's never been dirty an hour in his life." She sighed. "William couldn't stand the sight of a dirty child, not for a moment.

"I would bring Henry down with me, whenever travellers stopped nearby," she said. "We'd go down to greet them and wish them well. We'd bring them some bread or whatever we had in the house, and my heart would just soar, looking at the bright eyes of those delightful children, seeing how free they were. Seeing their skinned knees and hearing the clamoring rush of their squeals when they'd see us coming. Poor Henry was so pale beside them, so reserved and unsure, so buttoned-up. He didn't even know how to play with them, how to be that free. I always knew, then, that you were better off. No matter how much I missed you."

She pressed her palm flat against the carved surface of the rock, tenderly.

"There's a great comfort in these ceremonies we do," she said. "Whenever we have to say goodbye."

I leaned my head back against the rock behind me, and wondered if I could tell her about Grandda. Maybe she'd understand. "Do you know the way travellers burn the wagons after?" I whispered. "When somebody dies? That's our ceremony?"

"Yes," my mother said. "I've seen them burn. It's meant to free them, isn't it?"

"Yeah."

"What a beautiful thing to do," she said. "Such a poetic gesture, like a sacrifice. A pure, unbridled expression of grief. We don't have anything like that at all. We just bottle it up. Move on." She shook her head.

"Those were the things I loved about your father," she said. "The realness of him. The audacity. Even for all the hardships of his life, he was free in a way I could never be. And I knew I couldn't give you that. Or rather, I could. But only by letting you go."

I swallowed against the bump in my throat. "I want to tell you something," I said. "A secret."

My mother sat completely still beside me.

I closed my eyes, squeezed them shut. "We burned my grandda after he died." I felt my heartbeat in my chest. "Not just his wagon. All of him. His body. My cousin Martin and me did it. Well, Martin did it, really, but I got him to do it, because I just couldn't. Martin's always . . ." I dropped my head and my voice. "He's always braver, more fearless than me, and we thought Grandda would want it that way, that he wouldn't like to get buried. So Martin did it. He just took the leap and he did it. But I'm still not sure whether it all went wrong. Grandda mostly got buried anyway."

And there was something in that confession that deepened my grief. It reared up inside me. Monstrous. I opened my eyes.

My mother didn't gasp, or move away. She didn't even look surprised. She touched my ear, the same place where Dad's scar was.

"I don't know what's worse," I said. "Wondering if it was the right thing to do, or knowing that I didn't have the courage to do it."

"But none of that matters, Christy," my mother said. "You tried to do a beautiful thing for your grandda, and that's the important thing. I'm sure he knows that."

"You think so?" I breathed.

"I do."

Outside our rock-gap, I could hear the breeze sailing acrosst the steep hilltop. I could hear it ransacking the heather.

"I should do something like that for Jack," I said. "Some fierce ceremony, some vivid farewell." All my grief was gathering like a weight in my stomach. "He deserves something beautiful."

"He does," my mother agreed, folding her arm around my shoulder. "He didn't deserve what happened. Neither of you did."

I shook my head. I didn't want to cry again. I didn't want the exhaustion of spent grief. My mother touched my chin with her thumb.

"I wish I could be brave for him," I said.

"You will be," she said. "You are. And you'll think of just the right thing to do, and you will make it perfect for him. I have every faith in you."

We was quiet a while longer then, and I had the thought that I had never been so still before. Beneath me, I could nearly feel the earth rolling on its axle. I could feel us orbiting the sun.

"It's nice here," I said to my mother.

She smiled. "Of all the land, of all the hiding spots and getaways, this one is my favorite. I even came up here when I was pregnant with Henry, until I was too big to make the climb anymore. He likes it here too."

"Oh," I said. "You bring Henry here?" I wanted to be the only one.

"Yes, he's the one who painted in the letters." She pointed to a red stain sunk into my initials. It had peeled up in places. "He did that to surprise me once," she said. "Stole a bottle of my nail varnish, and came up here and painted it in for me."

I blinked at her in the shadows. "Henry did that?" I said. "Does he know about me?"

She nodded. "Yes," she said. "I thought it was important for him to know he had a brother."

A brother. It hadn't really occurred to me before. I had a brother. "And does he know I'm a traveller?" I asked.

"Yes," she said.

I took a very deep breath. "Were you not ashamed to tell him?" I asked.

She reached over and touched my forehead with her fingertip. She brushed my hair away from my eyes. "No, Christy," she said. "I was a lot of silly things, but I promise you, I was never ashamed of you."

I leaned my head against her shoulder and she tucked her arm around me. We stayed there for ages, and when we finally stood to go, she held my two hands in hers, and she pinned me into the rock with her pleading eyes. She took a very deep breath and gripped her fingers into me tightly. When she spoke, it was a word nobody hadn't never said to me before.

"Stay."

On the way back, my mother brought me to see her greenhouse, and I never seen a place more full of living ghosts than that. It was exactly the same as my dad had described: the hot, damp silence of the place, all green with dripping ferns, punctuated by brilliant fists of color. The musk of them flowers and spices was so strong it was nearly animal; it ambushed me at the door. Overhead, the sun shone high through the streaky glass, so's I didn't feel too trapped inside. Still, I stood very near to the door, to feel the reassurance of the outside breeze travelling through.

"This bamboo orchid is new," my mother said, bending over a fragile purple blossom. "I wasn't sure if she'd flourish here. But now I'm hopeful." She turned to smile at me.

"Like you," she said, and I think my own smile probably faltered, because my stomach was twisting with worry. "I can be hopeful, right?"

She wanted me to stay. And part of me wanted that, too. But it almost felt too big to consider, like she was asking me to jump to the moon. I bit my lip, and she held her two hands out to me, and gestured me over.

"Here," she said. "It's okay. I'm not sure either, how it would work. But now that you're here, I just can't imagine letting you go. I don't know if I can do it again." And she wrapped me up, snug inside the brace of her willowy arms.

"But I don't want you to worry," she said, and she folded her hand through my hair, kissed the top of my head. "I know it mightn't be possible. I know that. Whatever you decide, it's okay."

She leaned back to look at me, and I tilted my chin up to meet her gaze in that green and dappled sunlight.

"It's okay," she said again. "Just always know this is your home. Always know that I want you, and the door is open both ways."

She folded me in again.

And then, for a second, I could smell something like home here, behind the milky-cinnamon scent of my mother's embrace, behind the spices and blooms. I could smell the earthy soil that sustained them. And then, I nearly thought I could see my dad, there in the corner, sat down on that crate. Waiting for her, bent over a book, puzzling out the sounds and letters, breathing in all the scents of my mother's garden, hoping and hoping for her. Studying her, loving her, trying to work it all out. That sorta dream-poison of love making him think, for a small space of time, that anything was possible, that there might be a place where they could both survive, where they could make a life together. But that was just the dazzle of the afternoon sunlight before my eyes, and when I blinked again, he was gone. The crate stood lonesome. I would have to decide for myself.

After that, she brought me by the stables, to try and get me to pick out a new horse for myself. She insisted on giving me one, any one I wanted. But I wasn't ready. I couldn't even look them horses in the eye.

It was late afternoon by the time we returned to the house, and William Keaton said we should all take our rest while Kitty prepared the tea. The shock of the day had taken its toll on everyone, he said, and my mother needed to lay down for a while.

My mam took me back upstairs, to Henry's room, but when she

opened the door, the air inside was stagnant, like it had been closed in tight for too long. His curtains was opened and the light coming in from the bald window was too bright, somehow—ghostly and watery.

"Go on, come in," my mother said, stepping acrosst the threshold in front of me.

I hesitated in the doorway. I didn't know how to tell her how unused to rooms I was. The ceiling was too low overhead, the hinges on the door too rusty. I tried to breathe deep, but I felt choked. I felt a need to stretch at the shoulders. My mother reached her hand out to me, and I finally followed her into the room, like a baby taking his first steps.

The floor was carpeted in thick green, and all the furniture was a dark, varnished wood. There was a toy chest painted with a train, and then Henry's name on the lid. On top of that was a porcelain washbasin and some folded towels. There was a blue tartan quilt on the bed with its corners tucked and folded neatly. A fuzzy bear with glass eyes and a striped necktie leaned against the pillow. I picked him up.

"This is Henry's?" I asked.

"Yes," said my mother. "That's Baxter. Henry felt he was too babyish to take to school with him, so he stayed behind with us."

She took him from me, smoothed his tie, and then handed him back. "Did you ever have a bear like that?" she asked. "A special toy or a blanket?"

"No." I shook my head.

Baxter was soft and worn, with a chip in his left eye. He had a belly button.

"I never had nothing like this," I said.

I threw Baxter down on the bed. There was a chest of drawers on the far side of the room, and on top was a collection of family frames, all peopled with Henry's family. My family.

"Come and look," my mother said.

I stepped acrosst the room after her and she picked up the first frame.

"Here we are at his first day of school last year," she said.

Henry was about the same size as me, in a jacket, trousers, and shiny shoes. They could've been my jacket, my trousers and shiny shoes. He wore a striped necktie, the same as Baxter's. He looked like he might be sick. Behind him, my mother and William Keaton stood smiling at the camera, their hands on their son's sloping shoulders. They was all stood in front of a big, fancy iron gate, and you could see loads more boys in behind the gate, all dressed the same as Henry, some running, kicking a football, some carrying books and bags.

"Does Henry like it there?" I asked. "At the school?"

"He does now," she said. "He was a bit frightened that day, first time away from home."

I looked at the big stone building behind them in the photograph. "So that's where he lives, the whole time?" I asked. "Does he never be at home?"

She set the frame back on top of the dresser. "He does," she said. "He was home for three weeks at Christmas, and he'll be out again next Friday, for Easter. And then the whole of the summer as well. Oh, I can't wait for you to meet him."

I looked at her face, but despite everything, she was still mostly a stranger to me, and I couldn't read what she was thinking. I wondered what it was like to be Henry. To have this big, lovely house with a mam and a dad and a maid and your own stables with tons of horses, and then to be sent off to a big, lonesome boarding school without Baxter.

"Why does he have to go away to school?" I asked. "Isn't there schools close, where he could still live with you?"

"Yes, but they're not as fine as this school," she said. "Henry is receiving an excellent education there. If he does well, he could earn a place at Oxford."

"But do you not miss him, being away so much?" I asked.

"I do, of course," she said. "Sure I'm an expert at missing people."

She did her broken smile again, and I wondered how many times a day that sadness crossed her face, that it was so natural on her.

I shook my head. If I had a house and tons of money, I'd never send my kid away to school. I couldn't get my head around it, how easy she seemed to let go of people.

We looked at the rest of the frames, and she showed me her sister, Millicent, and her father.

"My grandfather," I whispered, looking at his face, his formidable jaw and piercing eyes.

Suddenly I could feel the warmth of my other grandda, all jolly and bright. I knew he was there with me.

"That's right," she said. "That's your granddad, God rest his soul."

Her voice was careful, reverent. She set the frame back atop the dresser, and fussed over it, til it was arranged just so.

"And what about your own mammy?" I asked then.

My mother pressed her lips against each other, and reached toward the back of the dresser, to draw out an ancient-looking brown-and-white portrait of a woman who looked just like her.

"Here she is," she said.

It was a formal portrait, so the woman sat straight, with her hands crossed daintily on her knee. She didn't smile, but you could tell she was happy from the light in her pale eyes.

"She looks just like you," I said.

My mother nodded solemnly.

"How come you're not in the picture with her?" I said.

"That was taken before I was born," she said.

I looked up at her in the watery light and I seen that her eyes was filling up. She blinked them. "She died when I was born," she whispered.

I stared at her. She swallowed and looked down at the floor. I knew her then. In that moment, I understood everything about her. I knew that guilt and sorrow she suffered, the same as my own, and I couldn't help wondering if Dad had done that on purpose. A gift, so's we'd have something in common. I touched the back of her hand.

"That wasn't your fault," I said quietly, and my mouth felt flooded with the words.

She shook her head and placed her mother's frame back among the others. "I never got past it," she said. "It's a thing I think you pay for all your life."

"I know," I said.

She turned and looked into my eyes. "That's part of it, too," she said. "Why I couldn't leave here, why I couldn't go with your dad. I couldn't do that to my father, not after I'd already taken his wife from him. She's buried here, in the family plot. I'll show you if you like. He grieved for her every single day until he followed her into that grave twenty years later."

She sighed, and I could see the breath coming out of her like a great weight.

"He always told me that I was like the sun and the moon to him." She smiled, but the tears was still stood in her mighty blue eyes. "He said Millie and I were all he had left in the world. He was stern with his ideas, strict with convention, but there was no question he loved us."

Then she gasped one little sob that was so quick it mightn't have been a sob at all, because the next thing, she was smoothing a swift hand acrosst her forehead and sweeping across the room to where the press stood with its doors closed and latched.

"There's something else," she said.

She opened the doors of the press, and the smell of Henry came out into the room. It was something like sticky caramel. She reached inside and drew a box down from the top shelf. She carried it to the bed and then sat down beside it. I sat on the other side of the box, and she lifted its lid. Inside was a knit baby blanket, raggedy and stained in faded blue. She unrolled it until a lump of tissue fell out.

"Open it," she said.

I lifted the tissue and carefully pulled it open. A silver rattle, about the length of my hand, with a long, slim handle, and a broad, round head. On one side was the face of a smiling sun, its rays spreading out to the scalloped edges. On the opposite side, a sleepy-eyed moon bound by stars. I shook it, and heard the captive noise of sand and pebbles.

"Do you remember it?" my mother asked.

"No." I shook my head. "I don't know." But the sound of it had made every muscle in my body go slack. I felt like a puddle.

"That was your favorite," she said. "You used to shake it when I'd come in to collect you in the mornings. You'd be crying for me to come and get you, and then in I'd come and you'd scuttle away from me til you'd find that little thing and you'd shake it at me. And you'd be as proud! Shaking it in the air and making a little O with your mouth, like you couldn't believe how clever you were."

I fingered the rattle, careful not to shake it again in case I would splatter.

"And this was your blanket." She stroked the faded blue yarn in a pile on her knee. "I never washed it."

She lifted it to her face and buried her nose in it, to try and smell me, that long-gone baby me, trapped in its threads. She handed it to me, and I sniffed, too.

"Smells like Henry," I said.

She laughed, and started to bundle it back into the box. "I guess it does now," she said. "That's what you smelled like one time, too."

"What do I smell like now?" I asked.

She leaned into my neck and breathed. "Like your father," she said. "Just like your father." And she touched my hair. But then she drew herself up quickly, and took a deep breath of house-air to remind herself.

"How is he?" she asked steadily, blinking her long eyelashes. She smoothed her hair back from her forehead, like she could tame that wildness out of her just by fixing her hair. The look on her face was like Dad's, when he told me I came in between the dragonwort and the jasmine. Her face was flushed.

"He's fine, I guess."

"Do you have other brothers and sisters?"

"No." I shook my head. "Dad's not married."

The flush rose up higher on her cheek. "He never married?"

"Nope."

She cleared her throat, but it wasn't enough to break the electric silence now, in the room. "So it's just the two of you, then?" she said.

"Yeah, us and then Finty and Brigid and Granny and Grandda and Martin," I said. "Well, not really Grandda now, I guess. And then there's John Paul and Maureen, but they's just babies."

My mother nodded. "Sounds like a lovely, big family, anyway," she said.

"Yeah, I guesso," I said. "It's just normal."

"Normal," she repeated.

And then maybe we both was thinking about how far away my normal was from hers.

"And do you go to school?" she asked.

"Yeah, we just started, me and Martin. We's going getting our Communions."

"Of course," she said. "You're Catholic."

"Yeah." I looked down at my bare feet on Henry's green carpet.

She followed my gaze down to my dirty toes. I set the baby rattle back in its blanket-nest and covered it over with the tissue. My mother replaced the lid of the box and put her hand on top.

"You remembered this, from all them years ago?" I said, pulling my Saint Christopher medal out from under my shirt.

"I do, of course," she said, taking it in her hand and spinning the orbiting rings. "Such a beautiful thing."

"It cost him all his wages, the whole harvest wages," I said. "He bought it for you."

She nodded, and her eyes was cloudy with remembering. She had a dreamy look about her, like it was a romantic, tender thing, to spend your whole season's wages on a trinket. She hadn't a notion of the hunger and hardship that would follow. She'd never knew the gnawing pain of a truly empty belly, how it follows you until you fill it, even into your hungry sleep and your unfed dreams.

She took my hand and pressed the medal back into my palm, closed my fingers around it. Her fingers was so clean and white next to mine. So soft, like the petals of a new flower. Mine was the hard, dirt-brown of wood and earth. Even our hands was foreign from each other. How had I come from her?

I thought of my Dad going into the jewelers with that fistful of money and throwing it down on the counter. I thought of his dirt-brown hands, like mine, tangled through my mother's hair.

"Do you still miss him?"

She glanced at the doorway and then back at my eyes. "I could never say a thing like that out loud, Christy," she said, but she grinned.

"You still love him!" I said.

"Shhhhh!" she said, and she stood quickly to close the bedroom door.

I gulped, and stared at that closed door like it was the inside lid of my very own coffin. She came back and sat beside me. She lifted my dirty feet into her hands so's I had to lay back on the pillow beside Baxter, and she rubbed them, one by one. My breath felt thin, but she didn't notice that no more than she minded the dirt on my feet.

"It's easy to love more than one person," she said. "The difficult thing is making the choice."

I picked up Baxter for a distraction, tugged on his tie. "So you love William, then?" I asked.

"I love things about him," she admitted. "And he loves me, to be sure. My life hasn't been as tragic as I once imagined. I'm content."

I closed my eyes and tried to picture what might've happened if she'd made the other choice. I tried to see her in the tent with me and Dad, out hawking swag with Granny, baking bread on the *greeshuk*, with her wild red hair plaited tightly at her neck, a beady pocket clacking 'round her legs. Her whole self worn out from one baby after another. Imagining that was like trying to shear a pig.

"And anyway, I'd no choice, really," she said. She tried to heave that weight out of her lungs again, but it stayed put. I felt the air in my own lungs filling, deepening, til I could breathe almost normal in that closed-door room.

"If I'd known my father was so near his end," she said sadly then, sounding almost afraid of her own words. "If I'd known how little my sacrifice mattered, that he would die anyway, that he wouldn't live to meet his grandsons . . ." She was shaking her head. "I might've had the strength to make my own decisions."

Her eyes was fixed and distant, like they was looking away back, at the past. She was wishing so hard. "I wouldn't have had to care, then," she said, her voice dropped to a whisper. "It wouldn't have mattered what anyone thought. Maybe then he would have stayed."

"Stayed?" I said. The word halted in my mouth. I'd never even thought of that. I'd been angry at her for not coming with us. The idea that my dad could have stayed never even occurred to me. Even now, it seemed like lunacy.

My mother looked at my face. "I know," she said. "That's like asking a wave to stay on the shore."

"But did you?" I said. "Ask him?"

"I did," she said. "We took turns begging each other. To stay, to go, to stay, to go. Then one day we just realized, it was impossible. The shore can no more go off with the ocean than the ocean can stay with the shore."

My mouth stood open.

"Your father was braver than me," she said. "He was strong for us both. He couldn't make a living here, I knew that. He'd no way to survive if he stayed in one place. No one would've employed him. We'd have ended up destitute. We'd have had to go on the road, and he knew what that would do to me, the guilt of failing my father, leaving my homeplace, all my world. I'd have been cast out. I wouldn't have known how to cope."

I couldn't believe it. My father, proud and brave, choosing his own course. All my life I'd believed he'd followed the lazy path, that he'd never made a difficult choice, that he'd never stood up to no-body, least of all a buffer. And all the time I'd believed that, the truth was, he'd done this thing: he'd left this beautiful woman behind, for her own good. He made the choice to let go of her because he loved her, because he knew that's what she needed him to do.

"I think your father knew I wouldn't last a week," she said. "He knew what a torture it would've been for me, and he didn't want to put me through it. He didn't want me to flounder and fail."

I'd never thought that, as hard as it was for me walking into a house, it might be just as hard for a buffer, taking out to the *tober*.

"He knew I could make a good life for myself here," she said. "Even if I didn't want to believe it then, that I could survive without him. He was right."

"And what about me?" I said. "Why did you not tell Dad about me straightaway?"

"I didn't know," she said. "I didn't know until he was gone, and it was too late." Her head collapsed a few inches.

"I didn't know what I'd do when I found out," she said. "It was terrifying, Christy. I mean, I was overjoyed, in a sense. But William asked my father for my hand only a few weeks after that, and it was a lifeline. I didn't love him then, but I knew I had to marry him, and not deceitfully. I told him the truth before we wed. I was terrified he would break it off when I told him, and if he did, I knew they'd take you from me. I couldn't stand it, the thought of that. I thought I would die."

"But you didn't," I said. "You gave me away anyway, and you didn't die at all. You barely even blinked."

She shook her head at me, but now she was smiling. "That was entirely different," she said, and she raised my hand up to her lips and kissed it. "You were with your father. There wasn't a greater gift in the world I could give him than you."

She leaned in to me. "That's how much I loved him," she said, stroking my forehead.

Like it was all quite simple, obvious.

"So then what about Henry?" I asked. "If everything had been different, if Dad had stayed, Henry would never've been born."

"That's true." She nodded.

"So who do you love more?"

"There's no *more*, Christy," she said. "There's no quantifying a thing like that. William saved my life, with one act of benevolence."

"Or one act of greed," I said. My mother looked at me sadly. "Well, he got all this land, didn't he?"

"He does have some good in him, Christy," she answered. "And then, when Henry came, he changed everything. He made it so William and I could live together in peace, so we could be like a proper family."

I closed my eyes and leaned back, and she went on rubbing my feet again, until she thought I was asleep. Then she kissed my forehead and whispered, "I can't believe it's really you."

TWENTY-TWO

After my mother closed the door behind her, Henry's ceiling started to feel lower and lower, and the scent of caramel got so heavy it turned a pain in my stomach.

I didn't cry in the traditional sense—there wasn't no sniffling or heaving or sobbing. But there was tears coming loose from my eyes anyway, and they was sliding down my face and they was dampening Henry's pillow. It was a fresh and throbbing grief I had now, and I couldn't even pin it down. I couldn't name it. I felt bound to my mam now, like a tree to the earth. But in truth, I felt bound to Dad like a tree to the sky, and that was the binding I needed.

I could never stay in this house, and maybe that's what I cried for. It wasn't in me to live inside walls, to put on Henry's shoes, and to sleep with my cheek against his pillow. If it ever had been in that faraway baby me, it was long gone now, and that was my mother's choice for me. She had decided.

It was easy to love more than one person, she said, and the difficult thing was making the choice. Maybe there was a way she'd understand this, then, that the ocean couldn't stay on the shore; maybe she was the only one who'd understand. I had to get out, out. I had to fill my lungs with outside air, to stretch my arms and swing my legs beneath me.

I sat up and wiped my eyes with Baxter's striped necktie. I chose the framed photograph of Henry's first day of school to bring with me. I unlooped my Saint Christopher medal from over my head and placed it on Henry's sodden pillow.

Outside, I walked barefoot toward the field where Jack had fell. When I reached the ridge of the hill and looked down, I could see the bloody patch in the matted grass where he'd fell, but his sleek, black body was gone. William Keaton and his grooms had moved his body away. I went down the hill anyway, paused at the spot where he'd fell. I got down on my two knees, in Henry's trousers, and I prayed to God for guidance and healing, I prayed for Saint Christopher to protect Jack on his travels in the hereafter, and finally, I prayed for forgiveness.

Jack hadn't got the death he deserved. He deserved a sleeping, old-man death like Grandda. Or a galloping into the seafoam-tide kind of a death, maybe. Or he could've died rescuing some childer from a fire. I could imagine a thousand better deaths for him than the one he got. The senseless, puncture-bullet, real one that was my fault.

I crossed myself and, when I stood up, Henry's trousers stuck to my knees with Jack's blood. The ground was still wet with it. I pulled the cloth away from my skin. But even then, in that horrible hollow moment, with my shoulders loose and my chest acheful with grief, I felt a bracing release. For the first time in all my life, I felt fitted into my skin.

I found my wellies where I'd left them in the forest—a few dozen paces into the tree line, where Jack and me had made camp. My rucksack was there, my jotter, *Gulliver* with the photo safely tucked in, my spoon, my bits and pieces still inside. I put the new photograph in its frame inside, too. I stuck my bare feet into the wellies, sat down, and wrote my mammy a note.

> Mam,
> I'm not angry no more. I guess you did the right thing
> when you gave me to Dad, because I think that's where
> I belong. I can't stay here, I just can't. Not with William,
> not after Jack. So I will take one of your horses now, like
> you said, and take it home to Dad. Don't be sad for me.
> I'll be okay now.
>
> *Christy*
>
> ps—tell Henry I said "how'ya" and tell him I left him a
> gift on his pillow.
>
> pps—you are the best mam I could ever have imagined
> in a million trillion years.

In the greenhouse, I opened my rucksack and pulled out *Gulliver* again, flipped to the back page, and found the purple Mother's Day card inside: the red, wax heart on the front, the charcoal letters M-A-M-M-Y. I opened the card and placed my note inside, then propped them both up beside the bamboo orchid.

Then I stuffed *Gulliver* back into my rucksack, and thought of Amy—not Finnuala Whippet, but Amy—back at Saint Malachy's. It was only Monday evening, and I knew she'd've missed me at school today. She'd've got my note. Everything felt different from yesterday. I wasn't going so far as to say I was in love with her or nothing mental like that, even though Finty was only three and a half years older than me when he married Brigid. But I kept thinking about what my mam said, about how sometimes you fall in love with the way a person makes you feel about yourself. And it was true that Finnuala Whippet made me feel braver. She made me feel *unworried*. And that feeling was something of a miracle to me.

The stable was throwing long shadows along the ground, casting its seam-grasses into a cool dark. I went right through the stable door, and with the animal scent of the sweaty horses around me, for a moment I felt like I was still the same boy who'd stolen out along the road and came here with Jack in the dead of night, but it was only a moment. And then I felt like someone quite different after that, someone new.

Suddenly I felt a calmness in my bones that came from my mam. I was half hers, and that half of me was tranquil. She was a hothouse flower, all splendor and spice, but at the end of the day, she was rooted, and it was them roots that defined her. She could only grow so far. And now, quite suddenly, I filled in. Like a pendulum coming to rest, I balanced. The other half of me, Dad's half, Grandda's and Jack's half, had been bound too tightly before, afraid to unfurl. In that moment, my soul uncoiled, spilled all through me like light, right out to my toenails, my earlobes, my eyelids. My mam and dad had fell in love over books, over sunlight and soil and simplicity, and I was the product of that bold, impossible love. I was the freest, happiest moment in their lives. I had always been their choice, but now I was my own choice, too. I knew I was an outside boy.

It was quiet except for the waiting sounds of the impatient animals, chewing, breathing, shuffling. Itching to get out and run. Like me. Inside that fancy stable, it was still a barn after all, with straw scattered underfoot, and that blessed blend of animal scents swarming up to greet me. There was high windows cut into the ceilings, so's the sunlight came sloping through at angles. It was always the same, no matter how humble or highfalutin, a barn was still a barn, and it felt safe and sacred inside.

"Hello?" I called to make sure I was alone.

And that's when I seen him, from the magnet corner of my eye.

The round black flank of him. That familiar curve I knew better than the shape of my own ear. Jack. I turned to look at him and he was there, laying down in the corner, covered over with a bit of hay, waiting for somebody to come and haul him away. Where would he go, I wondered. A butcher? A glue factory?

I went to him and kneeled down by him, and at first I wasn't sure whether to put my hand on him or not. I knew he'd be cold, and I wanted to remember him warm. I remembered the way Granny touched Grandda in the wagon, with such tenderness, like he wasn't dead at all. I hadn't been brave enough then.

"Jack," I said.

And then the tears came again. I couldn't believe I had any left to cry, but there they was—a thunderous swamp of waiting tears. And I leaned in to him, and I felt my lips part against each other, and I buried the weight of myself into his stiffened neck and I cried.

"I'm sorry," I said to him. "Jack, I'm so sorry."

And I wanted them words to feel like magic, and I wanted to breathe them into his nostrils and for them to heal him, but they wasn't. They wasn't magic at all. They was just bleary and snot-filled and hollow. Jack's legs was spread out carefully beside us, crossed—two and two. I wondered who did that for him, or if that was just the way he fell when they lugged him in here.

Past the grip of the rusty blood, I could still smell home. I grasped his mane into my fingers and I stroked him. I leaned my head against his nose and felt the nothingness where his breath used to be.

I sat up and looked at him then, kept my hand against his head. With the other hand, I wiped my nose, wiped my face. If he wasn't so cold, he could nearly have just been sleeping, he was that much hisself, just like Grandda'd been, in the wagon. I could be thankful that his eyes was closed, at least, that he was laying on the side where the bullet hole was. He looked peaceful and whole.

And then I had an idea, a good idea. The perfect ceremony I could do for Jack, to make things right, just like my mam had said.

"I won't let them take you," I said to him. "I can do that much for you, at least."

The farewell he deserved, like initials carved into a rock. I stood up out of the hay, and I was covered in it as well. It clung to me in patches.

"A proper send-off," I said. "For a traveller."

And all the times I'd said that word—traveller—all the times I'd tried before, in my life, to make it sound strong and proud . . . I'd never fully believed it before that day. That word had always been shadowed by the gloom of my own misconceptions, by a parcel of shame I never even knew I carried. I thought of Dad, outrunning them whizzing bullets in the dark of night. I thought of Martin, alone, terrified, taking a deep breath, and then lighting that match for Grandda. I took a deep breath of my own. There was strength where I came from.

"Traveller," I said again, louder. I stood up straight and dusted off my trousers then, looked around me at all the watching horses. There was eleven of them, I counted, not including Jack and me. They stood witness.

"Hello?" I called, once more, for good measure.

Nobody answered. I walked over to the closest stall and inspected the fella inside. He inspected me back. He seemed altogether unimpressed.

"Some house for horses," I said to him.

He snorted. I walked along the row of stalls then, pausing at one or two, reaching over to pat a nose or check teeth. It seemed to be growing louder inside, the horses stamping and snorting. Maybe they could hear the quickening of my heartbeat. There was agitation coming, whipping and slithering from stall to stall. My hands was sweating now and I could feel all manner of fluttering inside me, but maybe that's what courage was—to feel that trembling fear, and then to get on with it anyway. I stopped at the eighth stall door.

"You," I said.

I didn't have to inspect him at all. I knew just by the look of him, by the way his eyes lit on to mine and stayed there, unblinking. He looked back at me and whinnied. He pulled his head up at me and it was as simple as that.

"You're the one."

I reached over the stall door and jiggled the handle. The latches on the stalls was that elaborate, it took me a minute to figure out how to undo them. I started to get nervous in case the groom would come back from wherever he'd got to. Finally the latch came loose in my hand and I swung the door open for him.

"Hup," I said, but I didn't have to, because he was out like a shot and raring to go.

He seemed to know what to do. He went and stood by Jack and waited. After that first one, it was easier because all them latches was the same. I went down the line and unhooked the latches first, leaving the doors unlocked, but still shut. A couple of them horses didn't wait for me. They lowered their heads and shoved open the doors and went out milling in the middle of the stables. Two of them made for the outside door.

"Quick," I said to myself. "Hurry, hurry."

And I picked up my pace, racing along the row of unlatched doors then. I swung them open one at a time. I had to go inside the stalls for a couple of the shy ones who wanted to go lingering. I slapped their rumps and encouraged them toward the open door at the back of the stables. They filed past Jack. Some of them seemed to nod; they dipped their heads as they passed him.

I reached into my rucksack then, and found Grandda's photo, the original, still inside *Gulliver*. Baby me and Nora Keaton smiled out. The photo was cooling now. Grandda's ghost was leaving me. I took the new fella by the halter, and we had to be quick now, I knew, before somebody in the house seen and noticed. All them horses out to pasture. William Keaton would be angry, but my mam would understand what I had to do for Jack, I knew she would. That was all that mattered. I reached once more into my rucksack, and found a book of matches. I dropped into the hay on my two knees, crossed myself, and then, with my hand on his head, I whispered a quick, fervent prayer beside Jack. I leaned down and kissed his neck.

"Goodbye," I said to him.

I leaned up, flicked the match and watched the flame bite into the air. For a moment, everything felt suspended then, like me and Jack was a framed painting, hanging on the bookshop wall, and even with all its new grief, that painting was familiar. It was a mirror and an echo, and it sang all my life back to me. A torrent of memories came, dreams of purple horses, the rain splattering my bald baby head while my father sprinted barefoot through the muck, my mother standing like a shield in front of that shotgun, Grandda saving baby Jack in that faraway nighttime barn, Martin squaring his shoulders and lighting that match. It all led to this. My moment to be brave. My moment to give all my terror and hope and gathering courage to a single, reckless, defining act of love.

In my mind, I could hear my mother's reverent whisper. "There's a great beauty in the ceremonies we do, whenever we have to say goodbye."

I lit the corner of Grandda's photo, and the flames wasn't long making their way acrosst that short square of paper. I dropped it into the hay beside Jack's head. I knelt and put my hand on him again; I blessed him. Then I stood for just a moment, to make sure the fire would bloom and puff, to make sure it would glow and light the same way Granny's wagon had, when we'd tried to set Grandda free.

It was faster than I'd expected, the way the heat and the light scurried and leapt acrosst the scattered hay, the way fire can actually race and run, and soon each stall was harboring its own hot, little heartbeat of flame. The painted wood was already starting to peel and bubble and blacken. I leaned down and patted Jack's nose one last time. I stood and watched Grandda's ghost turn and shrink in the fire.

"Goodbye, Jack," I said.

I threw one foot up then, onto the swinging door of the nearest stall. Then the other foot, quick now, quick. I hoisted my weight up and swung my right leg acrosst the new horse. I was so quick I was like a flame myself, but I could feel his broad back scooped under me like a cradle. It was getting hot inside, the flames licking into every corner. Jack's bed was going up around him, like a brilliant purple wreath of flame. My new horse was jittery, waiting. We was ready, ready. "I might have to call you Traitor," I said to him, and he let out a great, rowdy whinny of a cheer.

There might've been voices as we swept thundering through that open stables door. There might've been shouts and whoops and peals of alarm. There might've been my valiant, gentle mother, standing still as ever in the middle of all that motion, letting me go all over again, with a small, free prayer. *Saint Christopher, protect him.* There might've been the confusion of horses and heat and pasture, and the broad daylight flames and smoke and grass and sky. A proud traveller's funeral.

But all I could hear was the fury of the wind, wild against my ears, and the free and heavy drumming of feet beneath me, flying, flying. Home.

EVENING WAS DROPPING TO NIGHT and exhaustion was creeping over me, but Traitor was stout and mindful; he was swift, purple in the gloaming.

He pulled me like a compass toward home, to the force and ferocity of my waiting father. Dad loved me like bricks and mortar. Stronger even.

I clenched my knees tighter around Traitor's neck, and guided him easy past twilight farms and crossroads. Two light fingers against his neck, that's all it took, and he'd bear left or right, bolting through the drooping, darkening towns.

Everything was hushed with sleep when myself and Traitor trotted softly down the Long Mile Road. There was the hedge gap, and beyond, the wide rise of cleared ground. There was our three wagons at angles, like rolled dice in the moonlight.

I swung myself down off Traitor's back and led him acrosst the gap to the pump. I filled up a bucket with water, and he drank. Beyond, the fire was lit low, in patient vigil.

My father sat waiting for me.

Jeanine Cummins is the bestselling author of the ground-breaking memoir *A Rip in Heaven*. She worked in the publishing industry for ten years before becoming a full-time writer. She was born in Spain, and has lived in California, Maryland, Belfast, and New York City, where she remains now with her Irish husband and growing family. *The Outside Boy* is her first novel.

THE **OUTSIDE** BOY

JEANINE CUMMINS

QUESTIONS
FOR DISCUSSION

1. Christy and his grandfather have a very special relationship, so when Grandda dies, it's a particularly difficult loss for Christy. What is it about their bond that makes the two of them so close? In what ways does Grandda, and even the memory of Grandda, enrich Christy's life, and make him feel less alone? Has the absence of Christy's mother made him feel less like a part of his own family?

2. Throughout the book, Christy struggles to find his place in the world, to become comfortable in his own skin. Would you describe Christy as happy, despite his uncertainties? Why or why not?

3. What things does Christy like about being a traveller, and living on the margins of society? Are there ways in which he is ever ashamed of his family or their way of life? Are there moments when he admires or even envies the settled life-style? Would Christy be happier if he lived in a house?

4. Are Christy's questions about his identity inevitable, or is there something about the family's extended stay in one place that ignites his struggle to figure out who he is, and where he belongs? How does Christy change during his stay in the town, and his time at school? Who and what are the catalysts for these changes?

5. Christy cherishes books and stories. How do language, stories, and books help Christy to define himself? In contrast, why is his cousin Martin so defensive about his illiteracy?

6. How are Christy and Martin similar, and how are they different? Which of the two boys has a more realistic view of life? Who is the more romantic character? Which of the two do you think is better prepared for the life ahead of him?

7. Is Christy's attitude toward his father typical, for a boy his age? Or is Christy's anger specific to his father's character and the circumstances of their life together? By the end of the book, Christy comes to find out that his father has lied to him about many things. Is this deceit justified by Dad's fears for Christy's stability, or are the lies indefensible? Is there ever a time when it's acceptable for parents to deceive their children?

8. Does Mrs. Hanley do the right thing in helping Christy to solve the mystery of the photograph, or is her choice a reckless one? She seems to know that she might be opening a can of worms; should she have spoken to Christy's father before agreeing to help?

9. During his stay in the town, Christy becomes very attached to both Sister Hedgehog and Mrs. Hanley, the bookshop owner, after they treat him with basic kindness. Is he looking for a mother figure in these women? Or is he simply grateful for their compassion?

10. Why is Christy unable to find a suitable mother figure among the female characters in his own family? The women in this community tend to have many children. Are Granny and Auntie Brigid simply overextended? Or is Christy looking for something beyond what they have to offer him?

11. Is Christy's budding romance with Finnuala Whippet a viable relationship, or is his friendship with a settled girl doomed by the same obstacles Christy's parents faced? Does this relationship have anything to teach him about his parents and their struggles?

12. Why does Christy react so impatiently with Beano? What is it about Beano that makes Christy so uncomfortable? Despite Beano's awkwardness, he seems to feel entirely comfortable with himself. Could Christy learn anything from Beano about self-acceptance and/or inclusion in society?

13. Christy has an incredibly strong bond with his horse, Jack. Is this a friendship that any young boy might have with his pet, or is there something special in Christy's circumstance or lifestyle that makes the attachment more intense? Who or what does Jack represent to Christy?

14. What is Christy's predominant emotional response when he finally meets his mother? Does he feel like he has things in common with her? If so, what things? Does he admire her, or feel disappointed by her? Or both? Why?

15. Christy is stunned when his mother reveals that she actually *asked* his father to kidnap him, when he was still just a baby. Why did she do this? Was it the right decision for Christy? Was it the right decision for Christy's mother, for his father? Was it a selfish act, or a selfless one? Does Christy understand why his mother did what she did?

16. In the end, Christy makes a decision that is a singular act of self-definition. Does Christy's extraordinary action at the end of the book make sense? Is it an act of joy or of grief, or of both? In his heart, Christy believes that his mother will understand the decisions he makes. Do you agree? Why or why not?

17. Christy makes the choice in the end to embrace himself as a traveller, and to return to the only life he's ever known. Is this the right decision for him? As a traveller, Christy comes to value his culture, his family, and his freedom. Do you believe there is intrinsic value in the traveller's nomadic way of life? Why or why not? What aspects of their culture are most valuable? And what features, if any, are dispensable?

18. The moral code of travellers is different from the moral code of the largely Catholic, settled community in Ireland. How can two cultures like these, with divergent ethical standards, learn to live together peaceably? Is there ever a time when one group's moral code should trump the other's?

19. Outsiders might be confused by the apparent dichotomies that exist within the moral fabric of the travelling community. For instance, most travellers are strict Catholics who observe their faith with rigor, but within the travellers' code of ethics, there are times when stealing is acceptable. This is a truth that Christy struggles to reconcile throughout the book. In the end, is he successful? What are your thoughts on these ethical disparities? Do similar discrepancies exist in our own moral code? Are these discrepancies harmful or reasonable?

20. Has this story changed your perceptions of gypsies in general, or of Irish Travellers in particular? If so, how?